Swell Time

for a

Swing Dance

All the Best!

Cindy Vincent

Also by Cindy Vincent

Bad Day for a Bombshell:
A Tracy Truworth, Apprentice P.I.
1940s Homefront Mystery

Yes, Carol . . . It's Christmas!

The Case of the Cat Show Princess:
A Buckley and Bogey Cat Detective Caper

The Case of the Crafty Christmas Crooks:
A Buckley and Bogey Cat Detective Caper

The Case of the Jewel Covered Cat Statues:
A Buckley and Bogey Cat Detective Caper

The Case of the Clever Secret Code:
A Buckley and Bogey Cat Detective Caper

The Mystery of the Missing Ming:
A Daisy Diamond Detective Novel

The Case of the Rising Star Ruby:
A Daisy Diamond Detective Novel

Makeover For Murder:
A Kate Bundeen Mystery

Cats Are Part of His Kingdom, Too:
33 Daily Devotions to Show God's Love

Swell Time for a Swing Dance

A Tracy Truworth, Apprentice P.I. 1940s Homefront Mystery

Cindy Vincent

Whodunit Press
Houston

Swell Time for a Swing Dance

A Tracy Truworth, Apprentice P.I.

1940s Homefront Mystery

Published by Whodunit Press

A Division of Mysteries by Vincent, LLC

For information, please contact:

CustomerCare@mysteriesbyvincent.com

This is a work of fiction.

ISBN: 978-1-932169-33-1

Printed in the United States of America

Dedication

To my fellow Houstonians who endured the wrath and then the aftermath of Hurricane Harvey. One of the very worst storms in history brought out the very best in humanity. May we always be "Houston Strong" and may God bless you all!

Houston, TX
January 15, 1937

Prologue

The air inside the basement of the Museum of Fine Arts nearly crackled with electricity as the small, select crowd of spectators, museum officials, and newspaper reporters buzzed with anticipation, like children waiting to dive into their presents on a Christmas morn. After all, it had been a year since museum benefactor, Miss Annette Finnigan, had traveled the capitals of Europe, like a treasure hunter on a quest, seeking and purchasing unique artifacts to ship home to the fledgling art museum.

Reports of her finds had caused quite a stir among members of the media, as well as the Houston Art League, the group that had founded the museum. For stowed within one of the four huge wooden crates that had just arrived were a golden gladiator myrtle wreath and a marble image from Greece that dated back to 2500 BC. And those were but a few of the priceless treasures that were about to be unpacked and then added to the museum's permanent collection. Now, not only would local citizens have the pleasure of viewing such rare antiquities, but the museum would also be well on its way to competing with some of the finest institutions in the country.

All thanks to Miss Finnigan's great generosity and her overseas exploits.

Of course, the timing of her trip couldn't have been better, considering the growing political unrest and military rumblings in

Europe. With the civil war in Spain and the rise of the Nazis—not to mention the Nuremberg Laws in Germany, which had stripped the Jews of their civil rights altogether—Americans wondered how much longer they'd be able to travel safely overseas. Naturally, there was plenty of talk that another Great War might be on the horizon.

But today at the museum, world politics was the furthest thing from anyone's mind. Instead, all were dying to view the new artifacts that had finally arrived, since no one but Miss Finnigan had even seen the items in person. The rest of the excited crowd had been forced to settle for the black-and-white images of photographs.

Yet as the crates were opened, and Miss Finnigan and the others stood by, excitement was also clouded by anxiety. Now came the question of whether these priceless antiquities had each arrived in one piece or not. After all, shipping them home wasn't as simple as plopping a few stamps on a brown-paper-wrapped package and dropping it in a mailbox on the sidewalk. The purchases had been taken to London to be handled by brokers Coomber and Dicken. From there they went to Antwerp, where they were stowed on board the SS Crawford and shipped on what seemed like a very slow boat to Houston. And who knew if such ancient items would withstand the rocking of a ship, let alone the changes in temperature and humidity?

With all eyes upon him, Mr. J.W. Sersby, the museum's man in charge of unpacking, started to dig through a box within a box within yet another box, to find the first delicate vase inside. The process was slow and painstaking, as layers upon layers of cotton and other packing materials had to be removed with the utmost of care. All the while, everyone in the crowd seemed to be holding their breath, as they waited to see if the items had arrived safely.

And as each artifact was uncovered and placed on a sturdy table, the crowd relaxed just a little bit more. That was, until an amphora wrapped in pale-blue linen was pulled from another box. While the blue cloth stood out from the rest of the packing materials, it was the dark, rust-colored stains on the material that instantly caused concern among the onlookers. Mr. Sersby himself frowned, as all began to wonder if the ancient amphora had survived the journey to Texas.

Was it possible the clay from the vase had gotten wet and dissolved, thus staining the outer area? Or had some of the paint rubbed off? Pulses picked up and hearts began to pound as the spectators inched ever closer, trying to see if the jar was, in fact, intact. After all, this wasn't some item that could be ordered from the Sears, Roebuck, and Co. catalogue. No, this was an ancient, one-of-a-kind piece that could never be replaced.

Hands appeared from behind Mr. Sersby, pulling the stack of packing material out of his way, to give him more room to work.

All eyes continued to be focused on him as he peeled more and more packing material away from the vase-like jar. Finally, after what felt like eons, the amphora was uncovered.

Thankfully, it was in one piece.

And no one noticed, or, for that matter, even cared, that the material it had been packed in had completely disappeared.

Houston, Texas
December 31, 1941

CHAPTER 1

Out with the Old and In with the Dead

The soft stage lights near the bandstand caught the sheen of my teal-green ball gown as Pete twirled me and led me expertly around the dance floor.

"Tracy Truworth, you are the prettiest girl here," he whispered in my ear when the music slowed down and we started to dance cheek to cheek.

"And you are the most dapper gentleman in the place," I murmured in return.

I pulled back just a bit so I could take in Pete's perfectly tailored tuxedo. I couldn't help but notice the way the double-breasted jacket emphasized his very solid shoulders.

"That's quite a compliment," Pete laughed, drawing me close again. "Considering how smart everyone looks tonight."

And he was right. The entire crowd had turned out in their evening finery. Even the band members were dressed in their white tuxedo jackets and black bow ties, as they sat behind their individual stage stands and played one of my favorite Tommy Dorsey songs, "You Taught Me to Love Again." A song that seemed especially fitting since I'd started to date Pete almost a month ago, right after my horrible engagement to Michael had come to a rather stormy end. Following my ordeal with my ex, I wasn't sure I'd ever find romance again. And in my world, being twenty-four and unmarried was moving me dangerously close to spinsterhood.

Yet here I was, out dancing at the fund-raising gala for the Museum of Fine Arts with this fair-haired, blue-eyed man. A man who was holding me much closer than usual, as we danced to nearly every song the band played.

At the rate we were going, we'd have to pace ourselves, considering we still had four more hours to go before the museum's giant clock struck midnight. And while most people looked forward to the big moment that signaled "out with the old and in with the new," I could have happily stopped that clock from counting down the last few hours of 1941.

But not because 1941 had been an especially good year. After all, less than a month ago our country had endured the worst attack on U.S. soil, when the Imperial Japanese Navy had bombed Pearl Harbor in the Territory of Hawaii. Thousands of people had been killed, leading our country to enter into the war against both Japan and Germany. And now, as time ticked on, that war was only growing and expanding, and likely to continue throughout the entire year of 1942.

At least.

Sometimes I could hardly believe all the changes our country had seen in such a short time. And while I knew we were tumbling headlong into a world that was very different from the one I'd grown up in, tonight of all nights, I wished I could have frozen that clock in place for just a little while. I wanted to memorize the twinkle in Pete's eyes, and the scent of his soap, and the feeling of being in his arms. Because it wouldn't be long before I couldn't enjoy even these very simple things.

Pete, like most of the fellas our age, was about to enlist and go off to fight in this nearly worldwide military conflict. Citizen soldiers from all walks of life—from ranchers to lawyers and from plumbers to businessmen—were leaving their homes and jobs in droves, in an effort to stop the fascism that had already invaded Europe and China.

My best friend's new husband and several of her brothers had already gone. And my own brother was just chomping at the bit to take off, the second he graduated from law school. Plus my dear father, an oilman too old to enlist, had been handpicked by Harold Ickes himself, the Petroleum Coordinator for War, to serve in a confidential assignment in Washington.

And now Pete was planning to leave, too. Of course, I wouldn't have had it any other way, and I couldn't have been more proud of him. But that didn't mean my heart wasn't aching with the mere thought of him going into battle in some foreign land.

Still, I tried my best not to think about it, so I wouldn't ruin what little time we had left before he went away. Instead, I focused on the ornately framed paintings on the walls and the beautiful holiday decorations here on the second floor of the museum. A huge Christmas tree towered near the bandstand, and the lights had been dimmed to create a soft, romantic mood.

I had to say, it was certainly working.

The band finished their song, and the orchestra leader announced a quick break.

But Pete and I still swayed in our own private dance, until it became a little bit embarrassing.

Finally, he stepped back and lifted my gloved hand to his lips, making the diamonds of my bracelet flash even in the dim light. Apparently it caught the attention of a photographer, who made a beeline for us. He snapped our picture while his bright flashbulb nearly blinded us for a moment.

"I'm taking photographs for the museum," the middle-aged man informed us. "Mind if I take another one of you two lovebirds? I promise I'll send you a copy."

"That would be awfully kind of you," Pete told him with a handshake.

Then Pete and I put our arms around each other and leaned together, smiling for the camera. I hoped and prayed the picture would be a keeper. Because someday, when Pete was far away from me and fighting in this awful war, photos and letters would be all we had to cling to.

And I wanted to remember our New Year's Eve together.

After we gave the photographer the address of my grandmother's mansion, where I lived, too, we thanked the man before he moved on to another couple.

"I suppose we should go back to our table," Pete murmured into my hair. "I hate to be rude to the others."

I smiled up at him. "I'm sure Nana will understand. She adores you, you know."

He smiled back. "Glad to hear it, because I think your grandmother is a pretty swell gal. And your boss, Sammy, is a real straight shooter. It's nice to see them having fun together. Do I detect a budding romance there?"

I laughed. "I'm not sure."

Especially since I knew Nana had been madly in love with my grandfather, Gramps. It had been so hard on her when he had passed away, almost two years ago. As for my boss, Samuel Falcone, P.I. (a man who was the spitting image of what Humphrey Bogart would probably look like as an older gentleman), well, it was pretty apparent that he was completely smitten with my grandmother.

Then again, who could blame him? Nana moved with the grace of a ballerina, and her navy-blue eyes (the same color eyes that I had been blessed with) twinkled with mischief whenever she laughed. Her hair had once been the same caramel color as mine, though it had now settled in to a lovely shade of silver, with plenty of shine.

She winked at me as Pete and I took our seats across from her and Sammy at the round table. Tonight she looked positively radiant in her cornflower-blue gown, along with her sapphire and diamond necklace and earring set.

She and Sammy were seated next to Nana's old friend, Eulalie Laffite. Eulalie was a local artist and art teacher, and she'd always been active in the Houston Art League. She was even a little bit famous in our community for her sculptures.

Sammy nodded at Pete and me. "You kids sure know how to trip the light fantastic. That was some pretty fancy footwork out there."

"Thanks, Sammy," I said with a smile.

Nana beamed at me. "You two look wonderful together, darlin'."

I was about to say the same about her and Sammy, but I decided to hold my tongue. Instead I replied with, "Pete's a great dancer. It's a lot of fun to be out on the dance floor with him."

I looked up into his face, and his laughing eyes met mine. Even though it was dark in the room, I could tell he was blushing slightly. He put his arm around me and scooted closer.

"Eulalie was just telling me about some of her sculptures," Nana went on. "She's been asked to create some pieces to display here at the museum."

Eulalie gave me her usual cat-that-ate-the-canary smile. I was pretty sure she was a few years older than Nana, yet she hardly had a wrinkle on her fair skin, and her dark hair had never grayed. Besides that, her green eyes sparkled as brightly as any teenager's, making her look far younger than what I suspected her real age to be.

"Congratulations," I told her. "What kind of works will you be showing?"

"It will be a celebration of my ancestry. Specifically, the great pirate, Jean Laffite. I am a direct descendant of the man, after all. And of course, I spell the name correctly, rather than with the mistaken use of only one *f* and two *t*'s, as I see so commonly written today." Eulalie let her black lace shawl fall to her shoulders, revealing a gold cross adorned with three nice-sized emeralds, hanging from a brilliant gold chain around her neck.

Pirate's booty if I'd ever seen it.

"How interesting," Pete commented.

"Yes, it is. Very interesting . . ." She looked him up and down, her gaze resting for a moment on his solid shoulders, and then his muscular arms. "One might even say, 'outstanding,' actually. The form, the curvature . . . something to truly appreciate," she sort of murmured to herself.

I raised an eyebrow and glanced at Nana, who had clearly picked up on Eulalie's visual scrutiny of Pete as well.

Nana gave me a wink along with a broad smile. "You know artists have a different view of the world, darlin'."

And apparently Eulalie was taking a nice, long "view" of my guy. While I've never been the jealous type, I hated to think I was going to start now, especially with a woman who was older than my grandmother.

Eulalie's study of Pete must have made him feel a little funny, too, since he leaned closer to me and tugged at his collar. My boss, on the other hand, looked like he was about to burst out with laughter, but he quickly suppressed it by taking a good gulp of his drink and then straightening his white dinner jacket.

Eulalie turned back to Nana. "While I am truly pleased to be creating a collection for the museum, I fear I am having great difficulty in finding a place to complete my pieces. My apartment is much too small, and the studio I once rented has been turned into a boardinghouse. What with all the people moving into Houston these days, and so many, many, many military men arriving . . ." She paused for a moment, with a faraway, dreamy look in her eyes, before going on. "And let's not forget all the other men arriving, thanks to the added jobs because of the war effort. As a result, there is simply no space available for an artist to work."

Nana's eyes suddenly lit up. "Eulalie, why don't you come stay with us?"

Eulalie pulled out a black lace fan, one that appeared to be an antique, and began to fan herself. "With you? Goodness gracious, I wouldn't want to impose."

Nana sat up straight. "Why, heavens, it would be no imposition at all! We've got plenty of room. With my grandson going to law school and my son spending so much time in Washington, it's mostly just Tracy and me rattling around my big, old mansion these days. Thankfully, we still have Hadley and Maddie, and even though they work for us, they're pretty much like family. But it would be wonderful to have a sculptress around the place. I would love to watch you work. I might even learn a thing or two."

Of course, what Nana failed to mention was that my mother was no longer there, either. Not since she had stormed off after a series of scenes that would've made Scarlett O'Hara proud. She'd gone right before Christmas and was now living in the "ancestral home," as they say, also known as her family's mansion in another part of town. Which, these days, was under the ownership of her brother and his wife. My mother had also taken our English butler in tow, and it was likely she would never return. Not as long as her love affair with champagne cocktails took top priority in her life.

Eulalie folded her hands before her in a prayer-like gesture. "Well, in that case, I accept. Provided I do not become a nuisance. And don't forget, I do have a calico cat that must come with me."

Nana patted Eulalie's hand. "It's settled then. Tracy and I love cats."

"That will be splendid," Eulalie told her. "Though I do hope you don't object to my having a gentleman caller every now and then. And just so you know, I will respond in kind, and not interfere with any romantic pursuits on your part." She motioned toward Sammy, who had chosen that exact moment to glance around the huge room.

You know what they say—you can take a P.I. out for an evening, but you can't stop him from keeping an eye out for something suspicious. Okay, maybe nobody really says that, but it applies just the same.

And as his employee and an Apprentice P.I., I figured I'd better follow suit, even though we were supposed to be here for enjoyment and not on the clock. So I glanced toward the tables at one end of the huge hall and "let my eyes do the walking," as Sammy would say, all around the room. But nothing stood out as being terribly out of place.

I saw ladies in evening gowns and gentlemen in tuxedos. Some stood in groups and chatted, while others sat at the myriad of tables that had been set up behind the dance floor. Some people drank punch from champagne glasses, and still others drank mixed drinks. I also noticed that few people held actual wine glasses tonight, which would have been normal at a gathering like this. But with most of France under the control of the Germans, French wine was just about impossible to get these days.

I had almost completed my visual tour of the hall when the little hairs on the back of my neck suddenly stood on end. Of course, I knew *exactly* what that meant. Like turning on the radio in our parlor and letting the tubes warm up, my feminine intuition was starting to kick in and send me a message. A coded message, maybe, but a message nonetheless. And while I had the feeling that something wasn't quite right, I couldn't put my finger on anything specific.

Yet.

But in my short time as an Apprentice P.I., I'd learned my feminine intuition was never wrong, and I would be wise to listen to it now.

Of course, that was a lesson I'd learned from the best. No, I wasn't talking about my boss, Sammy, who'd been a detective for decades, getting his start as a Pinkerton man. Instead, to be honest, I'd learned many of my sleuthing skills from the heroine in my favorite mystery novels—Katie McClue. I'd been reading her books since I was a young girl, and I found her latest episodes under my Christmas tree this year. Katie, of course, had spotted more than her fair share of bad guys by simply tuning into her own feminine intuition. Plus, she'd saved the police plenty of trouble by catching criminals almost before they'd even committed a crime.

Now as I glanced from one evening-gowned woman to the next, each wearing spectacular jewelry, I thought of Katie's most recent adventure, *The Case of the Diamond-Adorned Dowager*. Putting my hand to my own emerald and diamond necklace, it dawned on me that, just like in Katie's book, this party would be the perfect place for a jewel thief.

Not to mention, an art thief. Because there were plenty of high-dollar art pieces and antiquities here worth stealing, as well as an entire cloakroom full of furs and silk scarves downstairs. And while there were *also* plenty of museum guards in uniform milling about—and the walls with paintings were roped off and other items were kept in locked cases—it would still be difficult to keep an eye on everything. A clever thief could certainly abscond with some valuable item or another.

For a moment, I wondered why the museum had even agreed to host a gala here.

I was about to mention this thought to my boss, when a fella who was probably a little younger than me entered the room through the huge double doors that were flanked by Ionic columns on either side. The man wore a tan-and-gold checked sports jacket and a white scarf, and his reddish-blond hair was much longer than what most men wore these days. Though he moved swiftly, with the grace of an athlete, he used his umbrella as a walking cane while he held his Homburg hat in the other hand. He was the perfect picture of an English country gentleman out for a stroll. He practically glided across the floor to the table directly behind ours.

And frankly, I had to say, he stood out at this party.

Was it possible he'd come over from England? Maybe he was a victim of the Blitz, those horrible months from September 1940 to May of this last year, when Hitler had relentlessly bombed England.

After all, tonight's event had been organized to raise money for Bundles for Britain, a charity that gave aid to the Blitz survivors. Maybe he was a special guest of one of the hosts.

Or maybe he was someone else entirely.

Fortunately, I didn't have to wait long to find out. Because Eulalie had noticed the young man, too, and she followed him with her eyes, until she caught the gaze of the white-haired older gentleman he had joined. Then the senior man's eyes held hers, and she smiled and gave him a dainty little wave.

Whereby the older man's face was completely transformed, and he went from aged to infatuated in a matter of seconds. His hazel eyes twinkled and he put his hand to his heart. Then he stood up, fluffed out the tails of his tux, and headed straight for Eulalie, like a piece of metal being pulled to a magnet.

He arrived at our table, reached for Eulalie's hand, and immediately raised it to his lips. "Ah, my lovely Miss Laffite. I fear it's been far too long since I set eyes upon you."

"But I saw you mere days ago, William," Eulalie twittered.

"Yes, I am well aware, for I have counted the hours. If not the minutes."

"Dearest William, you are the knight of all knights . . . so handsome . . . so charming . . . so . . . Oh, but where are my manners?" she said as she turned her attention back to the rest of us. "Everyone, please allow me to introduce Professor William Longfellow, Ph.D. The Professor is the head of the Archaeology Department at the Rice Institute."

"Delighted," Dr. Longfellow pronounced to our table as he gave us a slight bow.

Pete and Sammy both stood to shake his hand while Nana and I smiled and said our hellos.

Eulalie glanced at the table behind ours. "I see you've brought those two delightful young gentlemen with you. Stan and Freddy."

"Yes, I have," the Professor told her. "When they heard I was attending tonight's gala, they both insisted that I include them. Of course, they had no idea how expensive their tickets were, since I purchased them myself. And I must say, tonight's fund-raiser *was* rather expensive. But I didn't mind paying for two such outstanding graduate students. Though until I saw Frederick walk through the door, I wasn't sure he would be able to attend after all. He had such a pounding headache earlier. The poor lad suffers from them so frequently. But it appears he has recovered, and I see that he is acting rather jovial now."

He glanced to the table behind ours, at the young man in the tan-and-gold checked jacket, who was laughing loudly and gesturing as he talked.

Eulalie nodded her approval. "It is a splendid idea to encourage young people to appreciate art."

"Yes, most certainly," the Professor went on. "Now, if I may, please allow me to make the proper introductions of my group to yours."

He turned and motioned to the guy in the checked jacket and another man whose light brown hair was trimmed in a close-cropped, "regulation" haircut. Funny, but until this moment, I hadn't even noticed the second fella, who looked to be a little older than the first—probably because he blended into the background next to the checked-jacket guy. Then again, lots of people probably did.

Both gulped down their drinks before walking over to our table.

Dr. Longfellow smiled and nodded to the second man with the short hair. "First, may I present Mr. Stanley Scott, a student with a tremendous knowledge of history, particularly the history of the world's religions. He has been an outstanding asset to the Archaeology Department."

His words caused Stanley to stand a little taller, while his cheeks glowed pink with pride, adding some nice color to his otherwise pale face with pale gray eyes. I noticed his charcoal-gray suit looked a little threadbare in spots, and suede patches had been sewn on the elbows of his jacket. Most likely to increase the life span of his wardrobe. And to help make ends meet.

In the years I'd gone to college, I'd seen so many of my fellow students barely manage to scrape by. That made me guess a graduate student must be even more strapped for cash, especially since this young man clearly did not come from great means.

Now Dr. Longfellow smiled at the second young man, the one wearing the tweed jacket. "Next, may I present Mr. Frederick Hoffmeister, a true prodigy, and one of the most brilliant archaeology students I have ever had the privilege to teach."

But instead of showing a sense of pride, like his counterpart had, I could have sworn I saw a glint of sadness in Frederick's eyes. It lasted for a mere moment, until Nana and Eulalie introduced the rest of us. Then hands were shaken and the usual "nice to meet you" greetings were exchanged.

I detected a hint of an accent from Frederick when he responded with a hearty, "The pleasure's all mine, chaps and lasses. Please call me 'Freddy.'"

Yet I couldn't pinpoint his inflection. Was it British? Or from somewhere else in Europe?

Before I could ask him where he was from, everyone seemed to start talking at once, seconds before the band began to play again. Naturally, Nana invited Dr. Longfellow and his students to join us at our table, and they'd barely pulled up some chairs when Nana started singing my praises, telling them that I was an Apprentice P.I. who worked for Sammy and his agency. While I'd seen Stanley react to such public praise with pride, and Freddy react with sadness, I, on the other hand, felt oddly uncomfortable when Nana bragged about me. Thankfully, I was spared any further awkwardness when the band broke into the Glenn Miller Orchestra's version of "In the Mood."

One of my favorite songs.

For that matter, it was a favorite tune of plenty of other people, too.

Pete was already up from his chair and holding his hand out to me. "Care to swing a wing?" he asked with a grin, knowing full well what my answer would be. After all, we never missed the chance to swing dance.

"You know I do!" I told him with a laugh.

Seconds later, there we were, on the dance floor, up front and near the band. Pete broke into a rock step and I immediately followed his lead. A few steps later, he sent me into a twirl, and then turned me and spun me the other way, making my gown flare out with each spin. All in perfect time to the music. It was so much fun that I couldn't help but smile.

A few other couples joined us and started to swing as well. Soon it seemed like the whole floor was filled with twirling, spinning, dancing couples, moving at a pace much faster than our grandparents had probably danced.

And then Freddy stepped onto the dance floor with a young woman. I couldn't help but notice what a striking pair they made—he with his strawberry-blond hair and baby-blue eyes, and she with her exotic black hair and dark eyes. But that was as far as their eye-catching union went. Because shortly after they started to dance, it became clear the two were not a good match. Freddy went into his rock step with such grace that his feet seemed to move separately from the rest of his body. He took the girl's hands in his and they completed two up-and-back motions before he turned them both so quickly and smoothly that it looked like he was on ice skates.

Yet his poor partner could barely keep up. She went wide-eyed in surprise and alarm with each new maneuver he made. To tell you the truth, I wasn't sure I could have done any better, since so many of his steps and tricks were ones I'd never even seen before. Especially when he wrapped one arm around her waist and stretched his other arm out, holding her hand in his. Then he twirled her around and around and around, while her feet sort of tripped over themselves. Clearly she was not used to dancing like a top being spun across the floor.

But that movement ended when Freddy suddenly released her. He jumped back and clutched his bicep while his partner put her hands to her cheeks in embarrassment. As near as I could tell, she'd made a misstep that had hurt his arm. Though I had to say, it was completely understandable, considering how hard it must have been to keep up with him and follow his lead.

Moments later, he was laughing, and then he grabbed her hand and they continued to dance. As they flew around the dance floor, I was in awe of each new move that Freddy made, and I started to wonder if he gave dance lessons. While Pete and I definitely knew how to cut a rug, it was always fun to learn some new tricks.

And Freddy had more tricks up his sleeve than a magician.

Even dancing near him, I noticed that Pete and I had naturally picked up the pace and danced a little livelier than we usually did. All the other couples around us did, too, and before long, the couples who'd been dancing more traditional styles ambled off the floor and then turned to watch. More and more people gathered to stare at

Freddy's performance, as obviously his dancing skills were like nothing anyone had ever witnessed.

At least not in person, anyway.

But definitely at the movies.

In fact, I immediately thought of Fred Astaire in *Swing Time*. Without the tap dancing, of course. Because the "Fred" here tonight could've easily given Fred Astaire a run for his money.

Unfortunately, Freddy's poor partner was no Ginger Rogers. Her face began to turn red with exertion, and her wide eyes made her look like a small animal staring down the headlamps of an Oldsmobile. Especially as more couples exited the dance floor, and before long, the only ones left were Pete and me, and Freddy and the young woman who now appeared to be panting.

When the song ended, Pete hugged me and laughed. "What a gas! That guy belongs in the pictures. I've never danced near someone who's that good."

As I rested in Pete's arms, I wasn't so sure Freddy's partner was as pleased about the whole thing as everyone else had been. The band had barely finished when she raced from the hall, as though running from an oncoming train.

Or a moving dancer, as Freddy appeared to be.

While the music had stopped, Freddy's feet had not. To my amazement, he didn't use any of his get-up-and-go to go after the girl he'd been dancing with. In fact, I wasn't sure he even noticed that she'd gone. Instead, he stayed out on the dance floor, practicing a few spins, slides, and maneuvers on his own, without music or a partner.

He reminded me of a runner who kept his muscles warmed up between races with calisthenics. He sashayed from side to side, dancing to some song that played only inside his head. And when the *band* began to play again—a second swing number—Freddy walked into the crowd and grabbed another young woman to be his partner. Then he started them off dancing double-time while Pete and I moved into a rock step and began to swing again ourselves.

To my surprise, no one else joined us and we remained the only two couples on the floor. The rest of the people chose to stay on the sidelines, with their eyes glued to Freddy.

Though honestly, I couldn't stop watching the guy and his new partner myself. I'd never been so close to someone who could dance like a movie star. And as he and his partner went around and around and around, before pulling back into a different maneuver, I had a hard time following Pete's lead.

All the while, I had to wonder, who was this Freddy and where had he come from? And where had he learned to dance like that? Obviously he was much more than just an archaeology student.

By now the crowd around the dance floor had grown larger, and ladies squealed in delight as Freddy made amazing move after amazing move, like he was dancing a routine that had been choreographed in Hollywood.

After the second song had finished, the entire group clapped loudly, and Freddy himself took a bow while his second partner wobbled from the floor. Though *he* was incredibly talented, so far the women he'd chosen for partners weren't up to his speed.

Then again, I wasn't sure if anyone but a professional dancer could dance as fast as he did.

While I was a pretty good dancer myself, I knew I'd never be able to keep up with a guy like Freddy. It made me all the more thankful for Pete, who moved at a pace that made dancing fun and not an Olympic event. I smiled at my beau, before I wrapped my arms around his waist and leaned into him, listening to his heartbeat.

Until Freddy danced his way over to us.

Even now, his feet seemed to have a mind of their own, and he kept moving and practicing at the speed of Superman. He also started to speak to us so fast that I could hardly understand what he was saying, in part because his accent seemed to be getting thicker by the second.

For the life of me, I still couldn't figure out where he was from.

But I didn't get a chance to ask him, because the band started to play Benny Goodman's "Sing, Sing, Sing." As near as I could tell, they'd probably picked another upbeat swing song so the crowd could watch Freddy dance again. Obviously, he was becoming the entertainment for the evening.

Though I hadn't seen him ask another girl to be his partner yet.

I was beginning to wonder whom he would pick, when he suddenly grabbed my hand and started to pull me to the center of the dance floor.

"Mind if I cut in?" he yelled to Pete.

"Sure. Be my guest," Pete said with a crinkled brow.

I shook my head. "No thanks. You'd better find someone else to dance with. I don't think I'd live up to your expectations."

But Freddy acted as though he hadn't heard a word I'd said. That, or he simply didn't care whether I wanted to dance with him or not. It was hard to tell which was the case, especially when his eyes clouded over with a sort of crazed wildness that scared me. Once he had us in position, he immediately started to twirl me, twice as fast as I was used to dancing. His rock step was ridiculously quick, and I fought to keep up with him, before he spun me one way and then turned me the other. He held my hands in a viselike grip, something a dance partner is never supposed to do.

I tried to pull away, but he had such a hold on me that I knew I'd probably get injured if I didn't just go along.

"Please . . . slow down," I hollered to him.

But my voice was drowned out by the music. Not that he would have heard me anyway. Because, strangely enough, he acted completely oblivious to me, as though he didn't even know I was there, his feet and body moving in an automatic, practiced fashion.

Only, he was going three times as fast as any normal person would ever dance. Even Fred and Ginger couldn't have moved at this speed.

And yet, amazingly enough, he moved faster and faster, laughing, like he was having the time of his life.

I, on the other hand, was *definitely* not.

"Please," I begged at the top of my lungs, "slow down!"

To which he responded by linking his elbow in mine and spinning me to his side, right before he rolled me over his back.

Not exactly a ladylike maneuver in an evening gown.

By now the room was going by in a blur, while Freddy kept up his frenzied pace, as though someone had put his personal gas pedal to the floor. I was pretty sure I was going to twist my ankle or fall to my knees. And with the death grip this guy had on my hand, and with the way he was yanking me around, I feared he might even dislocate my shoulder if I didn't at least try to keep up with him. I prayed for the song to end, but the band had gotten to the fast finale, which only seemed to energize Freddy even more.

"Stop!" I yelled to him. "Please stop! I don't want to do this! You're going to hurt me!"

But he ignored my cries. I was about to yell one more time when he twirled me again with one hand, under his uplifted right arm, and then spun me right into him. My back hit his chest with a *thunk* and completely knocked the wind out of me. It should have knocked the wind out of him, too, but he wasn't affected in the least. Instead, he just spun me out and yanked me back in again. I started to feel like a limp rag doll, completely at the whim of this maniacal man.

Then I felt a strong, muscular arm encircle my waist and use my own momentum to spin me up and around, all the while unlatching Freddy's hand from my own.

Finally, I was free from Freddy's grasp.

I turned my head to see who had stepped in to save me.

Pete.

My hero.

He set me on the ground again and glared at Freddy. "Say, chump, what's the big idea? That's no way to treat a lady! Dancing is supposed to be fun. Not dangerous."

With those words, Freddy's entire face contorted in rage. He charged at Pete, who raised his fist in reflex, ready to defend us both.

After that, everything happened in a heartbeat. As Freddy was about to tackle Pete, Pete swung his fist, aiming for Freddy's jaw. But Pete's fist missed its mark by a few inches when Freddy's head suddenly jerked back, and he lost his footing. While his feet continued to slide forward, his whole body fell backward and his face cringed in pain. He clutched a hand to his chest and landed on the floor with a *whump!* For barely a moment, he stared at the ceiling, right before his eyes rolled up and his whole body shook and spasmed.

And then it was over.

He was dead.

The mysterious swing dancer had danced his last.

CHAPTER 2

A Dead Body and a Baffled Boyfriend

The second the scene unfolded before us, I knew something was wrong. Really wrong.

Aside from the obvious, of course.

Because having someone die on the dance floor was never what could be considered a typical day-to-day occurrence. Or in this case, a *nighttime* occurrence.

But you didn't have to be a great scientist like Albert Einstein to figure out that Freddy's death probably wasn't due to natural causes. After all, his behavior had been truly bizarre before he'd suddenly keeled over. Then again, having just met the man, I guess I couldn't honestly say what *was* and what *wasn't* normal for him. Maybe he'd been soused, or maybe he was the kind of guy who downed five pots of coffee a day. I'd known plenty of students who drank a lot of coffee, to help them stay awake so they could study into the wee hours of the morning.

Even so, there was no good reason why a young man as alive and full of energy as Freddy should suddenly die like that. And I'd read enough Katie McClue novels to know when a mystery had landed smack dab in front of me.

Though in this case, it had been a little more literal than most, considering the dead guy had fallen onto the floor almost at my feet.

And he had barely hit the ground, in what could have passed for a Vaudevillian pratfall, when gasps and exclamations rose from the crowd. All the while, the band just kept on playing Benny Goodman's "Sing, Sing, Sing," until it came to the final note. And the final drumbeat. Clearly the bandleader had been unaware of the newest drama unfolding on the dance floor, or I'm sure he would have halted the music immediately.

Pete got to his knees next to Freddy in a matter of seconds, trying to revive him. Then a couple of tuxedo-clad gentlemen rushed in, too, and attempted to administer first aid. But it was no use. No matter how hard they tried, there was just no bringing Freddy back.

"Give it up, son," one of the men said to Pete. "It's over. The guy's a goner."

"I don't understand," Pete said, shaking his head. "I didn't actually hit him."

The other man let out a loud sigh. "I know. He fell over before your fist landed on his chin. But even if you'd slugged the jerk, the guy had it coming. He deserved a knuckle sandwich."

The first man put a hand on Pete's shoulder. "Son, you only did what a fella is supposed to do. This young guy was manhandling your girl, and you stepped right in and stopped it."

Those words, true as they were, didn't seem to make Pete feel better.

He stood up and stared at Freddy's form. "So why did the guy fall over and die like that? It just doesn't make any sense. Did I scare him to death?"

I touched Pete's arm. "If Freddy had been afraid, he wouldn't have charged you like that. Believe me, Pete, the guy was completely fearless, like nothing I've ever seen before. He acted like he thought he was Superman or something. And I know you didn't hit him. I saw the whole thing. None of it makes any sense to me, either." I rubbed my shoulders and wrists, which still ached from the way Freddy had been throwing me around.

Pete slid his arms around me. "Tracy, I'm sorry, I didn't even ask. Are you all right? I really thought that guy was going to hurt you."

"So did I. No matter how many times I told him to stop, he wouldn't let me go. The guy was a madman."

Sammy joined us and glanced at my hands. "You okay, kid? I thought that guy was going to tear you limb from limb."

I rubbed my right shoulder. "Me, too. And if Pete hadn't come to my rescue, I'm pretty sure I'd be headed to the hospital right now."

Anger flashed in Sammy's dark eyes. "Tell me the whole story, kids, starting with 'once upon a time' and ending with the grand finale here. And make it snappy. We don't have much time."

So we did just that. As we talked, Sammy squatted on the floor and began to examine the body. He checked Freddy's pockets and came up with a driver's license, a little cash, and a small aspirin tin. I noticed he palmed the tin while pretending to put it back into place. One of Sammy's old tricks. Then he examined the driver's license, before returning it and the cash to the pocket where he'd found them.

Finally, with a little more patting down, he pulled a folded piece of notepaper from another pocket. Again, Sammy managed to hang on to it with no one being the wiser.

By now a crowd had gathered on the dance floor, and people inched closer and closer, as they pointed and murmured. I could tell all the attention was making Sammy nervous, and he stood up and signaled to the photographer to join us.

"There's a ten-spot in it if you'll take a couple of photos for me," Sammy said, nodding at Freddy's body.

"Sure," the photographer told him. "Happy to help."

And happy to make an easy ten bucks, no doubt.

Which likely explained the smile on the photographer's face as he quickly took several snapshots from different angles. Each time, the flashbulb made its customary *pa-poof* sound and nearly blinded us all for a moment.

He had just finished when a short, broad-shouldered woman wearing a black-velvet dress stepped into his line of fire, so to speak. In other words, she managed to place her stout body between the photographer and Freddy. And both she and her lavalier necklace (with a diamond center stone that was so huge it could have doubled as an ice cube) were now front and center.

She pulled a hankie from her décolletage and started to cry hysterically, glancing occasionally at the photographer's camera, as though willing the man to snap her picture. Her performance was almost as attention grabbing as Freddy's swing dancing had been.

"I knew it!" she cried, with one hand on her cheek while the other hand pointed at Freddy's lifeless form. "That young dancer is dead. Gone. Taken in his prime!" She paused for a breath and then swung her arm in a wide arc until her forefinger now pointed directly at Pete. "And that man killed him! I saw the whole thing with my very own eyes." She emphasized the words by batting her lashes at the photographer.

Pete stared at her in disbelief. "Hold on just a minute, ma'am. I didn't actually hit him. And I certainly did not kill him."

"He didn't," I repeated. "I was right here and I had a front-row seat."

The woman took a step closer to us, and I got a better view of the diamond-encrusted combs holding the braids of her granite-gray hair in place. "Of course you would say that," she argued loudly in the nastiest of tones. "You're his girl. You have to defend him."

And that was the moment when everything went haywire.

Murmurs of "That young man killed the other one," and "He was jealous of that boy dancing with her," began to circulate throughout the crowd. Fueled by the woman in black velvet, the misinformation spread like wildfire.

Poor Pete was beside himself. "No," he kept saying as he turned from one person in the crowd to the next. "It's not true. I did not hurt that man."

But the diamond-adorned woman seemed to be on a mission to prove him wrong. And guilty. She started in on a loud litany of accusations that became more shrill by the second, as she succeeded in riling up the entire crowd.

Thankfully, Nana came to stand next to me, going to bat for our side. "That's enough of that, Ethel Barton," she declared to the loud-mouthed lady. "You don't know what you're talking about. Pete here wouldn't harm a fly."

"He's a vile young man who needs to be removed from civilized society," Ethel went on. "I shall call the police myself and have him dragged away in handcuffs."

Nana glared at her. "You think every man under forty is a murderer or a rapist or a bank robber. You need to find a different hobby other than reporting imaginary criminals to the police. I'm sure they've got better things to do with their time than to listen to your rantings."

"How dare you!" Ethel huffed. "I shall see to it that you, Caroline Truworth, are banned from the Houston Art League and this museum for life."

Nana laughed. "You don't have the authority, Ethel. You're just a member of the art league like I am. And nothing more."

"Ha! I am in charge of this event!" Ethel announced in a way that reminded me of a fire-breathing dragon. "As you well know, I hold much more status here at the museum than you ever shall! And I certainly have the connections and the power to have you barred from our group once and for all."

"You could try if you like, Ethel, but I wouldn't bother," Nana said, cool as a cucumber. "Because I have plenty of friends in the art league, too. And I'll bet the museum probably still appreciates my late husband's money."

More murmurs arose from the crowd.

Pete looked into my eyes, his face one of pure anguish. "How could anyone believe something so awful about me? I didn't hurt that guy. But there's no use telling these people otherwise. They want to believe I'm a killer and that's that."

"Well, I won't stand for it," I told him. "Because it's not true. You only stepped in to save me, so now it's my turn to return the favor."

"Tracy, don't . . ." he started to say.

Right before I put my hands on my hips and moved to the center of the floor. "Excuse me, folks, but I'm afraid you've got this all wrong. And accusing Pete of a crime he didn't commit is a crime in itself, and for that matter, just plain un-American. Remember 'innocent until proven guilty'? Well, that applies in this case, too. I personally witnessed the entire event, and I can tell you, Pete was only rescuing me from Freddy. Freddy collapsed right after he charged Pete."

But Ethel wasn't about to let me have the last word. "I saw him," she insisted, her voice going up a few more octaves. "He killed that young man. Frederick. You can't tell me otherwise. Fortunately, I happen to know a homicide detective personally, so I shall phone him and have this murderer arrested. Then I will testify against him in court. He will be swinging from the gallows before I'm done with him!" With those words, she turned on her heel and stomped off, dragging the train of her velvet dress with her.

All around us, different conversations broke out at once, and the crowd became louder than they had since Freddy had fallen at my feet.

I was ready to run after Ethel when I felt Sammy touch my arm. "Forget it, kid. There's no use duking it out with that dame. As near as I can tell, she's got a lotta pull around here. So getting your hackles up isn't going to help anyone. If you really want to help Pete, put your detective skills to work and take a good look at this crime scene."

My pulse picked up. "Crime scene? So you think Freddy was the victim of foul play, too?"

"I'd bet my bottom dollar on it, kid," he said as he studied the floor near Freddy's body. "I have a hunch somebody wanted to get rid of this guy. And it wasn't Pete, we all know that. But if you want to prove your fella is innocent, you'd better put your anger in your pocket. Then look at this like you'd look at any other crime scene."

And suddenly I knew he was right. Just like Katie McClue had once solved the murder of a man who appeared to have collapsed and died for no good reason, I had to figure out how Freddy had died. In Katie's case, the man had been hit by a tiny poison dart from a blowgun.

"I think we should check for puncture marks," I told my boss.

He tilted his head. "Blowgun dart? Good call, kid. Could be."

So we looked around Freddy's neck and behind his ears, but nothing was amiss.

And that's when I remembered something that had happened earlier. "Take a look at his upper arm," I told Sammy.

He shook his head. "Looks fine and dandy to me."

"No, look under the sleeve of his jacket. The right one."

Then together we pulled the front of his jacket over his shoulder and almost to his elbow, exposing the white shirt underneath.

Let me tell you, even in dim light, fresh blood on a white shirt stands out a mile.

"Bingo, kid," Sammy said with a little chuckle. "I've gotta hand it to you, you're a natural at this. Because it looks like we have a puncture mark."

And sure enough, we did. It was tiny, but enough to have left a small hole in his shirt, and probably a small hole in his skin as well.

"I know exactly when he got that puncture," I told my boss. "When he was dancing with his first partner."

"Good eye, kid," Sammy said, as he motioned for Pete and Nana to lean in.

"What can I do to help?" Pete asked, not wasting any time as he bent in to hear us better.

"Go round up the other two women this guy danced with," Sammy told him. "We need to chat with them. Take both girls to the table where we were sitting and stay with them. Whatever happens, don't let them leave."

"Got it," Pete said with a nod.

"Me, too," Nana added. "Anything to help my favorite detectives."

Then she wrapped her arm around Pete's. "Don't you worry about a thing, young man. That nasty Ethel is full of hot air. We all know you're a good fella, and Sammy and Tracy will prove you're innocent. They're the best there is."

"Thanks, Nana," I murmured just before she and Pete took off.

They were barely out of sight when a voice bellowed from across the room. A voice I recognized but wished I hadn't.

It belonged to a very tall and very large, barrel-chested man, and the crowd naturally parted at the mere sight of him.

It was Detective Denton of the police department's Homicide Division.

Right on cue.

He pulled his fedora from his head, revealing curly brown hair that stuck out everywhere. The sight of his unruly locks always gave me a chuckle, for as much as Detective Denton enjoyed being in control, it appeared his hair hadn't gotten the message.

He was followed by Ethel, who was about half his height. Yet judging from the way she carried herself with her spine perfectly erect, I got the impression she was working hard to stretch her short frame so she might look taller, even if it was only a quarter of an inch.

Detective Denton fixed one of his cold, steely gazes on me as he strode closer. "Well, well, well. Fancy meeting you here, girlie. Let me guess, you just happened to stumble over another dead body. You're racking up quite the numbers when it comes to corpses. We should send you over to fight the Germans. You could be Uncle Sam's best-kept secret."

His words succeeded in getting my hackles up. "Excuse me? But this is only the second dead body I have found. In a month. That hardly makes it some kind of pattern. And frankly, I had nothing to do with either death."

"Yeah, right, little missy. You looked suspicious then and you're not looking any better now. In fact, I'd say this is getting to be a whole new pastime for you. So how did you meet this poor slob?"

"I was dancing with him."

To which the detective snorted. "Of course you were. And then wouldn't ya know it, but the guy drops dead. So what did you do, dance him to death?"

I crossed my arms and tapped my foot. "No, but he practically tried to dance *me* to death. Or into the hospital, at least."

"Miss Truworth is right," Sammy said, taking a step toward Detective Denton. "I've looked at the body and near as I can tell . . ."

But Denton wouldn't even let Sammy finish his sentence. "Oh, who do we have here? Sammy Falcone. My least favorite Sam Spade look-alike. Well, let me tell you something, bub! I'm a real detective and I don't need any help from some two-bit phony gumshoe like you."

Sammy chuckled under his breath. "Then by all means, don't let me stand in your way. But if you try to pull a fast one, and do something outlandish like accuse one of my young friends here of murder, then you'll be dealing with the full force of the Falcone and Archez Detective Agency."

"Falcone and Archez? Whatever happened to your old partner, anyway? Somebody kill him, too? Maybe you unleashed your girl Friday here on him." He smirked in my direction.

Sammy's dark eyes practically burned holes through Denton's skull. "Last I heard, Abe Archez is still alive and getting three squares a day, compliments of Uncle Sam's Army. He's just waiting for his company to ship out so he can go fight in the Pacific."

His words silenced Denton. Nasty as Detective Denton could be, at least he had the decency to respect the men who'd given up their livelihoods and signed up to fight the Japanese and the Germans.

Ethel, on the other hand, had no intention of staying silent. "Aren't you going to arrest somebody?" she hollered in a voice that did not need a megaphone. "The girl didn't kill him! It was her beau!" With another huge flourish of her arm, she aimed her index finger directly at Pete again, just as he walked up to join us. I almost got the feeling she had practiced the movement in front of her mirror.

"Him!" she shouted. "That man, there! He's the killer. He was jealous of the other young man who was dancing with his girl. I saw it all with my own eyes," she repeated.

I took a step closer to Ethel. "And so did I. Pete didn't lay a hand on Freddy."

Denton squinted at me. "There's something about this whole mess that stinks to high heaven. Especially since *you* were right in the middle of it."

Beside him, Ethel stomped her foot. "Arrest and incarcerate that man," she screeched at an octave that I've only heard coming from an air-raid warden's whistle.

"What the heck," Denton said. "I'm game. Let's sort this out at the station." He reached for his handcuffs and grabbed one of Pete's arms. "I'm taking you downtown for questioning, chump. In the meantime, I want everyone away from the body. Until my boys have had a chance to do their work."

Then before I knew it, a bunch of uniformed officers swarmed in and took over the scene, while Detective Denton slapped his cuffs on my fella and began to haul him away.

I could hardly believe my eyes.

Sammy put his hand on my shoulder. "Don't sweat it, kid. We'll get him out of this mess. Now why don't you walk him out, and then get back here so we can finish poking around, before Denton's men put their paws all over everything. We'll join Pete down at the station the second we're done. A lawyer might not hurt, either."

I nodded and took off after them, doing my best to keep up as Denton led Pete from the exhibit hall to the hallway, with its curved ceiling, and then on toward the double staircase.

"Tracy, I can't believe this is happening," Pete tossed over his shoulder to me. "I didn't do anything wrong."

"I know you didn't, Pete. I'll have Nana call your dad's lawyer," I managed to get in as I followed along. "Sammy and I will be there shortly. Don't worry, Pete! We'll get to the bottom of this."

But the furrowed brows and set of his square jaw told me he was already pretty shaken up. And who could blame the guy? Especially since Denton's rationale for dragging Pete away was flimsy at best. Other than Ethel's accusations and insistence, Denton had nothing else to go on. Now I had to wonder if he was only doing Ethel's bidding, or if he was trying to get even with me.

For more or less showing him up on the last case.

Either way, taking it out on Pete was inexcusable.

I caught my last glimpse of my guy through the ornate wrought-iron railing of the left staircase as Denton practically forced him down the stairs with the speed of a runaway train. I prayed that Pete wouldn't lose his footing. At the rate they were moving, I was terrified Denton might send Pete tumbling downward, and he would have a broken neck before they even left the building.

Much to my amazement, a very smug Ethel now stood at my shoulder. "That's a despicable young man you brought to this gala, young lady. Yet I would expect no less from Caroline Truworth's granddaughter. The woman was not born to money, so she has no comprehension of class. You, on the other hand, should know better. You were raised with wealth."

Right at that moment, it took every ounce of self-control that I had not to strangle this woman before me. "If one were to use the argument that coming from wealth determined proper behavior, then you should be the kindest, fairest, and most decent person of all. But since you are none of those things, I'm afraid that's where your premise falls to pieces."

She blinked in befuddlement as I turned on my heel to go back to the exhibit hall and help Sammy. But I'd barely taken two stomping steps when the ball of my left foot landed on something and went skidding forward, sending me to the floor.

Behind me, I heard the echoes of Ethel's laughter as she headed down the staircase.

I rolled to the side and pushed myself up, with no help from Ethel. Or anyone else, for that matter. Then I felt around my skirts to see what had caused me to lose my footing. After a few seconds, I wrapped my fingers over a round, metal object on the floor.

Using the balcony railing, I pulled myself up and took a better look at the item.

It was a rhinestone brooch, though not an especially nice piece. It was the kind of thing that might have come from any five-and-dime store, and most definitely not the kind of jewelry you would expect to see someone wearing at a gala like this.

I turned the brooch over, to look for a stamp or a signature, though I had a pretty good idea I wouldn't find one on a cheap piece of costume jewelry like this.

Even so, I wasn't prepared for what I *did* see on the back. Or rather, what I *didn't* see. Chills suddenly raced up and down my spine as I stared at the object.

For the back of this brooch was missing something very important.

The sharp, pointed pin was gone. And it was nowhere in sight.

CHAPTER 3

Coming Up Missing and Counting Down the Minutes

Naturally, as I held that rhinestone brooch with the pin missing from the back, all I could think about was the pinprick on Freddy's arm. I racked my brain, trying to remember if either of his dance partners had been wearing a brooch.

Not that a brooch like this would have stood out in anyone's mind and memory in the sea of expensive jewels worn here tonight.

Yet I knew there was one way to find out for sure—I had to question Freddy's dance partners myself. And since Pete and Nana were supposed to have rounded up both girls, it was high time I talked to them.

So I ran back to the exhibit hall, and back to the gala.

Despite Freddy's unfortunate demise, the crowd hadn't thinned out at all. In fact, the entire place was on their feet and standing in clusters, while people talked in hushed tones that were very different from what you'd normally expect at a New Year's Eve party. As near as I could tell, most of the museum guards had come upstairs, too, probably to help if they were needed.

The musicians in the band appeared to be taking turns shrugging their shoulders and raising their eyebrows at each other, in a strange rhythm that might have been considered musical had any actual instruments been involved. It was clear they didn't know if they should stay or go, or if they'd even be playing again during the remainder of the evening.

In the meantime, a police photographer snapped some pictures of Freddy's body, while a few plainclothes policemen interviewed people and scribbled on notepads. Though, I had to say, none of them seemed to be putting much enthusiasm into their jobs, probably since they would've rather been out with their own friends and family, celebrating the New Year.

I also knew the police department was becoming more and more short-staffed by the day, with so many young men in Houston and around the country enlisting to go fight Hitler and Hirohito. In fact, I realized that most of the police officers here tonight were probably closer to retirement than to working their way up the ranks.

None of this boded well for Pete. Especially if Denton had already determined that Freddy was murdered. Because, unless his people were digging deep for any real evidence, Pete would be the closest and most convenient candidate to throw the book at.

Which meant that Sammy and I had to work fast.

Thankfully, I spotted him waving at me from our table, so I grabbed the skirts of my long gown and hurried across the room.

When I got there, I found Sammy standing behind Nana, who was sitting next to Eulalie, with the Professor sitting next to her. The Professor had both his hands wrapped around one of Eulalie's, and they appeared to be consoling each other. Stanley and a young woman looked on from the other side of the table.

I recognized the young woman as Freddy's second dance partner.

Sammy leaned toward my ear and gave me the scoop. "Your grandmother and Pete could only corral one of the dames that Freddy danced with. That's Dorothy over there. The other girl got away. Looks like she wasn't just a swing dancer, since she did a pretty nice tap dance to get out of here so fast. Her disappearing act seems a little fishy, if you ask me."

In light of Freddy's death and the broken brooch I'd found, I suspected Sammy was right.

He raised a dark eyebrow in Dorothy's direction. "That little bird has been beside herself since she perched on that chair. She's got a real case of the jitters. So I think it'd be best if you talked to her. I have a feeling she won't say much to me. But I'll listen in and see if I can pick up on anything."

"Got it," I told my boss. "Right after I send Nana on an errand."

Nana's ears perked up and she immediately glanced my way. "How can I help, darlin'? Just say the word."

"Would you mind calling Pete's dad? And arrange for his lawyer to meet Pete down at the police station? While you're at it, would you please tell his dad what *really* happened?" I finished with a sigh.

She scooted her chair back and gave my hand a quick squeeze. "I'll take care of it right away. There's a phone downstairs in the office and I'll look up the number in the phone book. And don't you worry—I'll make sure Harold learns the truth."

Of course, Nana knew Pete's parents, Harold and Mary, since our family and his all lived in Houston's experiment of a community, River Oaks. We belonged to the same country club, and Pete and I had gone to high school together.

"Thanks, Nana," I said, feeling a tiny bit of relief.

Still, I hated the thought of Pete having to endure the bare-bulb-and-rubber-hose treatment that Detective Denton was known for. Somehow I thought Denton enjoyed that part of his job a little too much. Maybe it was because he was past the age where he could enlist and go off to fight with the rest of the men. I wondered if he took out his fantasy of interrogating the enemy on any suspects here.

Nana gave me a kiss on the cheek and waved goodbye to Sammy before she strolled across the hall, moving with the swanlike grace of a ballerina. Sammy watched her for a moment, while I took the seat next to Dorothy and introduced myself.

She offered me a limp, clammy handshake. "You can call me Dot," she muttered before she quickly withdrew her hand and tucked an errant strand of pale blond hair behind her ear. "That guy who was taken away by the police asked me to sit here, so you could talk to me. But I don't have anything important to tell you."

She hugged herself with her arms, and as near as I could tell, she was trying to control the trembling that had taken over her thin frame. Judging by how nervous she was, I knew I'd better proceed with caution.

But before I could ask her a single question, the Professor suddenly threw up his hands and wailed loud enough for the whole table to hear, "It's a travesty! A complete travesty. That young man was well on his way to becoming one of the most preeminent archaeologists of our time. The world has lost a great researcher and a tremendous historian. Such a loss . . . Such a loss . . ."

Eulalie patted his arm. "There, there, William. Freddy will always be remembered for his work. So we must put on a brave face, for our country is at war now, along with most of the world. And just as we did during the last war, we must steel ourselves for the loss of more young men. The best we can do is let them live on in our memories."

I glanced at Stanley, who appeared to be as frozen as any archaeological artifact. He stared stone-faced into his punch, unblinking.

And that's when it hit me. I remembered that I'd seen both Stanley and Freddy down a glass of *something* before joining our table. But Freddy had only just arrived, which hardly gave him time to get a drink on his own. Meaning, someone must have had that drink already there waiting for him.

Had that same *someone* put some kind of pill or powdered poison into that glass? It certainly could have accounted for Freddy's erratic behavior. Although, to be honest, I'd seen a few drunks in my day, and I'd even come across a few drug addicts who took things like morphine or cocaine. But none of them had acted like Freddy did before he died.

Even so, it was an avenue that Sammy and I needed to explore.

I reached over and touched Stanley's hand. "I'm so sorry for the loss of your friend."

He barely mumbled his thanks and kept on staring into his glass. Though I had a hunch he didn't even see it.

"Stanley," I said softly. "What were you and Freddy drinking at your table?"

That's when Sammy suddenly tuned into my line of questioning, like a dial being turned on a radio. He leaned forward ever so slightly and slid his dark eyes in my direction.

Stanley blinked a few times. "I'm not sure . . . Oh, wait, now I remember . . . It was wine. White wine. Dr. Longfellow brought it."

The Professor immediately jumped in. "That's right. Not that it is anyone's concern. But yes, I had a lovely bottle of sauvignon blanc from the Loire Valley in France. I'd been saving it for a special occasion, since, after all, you realize we can no longer get such exquisite French wines these days."

Sammy nodded. "Not since the Nazis marched into France. So what was the cause for celebration?"

"One that you would hardly understand," the Professor replied with a huff. "And certainly none of your business."

"All right, then," Sammy said casually. "Would you mind confirming that you gave a glass to both the boys—Stanley and Freddy?"

The Professor picked a tiny fleck of lint from his jacket sleeve. "Yes, I gave them each a glass. I drank a couple of glasses myself, and that was the end of the bottle. Whyever do you ask?"

Sammy shrugged. "No particular reason. Just covering our bases. Mind if I see the bottle?"

The Professor sat up soldier straight and glared at Sammy. "What exactly are you implying?"

Sammy laughed. "You never know, Doctor. Could be somebody decided that wine needed a little enhancement. Maybe someone added something to it."

Stanley's eyes went wide. "Do you think we were poisoned? Am I going to die, too? Like Freddy did?"

I patted his arm. "Not to worry, Stanley. You're not acting like Freddy was at all, so I doubt you have anything to worry about. But if you like, we could have someone take you to the hospital and have a doctor look at you."

Stanley returned to staring at his glass. "No. I don't want to waste the money. Besides, I feel fine."

"I'm glad to hear you're feeling okay, because that's a good sign the wine wasn't tainted," I told him. "And I didn't mean to upset you. We're just asking some routine questions. After all, a good detective leaves no stone unturned."

Sammy focused in on the Professor again. "I'm waiting, Doctor. Mind directing me to that bottle of your fancy French wine?"

To which the Professor responded with a loud "*Harrumph!*"

He shoved his chair back from the table and stomped over to the table behind ours, where he, Freddy, and Stanley had first been sitting. Then he reached under the white tablecloth and pulled out an empty wine bottle that had been hidden from view. He returned to his chair and *thunked* the bottle down in front of Sammy with so much force that it shook the entire table.

Eulalie and Dot both jumped.

My boss, on the other hand, reacted with a chuckle and a wide grin. "Now, see? That wasn't so difficult."

The Professor pounded his fist on the table. "Confound it, you disrespectful ruffian! *You* are the one who is being difficult! Not to mention, insulting! One of my students has just died, and this is how you treat me?"

Sammy raised his hands. "Sorry, Doctor. I meant no disrespect."

With that, I figured it might be good for me to take the reins for a moment.

I turned to Stanley. "And what about the glasses that you were drinking from? Do you happen to know where they ended up?"

Stanley nodded and immediately jumped up to retrieve two glasses from the same table. He returned to his seat and placed the wine goblets before me.

"This one was mine," he said, pointing to the glass on the left. "And this was . . ." he finished in a whisper, unable to speak his friend's name.

"Thank you," I said gently. "You've been very helpful."

I glanced at Dr. Longfellow. "Would you happen to know where your glass might be?"

The Professor's face burned red with rage, reminding me of a character in a cartoon short before a movie. Any minute now, I almost expected to see steam bursting from his ears.

"Enough!" he yelled. "I will stand for no more of this charade. If this is how we are to be treated, then Stanley and I shall depart." He stood up and motioned for his very dazed graduate student to do the same.

But not before lifting one of Eulalie's hands to his lips, which gave me just enough time to pull my little notebook from my purse and get Stanley to write down his address and phone number.

Then Stanley mumbled a "good night" to us all, while the Professor kept up his theatrics.

"Parting is such sweet sorrow," he recited to Eulalie.

"That I shall say good night till it be morrow," she finished the Shakespeare quote with a sigh.

"I shall call on you soon." He gazed directly into her eyes for a moment, beaming his brightest smile, before he turned and glared at the rest of us.

Then he pivoted on his heels, gave a forward-march signal to Stanley, and the two of them took off. He in the lead, while Stanley trailed behind, like a soldier following a drill sergeant. Somehow I got the feeling the Professor preferred it that way. Though if nothing else, at least Stanley kept his head up and his shoulders back, showing some sense of confidence.

Once they were gone, Sammy flashed me a knowing look. Right before he partially wrapped the wine bottle in one of the huge cloth napkins at the table.

Then he turned to Eulalie. "If you don't mind my asking, Miss Laffite, does your pal there, Dr. Longfellow, always put on a real show like that?"

Eulalie waved him off. "William, I fear, is horribly upset. One of his favorite students has passed away, and as far as he's concerned, it's almost like he's lost a son. I ask that you excuse his ill manners in light of all that has taken place here tonight."

Sammy shrugged. "Sure thing. I can see how a guy might get a little hot under the collar. Under the circumstances."

In the meantime, the dramatic exit of Dr. Longfellow seemed to make Dot even more uncomfortable than she'd been before. Her eyes had gone wide and she'd become downright jumpy. I got the distinct impression she was ready to bolt.

That meant I had to convince her to stay put, if I hoped to get any information from her at all. It also meant I had to ask the right questions, and ask them in a way that would entice her to spill the beans, as Sammy would say.

I instantly thought of one of Katie McClue's earliest episodes, *The Case of the Unnaturally Nervous Nellie*, in which Katie had managed to get a very nervous deaf and mute girl to open up. Not verbally, of course, since the girl could not speak. But instead, Katie discovered the girl had tremendous artistic talent, a gift that had previously gone undiscovered. And with Katie's encouragement, the girl drew several perfect pictures of what she'd witnessed at a crime scene. Her sketches even played a huge role in court, and truly tipped the scales when it came to convicting the bad guy.

Thankfully, I remembered exactly how Katie had worked her magic. She had started by befriending the young girl, before drawing a few innocuous pictures herself, of things like the sun, and the moon, and a few flowers. With each picture she drew, she urged the girl to do the same. And on it went.

So I decided to try Katie's technique. Only, by painting mental pictures, so to speak, instead of *actual* pictures.

I rubbed my shoulder and groaned. "I don't know about you, Dot, but my arms and wrists are so sore from dancing with Freddy. He made me feel like a rag doll, the way he was tossing me around out there. I've never been jerked around like that on the dance floor before."

Dot nodded and straightened the skirt of her pink chiffon dress. "Me, either."

I mirrored her nod. "I went to see Spencer Tracy, Ingrid Bergman, and Lana Turner in *Dr. Jekyll and Mr. Hyde* last fall. Freddy kind of reminded me of the way Spencer Tracy acted in that movie. One minute he was a nice guy, and then he sort of turned into a monster."

Dot's chin practically dropped to the table. "That's what I thought, too! I saw the movie, and it was *just* as scary as the way Freddy was acting tonight."

"*Scary* is the word," I agreed. "No matter how many times I hollered for him to let me go, he ignored me. He just kept dancing faster and faster, like he was a madman."

She gasped. "He did the same thing with me!"

"I'd never met Freddy before tonight," I kept on. "I wonder if he was always like that."

"Nope," she said, shaking her head. "At least, I don't think he was. I'd seen him a few times on campus, but he was all business and he kept to himself. Sometimes I noticed a sort of sadness to him, and I thought maybe he was kind of shy. Definitely not like the guy you saw out there tonight."

From across the table, Sammy kept his eyes fixed on the chair where Stanley had been sitting. Yet I knew he was actually listening intently to our conversation.

"So you knew Freddy from school?" I asked Dot.

"Well, in a way. I knew who he was and I always noticed him. He stood out, with the way he dressed. While the other boys always looked nice enough, Freddy was different. Classy. Though I wasn't sure if he'd ever noticed me before."

"He must have noticed you tonight," I said in my softest tone.

A brief smile flashed across her face. "Uh-huh. I was pretty surprised when he grabbed me out of the crowd. I always wished he would ask me out. But I figured he just didn't have the money. You know, since we were in school and all."

I reflected her smile back to her. "So I'll bet you were happy when he asked you to dance."

She put her elbows on the table and rested her chin in her hands. "At first I was. But then he was so mean to me on the dance floor, and he wouldn't let me go. I guess I should have figured that out after watching him dance with the first girl."

As she spoke, I spotted a flurry of activity out of the corner of my eye. Then I saw what I presumed to be Freddy's body, covered in a sheet, being carted away on a gurney. It appeared the police officers were leaving, too.

Well, I had to say—that was fast!

When it came to clearing a crime scene, this one had been processed in world-record time. Especially since, as near as I could see, the area was not being cordoned off for any future investigation. And none of the gala guests were being asked to leave.

That left a couple of possibilities in my mind. Either Detective Denton believed Freddy had simply died of natural causes. Or, he believed Freddy had been murdered, and Denton thought he already had his suspect and all the evidence he needed to convict him.

Him, of course, being Pete.

I shuddered at the thought of Denton sending my guy up the river to the big house.

Dot watched the scene, too, and she turned even paler than before. For a moment I was afraid she might clam up again.

So I immediately returned to our conversation. "Did you know the first girl that Freddy danced with?"

Dot shook her head. "Nope, I'd never even seen her before. But Freddy seemed to know her. He went straight for that girl when the band started to play swing music. But I guess he must have been pretty mean to her, too. Maybe that was why she stabbed him with her brooch."

And that's when the hairs on the back of my neck suddenly stood at attention. "She did?" I darted a glance at Sammy and picked up on the slight rise of his eyebrow, which was just enough to let me know he'd caught every word.

"Yup," Dot went on. "She was real sneaky about it, too. She slipped off her brooch in one swift move, and when Freddy started spinning around with her, she stabbed him in the arm. I think she just wanted him to stop dancing."

That, or it was her version of a poison dart. But instead of putting deadly poison on a blow dart, she could have put it on the back of a pin.

I let out a low whistle. "My goodness! That would take a lot of talent to pull off a stunt like that. I can't imagine being able to slip off my brooch and stab somebody, all while dancing at the same time."

Dot's eyes went wide again. "Me, either! But that girl knew what she was doing, that's for sure."

I reached into my pocket and took out the broken brooch that I'd found. "Do you think this was hers?"

"Maybe. I didn't get a good look at it. I don't think she put it back on. And then she ran out of here so fast after the dance was over, so I don't know what she did with her brooch."

"Do you know if she left by herself?"

Dot shook her head. "I didn't see her with anyone. Then again, I came by myself, too. Someone sent me a ticket in the mail, though I have no idea who. When I saw Freddy walk in, I was hoping it might be him."

Somehow I doubted Freddy would have been the one to secretly send her a ticket, considering the price of admission.

Of course, there was no need to insult her with that bit of information, so I simply responded with, "That's interesting. So you never figured out who mailed it?"

For the first time since I'd gotten Dot to open up, she let out a little laugh. "It could have been anyone, because I always tell everyone how much I love to go dancing. Especially swing dancing. And I thought it would be nice to go out and ring in the New Year somewhere."

And then, as if the band had heard her, they suddenly started up again, playing Glenn Miller's "Moonlight Serenade," while the bandleader stood at the microphone. "Ladies and gentlemen, I know we've had a true tragedy here tonight. No doubt we can all agree that it's terribly sad for a young man to pass away like that. But even so, 1941 is nearing its final minutes, and we're about to enter 1942. Young men all across the country will be leaving us soon, going off to fight in this war. So let's please honor them by counting down to the New Year, which will hopefully bring peace and freedom to all!"

Cheers went up around the room, and a few couples even got up to dance, though they stayed near their tables or on the edges of the dance floor, avoiding the spot where Freddy had breathed his last.

At that very moment, I longed to be in Pete's arms. Not only was it one of our favorite songs, but I had so desperately wanted to be together when the clock struck midnight. With him about to enlist and leave for parts unknown, it might be years before we had the chance to do this again.

If we *ever* got the chance to do this again.

When the band finished playing their song, all eyes turned to the clock, and the bandleader started the countdown.

Then nearly everyone in the crowd chimed in. "Ten . . . nine . . . eight . . . seven . . ."

But instead of counting down the seconds till midnight, I was counting down the seconds until Sammy and I could get out of here and go join Pete at the police station.

"Four . . . three . . . two . . . one! Happy New Year!" the crowd hollered, followed by plenty of couples who partook of the annual tradition of kissing the second the New Year started.

The band broke out with "Auld Lang Syne," but only got through a few bars before Ethel came rushing into the room, pausing just inside the entrance to the exhibit hall. She let out a shriek as piercing as any scream I'd ever heard in any horror movie.

At once the band went silent and the crowd followed suit.

With all eyes on her, Ethel yelled in her megaphone voice, "Help! Help! We've been robbed!"

I moaned and dropped my head into my hands.

At this rate, Sammy and I would never get to the police station to help Pete.

Much as I hated to say it, 1942 wasn't exactly getting off to a good start.

CHAPTER 4

A Stolen Statue and Another False Accusation

Never in my wildest dreams could I have imagined that tonight would have turned out like it did. And to think, the night wasn't even over yet! But when Pete and I had decided to attend this fund-raising gala with Nana and Sammy, I thought we were in for a night of romance and dancing among beautiful works of art. A place and time where I could spend a few last precious moments with Pete, before he went off to war and I had to say "so long" to him at the train station. And like all the other women my age and older, who all had to say goodbye to their sweethearts—husbands, fiancés, or just steady boyfriends—we all knew full well that our fellas may never come home. Many of them would not survive the war.

But instead of a night of starry-eyed sighs, this night, of all nights, held a murder and a burglary—barely an hour apart from each other.

And both before the clock ran out on 1941.

To top it off, Ethel had managed to land smack dab in the middle of both crimes. Or, at least, she'd been the one to announce them both, something she was surprisingly good at, considering the volume of her voice. And just in case there might be any question about her abilities, she rushed to the center of the dance floor, tipped her head back, and released another ear-piercing scream.

Which meant, once again, that all eyes were on her and only on her.

Beside me, Dot nearly jumped to the top of the museum's very high ceiling.

Eulalie, on the other hand, practically seemed to be purring. "What an eventful evening this is proving to be," she murmured to no one in particular.

Unfortunately for the rest of us, Ethel wasn't finished with her performance. Now that she had everyone's complete attention, she spread her arms wide and repeated at the top of her lungs, "We've been robbed!"

The crowd finally erupted with gasps and exclamations, as everyone glanced at one another, trying to figure out exactly what had been stolen. Gloved hands reached up to finger jewels worn around necks and on ears. For a moment, I even involuntarily touched my own emerald jewelry.

Security guards immediately circled Ethel, before she pointed toward the door and announced, "No, not here, you fools! Downstairs. You'll see the empty display case."

And while the security guards rushed out, Nana glided back into the room, with her long gown flowing across the floor, giving the appearance that she was floating on a cloud.

Ethel's eyes went wide when she saw her, and clearly she wasn't about to let such a well-timed opportunity go to waste. She sucked in air, ready for another tirade, and then let it rip.

Hands on hips, she turned to face Nana. "Well, well, well, who do we have here? Why, if it isn't Caroline Truworth! Let me guess, you were practically all by yourself downstairs, weren't you?"

Nana did a little curtsy. "And what's that got to do with the price of tea in China?"

Ethel raised one arm up with a flourish, while she extended the other arm and pointed directly at Nana, in a position that reminded me of Errol Flynn about to engage in a movie sword fight. "Precisely what were you doing downstairs?"

Nana put a hand on her hip. "I was calling a lawyer for Pete Stalwart. You remember Pete, don't you? He's the young man you wrongfully accused of committing murder! The wonderful young gentleman whom you had hauled away by your police friend."

"I was only doing my civic duty, by saving our city from a murderer," Ethel scoffed. "As for you, the only place you could have used a telephone was in the office. And while you were there, you easily could have taken the key to the cabinet that held the statuette that was stolen. So obviously, you must be the one who stole that priceless piece! You and your kind are a menace!"

Nana offered a smug smile. "I'm a menace? I'm not the person having a temper tantrum in the middle of the room while falsely accusing people of crimes. I hear the Nazis are very fond of such tactics. There's no need for you to start that sort of thing over here in America."

Right about then, Ethel's face turned a shade of red I've never seen before on a human being. "How . . . dare . . . you!" she spewed forth, once again reminding me of a fire-breathing dragon.

Sammy rushed to Nana's side and flashed his P.I. license to Ethel. "Why don't you simmer down, Mrs. Barton. I would be happy to help you find whatever you believe is missing."

"Missing? Hardly!" she cried out. "It's been stolen, and we have been robbed! And I would never allow you, of all people, to help. I've seen what your kind can do. You were with that young man who is a murderer, so I would never trust you or any of your party to assist in solving a crime of this magnitude."

At that moment, I figured it might be a good idea if I joined forces with Sammy and Nana. So I patted Dot's arm and told her I'd be back. Then I took off across the floor and slipped in behind Nana, putting a hand on her waist.

Sammy chuckled under his breath. "Come now, Mrs. Barton. People misplace things all the time. Mind telling me *what* is missing? And what makes you think anything was *stolen* at all?"

Ethel sputtered for a moment. "Are you a complete imbecile? The burglary is as obvious as that thing on your face that you call a nose! There was a Greek statuette in a display case downstairs, one that stood in the middle of the room. And now that case is empty."

"Maybe it was empty to begin with," Sammy suggested, though I knew he was only trying to bait her into telling him more.

And she took that bait—hook, line, and temper. "I know precisely what item was in there! After all, it was around two thousand years old. A small statue, sculpted from white marble, of a turtledove. It's priceless. And the door on the case is now open, probably because someone either stole the key or picked the lock! Maybe that Pete character and his girl committed a burglary before they came up here to dance. Maybe that's why he murdered Frederick. The poor boy probably witnessed their crime, and Pete decided to silence him, once and for all."

Sammy responded with more chuckling. "And maybe you've been watching too many Cagney gangster movies."

"I know enough to recognize a reprobate when I see one," Ethel bellowed.

"Oh, is that so?" Sammy retorted. "It seems to me you can't make up your mind who you want to accuse. First you go after young Pete. Then you accuse Mrs. Truworth. And to top it off, you've even made mention of my apprentice here, Caroline's granddaughter."

But before the confrontation could go further, a uniformed police officer sauntered in to join us. The dark circles under his eyes made me think he could have used about two days' worth of shut-eye.

Sammy raised his brows at Ethel. "My, my, Mrs. Barton, but that was speedy. It seems you've got the cops at your beck and call."

She puffed out her chest, like a bird I'd once seen at the Houston Zoo. "Of course I do. And there should be several of them downstairs."

The tired officer removed his peaked cap, rubbed his balding head, and turned to Ethel. "Don't worry, Mrs. Barton. I'll have a man posted at every door. We'll ask people to leave group by group, and we'll check them as they go. If that statue's still here, we'll find it."

Sammy flashed his P.I. license to the officer. "My associate and I would be happy to lend a hand. Searching this crowd could take hours. And it could make for a pretty long night for you boys."

The officer let out a loud sigh. "Tell me about it. Still, it's a job and it's better than being in the soup line. But none of these people will be happy about us putting our paws on them and patting them down. Not to mention, looking in their purses and pockets and things." The officer cocked his head and gave Sammy the once-over. "Say, fella, you sure look a lot like Humphrey Bogart. Anyone ever tell you that?"

"He does, doesn't he?" Nana said as she glimmered up at Sammy.

My boss just grinned. "I hear it all the time. Though frankly, I don't see the resemblance. I think Bogey is a little shorter than me."

Ethel stomped her foot and glared at the police officer. "Enough! I do not want this man, whomever he resembles, to help out in any way, shape, or form. His *entire* group is nothing but a band of thieves and murderers. I ask that you check him and his companions first for the missing statuette. Then escort them out of the museum immediately."

Sammy turned his attention back to Ethel. "Fine by me. This party's taken a turn for the worse anyway. We're happy to go." Then he nodded to the police officer. "Come with me, pal, and I'll show you to our table. You can search the lot of us and then we'll be on our way."

Which was music to my ears, since I was dying to get to the police station to see Pete. Except now I was also worried about Nana, since Ethel had publicly pointed a finger at her, claiming she'd stolen an ancient artifact. So while I was chomping at the bit to leave and go help my guy, a very big part of me wanted to stick around and investigate, to see what we might uncover with what Ethel was calling a burglary.

But who knew if anything had actually been stolen or not? As far as I was concerned, it was very likely someone had simply taken the statue out and placed it elsewhere, maybe as they were cleaning the displays or rearranging things. I had a hunch that an hour of investigating would probably clear up that little "mystery."

Unfortunately, this was one crime scene we would not have a chance to investigate. Whether Ethel was really in charge or not, she had succeeded in having us kicked to the curb, in a manner of speaking.

Even the police officer seemed to feel funny about the situation, and once we were back at our table, he cleared his throat, barely able to hide his unease. "I'm sorry about this folks. I hate to embarrass anyone, but I've got to search each of you."

Eulalie immediately rose from her chair. "Embarrass? Not at all. The human body is a beautiful work of art, created by the Almighty Himself. You may search me first. I'd be delighted." She stood up tall and stretched out her arms.

The policeman froze in place for a moment, terror flashing across his face. Finally, he gulped and put his hands on Eulalie's waist. Then he proceeded to pat down her entire body, moving quickly, with motions that resembled someone trying to put out a hot ember, rather than search for a stolen statuette.

Eulalie giggled and smiled throughout the entire procedure. "If I'd have known I were to meet up with such a handsome specimen of manhood, such as yourself, why, I would have actually stolen an artifact or two."

Sammy bit his lower lip, and I could tell he was fighting hard not to laugh.

Eulalie winked at the officer when he had finished with her. "Perhaps you and I might try this again sometime. In private."

"Sorry, ma'am. But I'm spoken for," the poor man mumbled.

"Such a pity," Eulalie cooed while he looked in her purse.

Then the officer moved on to Sammy, probably since he seemed like a less-threatening subject. And while he checked Sammy's pockets and patted him down, I glanced at Dot, who sat with eyes the size of saucers. Her shallow breaths told me she might even faint.

And it also signaled that my interview with her was over. So I quickly asked for her address and wrote it down in my little notepad, along with the phone number to the boardinghouse where she was staying. Just in case I needed to talk to her later.

Thankfully, she didn't pass out when the officer checked her over next. After that, he moved on to Nana. And while she and I were being searched, the officer didn't notice my boss secretly stashing the goblets that Stanley had retrieved into his pockets. Nor did he see Sammy stuff Professor Longfellow's wine bottle up the left sleeve of his jacket and then hang on to the bottom with his hand. But I knew my boss well enough to spot his maneuvers, and I followed behind him as we left and our entire table was escorted out of the exhibit hall. Then I stayed behind him as we all went single file down the right side of the double staircase, so I could block Sammy's left side and no one would spot the bottle.

Once we got to the first floor, I noticed a couple of police officers dusting a display cabinet for fingerprints. And sure enough, that display case—with a wooden base and top, and four glass windows held in place by wooden frame—was empty. Whatever artifact had been inside the cabinet must have been important, for it to warrant a case of its own. I guessed it had been the home of the now missing marble turtledove.

But we weren't allowed to stick around long enough to find out. Even so, the officer leading us out did let us pause by the hatcheck room, where we all retrieved our coats and wraps. Yet not until those items had been searched, too.

While I slipped into my own wool coat, Eulalie insisted the officer help her don her sable, calf-length coat. The poor man gulped again but still obliged, quickly jumping away once she had the coat on.

Then we left via the front door.

And stepped out into the chilly and *very* foggy night air.

Sammy offered his right arm to Nana, before we all moved slowly and carefully down the slick front steps. As we went, my grandmother and Eulalie started to hammer out the details of her moving in to our mansion. A move that I was beginning to wonder about more and more. But it wasn't my place to question what my grandmother did. After all, she was a grown woman and she owned the mansion that she and Gramps had built. What she did with it was entirely up to her.

Still, I *had* promised my father that I'd stay at the mansion to watch over her, while he spent so much time in Washington. Now I wondered if part of that promise involved talking to her about her choice of houseguests. Though to be honest, I had no idea how to even broach the subject. I didn't want to give her the impression I was treating her like a child, and I certainly didn't want to sound like a snob, by trying to tell her who was "good enough" to come live under her very own roof.

My grandmother was the kindest person I knew, and practically famous for her generosity. She hadn't grown up with money, and it wasn't until Gramps had invented some oilfield tool that they became wealthy beyond their imagination. Yet Nana never forgot her roots, and she taught me to be charitable, but to do so in a way that wouldn't hurt someone's pride. So, when I was a child, Nana and I would sneak boxes of groceries onto someone's front porch, then ring the bell and run. Or, she'd hire a young boy to deliver a new radio or kitchen blender to a family who was down on their luck. To her, it was a great game to secretly send gifts to people who could use a helping hand.

Yet despite her attempts to keep her charity quiet, people still managed to find out. And those people had no intention of keeping her good deeds a secret. Even now, when we donated clothes and things to Bundles for Britain to help victims of the Blitz, a lady at our church always smiled and called Nana "the Angel of Kindness." Though it was a lovely name, my grandmother in turn quoted Matthew 6:3, the part of the Bible that mentioned not letting your left hand know what the right hand was doing when it came to giving. Then she would take me aside and emphasize that a person with true generosity in their heart was never supposed to brag about their donations.

And I had to say, I loved Nana for her thoughtfulness and generosity. It was just one of the things that made her so special to me. But sometimes there was a fine line between being generous and being taken advantage of.

I glanced at Eulalie as she neared the last step, and I wondered if she might be exploiting my grandmother for some reason that wasn't readily apparent. Just the mere thought of it made me realize I had no choice but to talk to Nana about it the next day. Once she'd gotten plenty of sleep, of course. After all, I figured she'd been through enough drama for one night, especially since she'd practically been accused of stealing a priceless artifact from the museum.

Though if she was upset about it, she certainly didn't let it show. I, on the other hand, was still seeing red over the whole situation. First Ethel Barton went after my fella, and then she went after my grandmother. She had crossed more lines in one night than Rita Hayworth's tennis ball. And I intended to make sure that all the wrongs she'd committed were made right.

Starting with meeting Pete at the police station. And from past experience, I knew I was in for a very long night.

Sammy paused when we all got to the bottom of the steps. I knew he'd be taking Nana home, and they'd probably drop Eulalie off first. But I had ridden with Pete, and even through the fog I could see his dark Cadillac was still parked along the street.

Sammy nodded in that direction, as though he'd read my mind. "Need a ride, kid?"

And that's when I remembered that Pete kept a key hidden on his car, just in case he ever got locked out.

So I shook my head. "Thanks, but I know where the spare key is stashed. I'll take Pete's car down to the station. Then he'll have a ride home when we're finished."

Provided he *would* be coming home tonight. And provided Detective Denton didn't just throw the book at him and toss him into a jail cell.

Nana put her hand on my arm. "Now don't you worry, darlin'. Pete's dad's lawyer said he'd be on his way. And if he doesn't get Pete out of this jam, then I know you and Sammy will."

I gave her a quick hug. "Thanks for the vote of confidence, Nana."

Sammy raised an eyebrow in my direction. "I'd better get these ladies home, kid. Then I'll join you down there at the O.K. Corral. Since you'll get there first, don't let 'em give you any guff. Make sure you come out swinging. Remember the last time you and Denton went a few rounds at the station."

How could I forget! It was on the case where I'd met Sammy and officially become an Apprentice P.I. And it didn't take me long to figure out that Detective Denton thought he was a regular Dick Tracy and God's gift to crime solving.

"Aye, aye," I told my boss, before saying a quick good night to Nana and Eulalie.

Then I headed for Pete's Caddy. Thankfully, I found the key right away, and I was behind the wheel in a matter of minutes. I pushed the clutch in with one foot and kept the other on the brake, while the engine caught and started to purr like a tiger. Next I pulled on the headlamps and saw beams of light shining right into the wall of fog before me. With such low visibility, it was going to be slow going. But no matter how treacherous the driving might be, I had to get to the police station tonight. So I put the car in gear, turned the wheel, and gave it a little gas.

Then little by little, I pulled away from the curb, just as a few more of the gala attendees trickled down the sidewalk. I had to say, this latest bunch that had just emerged looked furious. Probably as a result of the wonderful pat down they had just endured, compliments of Ethel and her outlandish accusations. And if the police hadn't let the rest of the patrons go, that meant the marble bird probably hadn't been recovered yet.

Yet something about the whole scenario still struck me as being fishy. Especially when I remembered one of Katie McClue's later cases, *The Mystery of the Midnight Robbery*. It was the episode where Katie and a whole crew had been searching for an ancient urn that a woman had reported stolen. But in the end, Katie had proven a maid had merely taken the urn from its display case in order to clean a spot from the lid—something the woman who owned the urn had known about all along. And yet she'd turned the whole thing into a federal case, simply because she wanted her picture in the paper.

Now I wondered if the situation might be similar with this artifact that was supposedly missing from the museum. Especially when I remembered how Ethel had acted. For as much as she screamed and yelled and accused everyone around her, in a strange way, she appeared to be enjoying the attention. Was it possible the turtledove statuette was only out for restoration, and Ethel had simply seized on that opportunity to make herself famous, in a sense?

Then again, maybe the artifact actually had been stolen. And if so, maybe the theft was somehow connected to Freddy's murder.

The idea kept playing through my head as I worked to keep the Caddy's speed down, forcing the car to practically crawl through the fog to the police station. Funny, but in all the rescue scenes I'd ever seen at the movies, I'd yet to see one where the car was going a mere six miles an hour.

But fast or slow, I was still on my way to rescue Pete from the clutches of Detective Denton.

I took a deep breath, steeling myself for battle, knowing full well that I was about to enter the lion's den.

One where I'd gone a few rounds before.

And who knew what might await me there this time?

CHAPTER 5

Interrogation and Shocking Allegation

I blinked my tired eyes as I drove Pete's Cadillac to the police station. Even though the Caddy handled like a dream, it was still slow going, and staring at all that fog made my eyes sore. So I fought to focus on the road directly in front of me, with the occasional glance from side to side as I tried to spot any landmarks along the way. Anything to give me an indication of where I was and how much farther I had to go. Thankfully, I'd been to the building a time or two before, so at least I was familiar with the route.

After what felt like hours, I slid the Caddy into a parking spot in front of the station. Then I went inside and did some pretty fancy "tap dancing," as Sammy would say, to talk my way into the interrogation room where they were holding Pete.

I found him sitting there alone, stretched out and leaning back in his chair, while he stared at a cup of coffee. At least they'd offered him that. It was a good sign. Meaning, they probably didn't think he was guilty if they were acting so hospitable toward him.

His face lit up when I swished into the room in my teal evening gown. Thanks to his well-mannered upbringing, he stood the second I walked in.

"Tracy, are you ever a sight for sore eyes!" He immediately wrapped me in his arms and kissed my forehead.

"Sammy's on his way," I murmured. "Sorry we didn't get here sooner."

"I'm just glad you're here at all. I can't believe Detective Denton let you in this room."

That made me laugh. "Let's just say he owes me one. Because he allowed a whole crowd in here one time when he interrogated me. And most of those people weren't helping me one bit."

"Well, you got here before my dad's lawyer did."

"Nana called him and he's on his way."

Pete leaned back and looked at me. "What a way to ring in the New Year, huh? I didn't even get to kiss you at midnight."

With those words, his pale blue eyes stared into mine, and I suddenly forgot all about the turmoil of the night. Not to mention, the fact that we were standing in a room at the police station.

Instead, all I cared about was that I was finally reunited with Pete. And all I could think about was the way he brought his face close to me, with his lips mere inches from mine. I closed my eyes, waiting to sink into the warmth of his kiss.

But then the door banged open and Detective Denton stormed in. "What kind of shenanigans have we got going on here?"

Pete and I immediately pulled apart.

"Just a New Year's Eve kiss," Pete explained, blushing slightly.

Denton pointed a chubby finger at me. "And you! It's bad enough that you weaseled your way in here, but to carry on like this in public is going too far!"

That got my hackles up. "Oh, *I'm* going too far? How about your dragging my guy out of the museum in handcuffs just because some woman claimed he is a murderer?"

Detective Denton sneered. "Well, maybe he is and maybe he isn't."

"Hey, wait just a minute . . ." Pete said. "If you'd hear me out, you'd know I'm innocent."

Now Denton jabbed a finger in Pete's direction. "Well, I'd be happy to hear you out, buddy. But you were being a real nuisance about it all when you said you wanted to have your lawyer present first. That makes me think you're guilty as sin."

I felt my eyes go wide. "Pete is not a killer. And you need to do the right thing and let him go this instant."

The huge detective put his hands on his hips. "I don't need some broad like you telling me how to do my job. You gave me enough trouble when I tangled with you last time."

I squinted at him. "Ah, yes, I remember it well. As I recall, that's when you accused me of shooting someone with a knife. Quite a feat. I haven't even seen a trick like that at the circus."

Denton looked from me to Pete, and then back to me again, sputtering. "Oh, yeah? Well, nobody likes a wise guy. Or, in your case, a wise girl. Now sit down!"

By now I figured I'd done my part in "coming out swinging," like Sammy had instructed. So I simply followed Denton's orders and took the chair that Pete held for me, before he returned to his own.

Just as Sammy knocked and walked on in.

Denton responded with an "*Aaaack!*" and threw his hands in the air.

Then he focused his Superman-like, X-ray vision stare at me. "Here we go again, with the Humphrey Bogart look-alike. Maybe I should take a closer look at his P.I. license to make sure it's real. For all I know, you just hired some actor to play your boss. You're a dizzy enough of a dame to do something madcap like that."

Sammy removed his fedora, placed it on the table, and took a seat next to me. "You can look all you like, Denton. Hey, for that matter, call the licensing board. You'll find out I was a detective when you were still in diapers."

But Denton didn't even get a chance to respond, since the door opened again and a tall, balding man with dark-rimmed glasses entered. Judging from the worn leather satchel he carried, I guessed he was Pete's father's lawyer. Though he wasn't exactly dressed for the part. He had on a blue-and-white striped pajama top under his suit jacket, and while he had on regular trousers, he wore bedroom slippers on his feet. What little hair he had left was sticking out in ten different directions, as though he'd forgotten to comb it.

"I'm Nathaniel Nedrick, the Third, Attorney-at-Law," he announced.

Then Pete made the rest of the introductions while the lawyer glanced at each of us in turn, unblinking, with a gaze that seemed to be looking right through us.

"Well, isn't this just fine and dandy," Detective Denton said with a newfound drawl. "Shall we lay odds on whether you can keep your client out of jail or not?"

The lawyer's eyes rolled in a complete circle, paused, and then started into a second one. "I got here as quickly as I could," he murmured as he stumbled into a seat and plopped his satchel on top of the table. "Only minutes earlier, the missus and I had returned home from a private party. I was just climbing into bed when Caroline Truworth called. So lovely to hear from her again. My, but she's a wonderful asset to our community of River Oaks. I remember her late husband well. A rather jovial fella. Anyway, I'm here now and I certainly wish I hadn't taken those sleeping pills before she phoned." Then his eyes slammed shut, like someone pulling the shades down on a window.

Pete sucked in air while my chin nearly hit the table.

Sammy chuckled and shook Nathaniel. "Wake up, pal. You can sleep later. Right now your client needs you."

The lawyer responded with a jump, and then began blinking his eyes and shaking his head. "Oh, heavens, so sorry for the mishap. Is that coffee I see you're drinking?" he asked, staring at Pete's cup. "Would you mind terribly if I had a cup or two? In fact, I could use the entire pot, if you would be so kind. I'd be happy to put money in the kitty for it."

He opened his satchel and reached for his wallet. He pulled out a few bills of various denominations and dropped them onto the table.

Then he blinked a few more times while his head started to wobble. "I'll take a slice of blueberry pie with that. À la mode, if you don't mind . . ." he mumbled before his eyes closed again and his chin dropped to his chest.

This time Detective Denton grinned before he glared at me. "Why is it that every time you cross my path everything turns into a Vaudeville act?"

"Hardly my fault," I said through clenched teeth.

Sammy shook the lawyer. "C'mon, buddy. Get your ducks in a row and help our boy here."

To which Nathaniel Nedrick the Third, Attorney-at-Law, blinked a few more times and slurred, "Did Santa bring me a new sled? I've been a very good boy." Then he dropped his head onto his satchel and started to snore.

Loudly.

So much for the idea of having legal representation.

Pete's eyes went wide. "Now what?"

Detective Denton laughed. "Well, sonny, I can put you in a cell and let you wait until morning. You can either call another lawyer or see if this guy wakes up."

Sammy waved him off. "No need, Denton. Because there's not much to the story."

"And Pete did nothing wrong," I added.

Sammy nodded to Pete and me. "Why don't you two kids tell him the whole tale?"

So we did just that. From the part where Freddy had been dancing like a madman with the first two girls, to the moment where he grabbed me and refused to let go. Then we told him about how Pete had hauled back with his fist, ready to defend us, seconds before Freddy had dropped dead.

Detective Denton leaned back in his chair and stared at Pete. "So you're saying you didn't actually hit the guy?"

"That's right, Detective," Pete said with a nod.

"But you were ready to give him a knuckle sandwich if he came any closer. To protect your girl?"

Pete sat up straight. "What guy wouldn't?"

"Believe me," Sammy added. "Freddy had it coming."

Denton shook his head. "That's not the story I heard. When I got the call—at home, I might add—we were told you were on that guy like a prizefighter."

Sammy chuckled. "Be reasonable, Denton. Look at the back of Pete's hands."

Pete put his hands palms-down on the table where everyone could see them.

Denton spread his long arms open wide. "Swell. Exactly what am I lookin' at?"

"Do you see any bruises? Scrapes? Blood?" Sammy demanded. "If young Pete here had whaled on the guy like you heard he did, or if he'd even punched the guy at all, Pete's knuckles would tell the tale. But as you can see, Pete doesn't have a mark on him. And the dead guy's face didn't have a mark on it, either."

"All right, all right," Denton said, waving him off and not bothering to keep the annoyance from his voice. "I'll let you go for now. But stick close to home. Don't leave town."

Pete leaned forward. "But Detective, I *have* to leave town. I'm about to enlist and do my part to help Uncle Sam."

And for the first time since the events of the evening had unfolded, I noticed a softening in Detective Denton's demeanor. "Give it a few days, will ya, son? Until we can get this wrapped up? Ethel Barton is a friend of the mayor's, and I've got to tread lightly here."

Pete frowned. "Tons of guys my age have signed up already. I don't want people to think I'm a coward."

"I know, son," Denton said with a sigh. "Ever since we were sucker punched at Pearl Harbor . . . hard to believe it was only a month ago . . . we've got guys leaving the force, right, left, and center. Going off to fight Hitler. And Hirohito and his nasty bunch."

Pete sat up soldier straight and looked Denton in the eye. "Then you *do* understand why I have to go. We've all heard about the horrible things going on in Europe. And you've read about the Rape of Nanking in China."

Sammy was already nodding. "Hundreds of thousands of innocent Chinese were raped and murdered by the Japanese Army. They went there to kill, kill, kill."

Pete's face clouded over with anger. "And look at the way Hitler bombed England. We could be next, you know. If we don't take a stand and stop these people. We didn't start this mess, but now that *they* did, we need to put a stop to it. Right away."

That's when I suddenly found myself fighting back tears. I was so proud of my guy. He was a hero to me already, with his determination to join the battle against the evil forces that were trying to take over the world. Our country included.

"Pete's going to leave a good job as an engineer for an oil company, to go off and fight for freedom," I said with much more emotion than I had intended. "He's willing to sacrifice everything, just like all the fellas who are enlisting right now."

Detective Denton nodded, and for a moment, I thought I saw a glimmer of pride in his eyes. "All right, then. All of you get out of here. For now." Then he glanced at Mr. Nedrick. "You can leave your lawyer and let him sleep it off."

As though on cue, Mr. Nedrick let out a loud snork before he continued his regular snoring. And I decided Detective Denton was probably right about leaving him until he woke up.

So we all stood up and gave some polite but stilted goodbyes. My feet felt leaden by the time we walked out of the police station. Dawn was breaking and the fog had burned off, though the mercury hadn't gone up one bit. If anything, it was even colder out now than it had been the night before. Thankfully, Pete kept his arm wrapped around my shoulders as we ambled toward our cars.

"Tracy, you were terrific back there," he told me. "I know you're still an Apprentice P.I., but you'll be a top-notch private investigator one day."

I smiled up at him. "Thanks, Pete."

Sammy put his fedora on his head and nodded toward me. "She's a natural at this. Good thing, too. With all the fellas going off to fight, I have a hunch the gals will have to step into the jobs our boys have vacated. Plus, according to Roosevelt, we need to build tons of planes, tanks, and ships. Just to play catch-up with Germany and Japan's military."

Pete nodded. "Uncle Sam is the underdog, all right. Did you know our military only ranks number eighteen in the world?"

Sammy raised his eyebrows. "That's pretty low on the totem pole. And that's why you'll probably see plenty of gals punching time clocks now. Our country needs them."

It was true. We women were going to have to step into the roles usually held by men. Much like I'd taken the place of Sammy's old partner who'd gone off to war.

I had to say, I did like the idea of chipping in to do my part, though it was a far cry from my upbringing. My mother had raised me to be a society girl, whose only real responsibility was to choose the right china pattern and crystal glassware for dinner parties, whereby I was supposed to be perfectly charming while I entertained my husband's colleagues. That, and I was supposed to serve on the boards of the proper clubs and organizations.

But I'd taken a different path and opted to become an Apprentice P.I. instead. My mother, with her gilded upbringing, was appalled by the mere idea of my being on *anyone's* payroll, something she considered to be a disgrace to our social status.

Yet when I heard Sammy talk about women filling the jobs normally held by men, because we were so badly needed, it sounded important. Like we were changing the course of history by becoming employed. Not to mention, having an impact on the security of our nation. It all felt so meaningful and patriotic.

It even reminded me of one of my favorite Katie McClue novels, *The Case of the Kidnapped Couriers*, where she'd been awarded a bronze medal from the governor for solving a case that had an impact on national security. The applause and standing ovation from the gathered crowd almost moved Katie to tears. And while one or two drops may have rolled down her cheeks, Katie didn't get to be the world's greatest girl detective by giving in to her emotions.

Hard as I might try, I wasn't sure I could ever be so stoic in such a situation. In fact, I almost shed a tear or two while just imagining what it would be like to receive a medal from the governor.

Thankfully, I was pulled out of my reverie when Sammy yawned and stretched. "Time to head home, kids. Denton hasn't got a case against Pete, and he's got too much on his plate to figure out what really happened to Freddy. So I'm betting Pete will be off the hook in a day or two."

"Music to my ears," Pete said before taking a deep breath of the cool air. "It's almost as good as a Glenn Miller number."

"You can say that again," I added.

Pete gave me an extra squeeze as we neared his Caddy. I was about to climb into the car when I noticed a newsboy on the corner. He was already hard at work hawking today's *Houston Star-Journal*.

I waved to him and reached into my purse for a dime. He made a beeline for me and then completed our transaction with the politeness of a society gentleman.

So I tipped him a quarter for his good manners.

His eyes went wide and he grinned before scampering off to another customer. His enthusiasm made me smile, too.

That was, until I unfolded the newspaper and took a glance at the front page. For a second or two, I could hardly breathe. Because right there, front and center, was the main headline staring up at me. "Murder at the Museum," it read. And directly beneath the huge block lettering was a picture of Freddy, lying dead on the floor. Next to that photograph was a picture of Pete and me, smiling, as though we were happy about Freddy's untimely demise. Then there was a picture of Pete, as Denton led him out the front door of the museum in handcuffs.

Of course, I immediately recognized the first two shots. They had been taken by the photographer who'd been at the gala last night. The very man whom Sammy had paid to take some photos for us.

Never in a million years would I have dreamed that the man would turn right around and sell those pictures to the paper. It was a lousy thing to do.

And judging from the way Sammy clenched his jaw as he stared at that front page, I knew he agreed with me.

Pete frowned when he saw it. "What in the name of Sam Houston . . . I can't believe this is happening. They'll never let me enlist now. Not with stuff like this being printed in the paper. I might even lose my job."

At that very moment, I knew there was only one thing to do—Sammy and I had to prove what had really happened to Freddy and clear Pete's name. If not, Pete would pay the price.

And I wasn't about to let that happen.

CHAPTER 6

Bad News and Bad Breaks

As Pete drove us back to River Oaks, he did his level best not to show how blue he was about the article on the front page of the paper. An article that basically accused Pete of killing Freddy. Of course, that story didn't really have much meat to it. Mostly it involved many, *many* quotes from Ethel, listing her as an eyewitness. Freddy was referred to as a "foreign-born man of mystery" and a "graduate student in the Archaeology Department." There was also a picture of the Greek turtledove statuette that had been stolen, a stock picture the museum probably kept in a filing cabinet somewhere.

And that was about it. Other than to say that Pete, the prime suspect, was currently being held by the police.

The entire so-called article, written by P.J. Montgomery, had a very melodramatic tone to it. Much to my amazement, the thinly veiled subtext of the article made the whole event sound suspiciously like *The Maltese Falcon*, the movie with Humphrey Bogart and Mary Astor that had come out a few months ago. A movie that was considered to be the best mystery thriller of the year. And much like *The Maltese Falcon* kept everyone guessing the identity of the murderer until the very end, the audience was also intrigued by the mysterious missing statuette that all the suspects had been hunting for.

Now here we were, with a real murder mystery on our hands and another missing bird statuette, something the reporter had immediately pounced upon. How very convenient. I was surprised P.J. Montgomery had failed to mention that my boss looked a lot like Humphrey Bogart himself. I was also surprised the reporter hadn't learned *exactly* which "foreign country" Freddy was from. Nor did P.J. list Freddy's next of kin. At least his age had been given, and I had to say, I had come pretty close to guessing it. It turned out he was just a year younger than me.

Which was awfully young to be considered such a rising star in the world of archaeology. Freddy truly must have been a prodigy, just like the Professor had claimed him to be. Yet with all Freddy's book smarts, he should've known better than to nearly dance me straight into the hospital. Who knew what might have happened if Pete hadn't come to my rescue?

I glanced at my handsome fella as he expertly turned the Caddy onto River Oaks Boulevard. "Don't worry, Pete. Sammy and I will get to the bottom of this whole mess, and then we'll get things straightened out with the paper. They had no business printing that article. Not without substantiating anything."

He shook his head. "I don't want to burden you with this, Tracy. What kind of a guy expects his girl to come running to his rescue?"

"It's not a rescue, Pete. Consider yourself a client of the Falcone and Archez Detective Agency."

For the first time since the entire swing-dance fiasco, Pete actually smiled. "A paying customer, that is. I wouldn't dream of letting you and Sammy investigate this for free. And I can't think of anyone else I'd rather hire."

I slid over on the seat and planted a kiss on his cheek. "I appreciate the vote of confidence. As for any kind of payment on your part, I already know what Sammy would say."

"Oh? What's that?"

"He'd say your money's no good here."

Pete chuckled under his breath. "Well, then, at least let me help out any way I can with your investigation."

"Deal. We could probably use another legman on this case," I told him as he turned into the driveway of Nana's mansion and drove past the wrought-iron fence that surrounded the property. It looked like Nana had lifted a few of the blackout curtains that she pulled tight every night, even when the local air-raid warden wasn't conducting a blackout drill. She'd had the curtains sewn the second the Office of Civilian Defense began broadcasting the idea last May.

Before Uncle Sam had officially become part of this rotten war.

I glanced out the Caddy's rear window to see Sammy's dark sedan not far behind us. He had insisted on following us home so we could have a little "powwow," as he'd put it, when we got there.

Minutes later, we were seated at our kitchen table, while Maddie, our cook, along with her young helper, Violet, fussed around us. They put plates of eggs and bacon and fresh-baked breakfast rolls before us, all the while asking for details about the night before. Apparently, Nana had already told them bits and pieces of the story. And they were dying to know the rest.

Maddie's naturally rosy cheeks became fiery red, standing out against her pale skin, when we told her how Ethel had accused Pete of murder and Nana of theft.

Maddie clucked her tongue. "You know what they say—'what goes around comes around.' One day that Ethel will get her comeuppance."

Yet while Maddie couldn't hide her anger, Nana, on the other hand, was a vision of calmness as she swept into the kitchen, wearing her favorite blue wool dress. She dropped a kiss on the top of my head and squeezed Pete's arm. Then she slid into a chair and flashed an adoring smile at Sammy. Maddie had a cup of coffee in front of Nana mere seconds after she'd landed.

Sammy winked at Nana before he turned back to Pete and me. "Near as I can tell, Denton plans to stick his head in the sand on this case. But that doesn't mean we're out of the woods, not with the press making Pete out to be a cold-blooded killer. And not if Ethel throws a fit and puts the screws to Denton."

I took a sip of my orange juice. "So we'd better figure out what really happened to Freddy. And the Greek statuette from the museum."

Sammy nodded. "You got it, kid. Then we'll hound the press until they print a retraction. So Pete here won't spend his entire life being stared at like he's the 'killer who got away.'"

Pete wiped his mouth with his napkin. "I can't even tell you how much I appreciate all you're doing, and I hate to be such a royal pain. I wouldn't even let you bother with this if I weren't in such a jam. Especially since I'm still wondering what will happen if my boss sees the headline on the front page of the paper. He'll probably fire me. And I'm afraid the fellas at the recruitment office will show me to the curb if I even set foot inside the building."

"I know, son," Sammy said. "You're getting a lousy deal and then some, being accused of something you didn't do. So I'm just happy to set the record straight. And I know Tracy is, too."

I smiled at Pete. "Personally, I'm looking forward to watching Ethel eat her words."

"Preferably with lemon juice sprinkled on top," Nana added as she dropped a couple of sugar cubes into her coffee. "That Ethel is a real sourpuss. She has no business acting so high and mighty. When this is all over, I'll call a special meeting of the art league and make sure Ethel is given the boot."

"As she rightfully deserves," Maddie jumped in. "After the way she treated the lot of you. And at a New Year's Eve party, no less!" She pushed a wayward bobby pin back into her braided gray hair.

Nana inhaled deeply from her coffee cup. "Ethel and I go way back. She's always had it in for me. She knows I came from humble beginnings, and she's determined to remind me every time we cross paths. Evidently she believes her blood runs blue simply because she comes from 'old money.' And she has a lot of it."

"Rich and ruthless . . ." Sammy murmured. "Not the kind of dame I care to tangle with. So let's get down to business and look at all the angles of this case." He raised an eyebrow to me, his apprentice. "Let's hear what *you* think, kid. How would you suggest we start our investigation?"

I gulped the last bit of my orange juice. Much as I hated being put on the spot, I also appreciated that Sammy thought enough of me to ask my opinion. Besides, I'd read plenty of Katie McClue books to know *exactly* where to start on a case.

With the victim.

So I sat up straight and told my boss, "I think we should find out more about Freddy. I detected an accent, though I couldn't quite place it. I'd like to know where he was from and how someone so young could be so accomplished in his field. Then I'd also like to find out who might have had it in for him."

Sammy nodded. "Good plan, kid. Let's start by interviewing people who knew the guy. But let's hold off on talking to that professor fellow. He was putting up quite a fuss. Maybe he's just an egomaniac, or maybe he's trying to divert us from what he really knows. Either way, we don't want to spook him and have him clam up once and for all."

"But Freddy's friend, Stanley, was pretty cooperative. Maybe I could visit him first," I suggested. "He could probably tell me lots about Freddy. Starting with where Freddy lived."

Sammy took a drink of his coffee. "I like it. Any other ideas?"

I stared at the collar of Sammy's white tux jacket and smiled. "We could look at those items you removed from Freddy's pockets."

This caused him to grin. "Good eye, kid. I didn't realize I'd been spotted."

I couldn't help but chuckle, knowing my boss the way I did. "Well, I guess I've learned what I should watch for. I saw you palm a little aspirin tin and a folded piece of notepaper."

Sammy kept on grinning while he pulled the two items from his breast pocket. "You might say I saw the writing on the wall, before Denton even got there. I had a hunch he wouldn't be willing to do the legwork in a strange case like this. So I snagged a few things off the body. The aspirin tin was empty, and I couldn't make heads nor tails of the note. But why don't you all see for yourselves."

He handed the folded notepaper to me, before he opened and shut the aspirin tin, to show that it was empty. Then I unfolded the note and put it on the table so everyone could see it.

And there, written in the most beautiful penmanship I think I'd ever seen, were the words: "La-la. 8:00. 2/1/42. Frenchtown."

"La-la?" Pete, Nana, and I practically said in unison.

"What in the world does that mean?" Pete asked.

"Maybe it's an expression, where Freddy came from," I said, thinking out loud. "Or maybe Freddy spoke another language."

Nana crinkled her brows. "In French or Spanish, 'la' would just mean 'the.' So I doubt it's either of those languages. Otherwise the note would read "The-the.""

"So I guess we can rule those out," I murmured. "Maybe these are song lyrics. Or it's the name of a movie theater somewhere. And Frenchtown . . . well, there's a Paris, Texas. Maybe that's what the note is referring to."

Pete stared at the paper. "If he was an archaeologist, maybe it's a clue to the location of some kind of artifact. Or an archaeological dig or something."

Sammy rubbed his five o'clock shadow, which had turned into a seven a.m. stubble. "Could be the time, date, and place of a secret 'rendezvous', as they say in the movies. Possibly a chance to buy or steal an artifact."

"Like the one that was stolen last night?" I offered.

"Could be," Sammy said with a nod.

"Maybe Freddy stole the statuette before he came into the gala," I went on. "After all, he walked in late. Maybe that was why."

Pete nodded. "And maybe the person he was selling that marble bird to showed up early. Then they killed him to cover their tracks."

"Could be . . ." Sammy closed one eye and stared at the notepaper. "Though it would have been awfully gutsy, considering there were plenty of guards down there at the time. Even so, I suppose it could be done. Stranger things have happened. Especially if Freddy took it out of the building to sell it."

Nana sat up straight. "Or, instead of selling it last night, he could have simply taken it outside and hidden it. In someone's car, perhaps."

I leaned forward in my chair. "And maybe this note gives the time and place where he was supposed to deliver it."

"But someone else stole it and then killed Freddy instead," Pete added.

Sammy shook his head, slowly. "That's an awful lot of ifs, buts, and maybes. All of which could send us on a whole lot of wild-goose chases. My money says we'd find out more if we could decode this note and figure out where Freddy was supposed to go. So we could show up there instead."

I sighed. "Unfortunately, it looks like he wasn't supposed to be there until February 1. That's a month from now."

Maddie pointed to the note. "Maybe not. In America, that date would read February 1, 1942. But where I grew up, in Ireland, it would read January 2, 1942. Because they put the date before the month. Many European countries do."

"That's right!" I practically shouted. "And today is Thursday, the first."

Nana's eyes danced. "So, if that were the case, Friday would be the second."

I couldn't help but smile. "Meaning, it's very possible that Freddy was supposed to be somewhere on Friday night. Maybe Stanley will have some idea where he was supposed to go."

Pete stretched his arm across the back of my chair. "I still wonder how the guy died. He was acting pretty strange before he came at me."

"Poison can make people do strange things," Sammy said.

Pete's mouth fell open. "Poison?"

I nodded. "Dot told me the first girl he danced with stabbed him with the pin of her brooch. Dot actually saw it." I pulled the broken brooch from my pocket and put it on the table for everyone to see. "I found this near the top of the staircase at the museum, and, as you can see, the pin has been broken off the back. I think it might have belonged to Freddy's first dance partner. And I'm guessing there was some kind of poison on the pin part that's missing."

"Very likely," Sammy agreed as he picked up the brooch and examined it. "We saw the puncture wound on Freddy's arm. Could be what killed him. But we can't be sure since we don't have the pin. So, just to cover our bases, I'm going to send that wine bottle and those glasses I brought back to a buddy of mine who works at a lab. He owes me a favor. I'll have him examine the whole shebang, and see if he finds anything that doesn't belong. Like poison."

In my mind's eye, I remembered Freddy and Stanley downing their drinks before they came over to our table. "But if there was poison in the wine, wouldn't the Professor and Stanley be dead, too?" I asked my boss.

"Just depends," Sammy answered with a yawn. "On who drank what and when. But I'd suggest we hash this over after we all get some shut-eye. Because none of us will be much good if we don't catch a few winks."

I had to agree, since I was more than ready for a visit from the Sandman myself.

Then without another word, Sammy and Pete and I slowly scooted our chairs away from the table. I could hardly believe how heavy my feet felt by now. And my shoulder had started to throb, thanks to the way Freddy had mistreated me on the dance floor.

But Nana practically bounced to her feet. "While you sleepyheads go off to dreamland, I'll be helping Eulalie move in. Because I got plenty of sleep while you were all at the police station. I've already got her room ready, and Hadley's gone over to get some of her things."

Nana had barely spoken the words when in walked Hadley, our chauffeur, carrying a large box. He set it on the table and wiped his brow.

Hadley was an older black man with gray hair and large glasses, and he lived in the substantial apartment over our equally substantial garage. He had practically become Gramps' right-hand man when he worked for him in the oilfields, back in Gramps' wildcatting days. But before that, Hadley had taught literature at a high school, and to this day he loved the classics. He forever kept me guessing with his endless supply of quotes.

"Greetings, all!" he announced. "Only that day dawns to which we are awake. There is more day to dawn. The sun is but a morning star."

"Emerson?" I guessed.

Pete tilted his head. "Nope. I think it's Thoreau."

"Correct, young fellow," Hadley said with a half bow. "And as I understand it, you've had some strife during the night."

"I have," came Pete's reply. "Here I am, all ready to enlist and go fight for our country. And now I've been sidetracked."

Hadley frowned, his gray-brown eyes filled with concern. "Only momentarily, let us pray. Even my own grandson, Alistair, is chomping at the bit to go fight against the Nazis. He's becoming a pilot in Tuskegee, Alabama, in a program supported by Eleanor Roosevelt herself. Apparently, my Al is near the top of his class."

Nana smiled. "That doesn't surprise me one ounce. Al has always been brilliant. And fearless."

I also smiled up at Hadley. "A chip off the old block, as they say."

Hadley laughed. "I should hope so. But Al and I—like you, young Mr. Peter Stalwart—have overcome a number of obstacles in our lifetimes. 'The greater the obstacle, the more glory in overcoming it.'"

"And that would be a quote from Molière," Eulalie chirruped as she walked in, carrying a huge, longhaired calico cat. "And one of my favorite quotes of all." She spotted the piece of notepaper on the kitchen table and stared at it for a moment.

That was, until she turned her unblinking gaze toward Pete.

Her scrutiny clearly made him squirm, though it didn't stop him from being a gentleman, as he and Sammy jumped to their feet to help Hadley with the rest of the boxes and suitcases. Then Nana directed them all, as box after box came through the kitchen door, and things were sent to an upstairs bedroom, down the hall from mine, where it appeared Eulalie would be staying. Other boxes were sent to the conservatory, where I learned Eulalie was about to set up her studio.

A metal container filled with sand was also carried inside and taken to the conservatory.

"That's sort of an indoor toilet for my cat," Eulalie explained to me. "She jumps in, digs, and then completes her morning constitutional in that open box. Though, of course, it's not always in the morning. Later, I scoop out the results with a trowel and toss it into the garden."

I reached over and petted the top of the cat's head. "Sounds much easier than always having to let the cat in or out. What is her name, by the way?"

Eulalie passed her cat to me, and the large animal immediately snuggled in and started to purr. "Miss Tracy, meet Miss Opaline."

The cat continued to make herself at home in my arms, much like Eulalie clearly planned to make herself at home in our house, judging by the steady stream of boxes and suitcases and trunks that were being carried in and carted off to the correct rooms.

I had to say, I was amazed at how quickly she had managed to get her things together. After all, Nana had barely invited her to come stay with us the night before.

But I also wondered how *long* she planned to stay, considering the number of items she'd brought with her.

When the last of the load had been sent off to the various parts of the mansion, Eulalie stepped closer to the kitchen table and pointed at the piece of notepaper we'd left there.

"I see there's a La-la," she commented as she turned her gaze to me. "On Friday night? Am I to assume that you and your young beau will be attending?"

Right at that very moment, I truly wished I could have answered her. Unfortunately, I'd suddenly seemed to have forgotten everything I knew about forming words. Mostly because I was in complete shock from finding out that Eulalie knew what the word "La-la" meant.

Now, I only prayed I could stop sputtering long enough to ask her to explain it to me.

CHAPTER 7

Lousy Time for a Break-in

"Eulalie . . ." I finally managed to utter as I set Opaline on a chair. "You know what a La-la is?"

She stared at me with eyes full of curiosity, and once again I was amazed at how very young she looked for her age. "Why yes, my dear child. Of course I do . . ." she started to say.

And I knew she was but a split second away from following up with an explanation, one that I was so desperate to hear.

And I was just sure that very explanation would be pertinent to our case, and set us on the path to finding some significant clue. And that clue, no doubt, would be *the* clue that could make all the pieces of the puzzle fall into place.

In that exact moment, my mind flashed onto a scene from one of my favorite Katie McClue novels, *The Case of the Incredibly Important Evidence*, in which an innocent bystander gave Katie a vital piece of information, completely out of the blue, that set her on a path to unravel an entire chain of clues, much like someone might unravel a row of knitting.

So now as I kept my eyes glued to Eulalie, I knew in my heart that the very same thing was about to happen to me.

And it might have, had it not been for the commotion that followed, when Hadley suddenly burst into the room, wild-eyed and waving his arms to get our attention.

Pete and Sammy rushed in after him.

"We've had a break-in," Hadley hollered, out of breath.

This led to gasps and screams from Maddie and Violet, and well, all of us girls in the kitchen. Including me, much to my annoyance.

And I do mean *annoyance*. After all, what kind of an Apprentice P.I. was I, to let out a little squeal in the face of peril? I was supposed to stay cool, calm, and collected. Like my boss.

"He could still be in the house," Hadley went on.

"I've got my gun in my car," Sammy said, not wasting a second as he ran out the door.

Which made my heart start to pound like a bass drum.

I grabbed Pete's arm. "What happened? Do we have burglars? Are we in danger?"

His pale blue eyes met mine. "Someone broke in to the conservatory. We didn't see them but we saw the mess they made. We don't know if they're still here or if they took off. And we have no idea who or how many there were. It could have been one person, or it could have been several."

I glanced out into the hallway. "That's pretty strange. We don't have much crime out here in River Oaks."

"Almost none," Pete agreed. "And we have no idea if the person who broke in is just a common burglar. Or something much worse."

"Like a homicidal maniac," I added. "So we need to protect ourselves."

Pete's mouth was set in a grim line. "Do you or your father have a gun?"

"Yes," I managed to say, though I could barely hear my own voice over the pounding of my heart. "I have a pearl-handled revolver that my father gave me. And he has several guns. They're locked up in the gun cabinet in his study, just down the hall. I think we should go get them, even at the risk of running into our intruder."

"I'm game," Pete told me. "I'd rather be a winging duck than a sitting duck."

While Eulalie picked up Opaline, I turned to Hadley. "Would you please stay here with the other ladies and do your best to keep them safe?"

"Most definitely," came Hadley's reply. "While the pen may be mightier than the sword, I'm not averse to a bout of fisticuffs when the need for protection arises." He demonstrated by striking a boxing pose.

Nana grinned at him and grabbed a cook's knife from a drawer. "Count me in to help hold down the fort!"

"Thanks, you two," I said before turning to Maddie. "Please call the police and tell them to get over here right away."

"Consider it done," she said as she ran for the phone at the far end of the kitchen.

"Make sure you all stick together," were my final words before Pete and I stepped out into the hallway.

We glanced both ways and then raced across the black-and-white marble floor of our mansion. We ran past the parlor and huge staircase and the dining room. Once we reached my father's study, we stood on either side of the French doors leading into the room. I carefully peeked through the glass panes, and as near as I could tell, no one was there. So we quickly pushed one of the doors open and tiptoed inside, shutting the door behind us as quietly as we could.

Seconds later, I handed a loaded pistol to Pete and grabbed my own revolver. I checked to make sure it was loaded, too, before I locked the cabinet and returned the key to the hiding spot in my father's desk.

"Tell me about this break-in," I whispered as we glanced out into the hallway again. Goose bumps suddenly popped up on my arms and the back of my neck.

I fought the urge to roll my eyes, since it was becoming more apparent by the moment just how much I needed to work on my "cool, calm, and collected" skills.

Pete leaned in to my ear and spoke barely above a whisper. "We'd just taken a load of Eulalie's art things to the conservatory and were headed back for more. We weren't even gone that long. But when we got back, the conservatory door to your backyard was wide open. That's when we noticed someone had broken a glass pane right by the door handle, so they could unlock the door and get in."

I kept my eyes focused on the hallway, watching for any movement that might indicate someone was out there. "In all the years we've lived here, no one's ever done something like that."

"Whoever it was, it looked like they were in a big hurry. Because they dumped everything right out of the boxes we'd brought in. Eulalie's stuff was everywhere."

I cocked my gun and we carefully stepped out of the room and into the hall. "That is really strange. Who would want to go through Eulalie's art supplies?"

"Beats me. But they weren't going to wait until she had a chance to unpack them. They were probably watching us when we brought the boxes in there."

"It gives me the creeps," I murmured as we hugged the wall and made our way to the conservatory. "Now, the big question is—are they still in my grandmother's mansion somewhere, searching for whatever it is they were after?"

"And," Pete added, "do they have their own guns or weapons?"

"Another good question," I whispered, as an ice-cold chill raced down my spine.

At long last, we reached the glass door of the wrought-iron and glass-walled conservatory. I could see Nana's huge potted palms around the room, as well as plenty of other houseplants. But what stood out the most were the empty boxes that had been tossed randomly about, leaving art supplies and utensils spread across a very wide swath of the floor. Eulalie's things now looked more like the debris I'd seen in pictures of the Great Galveston Hurricane in 1900.

As we carefully stepped inside the room, the scene suggested one thing to me—like Pete had said, whoever had done such a thing had done so in a very big hurry.

And with great purpose.

Meaning, they must have been looking for something specific. And whatever that *something* was, it clearly couldn't have been fragile, given the rough treatment Eulalie's items had received.

Now I had to wonder, had they found what they'd been looking for? Did they take anything? Only Eulalie herself could tell us if something was missing.

Pete and I moved a little farther into the room, and I could finally hear sirens off in the distance, coming ever closer.

Then footsteps sounded down the hall and Sammy strode into the room to join us. "It's a mess, isn't it, kids? Now we'll have to search this place from top to bottom, and north to south. And east to west. To make sure whoever decided to pay us an unwanted visit isn't here anymore. We'll get the police in on that little chore."

Which was one of the big downfalls of living in such a huge mansion. There were so many places for someone to hide. And there were plenty of doors through which some depraved person could sneak in and out, and stay two steps ahead of people scouring the house for an intruder.

A fact that didn't make me feel any more comfortable, even after the police showed up. Once we'd explained the situation to them, we all started to go from room to room, on all three floors and in the attics, too, to see if any criminals might be hiding somewhere. We checked closets and under beds and even in the showers. We looked behind old trunks and bookshelves in the attic.

Funny, but now that we were on the hunt for some criminal, I realized just how gigantic Nana's mansion really was. As a child growing up here, I'd never thought of the place as being so huge. To me, it had simply been home.

After a full hour of searching, we didn't find any suspicious person or persons hiding in an armoire, or lurking behind a bathroom door, or anywhere else, for that matter. And as near as we could tell, the only evidence that a break-in had occurred at all was in the conservatory, where it appeared our intruder had only gone through Eulalie's boxes.

And nothing else.

Even so, I could hardly believe the mess the crook or crooks had made in such a short time. I took a last glance around while one uniformed policeman interviewed Eulalie, and another checked the door and the grounds. From what I could overhear of the conversation, Eulalie didn't think anything had been stolen.

"Someone is trying to prevent me from creating my exhibit for the art museum," she insisted to the officer. "Clearly there are dark forces at work, doing their level best to inhibit my creative process!

But they shall not succeed in deterring me, for true artistry can never be stifled."

And while I realized Eulalie might be right, that someone was trying to put the kibosh on the exhibit she was supposed to create, breaking in today seemed like a strange way to go about it. Instead, if someone wanted to sabotage her art, common sense said they'd be more likely to break in *after* she'd created a few pieces.

Whatever the case, nothing appeared to be missing, and no burglar had been found in the house. Even so, Sammy and Hadley decided to give the place one more going-over, just for the sake of our safety.

As for me, well . . . my spirit was willing but my flesh was weak. Or tired, rather.

Completely exhausted was more like it.

Pete and I returned our guns to my father's study, and after that, I barely remembered him leading me into the parlor and insisting that I sit on the sofa. The swish of my evening gown sounded strange to my ears, like it was coming from a long way off. My eyelids were so heavy they felt like they weighed a hundred pounds each. And no matter how hard I fought, I just couldn't keep them open any longer.

I was vaguely aware of Pete leaning me back, until my head rested softly on a throw pillow. Then he lifted my legs to the other end of the sofa and pulled off my shoes. He covered me with a blanket, before he took off his tux jacket and tie, and practically flopped into a wing chair next to the sofa.

And like the saying goes, that was all she wrote. Because I went off to dreamland while the world went on around me.

Finally, I woke up to the sound of an engine running. I wondered if Nana had started her 1940 maroon Packard, though she rarely drove it these days. Mostly she just loaned it to me, and I had the privilege of tootling around town in it.

But after something wet and cold touched my nose, I knew the sound I'd heard wasn't the purr of an engine at all. Instead, it was actual *purring*.

From a cat.

I opened my eyes to see Opaline's green eyes staring at me, and I realized she'd planted herself on my chest while I'd been sleeping.

And for the first time since I'd met this beautiful feline, I fully understood her name. Because her eyes were positively luminescent, with a shine all their own. She was a cat with a coat of many colors, and her long fur was more stunning than any mink coat I'd ever seen.

I put my arms around her and hugged her. "Are we to be friends, Miss Opaline?"

I took her chirruped meow to mean, "Yes."

Then I glanced over to the wing chair where I'd last seen Pete, only to find that he'd already gone. I fought the disappointment that welled up within me, fully aware that he'd probably just gone home for a shower and a change of clothes. And well, to go on with his day-to-day life, like all grown men did.

Yet there was something about the knowledge that he might be signing up for the service and leaving soon that made me want to cling to him. Most likely he would be stationed somewhere in the world that I'd never even heard of before, and wherever he ended up, he would probably be in danger. Along with all the other fellas there with him.

The thought of it gave me a sick feeling in the pit of my stomach.

Especially since there was an added complication where Pete and I were concerned. I couldn't help but wonder, what would become of our romance after he left? Since the Japanese had attacked Pearl Harbor less than a month ago, tons of young couples had been making a beeline for the courthouse, to hurry up and get married before the guys shipped out. In fact, couples who barely even knew each other had been tying the knot in a hurry. Or, at least, getting engaged right away. These days, a quick courtship was perfectly acceptable.

Yet the idea of getting married to Pete before he left didn't exactly feel right to me. For that matter, I wasn't sure if getting engaged was the proper thing to do, either. Sure, I'd known him for years, but we'd only officially been dating for less than a month. We hadn't even said our "I love you's" yet, even though I was pretty sure we both felt it. And if it weren't for the war, we'd probably date for a year and then think about getting engaged.

But this crazy war was speeding up romances like they were an Olympic track event. Even my best friend, Jayne, and the love of her life, Tom, had recently resorted to a courthouse wedding, shortly before he enlisted. Though their situation had been a little different, considering they had been engaged already, and they'd been planning to get married long before our country went to war and our whole lives changed.

Unfortunately, Pete and I didn't have the advantage of months of dating. And I wasn't sure if we were far enough along in our relationship to take the next step.

On the other hand, if we didn't have some kind of a commitment, what would happen to us as a couple, when we'd be separated by so many miles? And very possibly, through so many years? Could two people stay true-blue without some kind of a pledge?

I shook my head. It was all so hard to believe. Here I was, in training to become a private investigator, and I'd already helped to solve a few mysteries. Yet the mystery of what to do about our relationship was a puzzle that had me stumped. In fact, I wasn't even sure where to start when it came to dealing with our dilemma.

But I did know one thing for sure—our timing in getting together was lousy.

Very lousy.

The war had changed everything, including the rules for a relationship. These days, there was no such thing as a "convenient" time. Because nobody knew what tomorrow might bring, or if there would even *be* a tomorrow. Our generation didn't have the luxury of waiting, like generations before us had.

So, deep down in my heart, the truth was, I knew I'd say yes if Pete asked me to marry him. For that matter, much as I thought it was a little early, I knew I'd even *get* married to him before he left, if he wanted to.

Which, oddly enough, brought up the other part of the complication—what if Pete didn't ask me for some kind of commitment? Would I be disappointed?

Something inside said I already knew the answer to that question. Yes, I would be terribly disappointed. It might even make his leaving that much more difficult.

Provided, of course, that he even got to leave. First, Sammy and I had to work to clear his name, so Uncle Sam would want to accept him.

Funny how that all worked. Here I was, racking my brain to solve a case, all so my fella could leave me.

"I should have my head examined," I said to Opaline.

I put her on the floor and fumbled to my feet, noticing my once gorgeous gown had now turned into a wrinkled mess. I was pretty sure the rest of me probably matched. Not that I especially cared at the moment, as I headed for the kitchen, hoping to find someone to give me an update on the break-in.

And, to ask Eulalie what a "La-la" was.

When I got to the kitchen, Maddie, Violet, and Nana were the only ones there. Maddie was peeling apples while Nana rolled out some dough. Though Maddie was officially our cook, Nana had grown up cooking for her family, and to this day, she still enjoyed baking goodies for us all.

"Sammy went home for some sleep," Nana told me, wiping her hands on her apron. "And Eulalie went out for a bit, though I'm not sure where. She said something about visiting some friends."

So much for asking her what the phrase "La-la" meant.

I sighed and rubbed the sleep from my eyes. "What about Pete?" I glanced down to see that Opaline had followed me into the kitchen. I reached down to scratch her back, and she purred in return.

Nana poured me a cup of coffee. "Pete left you a note," she told me with a twinkle in her eyes as she pointed to an envelope on the counter with my name on it. "I gave him some of your father's stationery."

"That beau of yours is a true gentleman," Maddie said with a smile. "He's got my vote for being the one who takes your hand in marriage."

Her comment made me smile. "We'll see, Maddie. But thanks for the vote. He's a swell guy, all right."

Pete's note was sitting next to the broken brooch, the folded piece of notepaper, and the aspirin tin that Sammy had found on Freddy's body. I put the last three items in my pocket, before leaning against the counter and pulling Pete's letter from the envelope. It was written in his perfectly neat handwriting, with just a slight flair to the loops and capital letters.

Dear Tracy, it read, *you were sleeping so peacefully that I didn't want to wake you. I know the New Year didn't exactly start out the way we had planned, full of romance and music and a long stroll under a starry sky. But honestly, being with you is all that really matters to me. Regardless of what is going on around us. I'll call you later, after we've all had some sleep. Welcome to 1942.*

Then he signed his name with a flourish.

And that's when it dawned on me—this might be the first in a long, long series of letters that we'd write to each other, as soon as Pete was able to leave for the service. We would probably write every day, just like my friends Jayne and Tom did. Jayne's days evolved around that moment when the mailman showed up at her apartment building, and I had a hunch that Tom could hardly wait for daily mail call.

Once when we were at the movies, Jayne was so sure she'd seen Tom in a short before the feature. In fact, seeing those newsreels gave us a whole new view of the war, with moving pictures instead of mere still photographs in newspapers or magazines.

Now I wondered if I would see Pete in one of those newsreels someday, too.

I held the letter to my heart and took a deep breath. Suddenly tears stung at the corners of my eyes and threatened a full-blown eruption. But I didn't want to dissolve into a big, blubbering ball of self-pity. Especially since I didn't have it any rougher than anyone else.

So I took a few deep breaths and fought to focus my mind on Pete's case. "I guess the police have gone already," I said to Nana.

Using a rolling pin, she lifted a piecrust onto a pie pan. "They finished hours ago. Hadley is back there repairing the door. And he helped Eulalie get all her things back into the boxes. Thankfully, nothing was missing, according to Eulalie. We still don't know what any burglars were after. With all the things they could steal in this house, why they'd go after those art supplies is beyond me."

I had to say, it was beyond me, too. Maybe Eulalie was right, maybe someone *was* trying to discourage her from creating pieces to show at the art museum. Though no matter how I looked at it, the whole idea still seemed pretty farfetched to me.

"I've never been nervous living here before," Maddie said. "But this place feels so empty these days, and there would be plenty of places for someone to hide."

Nana smoothed the piecrust into the pan. "One thing's for sure—this house is too big for just the few of us. Especially with Benjamin out of town for the holidays."

"Thank goodness he'll be back to finish law school," Maddie added. "At least then we'll have another man about the house."

While she had a point, I wasn't sure how much help my older brother would be when it came to defending us. He'd been the golden child and my mother's favorite when we were growing up. And now that we *had* grown up, he seemed more interested in pursuing his own personal pleasures rather than looking out for others. Besides that, he was hardly ever around anymore, considering law school and his social activities took up most of his time.

Though, in all fairness, he was anxious to enlist just as soon as he finished his final semester of school in the spring. That in itself was a true act of selflessness. So maybe Benjamin was going to grow up after all.

"I'm thinking about bringing in some boarders," Nana went on. "Since all the people moving here to get jobs with the war industries are having a tough time finding a place to live. And I could help out by renting a few rooms. Of course, I'll need to bring in a full-time housekeeper, too."

Then, right on cue, as though someone had written it as part of a script, a very loud knock came at the door.

Nana and Maddie and I all glanced at each other while Violet stared at the door with saucerlike eyes. Right at that moment, I sincerely wished I hadn't locked up my gun.

"Let me take a look," I said quietly.

So I did. And there on the doorstep was a short, plump woman, who looked to be of Latin descent. She was carrying suitcases in both hands, which also meant she wasn't holding a weapon of any kind.

Meaning, she probably wasn't an immediate threat to us.

I opened the door and stepped outside. "Yes? May I help you?"

Her smile glowed a brilliant white as she put the suitcases down and held out a hand to shake mine. "My name is Consuela Isabella Guadalupé Vazquez. But you can call me 'Lupé' for short. I am from Argentina. I have come to be your housekeeper."

Waves of shock washed over my body, and I think my chin practically hit the ground. Before I could even recover, Nana was already behind me, motioning to the woman.

"So delightful to meet you, Lupé," Nana cooed. "Your timing is wonderful. I was just saying that we were going to need a housekeeper. And there you are, as though you appeared from out of thin air. You've saved me the trouble of working with an agency. Please, do come in."

And so she did, despite all the wild-eyed looks and facial expressions I directed toward Nana. After all, we didn't know Lupé from Adam.

If that even *was* her real name. Or maybe I should have said, her real *names*.

But Nana didn't pick up on my concern. Instead she simply treated Lupé like they were old pals who'd known each other for decades.

Yet they hadn't.

Now I had to wonder, who was this woman who had suddenly shown up at our house? And how did she just happen to land on our doorstep exactly when she did?

While I had plenty of unanswered questions, there was one thing that was coming through loud and clear—namely, the warning bells that were going off inside my head.

CHAPTER 8

The Mysterious Maid and a Roommate's Revelation

For a moment or two, I stood frozen to the spot while Nana invited a complete stranger into our mansion, only hours after someone had tried to break in. For all I knew, Lupé could have been that "someone." Or even part of a team of "someones." Maybe the break-in hadn't produced the results she'd been hoping for, so she decided to show up under the guise of someone looking for employment. And who better to go through all the valuable items in our house and steal whatever they wanted than a housekeeper?

Of course, it didn't help that all this happened on the heels of Nana inviting Eulalie to come stay with us. As near as I could tell, Eulalie had enough oddities of her own, and could've practically passed for a character in a *Dick Tracy* comic strip.

At the rate Nana was taking in suspicious characters, she'd probably have the entire cast of *The Thin Man* living with us before long. And while I especially enjoyed that movie, based on the novel by Dashiell Hammett, it didn't mean I wanted to share my upper hallway with any dubious suspects. But more importantly, I didn't want my grandmother to be subjected to any kind of danger.

Yet my grandmother seemed completely oblivious to any potential problems whatsoever, since she now flashed me her brightest smile. "Tracy, would you please shut the door while I get our guest some coffee?"

I decided to do as I was told. For the moment, anyway. But I was also determined to pull Nana aside and have a little chat with her later.

Nana paused in the center of the kitchen, standing with the posture and grace of a ballet dancer ready to perform. "Allow me to make the introductions, Lupé. I'm Mrs. Truworth, and my granddaughter here is Tracy. Maddie, or Matilda, is our cook. And Violet is her helper."

Lupé nodded and smiled to us one by one. "So nice to meet you. Thanks be to you for letting me come in."

"Please," Nana said, "have a seat. Make yourself comfortable."

Lupé put her suitcases to the side of the worktable in the center of the room, and then took the stool that Maddie pulled out for her. "I have reference papers from the Hamiltons down the street. When Mr. Hamilton and their sons left to go to the war, Mrs. Hamilton said they no longer needed me. They told me to come here and talk to Mrs. Truworth, and maybe you need someone. And I need a job. Please. I promise to do very good work. Otherwise I will have no place else to go." She made the sign of the cross with her right hand.

"Ah, yes," Nana said with a nod as she put a steaming cup of coffee before Lupé. "I know the Hamiltons. Though I haven't been to their house in years. How long were you with them?"

Lupé took a drink of her coffee. "This is very good coffee, Mrs. Truworth. For coffee in America. I could never get the Hamiltons to buy good beans. I was with them for seven years. About a year after I moved here from Argentina."

"What made you want to come to the United States?" I asked as casually as I could.

Lupé grinned. "Land of the free? Who would not want to be here? Our economy was so bad in Argentina, after the military dictatorship took over."

I tilted my head. "Even though our country was in the middle of the Great Depression?"

She slid her eyes in my direction and took another sip of her coffee. "There was much political unrest in my country. And my husband was killed. So I came here. Where I'd be safe."

"Tracy, don't be so rude to our guest," Nana admonished in her most genteel tone. "Argentina has had a lot of turmoil over the years. Who can blame a woman for wanting to leave?"

Lupé grinned at Nana again and Nana smiled back. And before I knew it, arrangements had been made for Lupé to start working for Nana on a trial basis. She would be living in the housekeeper's quarters on the third floor.

Maddie flashed me a questioning look before she took Lupé upstairs. And that's when I took Nana aside. Or, more specifically, to my father's study.

My pulse was pounding even faster than the ticking of the grandfather clock in the paneled room, when I leaned against the back of my father's huge desk. "Nana, I'm really concerned about you. What do you even know about these women that you've allowed to move in? Eulalie and Lupé? We've never had a break-in before, and now, seconds after Eulalie gets here, somebody breaks in and ransacks her stuff. Then Lupé shows up out of the blue. This all looks pretty suspicious, if you ask me. It makes me worried about your safety."

To which Nana just smiled and leaned back on the leather couch. "Tracy, darlin', I appreciate that you worry about me. But I think you might be overreacting just the tiniest bit. I've known Eulalie forever, and yes, I realize, she's what you might call 'eccentric.' All artists are. As for Lupé, well, I was ready to hire a new housekeeper, ever since our old one left. So, I'm willing to give Lupé a chance."

I folded my arms across my chest. "But don't you find it odd that Lupé showed up only minutes after you mentioned the idea of hiring a new housekeeper?"

Nana laughed. "I've lived a long time, my dear granddaughter, and if there's one thing I've come to understand, it's that coincidences really do happen. Let's just call it a blessing and not second-guess it."

I sighed. "All right. It's your house. Even so, Nana, it doesn't stop me from being concerned about the situation."

Nana leaned forward. "I can see that, darlin'. But don't fret over me. Instead, think of those who are far less fortunate than we are. Remember that our country has been through so much in the last decade—first the Great Depression and now another war. So we've got to do our part in helping others. And don't forget, I'm giving Lupé a *job*, not a *handout*."

"But what if you're putting yourself in harm's way by trying to help someone else? You know I'd be devastated if anything ever happened to you."

She waved me off. "I don't think we're in any great danger here. Besides, I like the idea of having a bunch of people living under my roof again. It sounds like fun."

She stood up and smiled, which I knew signaled an end to this conversation. She had just ever-so-delicately put her foot down. The subject was now closed for discussion.

We shared a quick hug before she took off and I sat pondering the events of the last twenty-four hours. Freddy's frenetic dancing and death. A priceless statuette stolen. A break-in at our house. Not to mention, the appearance of Lupé. Somehow I couldn't help but wonder if everything was connected. I also couldn't help but worry about Nana. I wasn't opposed to her bringing in a few roomers, especially if those people kept her company. I only wanted her to be careful about *whom* she brought in.

But how I would ever convince her to be more wary, I had no idea.

Katie McClue had encountered a similar scenario in *The Mystery of the Suspicious Houseguests*. That's when a group of people had come to stay at her aunt's ranch, and Katie soon discovered the visitors were actually there to hide out from a whole gang of bank robbers. Probably because the visitors had stolen the loot that the bank robbers had stolen in the first place.

Naturally, Katie unraveled the tangled web and took care of the situation—but not by convincing her aunt to kick out the criminal houseguests. Instead, she uncovered evidence from the first crime and put the bank robbers behind bars. This, in turn, had the effect of exposing the people who had robbed the robbers, and soon they were hauled away in a paddy wagon, too.

Now I wondered if a similar approach might work for me, too. Maybe if I solved the mystery of who had killed Freddy and why, and what the statuette had to do with it all, the issue of Nana's new housemates might sort itself out.

Then again, maybe Freddy's death and the stolen statue had no connection whatsoever to Nana's new roomies.

With a heavy heart, I trudged up to my room. I shut the door behind me, reached into the pocket of my gown, and pulled out the aspirin tin, the folded notepaper, and the broken brooch. I gave them all a good going-over before I wrapped them in tissue and placed them inside the top drawer of my dressing table. Then I took a quick shower, put on a sleek plum-colored suit with matching felt hat and gloves, and went back downstairs for a very late lunch.

Shortly afterward, I motored out of our driveway in Nana's Packard Super Eight sedan. Gramps had bought the maroon car for her, since the Packard was the first to offer air conditioning, something that was extra nice during the hot Houston summers. Though to be honest, I always thought he really bought the Packard for her since lots of Hollywood movie stars drove them, and he always said Nana was so beautiful that she belonged in pictures. And while she rarely drove the car anymore, it was one of her last connections to Gramps. So I made sure it got the very best of care.

Of course, I loved to drive the Packard because Katie McClue drove a Packard. Though hers was an older, sportier model in a brilliant shade of red. And thanks to the Packard's great performance and her own superior driving skills, Katie had either outrun or chased down many a bad guy. She'd even helped the police now and then with car chases, since her car was so much faster than standard police automobiles.

Today I took advantage of that Packard horsepower as I sped out of River Oaks and headed toward Stanley's place. I figured he'd be up by now, depending on whether the police had stopped in to question him or not. Yet somehow I doubted they had, since, in Sammy's estimation, he didn't think the police would pay much attention to this case. Especially when they were so short-staffed. Even so, the article in last night's paper might have changed their minds.

But that didn't mean they would have found Freddy's friend, Stanley, already, and I hoped I might get a chance to ask him some more questions before the police got to him. To be honest, I hated to barge in on the guy like I was planning to do. As a girl who was raised to be well mannered, I knew it would've been polite if I had called first to let him know I was coming. But as an Apprentice P.I., I also knew that my "interview" with him would be much more honest if I caught him off guard.

Which was exactly what I did when I arrived at the boardinghouse where Stanley lived near campus. Thankfully, the place was deserted, probably since the school was on break for the holidays. And a near-empty house meant there wasn't much chance of me being recognized from my picture in this morning's paper.

Even Mrs. Chapman, the owner, barely gave me a second look before she led me up the stairs and down a dark hallway to Stanley's door.

"The poor lad," she said. "He just lost his best friend, in case you didn't know. Though I can't say I'm surprised that poor Freddy died. He came wandering home right around dinnertime yesterday with such an awful headache. He skipped dinner because he was too sick to eat. Then later, sure enough, there he was, coming out of his room, full of pep and vigor. He said he took some aspirin tablets and felt better. If you ask me, he shouldn't have gone out to that dance. But he was determined to go."

"So Freddy lived here, too?"

"That's right. Freddy and Stanley were roommates."

For some reason, that information surprised me. Though I wasn't sure why.

"Did you know Freddy well?" I asked.

She rapped on a door near the end of the hallway. "No more than any of the other kids who live here and go to school. Most of them went home for Christmas and haven't come back yet, since school is still on Christmas break. In fact, Freddy and Stanley were the only ones around. I heard they went to their professor's house for Christmas Day dinner."

"That was nice. So it sounds like Freddy *did* talk to you somewhat."

She shook her head, before knocking on the door again. "Very little, though. Freddy was never one to share much. He never said a word about his home or his family. All I really knew was that he was a hardworking student who paid his rent on time. In cash."

Mrs. Chapman raised her hand, ready to knock again, when Stanley finally pulled the door open a crack and poked his head out.

It was clear we'd woken him up, since he was blinking the sleep out of his eyes. He had on a ratty sweater over a shirt with a stained collar, letting me know he wasn't expecting company.

"Now, mark my words," the landlady said, shaking her finger at me while Stanley opened the door wide enough for me to enter. "I want no funny business. I run a clean establishment here. And, to be honest, I don't much care for young ladies visiting young gentlemen without a chaperone. I wouldn't have even brought you up here if I didn't know how upset Stanley was over losing his friend."

"I assure you," I told her, taking a pen and my little notepad from my purse, "my visit is strictly professional. I'm here on behalf of the Falcone and Archez Detective Agency."

"Why would an agency send out a secretary instead of a detective?" she smirked.

"They didn't," I said, fighting to keep my cool. "I am an Apprentice Private Investigator."

To which the landlady merely grumbled something under her breath about women not being capable of doing men's jobs. Then she turned on her heel and ambled her large frame down the hallway toward the stairs.

Stanley shook his head. "Good old Mrs. Chapman. She runs a tight ship."

"I can see that," I said, just to be agreeable.

Though in all honesty, I wasn't exactly sure how tight that ship was. But I politely held my tongue as he let me into the small sitting room of what appeared to be a suite arrangement, with two small bedrooms on either side. I guessed the bathroom was probably a community one down the hall.

"Thanks for seeing me unannounced, Stanley. How are you holding up?" I asked him.

He shook his head, as though struggling to find the words. "I, um . . . well . . ."

"Let me just tell you again how sorry I am for your loss," I said as gently as I could. "I didn't realize you and Freddy were roommates."

Stanley nodded. "Yes, we were. We shared this apartment. That's his bedroom on the right."

I glanced into Freddy's room, and noticed books and papers and notebooks stacked everywhere. With all the stuff on his bed, I was amazed he even found room to sleep.

Stanley sighed. "Would you like to sit down? I'd offer you something to drink, but I'm afraid we don't have anything around here. We were a little low on funds. Though I'm sure Mrs. Chapman could make some tea for us, but I'll have to go downstairs to get it."

"Thanks, Stanley. But I'm fine," I said as I slid onto one of the mismatched club chairs that he offered.

He dropped into the other, leaned his elbows on his knees, and stared at the floor. Clearly he was in such a state of grief that he didn't even bother to ask me why I'd come.

I waited a second or two before I started in. "Stanley, I know this is difficult, but would you mind if I asked you a few questions?"

"Sure. Go ahead."

"I wanted to know more about Freddy. How long were the two of you friends?"

That's when Stanley finally smiled. "I met him in '36. He was the smartest fella I've ever known. He was years ahead of his time in school. A true genius. Everybody knew it. His father was a professor, and Freddy started his formal university studies when he was in his early teens."

I gave him a nod of encouragement. "Is that how the two of you met? Through your studies?"

"Uh-huh," Stanley went on. "I had gone to Berlin with my uncle to the '36 Summer Olympics. And when we stopped by the university, that's when I got introduced to Freddy."

For a moment, I wasn't sure if I'd heard him correctly. That, or maybe I'd missed the details I needed to connect the dots and create the big picture.

"Excuse me," I said carefully, "but did you say you were in Berlin, and that's where you visited the university? Do you mean that Freddy was going to school in Berlin?"

Stanley sat up and stared at me with wide eyes. "Well, yes. Didn't you know? Freddy was German."

And right at that moment, I nearly fell out of my chair. At long last, I finally understood Freddy's accent.

But what in the world was a young man from Berlin doing over here? Especially now, when we were at war with Germany? Was it possible that Freddy had been an enemy agent?

A spy?

CHAPTER 9

Sorted Papers and Hidden Spaces

"How . . . what . . .?" I sort of sputtered, all the while wondering about the possibility of Freddy being a spy.

Stanley kept his eyes on me, and I got the feeling he was almost reading my mind.

"Freddy wasn't a Nazi," he said. "He didn't even like Hitler. Not even when Hitler hosted such a grand show with the Olympic Games. And believe me, it was quite a show."

I knew exactly what Stanley was talking about. According to the pictures I'd seen in the papers and magazines, as well as the newsreels at the movies, Hitler's Summer Olympics truly had been a dazzling spectacle. It started with a well-publicized torch relay, where the Olympic flame had been passed from torch to torch, being carried by runner after runner, all the way from Greece to the brand-new stadium that Hitler had built. The opening ceremony itself included a parade of the nations, with all the athletes wearing costumes representing their own countries. Plus, the dirigible *Hindenburg* flew over the stadium, towing the Olympic flag. From what I'd heard, the crowds were completely wowed by the show that bordered on being a theatrical event.

Strangely enough, right afterward, plenty of people changed their minds about the Nazis. Or, if nothing else, they suddenly seemed indifferent to all the warning signs that came along with the mushrooming empire. Especially when it came to their treatment of the Jews.

Yet it was the treatment of the Jews and the Jewish athletes in the first place that had caused many citizens of the United States and other countries to boycott the Berlin Olympics before they even got started. Clearly some people had seen past the propaganda to the writing on the wall. Yet in the end, the president of our own American Olympic Committee, Avery Brundage, fought against that boycott. He argued that the Olympics were about the athletes, not about politics.

I wondered if he still felt that way today, now that those "politics" had spiraled the entire world into war.

I blinked a few times to get my bearings. "So . . . I'm guessing Freddy must have left Germany of his own accord."

Stanley shook his head. "Not entirely. He basically escaped with a few clothes and a hundred dollars in his pocket. Late last summer."

"I don't understand. Why did Freddy have to escape?"

"He was about to be put into a concentration camp."

The very image of that brought forth a sobering reality. Americans were well aware of the way Hitler had been taking Jewish people from their homes, putting them on trains like cattle, and then shipping them to concentration camps.

The mere thought of it made me shudder. "Was Freddy Jewish?"

Stanley shook his head. "Nope. He had been arrested because he was one of the *Swingjugend*."

I had heard that name before. "The Swing Youth."

Stanley nodded. "That's right."

I raised my eyebrows. "I guess that accounts for Freddy's talents when it came to swing dancing."

A small smile crossed Stanley's face. "He was a Swing-Boy, all right. He told me how he and his crowd went out dancing almost every single night. Not only was he a prodigy when it came to archaeology, but the fella could dance like nobody's business."

"Sounds like he got in a lot of practice. And that would certainly make him an excellent dancer. But I never would have guessed he was German. I thought he looked British."

Stanley glanced at a tweed jacket hung on a coatrack in the corner. "The Swingity were obsessed with English and American culture," he went on. "Most of them dressed like they were from England. Freddy refused to cut his hair and join the Hitler Youth."

"And that's what got him in trouble."

"He rebelled against Hitler and the Nazis. So did his whole group."

"I read about them. The Nazis arrested over three hundred of them because they wouldn't conform. Many of them went to concentration camps. That must have taken some doing for Freddy to get away from the Nazis."

Without speaking, Stanley just nodded, his mouth forming a thin, straight line.

At that moment, I wondered if we were both thinking the same thing—that Freddy had escaped Nazi Germany only to be murdered here on Uncle Sam's soil.

But I didn't say the words out loud. After all, Stanley looked upset enough. There was no need to rub salt in the wound.

I decided to pursue another line of questioning. "Stanley, would you happen to know if Freddy was planning to go somewhere on Friday?"

Stanley gave me a quizzical look. "Huh?"

"I just wondered if Freddy had plans for that night."

He shook his head slowly. "None that I know of. And we usually kept track of each other. He knew my schedule and I knew his. Why do you ask?"

"No reason. Just standard questioning," I told him, though I wasn't sure if he believed me or not.

Even so, I had learned one thing—either Freddy didn't share everything with Stanley, or Freddy hadn't had a chance to share the information on the note we found in his pocket.

And since Stanley was still staring at me with questions in his eyes, I figured it would better for me to just change the subject.

"Would you mind if I take a look around Freddy's room?" I asked him.

Stanley shrugged. "Please, go ahead. But I don't think you'll find anything. Nothing useful, anyway. To prove what happened to him. There's nothing there but papers and books on archaeology."

"So you've gone through his things?"

His eyes slid toward the door of Freddy's room. "Uh-huh. Freddy was doing some important work. I hate for all his research to go to waste. I want to make sure it's all preserved."

"That's very thoughtful, Stanley. I bet Freddy would have appreciated it," I said softly.

"It's the least I can do," he said, staring at his shoes.

I raised an eyebrow. "Have the police been here to ask questions?"

Stanley snorted. "The police? They won't care. Especially when they figure out that Freddy was German. So to answer your question, no, they haven't been here. I'm not exactly expecting them."

I merely nodded before getting up from my seat. "Could you show me what you've found in his room?"

He let out a loud sigh. "Sure. But you'll probably be bored. Most girls find this stuff to be incredibly dull."

With those words, Stanley got to his feet and led me to Freddy's room. And if I had thought the room was a disaster when I'd looked at it through the doorway, well, it didn't even compare to the experience of actually *stepping* into the space. I could hardly believe what a mess it was. The place looked like it had been hit by a hurricane—just like our conservatory. In fact, having just seen what someone had done to Eulalie's things, I suddenly wondered if someone had done the same to Freddy's room.

But Stanley was already shaking his head, as though he could read my mind. "Freddy may have been an absolute genius in the world of archaeology, and he may have had an incredibly brilliant mind, but unfortunately, he was also a complete and total slob."

I gasped. "He kept the place like this? On purpose?"

Stanley let out a little laugh. "Freddy wasn't a real stickler for organization. He believed it was a waste of time to sort things or put them away. To tell you the truth, it kind of annoyed a lot of people."

"I could see that. But how did he ever find something if he was looking for it?"

"That was part of Freddy's brilliance. He knew exactly where he'd put everything. He never had trouble finding a thing. Freddy was pretty eccentric."

"And now you're going to have one heck of a time sorting all this out."

"You can say that again."

For once, I was definitely tempted to. Especially after I stepped over to a stack of papers on his bed and began to dig through the pile.

Stanley joined me. "You'll find that bunch of stuff is all on Roman Catholic history. You probably already know that the Vatican houses artifacts that no one has seen in centuries."

"Interesting," I said, just as I stepped onto an errant piece of paper and my foot slid a few inches under the bed.

Stanley caught my arm and helped me to stand upright again.

But not before I was sure I'd felt the floorboard beneath the bed soften a bit.

He let go of my arm and pointed toward a small desk in the corner. "As near as I can tell, that bunch of notes and papers over there is mostly relating to Greek history and artifacts."

I let him lead me over to the desk, and together we sifted through lots of books and papers. Until we came upon something that truly seemed out of place. It was a wide, leather-bound book.

A bookkeeping ledger. One that showed sales and purchases. At least, that's what I thought it was, considering I could only make out numbers in various columns. But I couldn't read the words, since I wasn't familiar with whatever language it had been written in.

"Did Freddy have his own business?" I asked Stanley. "Otherwise, why would he have someone's business books?"

Stanley tilted his chin. "No, Freddy didn't do any buying and selling. None that I was aware of, anyway. I'm not sure how he got his hands on something like this. But he might have been trying to track down artifacts that had been sold and taken out of their native country."

"Like in the case of a museum buying some artifacts?"

"That's right," he said with a nod. "Museums or private collectors might buy these artifacts. Sometimes the purchases are made through brokers."

"Are there always records of the artifacts that are taken from a country?"

Stanley shook his head. "Absolutely not. Artifacts are sold on the black market all the time."

I picked up the ledger and glanced through it. "So how do you figure out where black-market items went?"

"That's where detective work comes into play. Sometimes you have to meet the locals and talk to the right people who might know something."

"Criminals, I would guess."

Stanley nodded. "That's about the size of it."

"Mind if I borrow this ledger?"

"Go right ahead. I've already looked through it and there's really nothing in there of any great significance, anyway. It won't mean much to you unless you speak Greek."

Which I didn't. But I knew someone who did—Mildred, the secretary who worked for our agency.

"Thanks," I said to Stanley. "Now, what else did you find in this room?" I moved back to the bed, and tried to clear out a little area where I could collect the items I might want to take with me. For further study.

And just as I did, I stepped on that soft spot in the floor once again.

By that time, I had a pretty good idea what I'd been stepping on. After all, I'd seen this sort of thing on another case.

So had Katie McClue, in *The Case of the Hidden Evidence*, where she'd found a critical clue hidden beneath a floorboard. And, after being an Apprentice P.I. myself for a short time, I'd learned that floorboards made excellent hiding places, something lots of people took advantage of. So, in the words of my boss, I would've bet ten to one that there was something important hidden just below my feet.

I also would have bet that Freddy was the one to hide it there. And while nothing would have made me happier than to reach down and find out for myself, I couldn't help but wonder if Stanley knew about the hiding place. Or had Freddy kept Stanley in the dark about that, too?

And if that were the case, then why? Was there something he didn't want his friend and roommate to know about?

Yet as Sammy would have said, I was doing more guesswork than legwork, which meant I wasn't getting anywhere.

The only problem was, I couldn't exactly check out a possible hiding place with Stanley standing right there. And I especially didn't want to give away my potential discovery, in case Stanley didn't know about it.

So I moved to the other side of the room, giving myself time to formulate a plan. "What else have you found among Freddy's things?"

I'd barely spoken the words when I wished I hadn't. Because Stanley took that opportunity to practically give me a short course on archaeology and religious artifacts, and how and when they were unearthed.

In fact, while Stanley could have been the model for Caspar Milquetoast from *The Timid Soul* in the Sunday comics, the guy was completely transformed when he talked about his work. Not to mention, transfixed and transported. For a few minutes there, I could hardly believe he was the same Stanley I'd seen obediently following his professor from the art museum last night.

And while he took me from pile to pile of papers and books, as near as I could tell, none of the information he was offering might have had a bearing on the case.

On the other hand, anything that might be hidden below that loose floorboard could be promising.

I pretended to shiver and hugged myself with my arms. "Stanley, would you mind if I took you up on that offer of some hot tea after all?"

He crinkled his eyebrows at me. "I'll have to ask Mrs. Chapman to make some."

I beamed my brightest smile. "That would be lovely."

"Oh, okay. Sure. I'll be right back."

"Thank you. I'll just stay here and wade through Freddy's things."

I waited until I'd heard him shut the door to the sitting area and then listened for his heavy footsteps to go down the hallway. Once I was sure he was gone, I didn't waste a single second in getting to work.

Pulling the bed away from the wall took some doing. Much to my amazement, the landlady must have had a fear of people running off with her furniture, since she'd clearly bought the heaviest bed ever made on the planet. The thing belonged on a battleship, since it was so bulky and solid that I doubted even the largest waves in the ocean could have made that thing budge.

But after a few minutes of tugging and pushing, I finally had the bed moved enough to get a good look at the floorboard below.

And that's when things got interesting. I got down on my hands and knees, and I suddenly spotted a little cut across the board, about a foot from the end. And I could also see there wasn't a single nail in that entire foot-long section. Both were telltale signs that Freddy had used this spot as a hiding place.

My heart began to race as I tried to figure out how to pull that board up from its spot. The gap between it and the next board wasn't wide enough for me to hook it with my fingers, and when I tried using my nails, I didn't have enough strength to pull it up. In fact, I ended up breaking one of my nails in the process.

Amazingly, that broken nail gave me the obvious solution to my problem. I ran to my purse and grabbed my trusty nail file. Then I got back on my hands and knees and stuck the file into the small gap between the boards. All the while, I kept an ear out for Stanley's return.

Within seconds, I had enough leverage on that board to maneuver it right out of its spot. I pulled it up and gasped the second I saw what was hidden there.

Money. American money. All in bundles of twenties. I pulled one of the stacks out and did a quick count of the bills. Twenty-five in that bunch. Then I counted out ten stacks, meaning there must have been about five thousand dollars there.

That was a lot of money for a young man in graduate school. Especially one who had supposedly escaped Germany with barely a hundred dollars. Something was amiss, that much was certain.

So how did Freddy get all that cash?

My heart began to pound like a bass drum, making it difficult for me to listen for Stanley's footsteps in the hallway outside the apartment. I knew I probably didn't have much time left, so I quickly pulled out a few more stacks of bills until I could see the bottom of the hidey-hole.

And that's when I saw the book. At first I wasn't sure what it was. But when I pulled it out, I saw it was a blue leather-bound book with a filigree border in gold. The cover looked a little shabby and some of the gold had worn off. Clearly it was something that had gotten a lot of use.

My first thought was that it might be a book of poetry, or a prayer book. But when I opened it to the first page, I read the words, "Diary of Frederick Hoffmeister."

Chills raced up and down my spine with the speed of the Packard on an open road. Especially when I realized the entire thing was written in English.

Which truly seemed odd to me, considering Freddy was supposed to be from Germany. And any way I looked at it, the whole thing just didn't add up.

But I had a good idea that it might, if I had more time to peruse the diary.

Privately, without Stanley or anyone nearby.

Or at least, that was my hope, which began to fade fast when I heard footsteps coming down the hall, along with the voice of Mrs. Chapman.

And that's when I flew into action like Superman racing a speeding train. I quickly hid the diary between the pages of the ledger I had already planned to take with me. Then I stashed the stacks of money back where I'd found them. I dropped the floorboard into place and started to work on that ten-ton bed. I pushed and shoved for all I was worth, and barely got it back against the wall when I heard the door to the apartment open.

I plopped onto the bed, sitting up straight and crossing my legs. I'd moved so quickly that I was breathing hard, and a glance in the mirror showed my face was flushed, and my hair and hat were askew.

Very askew.

Mrs. Chapman took one look at me and let out a little scream. No doubt, she'd gotten the wrong idea about my current state of exertion, and she practically dropped her tea tray onto a small table. Tea and cream sloshed everywhere.

"Well, I never!" she hollered in a strange sort of gurgling yell. Then she took a deep, raspy breath before she went on. "Working for a detective agency, my eye! I know exactly what kind of detecting you've been up to, missy! And I already told you, I don't want any funny business here. I run a clean establishment. Clearly you have no respect for proper morals and behavior. I will ask you to take leave of my house, thank you very much. Immediately. Your kind is not welcome here."

"My kind?" I half laughed.

"Now that you've practically forced me to say it, I will. You're a tramp," she huffed.

Stanley poked his head around the landlady. "Please, Mrs. Chapman. Tracy is *not* that kind of girl."

"Oh? I can see with my own eyes exactly what kind of a girl she is!" Mrs. Chapman put her hands on her hips. "Just like a lot of these young women nowadays. These so-called Victory girls, ones who have relations with any man in the military. Or any man even *going* into the military. Some think it's their patriotic duty to commit such acts. Why, in my time, such a young woman would have been scorned and shunned for life."

"I am not a V-girl," I said as calmly as I could.

"I don't care if you're the second-coming of the Virgin Mary herself. You shall leave my establishment."

And so I did. Since obviously, there was no use arguing with her. I grabbed the ledger and hugged it close to my chest, so no one might notice it was now bulging a little more than normal, thanks to the diary I had stashed between the pages.

Then I thanked Stanley and told him I'd be in touch if I had any further questions. I turned on my heel at the open door of the apartment and headed down the hallway, with Mrs. Chapman following me the whole way.

Following and talking.

Before long I'd heard every possible name for the type of woman she had determined me to be. Everything from tramp to tart, and well . . . I'll spare you what soon became some rather colorful word choices. Some that I'd never even heard before.

You might say I walked out the front door having gained a whole new vocabulary.

Now I only hoped I might learn as much from Freddy's diary.

CHAPTER 10

A Dead Man's Diary and a Ruthless Reporter

After my interview with Stanley, I hopped back into the Packard, put it in gear, and drove directly to our office in the six-story Binz Building, on the corner of Main Street and Texas Avenue. The building was famous for being Houston's first skyscraper, and our offices were on the top floor.

Funny, but when I'd first met Sammy, I'd pictured his office as looking exactly like the kind of P.I.'s office that you'd see in the movies. I expected a smoke-filled room with battered secondhand furniture and grimy walls. Something similar to Sam Spade's workplace in *The Maltese Falcon*, especially since Sammy looked so much like Humphrey Bogart himself.

But much to my surprise, nothing could have been further from the truth. Because the offices that housed the Falcone and Archez Detective Agency were perfectly clean and well organized, with expensive art on the walls and an ornate Victorian desk in the front office. There were even a variety of plants happily growing around the place, including some large potted palms.

Of course, most of that had to do with our secretary, Mildred, a Jewish woman who had gotten out of Germany just before *Kristallnacht*. Many of her friends were murdered or arrested on that horrendous November night in 1938, when the Nazis vandalized Jewish homes, businesses, schools, and synagogues. Altogether, nearly one hundred Jews were murdered during the "Night of Broken Glass," as it came to be called, while around thirty thousand were arrested.

For no other reason than the fact that they were Jewish.

And much as I hated this war, I was proud that Americans were willing to risk everything to stop such atrocities, so that people could be free. And so they could live without fear of being murdered or imprisoned by a fascist regime.

I was also very happy that Mildred had managed to leave Germany before it was too late, and that she'd gotten her valuable possessions out, too.

Thanks to my boss.

Once I arrived at the top floor of the building, I stepped out of the elevator and made a beeline to our door, still clutching the ledger and the diary that I'd gotten from Freddy's room. I guessed Mildred wouldn't be in today, since it was New Year's Day. But I had a hunch that Sammy would be there.

And as soon as I entered the front office, I learned my hunch was right. Because the door to the back office was open, and Sammy's coat and fedora were hanging on a hall rack.

He leaned over from his desk and waved at me, motioning for me to join him. "I see you come bearing gifts, kid. What'd you find out?"

"Lots." I strode into the back office and handed him the ledger and diary.

A grin slid across his face. "Ho-ho! A diary. You can't beat something like that when it comes to finding a clue or two. Or even cracking a case, for that matter. Good work, kid."

Then while he glanced through the things I'd brought him, I *also* brought him up to speed. I told him about Eulalie and her reaction to seeing the word "La-la." And I filled him in on my adventures at the boardinghouse, including the sneaky way I managed to discover the diary, without Freddy's roommate being any the wiser. And I also told him about the money I'd found.

Sammy held up the diary and looked at the leather binding. "So the dead guy *wasn't* broke. But he *was* German. Yet his diary is in

English and the ledger is in Greek. We seem to have a whole lotta nationalities mixed up together in this case. Talk about a world at war."

I was already nodding. "Uh-huh. And I wondered why he wrote his diary in English. Don't people usually put their most personal thoughts down in their own language? Their native tongue?"

"Seems like the normal thing to do, kid. But from what you've told me, Freddy wanted to be like the British. He dressed like them and he acted like them. Maybe he decided to write like them, too."

"That would make sense," I murmured. "You know, if Freddy had escaped from Germany, maybe he was afraid of the Nazis finding him. *And* his diary. Because it might be full of incriminating evidence that they could have used against him. Maybe that's why he kept it so well hidden."

Sammy shook his head. "But not hidden well enough, kid. After all, *you* found it."

"So maybe writing his diary in English just added another layer of protection. Since any Germans who got their hands on it would have to be pretty fluent in English to understand what he'd written there."

Sammy frowned. "And as long as we're hopping on that train of thought, it's possible that Freddy was afraid of Nazis operating right here on Uncle Sam's soil."

My pulse picked up. "You mean the German American Bund?"

"Could be, kid. We've had run-ins with them before."

And Sammy was right. We had had some rather nasty encounters with the German American Bund in the past. A branch of the German Nazis, they had openly operated on U.S. soil since the 1930s and even held a rally at Madison Square Garden just a couple of years ago. They'd bragged about having tentacles that stretched clear across the nation, and they'd done a pretty good job of trying to make the Nazis look like nothing more than a fun bunch of guys out to make the world a better place.

Then again, what could anyone expect from a group who were experts at deceiving people about their real purposes? And even though the group had recently been outlawed, and their leader, Fritz Kuhn, had gone to jail, that didn't mean all the members had gotten their pink slips in the mail. As near as we could tell, remnants of the organization were still around. To top it off, they were every bit as dangerous and determined as their Nazi counterparts in Germany. The only difference was, the Nazis operating over here had to be sneakier about their intentions and activities.

Meaning, they had gone underground.

Sammy raised an eyebrow in my direction. "We've got to be careful here, kid. Those Bund boys are dangerous. And if Freddy escaped from Germany, the Nazis probably had a real chip on their shoulders. And the Bund might just be the bunch who did him in. But it's too soon to zero in on any one angle in this case."

I nodded. "Because there are an awful lot of angles."

"You've got it, kid. We've barely pushed off the starting block, when it comes to finding all the pieces to this puzzle. But I'll bet we pick up a clue or two from this diary you brought me. Why don't you take it home and give it the once-over. See if anything sticks out like a sore thumb."

I gave him a little salute. "I'm on it."

He grinned. "Then try to find out what Eulalie knows about this 'La-la' thing. It could be a real feather in our cap if we can figure out where Freddy was supposed to go on Friday night. Then we can show up in his place."

"We could be walking into a trap," I suggested.

Sammy raised an eyebrow. "Could be, kid. But there's only one way to find out."

A shiver ran down my spine.

Sammy, on the other hand, seemed unfazed. "When Mildred gets in tomorrow, I'll have her look at this ledger you picked up from Freddy's place. Mildred speaks Greek, so I'm betting she can decipher this."

"I'll be interested to see what she finds."

"You and me both. I also want to see what's what with that wine bottle and those glasses. Tomorrow, I'll run them over to my friend who works at a lab. I'll have him go over them with a fine-tooth comb. I'm not sure if I believe the Professor's story about the wine, since he wasn't exactly the cooperative type."

I raised my eyebrows. "He didn't like being questioned, that's for sure."

Sammy chuckled. "He was some piece of work, all right. But you never know if the guy's just a crumb with a fancy degree, or if he likes to kill people for a hobby."

The idea of that made me wonder about Eulalie once more. Because she certainly didn't appear to be bothered by Dr. Longfellow's behavior, and she certainly *did* seem to find him attractive.

Then again, she seemed to find nearly all men attractive. Including my Pete.

Thankfully, she hadn't taken a liking to Sammy, who I knew was sweet on Nana. In fact, when I thought about it, I realized Sammy also had a very effective way of steering clear of Eulalie, and making sure he was never standing or sitting right next to her.

I had to wonder, did he think Nana was taking a risk by letting her move in?

"Sammy," I began carefully, "what do you think of Eulalie? I'm not sure it's a good idea for Nana to let her come stay with us."

Sammy looked at me much like my Gramps used to look at me. "Your grandmother is one of the most good-hearted people I've ever met. Having money hasn't changed her from being a real swell doll. But I wouldn't dream of telling her what she should do with her house. Or her life."

I nodded and stared at the floor. "I know, I know. She's a grown woman. She can do what she wants."

"You got it, kid. But make no bones about it—that doesn't mean I wouldn't protect her from anyone who wants to harm her."

"I'm glad to hear it," I said with a slight smile.

"Which means I've got a nasty bee in my bonnet when it comes to that Ethel character. I didn't much care for the way she talked to your grandmother last night. And I haven't exactly ruled Ethel out in the foul play department. I just spent the last couple hours making phone calls to art league folks, after your grandmother gave me a list of names and numbers. So far I haven't learned much. *Except*, everyone seems to think it was Ethel's idea to host the big shindig last night."

"Hmmm . . . she likes being in charge. That's pretty clear."

Sammy chuckled. "More like she enjoys having people under her thumb. And maybe Freddy was one of those people. After all, she seemed to know his name. I'd like to know if she had a connection to the guy."

"Maybe it would help if I stopped by the newspaper offices and talked to the reporter who wrote that hit piece on Pete last night. Since, as near as I can tell, most of the information came from Ethel herself."

"Good idea, kid," Sammy said with a nod. "I've gotta say, this case is making us good and dizzy. We're already running in ten different directions at once. But, if nothing else, at least we've got some good jumping-off points."

I had to agree. This case *was* making my head spin, like I was on a carnival ride.

Funny, but until this moment, I would have said that I *liked* carnival rides. Now I wasn't so sure.

With plans to touch base later, Sammy and I said our goodbyes. Then I was on my way to the *Houston Star-Journal* building.

Much to my irritation, I was recognized the minute I walked in.

"You're the girl in the photo," a man wearing a plaid sweater-vest and a red bow tie said with great glee, almost like he'd just won a prize. "I'll give you a thousand dollars if you tell me how you and the boyfriend did it."

"I'm afraid you'll have to save your money," I said in the iciest tone I could muster. "Because we didn't kill anyone. I assume you must be P.J. Montgomery?"

The man snickered. "Not even close. She's right over there."

He pointed to a desk where a young woman was pounding furiously on the keys of a black Underwood, with her fingers flying so fast she was a regular tornado on that typewriter. She had a pencil clenched between her teeth like a dog chomping down on a bone. And with her dark hair and perfectly arched eyebrows, she was doing a pretty good impression of Rosalind Russell in the movie *His Girl Friday*, which featured one of my favorite movie stars, Cary Grant.

I sauntered straight over and stood smack dab in front of her desk. And sure, I knew I was supposed to be here in a professional capacity as an Apprentice P.I., but as soon as I saw her, my professionalism went out the window to make room for the anger that basically took over my mind and body.

Which truly surprised me.

Especially since I consider myself to be a pretty levelheaded girl, one who is very good at keeping her emotions in check. But when I thought about the way P.J. had upset Pete, and how she'd done her level best to publicly ruin his good reputation, I could have gone about ten rounds in a boxing ring with her.

And with all the fury swirling around inside me, I figured I would've delivered a knockout punch on the very first swing.

I didn't even wait for her to acknowledge me. "How dare you write such a libelous article," I said in a staccato beat. I could practically feel my eyes burning holes into her, with Superman-like heat vision.

She glanced up and the pencil dropped from her mouth. "Well, I'll be a monkey's uncle. If this ain't my lucky day. A cold-blooded killer has come to confess. It'll be the scoop of the century. Here I've only been on the job three days, and I'll be more famous than Brenda Starr. She may be just a comic-book gal but she's set the bar pretty high for the rest of us."

"Do you always accuse people of horrendous crimes without a shred of proof?" I shot back. "I hate to burst your bubble, but I didn't kill anyone. Now I'd like a full apology as well as a written retraction."

She leaned back in her chair, with a giant grin on her face. "No can do, sister. I'm not about to let this story go. Not when it's my ticket to the big time."

"Even if you hurt a lot of other people in the process? Innocent people?"

"Ha! Innocent, my eye! I know a guilty person when I see one. Though just to clarify, I know you didn't act alone. You had your fella with you. I'm guessing he did the dirty work and you went along for the ride. Am I right? You two are a regular Bonnie and Clyde."

I crossed my arms and glared at this young woman who was about my age. "I'm afraid you may be in the wrong line of work. Clearly you do a better job of writing fiction, rather than real news."

"Honey, the more papers I sell, the more my boss wants to keep me around. And considering I'm now in a job that used to be held by a man, I've got to prove myself. And so far, I'm on a roll. Thanks to my article, we're selling almost as many papers as we did the day

Japan blew our ships to smithereens at Pearl Harbor. Not too shabby for a girl straight out of journalism school."

She glanced to the far corner of the room. "I can see the billing now. Small-town girl rises from the steno pool to take the top spot at the City Desk."

"I thought you said you were fresh out of journalism school."

"All right, fine. So I'm a little stale, like day-old doughnuts. But it's close enough. And I'm also close enough to having a regular *Maltese Falcon* on my hands, when it comes to reporting this story."

"So, that's your motto? 'Close enough'?"

"I don't know what you're so sore about. After all, I'm making *you* famous, too. Did you see your picture in the paper? You looked gorgeous, like a regular Betty Grable."

"Betty Grable is a movie star. But you're accusing me of being an accomplice in a murder. There's a huge difference."

She shrugged. "Fame is fame."

"And lying is lying. So where did you get your information? As near as I can tell, Ethel Barton was your only source. Did you even do any background research on her? Her motives for accusing Pete were personal—she's got a beef with my grandmother."

"Give the old broad a break, would ya? From what I've been told, Ethel has been trying to get her name in the paper for decades. And she was pretty excited when it finally happened. She only wants some fame for herself. Why not make her happy?"

Apparently, I'd been right about Ethel. She wasn't as upset about the missing statue as she'd let on. She was mostly just enjoying her moment in the spotlight.

And the woman sitting behind the desk before me had placed Ethel right in the center of that very spotlight.

Which left me once again fighting the urge to take a swing at Miss P.J. Montgomery. "So you made Ethel famous by printing a story that ruins someone else's reputation. Pete may lose his job. And on top of it all, he's ready to enlist and go fight for Uncle Sam. Now he'll probably be denied entry."

She waved her hand in the air. "Oh, pishposh. I'm making Pete famous, too. And that guy comes from money, just like you do. So he doesn't even need to work. And why would he want to go off and fight in some silly war when he'll have women falling all over him here? Because there's nothing that attracts dames faster than a good-looking bad boy. Why, soon Pete will be more popular with the ladies than Howard Hughes."

A gasp escaped from my lips. "But he's *my* guy!"

She leaned forward, resting her elbows on her desk. "Oh, yeah? The two of you aren't married, are you? Are you even engaged?"

"Well . . . no . . . we haven't been dating that long," I sort of muttered, stumbling over the words, while I wondered why I was even explaining this to her.

She chuckled. "Then get in line, toots. Every single gal in the city of Houston is about to go after him. Heck, I might even take a shot at the guy myself," she finished with another huge grin.

To be honest, I wasn't sure what shocked me more—the fact that she'd just told me she was going to chase after my fella, or the fact that she'd done so with a big smile on her face. And since the status of my relationship with Pete had *already* been weighing heavily on my mind, her words cut me right to the core.

Now I started to wonder if she had a houseful of flying monkeys at home, just waiting to do her evil bidding. Much like a certain green-faced biddy in *The Wizard of Oz*. Because just like the Wicked Witch of the West, Miss P.J. Montgomery was a ruthless woman, one without any morals or human decency whatsoever.

I leaned in a little closer and rested my hand atop her typewriter. "You have made it quite apparent that I can't appeal to your humanity." I paused for a moment and refrained from adding, *because you don't have any*, before I continued with, "I also can't appeal to your sense of right and wrong." Again, I held back from adding, *because you don't know the difference*. Then I finished with, "But maybe you'd be willing to do this much—print a full retraction once my partner and I have solved this case. If I promise to give you the scoop on the whole story. Including 'who' really killed Freddy Hoffmeister. And how."

This suggestion was received with a huge snort from Miss Montgomery. "That'll be the day! And yes, I know you're supposed to be some kind of Apprentice P.I. I did my homework on you. Poor little rich girl, playing at being employed. I know your type. I've been put down by rich girls all my life, since I've had to scrape and fight for every dime I ever got."

"So you have a chip on your shoulder, a real grudge against girls like me? Is that the real reason you wrote your article?"

Her reaction told me I'd hit a bull's-eye. Because P.J. started to huff and sputter, clearly unable to come up with a witty retort.

"Fine," she managed to spout. "You bring me the genuine story and I'll print a retraction. Provided the story you bring me is interesting enough for a front-page spread."

Then she pulled a desk drawer open, grabbed a business card, and shoved it my way. I took it from her and read her full name: *Polly Jane Montgomery.*

I gave her the best smile I could muster at the moment. "Thank you, Miss Montgomery. I will be in touch as soon as we've solved this case."

Without waiting for her to reply, I turned on my heel and headed straight for the elevator. My head was still spinning as I rode it down to the street level. And as I walked to the Packard, no matter how many times I closed my eyes and tried to shake the entire experience, I couldn't come to grips with what she'd said to me. Especially the part where she'd mentioned my bringing her the "genuine story." From that, it was pretty apparent she knew the story she'd written wasn't real. It was nothing but pure fabrication. Except for the part about Freddy dying.

Now I had to wonder, would Miss Polly Jane Montgomery continue to look into this case, maybe to supply her readers with more tainted information? In hopes of selling more and more papers?

The thought of it made me cringe. First, I didn't want her to interfere with our investigation. And second, I couldn't help but question—exactly how much damage could she do to Pete, and to me, for that matter, before she was finished?

CHAPTER 11

Shedding Light on the Elusive La-la

The sun was setting on the horizon by the time I drove back to River Oaks, with Freddy's diary next to me on the bench seat of the Packard. Unfortunately, much as I fought to keep my spirits up, my normal, look-on-the-sunny-side disposition had faded along with the daylight. Mostly because I was still in shock after meeting Miss Polly Jane Montgomery. How someone could purposely ruin another person's reputation for their own selfish gain was beyond me. Our minister had preached on something similar in church the week before, when he talked about the Ninth Commandment: "Thou shalt not bear false witness against thy neighbor."

And now that Pete was on the receiving end of Polly Jane's brand of "false witness," I truly understood the harm that could be done. It was a good thing that Pete was a pretty tough fella who had plenty of backing from both our families—and from Sammy and me. Otherwise, Pete might have been even more shook up than he was already.

And seeing Pete so upset ignited a fury in me like I'd never felt before. Yet my ire against Miss Polly Jane only served to spur me on, and I was more determined than ever to solve this mystery. Much like Katie McClue had once solved a mystery that involved a couple of crooks who tried to pin their crime on an innocent man. In *The Case of the Blameless Bystander*, Katie had proven the man's innocence, despite the press doing their best to ensure the man found himself seated squarely on the electric chair.

And just like Katie had uncovered the real crooks in that case, I knew I needed to do the same for Pete.

But how exactly?

Questions began to swirl through my mind as I drove the Packard into one stall of our six-stall garage. I looked over to see my father's black Cadillac Sixty Special, which had been sitting untouched since he'd gone to Washington.

Hadley was in the garage waiting for me. "'Life is a journey that must be traveled,'" he said when I turned the keys over to him. "'No matter how bad the roads and accommodations.' Oliver Goldsmith."

I sighed. "The roads and the accommodations aren't the problem, Hadley. It's a few of the fellow travelers that are giving me trouble."

Hadley nodded slowly. "Ah, yes. 'We are all travelers in the wilderness of this world, and the best we can find in our travels is an honest friend.'"

"Robert Louis Stevenson," I murmured. "Wish I'd found a few honest friends today."

He gave me his grandfatherly smile. "Well, you're home now and back among friends. Though apparently we've added a few new names to the list."

"Lupé and Eulalie."

"A couple of characters who should prove to be interesting," Hadley added.

"Have they both moved in?" I glanced at the house and spotted Violet in an upstairs window, as she started the nightly routine of closing the blackout curtains.

"Lupé has gone for her things and is expected back this evening. And Eulalie is most definitely making herself at home. She already borrowed a shovel and is apparently planting something in the garden. Though, to be quite honest, this seems like an unusual time of year to be planting *anything*. Especially when the gardens are already full of azaleas and rosebushes and shrubs."

I tilted my head. "That does seem odd. But, like Nana keeps telling me, artists are eccentric."

Hadley smiled. "Then Eulalie fits the picture perfectly."

That's when I remembered I had wanted to ask her about the "La-la."

I stepped out of the garage and glanced around. "Is she still in the garden?"

"That she is," Hadley said, before pointing me in the general direction.

I bade Hadley goodbye and took off, starting out on a flagstone path that led me behind the house. The walkway took me past a grove of trees and an azalea garden, before winding around behind a huge oak tree and on to another sitting area. But it wasn't until I made the final turn to the far corner of our property that I met Eulalie coming my way. I couldn't help but notice that she had the gait of a woman half her age.

"Well, hello, dear child," she said with a smile.

I took one look at her shovel and saw it was covered with dirt. "Hadley says you've been out planting something?"

"Hardly," she corrected me. "It's not planting season, of course."

I pointed to the shovel. "Was there something you were digging up then? Maybe a shoot or a cutting to start a new plant?"

Now her smile took on a mischievous gleam. "Horticulture is not a hobby of mine. I prefer to use the soil for more depository purposes. Like I told you, I'm a direct descendant of the famous pirate who once operated in Galveston, Jean Laffite. Burying gold is in my blood."

For a second or two, I couldn't quite connect the dots with what she was saying. But then the light finally dawned. A bright, *golden* light, you might say.

"You buried some gold in our backyard?" I blurted out, without thinking. "Maybe that's why someone broke into our house earlier. Maybe that's what they were after."

She laughed. "I'm afraid not. No one knows what treasures I may harbor. You see, my dear, I am terribly good at keeping secrets."

Except that she'd just let *me* in on this bit of confidential information. And I suddenly wondered why she had. Was it because she trusted Nana and therefore trusted me, her granddaughter, by extension? Or maybe she wasn't as good about keeping secrets as she claimed.

"You know," I said gently, "I'm sure Nana would let you keep your things in her safe."

But Eulalie was already shaking her head. "A safe is hardly safe. Not after Roosevelt took all the gold back in '33."

I raised an eyebrow. "Roosevelt took all the gold? Are you sure, Eulalie?"

Her green eyes turned dark. "Of course I'm sure. I lived through it, you know. It all started back in the late '20s, when plenty of financially educated people saw the writing on the wall . . . *Wall Street*, that is. And plenty of people predicted a collapse in the stock market, so, in preparation, they used their cash to purchase gold. Then a few years after the big crash of '29, cash was worthless but gold still held its value. That's when Roosevelt passed Executive Order 6102, making it illegal for citizens to own gold. And people were forced to sell their gold to the United States government for just under twenty-one dollars an ounce. In other words, the government essentially stole money from its citizens. It was hard-earned money that people had put away to support themselves during the Great Depression. Though a person was allowed to own up to one hundred dollars' worth of gold, and you could keep your jewelry, but that was the extent of it."

Yet somehow I guessed that Eulalie had managed to hang on to any gold that she had "obtained." Through fair means or foul, I suspected.

Again, I had to question why she was letting me in on all this. In the strangest way, I felt like she was testing me.

"I didn't know about that executive order. Though I probably should have," I commented with a smile, all the while wondering exactly how much she'd just stashed somewhere underground in our garden.

"Never trust the government, dear child. For the government isn't some great, divinely inspired entity. No, the government is simply made up of people. Mere human beings. Not gods. And most of them are more interested in serving themselves than serving mankind."

"That's an intriguing way of looking at it."

"I'm afraid it's an *educated* way of looking at it. It's a perspective that I've developed over many, many decades."

I glanced at her flawless skin and tried to figure out precisely how many decades she might be talking about.

"Would you like me to return the shovel for you?" I offered.

"That would be lovely," she replied with a sly smile.

I took the shovel from her hands, and together we started walking back toward the house.

"Tell me," she said, "was there a reason you came in search of me?"

And I suddenly remembered there was. "Yes. I wanted to ask you what the phrase 'La-la' meant."

She nodded as we walked along the path. "Oh, of course. La-la's are dances that are held in Frenchtown."

"Where is Frenchtown? I'm afraid I've never heard of it." That was, except for reading the name on the notepaper we'd found on Freddy's body.

"Many people haven't," she informed me. "It's not really a town, per se. 'Frenchtown' is simply a community in the far northeast section of the city, and it's made up mostly of Catholic Creoles who moved there from Louisiana. And naturally, they speak a great deal of French. Much like my ancestor, the great pirate Jean Laffite, who was born in France and operated out of New Orleans—before he moved to Galveston and started his pirate colony."

"What a colorful family history," I commented. "It's wonderful that you know so much about it. Does the Frenchtown community also have the same pirate history?"

She shook her head. "Hardly. They're simply a group of people who moved there after the Great Mississippi Flood of 1927. That disaster put people out of their homes, and many had to live in tent camps. So they came here in search of jobs. Now they're all quite gainfully employed, either in the shipyards or the oil industry. Or the railroad."

"That's an extraordinary story."

"It's quite an extraordinary community. They're rather close-knit and happy to provide assistance to one another. The people of Frenchtown are also a jovial bunch, having brought their music and cuisine with them."

"What are these La-la's like?"

Eulalie hesitated a moment, taking in her surroundings. "Dancing at a La-la is very much like swing dancing, though the music is different. I've even heard the phrase 'Zydeco' bandied about. It's got an unmistakable and truly infectious beat, and the washboard and accordion are prime instruments. One can't help but tap their feet and feel an overwhelming urge to dance."

"Sounds like fun," I said with a laugh.

And while the La-la did sound like a gas, as Pete would say, I had to admit I was slightly disappointed in finding out what the word meant. Because it was very likely that Freddy simply had the information in his pocket because he wanted to go out for a night of dancing. Meaning, it might be nothing but a dead end when it came to our investigation.

Still, there was only one way to find out for sure—we had to attend the dance. Provided, of course, that Eulalie would tell me how to get there.

But she saved me the trouble when she asked, "Would you like me to take you tomorrow night? I can certainly arrange for an invitation. Especially if you'd be willing to make a donation to their cause. These La-la's are held to raise money for their church."

"Why, I'd be happy to," I told her.

"Perhaps your young man, Peter, might also like to join us."

Somehow, judging from the way Eulalie made Pete squirm when she looked him up and down, I doubted he'd actually be *dying* to go. But since his freedom and reputation were at stake, he might have to make some sacrifices, so to speak. Even if it made him uncomfortable to go to the dance with Eulalie in tow. Like it or not, solving this case might depend on it.

So I crossed my fingers behind my back and told Eulalie a doozie of a lie. "I'm sure Pete would love to go. But I'll call him later just to make sure."

"Then we shall plan on it."

By now we'd reached a fork in the flagstone path. Eulalie headed left to go into the house and I went right, to return the shovel to the garage.

"Please tell Nana I'll be right in to change for dinner," I called over my shoulder. "Just as soon as I put this shovel away."

"I will be happy to," Eulalie said with a smile.

But her smile quickly dipped when a dark car pulled up and Lupé emerged from the passenger's side.

CHAPTER 12

Scary Screams Beneath the Yellow Moon

Dinner that night was a strange affair, with just the three of us—Nana, Eulalie, and me—eating at the formal dining table. To be honest, I fought against the sense of sadness that tried to invade my spirits, considering things were so different this New Year's Day dinner than they had been in years before. Sure, I wore one of my favorite dresses, a pale blue gown with a chiffon outer skirt, and Nana and Eulalie both wore elegant dinner dresses with plenty of jewelry. And the candelabras gleamed and the cut-crystal stemware sparkled. Even so, it was a far cry from the lively, formal affair I'd been accustomed to on this holiday dinner.

I glanced at the empty seats that normally would have been occupied by my brother and my father. Tonight, I missed them both beyond measure. And once Benjamin enlisted and my father kept up his war work in Washington, I knew that "missing them" would become part of my day-to-day world. For a long time to come. Though I couldn't say the same for my mother, who would have downed at least a dozen champagne cocktails by now and started in with her drunken insults. Usually directed at me.

My thoughts then turned to Pete, who would be sitting down for dinner with his own family right about now. I knew they would do their best to cheer him up, and give him the kind of encouragement he needed to get through his ordeal.

I'd known his parents for ages, since his family and mine were both part of the River Oaks Country Club set. They also lived in a mansion, one that was about half the size of ours, though every bit as elegant. While his parents had always been busy with a full social schedule that usually left Pete and his younger brother under the care of a nanny, they were still loving parents and levelheaded people. Ones that Pete could count on.

Of course, he knew he could count on me, too. And more than anything, I wished he were here with us tonight. I couldn't believe it, but even though I'd seen him just this morning, I already missed him.

If this was how I felt after less than a day apart, how would I ever survive without him for an entire war?

Across from me, Nana and Eulalie were clearly having a grand time catching up on the "good old days." Yet no matter how many times they tried to engage me in the conversation, my heart wasn't in it tonight. I contributed just enough to be polite and then excused myself before dessert.

Nana gave me one of her "concerned" looks, and I gave her the best smile I could muster as I left the dining room and made a beeline for the telephone. Even though I knew social mores dictated that girls were supposed to wait for a fella to call them, Pete's situation canceled out that old ridiculous rule. I wasn't calling him for a real date. I was calling him to help out on this case.

His case.

But before I could pick up the receiver and spin the numbers around the rotary dial, the phone rang all by itself. Much to my happiness, it was Pete on the other end of the line.

I laughed. "Pete, I had the phone in my hand and I was about to call you."

"Well, you know what they say about great minds . . ."

"They think alike. And hopefully they're going to do the same now, because I've got something to ask you." I leaned against the wall, pulling the cord of the phone taut.

"That's swell, because I've got something I need to talk to you about, too. But you go first. What did you want to ask me?"

"I wondered if you'd be my date tomorrow night. Though it's *part* date and *part* investigation."

He chuckled through the line. "I would expect no less. I'm guessing you must have figured out what and where this La-la is."

"I have."

"I always knew you were more than just a pretty face. You've got brains, too."

"Thanks, Pete. Now hopefully I've got enough brains to solve this case."

And then I proceeded to tell him all about the La-la. Or, at least, what little I knew about it, anyway.

"I'd be happy to go," he said when I'd finished. "Just promise me you'll stand between me and Eulalie. And please don't let her ask me to dance. I know she's your grandmother's friend, but she gives me the willies."

I couldn't help but grin. "I promise. Why don't you come over for dinner first and then we'll leave from my house."

"You're spoiling me, Tracy. I don't know how I got so lucky to end up with a girl like you."

Words that could go straight to a girl's heart.

Of course, I didn't think it was necessary for me to point out that, were it not for Pete hanging around with a *girl like me*, he probably wouldn't be in this predicament in the first place. Though I could hardly be responsible for Ethel's obnoxious behavior. Nor could I be responsible for someone taking the life of another.

"I'm the lucky one," I told my beau. "Now tell me what you wanted to talk to me about."

"I'd rather talk to you in person. Mind if I come over and see you?"

"I wouldn't mind one bit," I said with a laugh.

"I'll be there in a short. It'll only take me a few minutes to walk over."

We'd barely said our goodbyes when I suddenly wondered *what* Pete wanted to talk about. From the sound of his voice, I got the feeling it must be something pretty important. Yet, with everything going on in the world these days, as well as the madness of our own lives lately, it seemed like everything had a lot of significance attached to it. Much more so than in years gone by.

Meaning, our lives had become one big, gigantic roller coaster of a ride.

Yet I knew there was one thing that might smooth out the bumps a little—figuring out who murdered Freddy. And that's when I remembered I'd left his diary on the front seat of the Packard. Thankfully, I had just enough time to retrieve it from the car before Pete arrived. So I headed straight to the garage, not even bothering to grab a coat from the armoire by the back, side door.

I passed Lupé along the way. With an oiled rag and a feather duster in hand, she was already hard at work with the housecleaning. Even though it was evening and not a time of day when she would be expected to work.

She paused when she saw me approaching. "Your grandmother has been so kind to give me a job," she said with great seriousness. "Now I want to earn my keep. I'll make this house sparkle like a diamond before you know it."

"But you just got here, Lupé. I'm sure Nana wouldn't mind if you got settled in first, before you started cleaning."

"No, no, no," she corrected me. "First I do my work."

Something in her tone told me there would be no convincing her otherwise. So I merely waved goodbye and left the house. It was dark outside, especially with no light emanating from the mansion, thanks to Nana's blackout curtains.

But a huge, bright yellow moon, one day away from being full, had already begun to show itself on the horizon, and gave off enough light for me to see where I was going. Once I reached the dark garage, I punched the button for the light, so I could make my way to the car. I went straight to the Packard and pulled the passenger side door open. Then I looked around in the dim light for the diary.

Only to find the front seat was empty.

I gasped, mortified, as I continued to stare at that empty seat. I knew full well that I'd put the diary beside me when I'd driven home. Had the book gone sliding off the seat and onto the floorboard when I came to a stop? In my mind, I knew it was the most likely scenario, but that didn't prevent my heart from pounding full force as I continued to search for the diary.

Yet no matter where I looked—from the floor to under the seat, and on the floorboards in the back—the diary was nowhere to be found. I sank onto the front seat, fighting back tears. I'd worked so hard to uncover that diary, something that might have been our first big break in the case, and I'd already lost it. Or misplaced it.

Or left it where someone else could run off with it.

But who would have wanted to steal Freddy's diary?

And how would I ever break this news to both Sammy and Pete?

I shut the Packard's door and left the garage, with my feet feeling like they weighed at least a ton each. I sighed and stepped slowly back to the house, trying to sort things out in my mind. When I was halfway there, I caught a movement out of the corner of my eye, and I turned to see someone on the sidewalk across the street, about half a block away. The person was standing next to a huge shrub, and half-hidden by the branches. And as near as I could tell, he or she was staring at our property.

At first glance, I guessed it must be Pete. Though it seemed strange to me, since he usually walked to my house from the other direction. Nonetheless, I waved and called out.

But instead of waving back, the person turned and hoofed it away in a hurry. And for just a moment or two, when the person glanced backwards, I could tell it was a woman. A young woman. With dark hair.

Could it have been Miss Polly Jane Montgomery? Possibly spying on my family? Or was it someone else?

For a moment, I toyed with the idea of going after her. That was, until Pete walked up from the opposite direction and waved to me.

"Boy, are you a sight for sore eyes," he called out as he came closer.

"Rough day?"

"Not the best. Everywhere I went, people recognized me from the newspaper. And it was the strangest thing—their reactions seemed to be one extreme or the other. They were either fascinated or terrified. They either threatened me or wanted my autograph. It was enough to make a guy want to stay home."

"I'm glad you left and came over to see me."

"When I'm with you, Tracy, I *am* at home."

Then before I knew it, I was in his arms, and his warm lips were on mine. There was something so sultry about that kiss in the moonlight, and there was something about the caress of his hands on my back and the way he held me even tighter than usual that made me forget all about the missing diary. And Polly Jane Montgomery.

In fact, as near as I could tell, if Pete and I remained like that forever, nothing could ever harm us and the world would be a perfect place.

Finally, we broke away from our kiss. I rested my head on his solid shoulder while he continued to hold me in a warm embrace.

"Tracy," he murmured, "there's something I need to talk to you about."

"Mmmm . . . Do we really need to talk? Because kissing is very nice. Besides, you know what they say, 'Talk is cheap.'"

I could feel his laughter. "Not this time. At least, I hope not. Because something has been weighing on me, and it's getting awfully heavy."

I pulled back and looked up into his smiling face. "Well, let's go into the parlor, and I'll have Maddie make us some hot chocolate. Then we can talk for as long as you like."

But he shook his head. "I'd rather we sat on your porch, because it will be a whole lot easier for me to say what I need to say in the dark. You can have my coat, and I'll keep you warm. I promise."

"Okay," I said softly, all the while wondering what he had on his mind.

I truly hoped and prayed that he didn't want to talk about the case right now. Not after I'd made such great headway by finding Freddy's diary, only to lose it. I hated to tell him what had happened, and it made me sick just thinking about it.

Pete took my hand and led me back to the side porch, where he put his coat over my shoulders, and together we sat on the wooden porch swing.

By now the moon had risen higher above the treetops, while the stars made the night sky look like it was littered with diamonds. The air was cool and crisp, and I detected the faint smell of smoke coming from fireplaces in the mansions near ours.

Pete wrapped an arm around me and pulled me close. "Tracy, I know this world has become a pretty topsy-turvy place. And times have changed. Things aren't the same for us as they were for our parents."

I leaned back and looked into his eyes. "No. They're not."

Pete gulped and went on. "Normally, it would be acceptable for a couple to meet and date for a while. Then after a time . . ." He hesitated, as though he were searching for the right words.

"Yes?" I asked, feeling emotional all of a sudden.

"Well . . . This war has changed things. And the rules have changed with them."

I sighed. "They sure have."

He took a deep breath. "Right now we have no idea what tomorrow will bring. Or if we'll even have a tomorrow, for that matter."

Tears pricked at the back of my eyes. "I know. It's not easy to face up to. But it's the truth."

"So Tracy, here's what has been weighing on me. If these were normal times, I know it would be far too soon for us to talk about this . . . but, well, to be honest, I know how I feel about you. I know how I've *always* felt about you. I also know there's no other woman in the world for me but you . . . and well . . ."

"Yes?" I asked barely above a whisper.

And that's when we heard it. A woman's scream. The sound pierced the night and startled us so much that we both jumped a mile. It was so loud that it might as well have been an air-raid warning siren.

Then the scream came a second time, even more shrill and terrifying than the first one.

And it was coming from right inside our mansion.

CHAPTER 13

The Disappearing Diary and Divinity in an Armoire

After the second scream, Pete and I leapt to our feet and raced into my house by the front door. Then we flew across the black-and-white tiles of the marble floor, running past one room after the next, in search of the source of the screams.

All the while, a million thoughts ran through my head. Had someone tried to break in again? Or had someone been injured? Images of Nana being hurt flashed across my mind like pictures on the front page of a newspaper.

At long last, we spotted Nana and Eulalie, standing in the hallway just outside the dining room. I almost fainted with relief when I saw that Nana was okay.

"Who screamed?" all four of us asked at the exact same moment.

"I think it came from the back hallway," Nana said, pointing.

Then Pete and I took the lead as we raced to find whoever had been hurt or harmed. Much to my amazement, Eulalie almost kept up with us while Nana lagged far behind.

Finally, when we got to the hallway that led to the back, side door, we found a teary-eyed Lupé down on her knees, staring at the armoire that held coats and hats and gloves. Judging from the way she was trembling, I was sure the screams must have come from her.

Though clearly, she was not injured.

I was almost giddy with relief to at least know that much. "What is it Lupé? Did you see a mouse?"

Eulalie stared at the beautiful art-deco piece, with huge burl-wood panels that held a swirling, meandering design in the grain. "Not to worry. I'll have my cat, Opaline, on the case in an instant. She's excellent at catching mice, and she's quite successful at eliminating insects, too."

"In there . . ." Lupé uttered just above a whisper. "In the armoire." Tears rolled down her cheeks as she clasped her hands before her, prayer-like.

Pete took two quick steps toward the tall cabinet and offered his hand to Lupé. "You're safe, ma'am. I won't let any of the little critters harm you."

But Lupé shook her head and refused his hand. "It's Hay-seus," she whispered before making the sign of the cross.

"Hay-seus?" we all repeated dumbly.

"Sí, sí," she said, nodding her head. "Hay-seus. Jesus. In the armoire."

My mouth fell open wide, and Nana let out a little gasp. Pete crinkled his eyebrows while he looked at the plump woman who remained on her knees.

Eulalie, on the other hand, tilted her head and studied the armoire sideways. "Well, it is a rather enormous piece of furniture. I suppose someone *could* be hiding in there."

"No, no," Lupé cried out. "Not just *someone*. It is our Lord and Savior. Jesus."

Then she crossed herself again, and for some reason, we all followed suit, though I wasn't exactly sure why.

And I also wasn't sure if Lupé had actually seen something or not. It was possible she'd gotten things mixed up, and it was our attempted burglar from earlier today who might be hiding in there now. If so, I decided it was high time for us to find out for sure.

So I stepped right up and grabbed the Bakelite handle of the door.

"Wait!" Nana yelled before I opened it. "Someone else might be in there, and they could have a weapon!"

Somehow, it was a chance I was willing to take. So I yanked the door wide open.

Only to find there was no one hiding in there at all. Aside from the coats and hats and things, there wasn't a single soul inside.

"Lupé," I said softly, "I don't think He's in here."

"Oh, I don't know," Nana countered. "Jesus is supposed to be everywhere. Maybe not in physical form, but in spirit. If Lupé says Jesus is in our armoire, then who are we to say otherwise?"

I had to admit, Nana had a point, and there really wasn't any argument to that statement.

But Lupé shook her head. "No, no. Not there."

She finally got to her feet and shut the door again. Then she pointed to a design in the burl wood, making an outline with her fingers. "There!" she exclaimed. "Can you see it? It's Jesus. There is his face and his robe. There's his beard."

And sure enough, she was right. It was the very image of Jesus in the grain of the wood.

"Well, I'll be," Nana laughed. "I always did like that armoire. I knew I bought it for a reason."

I gasped. "I see it, too, Lupé. Now that you point it out. I can make out the image of Jesus there perfectly."

"Me, too," Pete added, his arm sliding across my back.

Only Eulalie stood by silently, tilting her head from side to side, and staring at the wood with a small smile on her face.

"It's a miracle . . ." Lupé breathed.

At that very moment, I was about to say otherwise, that it was probably just the luck of the draw that the image happened to show up in the wood. But I held my tongue. After all, I wasn't exactly the world's greatest authority on miracles. Some said that life itself was a miracle. Others said that flowers and a beautiful sunset were miracles. Whereas still others only believed a miracle involved something more on the line of the parting of the Red Sea.

Yet as far as I knew, life probably held plenty of miracles that most of us didn't even pay attention to.

And if Lupé believed she'd just witnessed a miracle, I wasn't about to take that away from her.

So for a few moments, we all simply stood there staring. Until Pete caught my eye and motioned to the other end of the hallway, in the direction from which we'd come. I nodded, and together we quietly slipped away, leaving the women to continue gazing at the image in the armoire.

"That was an interesting turn of events," Pete murmured once we were out of earshot.

"A real surprise to me," I had to admit.

"You mentioned something about some hot chocolate earlier. Does that offer still stand?" Pete's voice held a slight warble to it. "I'd like to go back outside and . . . finish our conversation . . . if that's all right with you. The moon is especially beautiful tonight."

"Sounds perfect," I told him.

So we headed straight for the kitchen, where it turned out Maddie *had* been making hot chocolate for all.

She ladled out two steaming cups for us and topped each one with whipped cream. "Be careful, now, young ones. It's very, very hot. Don't spill it or you'll burn yourselves."

"Thanks, Maddie. We'll be careful," I promised before we left the kitchen and made our way to the front door.

Always the gentleman, Pete held the door for me, and together we stepped outside. Stars shone brightly above and the moon glowed even more golden than before as we started back to our spot on the side porch. We had barely taken another step when . . . *pa-poof!*

A huge flash of light blinded me. It was so shocking that I immediately spilled hot chocolate all over my front. I screamed, since the scalding hot liquid felt like burning lava as it splashed onto my neck and upper chest, as well as my dress. Then another bright flash lit up the night and I heard the crash of Pete's cup hitting the brick of our front porch, and I nearly dropped my own cup.

To make matters worse, I couldn't see a thing, while my skin burned in pain.

And more and more light flashes went off before us.

Yet for the life of me, I couldn't make sense of what was happening. Were we under some kind of attack? Had the Japanese or Germans hit the mainland?

That's when I finally recognized that *pa-poof* sound, followed by the crackling of a flashbulb, and I suddenly realized someone had been taking pictures of us. We had been ambushed, and the photographer must have been hiding in the shrubs.

Not to mention, trespassing on our property.

"Tracy, take my hand!" I heard Pete holler as his fingers found mine, and he began to pull me along behind him. "I'll get us back inside!"

And so I stepped along blindly, letting Pete guide me. From the sounds that I heard next, I could tell the front door had opened, and then I felt Pete pull me into our house. All the while, afterimages from those flashes kept replaying before my eyes. I could hear Hadley and Eulalie exclaiming and running toward us, though I couldn't see them. I put my hand to my neck, which felt like it was still searing, since the chocolate had been horribly hot when it hit my skin. To top it off, I could tell that my dress now clung to me in a big sticky mess.

And though I'm usually a pretty levelheaded girl, for once in my life, I started to cry. Openly.

Pete instantly had me in his arms. "It's okay now, sweetheart. We're safe. I'll protect you. It was just some creep taking pictures."

"Someone taking pictures?" I heard Hadley holler. "They're trespassing. They have no business being on our property and committing such an act. I will personally apprehend them."

With those words, I heard Hadley's footsteps heading for the door, right before I heard the door open and shut again.

Pete released me, saying, "My eyes are adjusting, so I'd better go help catch this guy." Then his footsteps thumped across the threshold and out the front door as he raced to join Hadley.

By now Nana was there, too. "Oh my goodness, darlin'. What in the world happened? Your chest and neck are red and that dress is ruined. Did you get burned?"

At long last, the room came into focus, and the flashes from the afterimages started to subside. Nana took my hand and led me to the kitchen, where she, Eulalie, and Maddie began to fix me up while I filled them in on the whole story. What little I had to tell, anyway.

"That's a nasty burn," Maddie told me. "Now hold still while I put some butter on it. I've had many burns myself from boiling water or grabbing a pan out of the oven without pot holders."

Then in a matter of minutes, she had butter slathered on my neck and upper chest, and I realized I was now covered in both butter and chocolate. Not exactly the most attractive thing for a girl to be wearing when she wanted to impress her fella.

Especially a fella who'd been trying to tell me something important all night.

To be honest, with a little reading between the lines, I had a pretty good idea what Pete had wanted to talk about. Namely, our future. And I got the impression he either wanted to get engaged or married. Or maybe he only intended to ask me to go steady.

Then again, maybe I wasn't very good at reading between the lines and I'd gotten it all wrong. Maybe what he was really getting at, in a roundabout way, was that he wanted to end our relationship, to make things less complicated for us both when he went off to war.

Funny, but even though Pete and I hadn't been dating all that long, the thought of no longer having him in my life made me sick to my stomach.

Which made me realize more than ever how I felt about the guy.

Like it or not, I had fallen head over heels in love. In my heart and mind, Pete had become my O.A.O. *My one-and-only.*

Did he feel the same way?

Though one thing was for sure, I wasn't going to find out tonight.

Nana and Eulalie walked me to the front of the house, on our way to the staircase, just as Pete and Hadley came back inside, half dragging a man with a camera slung over his neck.

Then Pete pretty much forced the guy into a chair near the entry. But I couldn't get a very good look at the man, since he pulled his bent fedora low over his face and slouched down, as though he was trying to sink farther into his rumpled trench coat.

"We apprehended one of the scoundrels," Hadley informed us. "But I fear he had an accomplice."

"I'll call the police," Eulalie announced before turning on her heel and racing from the room.

"Unfortunately, his pal got away," Pete told us. "But not before this meatball threw a film canister over the fence to him. Or her."

"So the pictures went off with his partner in crime," I sighed. "Meaning, this guy will probably get paid since he fulfilled his part of the bargain."

"I'm afraid so," Pete said, glaring at the disheveled guy, who was now doing his best to become the *Invisible Man*.

The photographer's dark eyes peeked out from under the brim of his hat, darting around the room until he caught sight of me. Then he practically jumped out of his skin.

That's when Pete turned and got a good glance at my glamorous new makeup. "Holy mackerel! Tracy, you're hurt! Is that blood all over your dress?" Shock and concern filled his eyes.

I gave him the brightest smile I could muster, though I knew it was wobbly at best. "Not blood. Just chocolate."

"Hot chocolate," Nana added. "Her dress is ruined and she's got burns on her neck. They'll take some time to heal, and hopefully they won't leave any scars."

Pete clenched his jaw as well as his fists as he moved closer to the photographer. "Are you happy now, pal? You've injured my girl! Why, I oughta give you a knuckle sandwich. Don't you know that's no way to treat a lady?"

The trench-coat man hung his head. "I'm so sorry, miss. I really didn't mean for that to happen. I just got hired to take some pictures, that was all. I didn't mean to hurt you."

By now Pete was angrier than I'd ever seen him before in my life. "What did you think would happen, huh? Scaring a girl half to death like that? When she had just walked out of her house in the dark? You should be ashamed of yourself."

The man shook his head. "I am. Believe me. I am so very sorry."

"Mind telling us who you were working for then?" Pete went on.

The man took a ragged breath. "Some dame. That's all I know. She has dark hair and she's a smart dresser. She wouldn't even give me her name and she didn't tell me why she wanted the pictures. She just offered me a lot of money if I got a picture of you and your gal. I wish I'd never gone along with her shenanigans. Really I do."

He had barely spoken the words when Eulalie walked in, followed by a uniformed police officer. Down the hallway, I could see Lupé was busy dusting, just within earshot. I had a pretty good idea that she was listening in, though probably not wanting to overstep her bounds by joining in the fray.

"We seem to be making this a habit," the officer said. "Who broke in this time?" Then he took a good look at me. "Is that blood, miss? Looks like you need a hospital."

I shook my head. "It's hot chocolate."

"And it's not a break-in," Eulalie corrected him. "Instead, this man ambushed Tracy and Pete here with his camera. Just outside the front door. The surprise of the flash made her spill her chocolate, giving her a burn."

The officer moved over to the trench-coat guy. "Are you the person responsible for the break-in here earlier? Did you come back to finish the job?"

The man bounced to his feet with a wild look in his eyes. "Break-in? I didn't do any breaking in! I may have acted like a jerk trying to take the pictures, but I'm not a crook. Don't try to pin something on me that I didn't do."

The policeman shoved him back into the chair. "That's what they all say. Let's see if you sing a different tune down at the station."

"Honest, officer. I didn't do it." The photographer took off his hat and held it against his chest, and for the first time, we all got a good look at his face.

"You look familiar," the policeman commented, crinkling his brow. "Have I arrested you before? Time to tell me your name, bub, and make it snappy."

Then, as if on cue, my boss entered the room. "His name is 'Two-Bit Louie.' They call him that because he's a cheap hire. He'll work for any P.I. or any sleazy rag that practices yellow journalism. He specializes in blackmail and bad luck."

"That's good enough for me," the officer said. "I'll take him downtown."

And for some reason, now that Sammy was on the scene, everything turned into bedlam. Everyone started to talk at once, trying to get answers from Louie. While Sammy, of course, wanted details on what had happened tonight, from start to finish.

In the middle of it all, Nana turned to me. "Let's get you upstairs, darlin', and get you cleaned up. I've got some cream to put

on that burn. Then I'm going to insist that you call it a night and go
to bed."

Much as I hated to admit it, I knew my grandmother was
probably right. So I blew a kiss goodnight to Pete, and he gave me a
sad smile in return.

I had a better idea why when I got upstairs to my room and
looked at myself in the mirror. My mascara had run in great black
streaks down my cheeks, and the hot chocolate on my dress really did
look like dried blood. Besides that, the butter that was smeared all
over my neck and upper chest gleamed with greasiness, and only
emphasized the redness of my skin, making me look like I had a very
bad sunburn. All in all, I could have easily passed for a character in a
horror movie.

And though I knew most of the damage could be cleaned up
with soap and water, I only hoped the burn wouldn't leave a scar.

Nana ran a bath for me. "I think that dress is pretty much
ruined, don't you?"

I just nodded.

"Then let's get it off. Maybe we can salvage enough for Lupé to
use for cleaning rags."

Nana helped me out of the dress, and that's when I noticed burn
spots on my stomach, too.

But I also noticed something else.

Because, sitting right there on my dressing table was a leather-
bound book. One that hadn't been there before.

It was Freddy's diary.

CHAPTER 14

A Suspicious Priest and a Surprise Bouquet

That night, my sleep was fitful, and it seemed like I tossed and turned the whole time. Nana had covered my burns in some kind of cream and demanded that I wear one of my father's old undershirts, to keep the salve in place. Then she'd insisted on giving me a couple of aspirins for the pain and a sleeping pill to make sure that I slept. And though I was dying to dig into Freddy's diary, I knew I was in no shape to argue with my grandmother's orders when it came to medical care.

But at least I'd had the good sense to hide the diary in my closet before going to sleep.

Though to be honest, I wasn't sure if the torment I'd gone through during the night even *qualified* as sleep. Because my night had been anything but restful. Instead, it felt like I had drifted from nightmare to nightmare. At one point, I dreamed I was back at the newspaper, where I was surrounded by reporters, all clacking away on their typewriters. The next thing I knew, Pete was there, too, and the newspaper people were laughing while a group of Nazis pointed guns right at us.

Another time I dreamed the air-raid sirens had gone off and we were under attack by the German *Luftwaffe*. I kept seeing flash after flash of lights, as more and more bombs exploded all around us. And though I tried with everything I had to run, I was frozen in place, since I was so blinded by the flash of lights. Then Eulalie silently floated into my nightmare and covered me with a thin, blue cloth stained with chocolate, much like the dress I'd been wearing the night before.

I awoke in the morning to the sound of thunder, and looked outside to see rain clouds had filled the sky.

Which, oddly enough, fit my mood just perfectly.

Especially when I knew it was time to face the music and check out my burn in the mirror. Naturally, I'd been too upset the night before to take a really good look.

But things always seemed different in the light of day (even a dark, cloud-filled day like today) and I knew I needed to find out the truth.

So I took a deep breath and stepped before my wall mirror. A million thoughts ran through my mind. Would I have scars that lasted a lifetime? Would Pete still find me pretty? Then again, maybe it wouldn't be as bad as I feared. Besides, I probably didn't have room to complain, anyway. With all the dangers and horrors our servicemen had to face every day, I could hardly bellyache about something so minor in comparison.

Even so, I said a little prayer before removing the undershirt.

Only to find that the burn was completely healed. Gone without a trace. There was nothing to indicate that I'd been injured at all. In fact, my skin looked even better than it had before. A small scar that I'd gotten as a child while roller-skating had disappeared, too. Vanished.

How was that possible?

For a moment or two, I just stood there staring in disbelief. When reality finally sunk in, I could hardly wait to share my news.

So I jumped in the shower and got ready for the day. Wearing an indigo-blue suit, I practically danced down the stairs and into the kitchen for breakfast. Nana and Hadley were already seated at the table, and their dour faces took me by surprise. And when Maddie turned from her cooking and gave me a look of pure pity, I knew something was up.

My first thought was that everyone might still be upset about the events of the night before. But then I wondered if something else had happened between the time I'd gone to bed and the moment I'd gotten up.

Nana squeezed my hand as I joined them at the table. "How's the burn?" she asked.

I couldn't help but smile. "You'll never believe it. But I'm as good as new! Even better. No scars."

She gave me a wan smile. "Well, at least *that's* some good news."

Much to my surprise, nobody acted all that happy to hear about my recovery. And while I didn't want to be a self-centered brat, I thought a little joy over my amazing healing might be warranted.

Yet Hadley simply took a sip of his coffee without saying a word, and Maddie suddenly became very busy with her cooking. Obviously something was bothering them. And I soon learned what that "something" was when Nana handed me the morning's paper.

The front page immediately caught my eye. Then again, it was hard to miss the huge picture of Pete and me, front and center at the top of the page, with a caption that read, "Is Bloody Dress Proof That Society Couple Committed Murder?"

For a moment or two, my mouth seemed incapable of forming words. Instead I just sat there, sputtering, trying to speak. And I couldn't stop staring at the picture before me.

In the photograph, my face had been contorted in shock and surprise, probably as I'd reacted to the sudden flash of light. Not to mention, the pain of being burned by hot chocolate which, in the black-and-white photo, could have easily passed for blood on my light-colored dress. Beside me, Pete looked furious while he held his hand out before him, trying to shield his eyes from the next flash.

When I finally managed to pull my eyes away from the picture, I started to read the article below it. A piece that was, once again, written by P.J. Montgomery. It was mostly a reiteration of the article from the day before, though this time P.J. used the so-called "fact" that I'd been caught wearing a "bloody dress" as proof that Pete and I had just gone on some kind of killing spree.

"So Polly Jane hired Two-Bit Louie to hide in our shrubs and photograph us," I sort of murmured. "That was a rotten thing to do."

Though I could hardly say I was surprised, considering she was a *rotten* person.

And it was bad enough that she'd hurt me, but with this newest article, I knew Pete would never be allowed to enlist. Not unless he went to a recruiting station on the other side of the country. For that matter, I figured he might not have a job if his employers got a look at the paper.

Which was highly likely.

Nana put her hand on my arm. "I'll call my lawyer this morning and have him put a stop to this madness. We'll sue the paper for libel."

I got up and poured a cup of coffee, still in shock over what I'd seen in the paper. "Thanks, Nana. But it won't prove Pete's innocence, and we'll just end up in a long, drawn-out court battle. None of this will be good for Pete. Or me." I returned to the table and drizzled cream into my coffee, before adding a couple of sugar cubes and stirring it all with a spoon. "No, our best bet is for Sammy and me to figure out what really happened to Freddy. Then we can get Miss Polly Jane Montgomery to print a full and complete retraction. Though to be honest, I'm not sure I'd even trust her to do that. I'd probably be better off taking the story to a competing paper."

"That's the spirit," Nana said softly while Maddie beamed at me with a teary-eyed smile.

Hadley grinned, too. "It's not the size of the dog in the fight, it's the size of the fight in the dog."

"Mark Twain," I said with a laugh. "Hadley, I hope you're not comparing me to a dog."

"Not at all, my child. It's simply a quote that my grandson happens to cherish. I pray it will give Alistair courage when he and his group, the Ninety-Ninth Pursuit Squadron out of Tuskegee, go into battle."

I took a sip of my coffee. "Well, if that quote works for Al, it should work for me, too."

"Speaking of dogs . . ." Hadley went on. "Creatures who have a penchant for burying bones . . . Would you happen to know where the shovel I lent Eulalie yesterday may have ended up?"

His question took me by surprise. "Why, yes. I returned it to the garage last night before dinner."

He crinkled his gray brows. "Hmmm . . . it appears to be missing. Perhaps you might help me locate it after breakfast?"

"I'd be happy to Hadley."

I'd barely spoken the words when Maddie served us eggs, bacon, and fresh biscuits. "You'd all better eat up now. I've heard talk of rationing in our future. Soon we may not be able to get this kind of food. Too bad Eulalie didn't come down for breakfast."

I unfolded my napkin. "Will Lupé be joining us?"

Nana was already shaking her head. "She only had toast and coffee before she went to church this morning. But Maddie's right—we'd all better enjoy this kind of food while we can, because I've heard talk of rationing, too. Flour, sugar, and coffee will probably be the first on the list."

Hadley held up a slice of bacon and looked it over. "Much of our agricultural resources will be funneled toward feeding our troops. We must all make sacrifices to keep our military strong."

"Just another way we can do our part," I murmured.

Hadley nodded. "Apparently, a record number of men signed up for the service in December, according to a more reliable article in this morning's paper."

Maddie sniffled. "I couldn't be more proud of our boys. We didn't start this war, but we'll go in and win it."

"That's right," Nana agreed. "We'll win this war. And we'll bring peace and freedom back to the world. But we'll all need to pitch in and help, from the homefront to the front lines."

"Hear, hear," Hadley said, holding up his glass of orange juice for a toast. "To winning the war."

"And to doing our part," Nana added.

Then we all clinked our glasses and took a good gulp of our orange juice. I, for one, couldn't help but wonder if I was doing *my* part to help out.

Then again, maybe I was helping more than I realized by trying to solve the murder of a young German swing dancer. Especially when my feminine intuition told me there was much more to this case than any of us had realized. For all I knew, there might even be some connection to the war.

That very thought stuck with me, even after breakfast, when Hadley and I headed for the garage to search for the lost shovel. We had just stepped into the back hallway when we spotted Lupé having a quiet, but intense, conversation with a priest and a nun. They were all standing next to our armoire and giving it a thorough examination.

While I could certainly appreciate her wanting to show off the "miracle" she'd found, it would've been appropriate for her to get permission from my grandmother or me first. Or, at the very least, notify us of the arrival of her friends.

I waved to them as Hadley and I approached, though they didn't return the greeting. Instead, the priest just stared at me like I was an intruder. His stare was all the more menacing given he was a very tall and very large man with salt-and-pepper hair. The nun on the other hand, blinked her vivid blue eyes and bit her lip that was covered with bright red lipstick.

Funny, but of all the nuns I'd ever met, I'd never met one who wore lipstick.

I held out my hand to the priest. "Hello, I'm Tracy and this is Hadley. My grandmother owns this mansion. May we help you?"

To which the three of them responded with complete silence.

A silence that grew awkward in a hurry.

Finally, the priest spoke up. "I'm Father Phillip. And this is Sister Gertrude. From what we can see, it appears you've got a full-blown miracle right here in your home. You must be utterly ecstatic. But I'm afraid we'll need to cordon off your hallway and have it properly investigated."

I let out a little laugh. "Well, yes, it is an extraordinary image in our armoire, and we *are* very pleased. But this is a private residence and *I'm afraid* we won't be cordoning off anything. Besides, we've been storing things in this armoire for as long as I can remember, and this wood has never been harmed by our use."

He clasped his hands before him and frowned. "Then we will need to talk to the homeowner about this."

"I'm sure my grandmother would be happy to speak with you," I replied. "Provided she's finished her breakfast. And by the way, you never said what church you're affiliated with."

He gave me a slight smile. "I hate to be a bother and waste your time. If you would be so kind, could you please direct me to your grandmother?"

At that very moment, it took every ounce of good manners I had to restrain myself from asking this man of the cloth to leave our house. Clearly he realized he'd run up against a brick wall in dealing with me, and he probably had the idea that my grandmother might be more malleable.

Unfortunately, I knew he was probably right. After all, my sweet but naïve darling of a grandmother had already allowed Eulalie and Lupé to come stay with us. So I figured she'd probably accommodate this priest and nun in any way they wished.

But before I could say another word, or draw the battle lines with these two, Hadley intervened. "Lupé, would you please lead the father and sister to meet Mrs. Truworth? I'm sure you'll find her in the kitchen."

Lupé smiled and curtsied. "Sí! Sí! Please come with me then."

And without another word, their little procession headed in the direction from which we'd just come.

"Hadley, does anything seem suspicious to you? About those two? For a priest, that man was downright dismissive."

"I thought so as well," Hadley replied as we walked to the back door. "'Things are not always what they seem; the first appearance deceives many.' Phaedrus."

"That seems to be a regular theme around here lately. Did you notice that nun was wearing lipstick? I thought nuns weren't supposed to wear makeup."

Hadley chuckled. "Clearly your P.I. training is paying off, for I hardly perceived such a subtle detail. You, on the other hand, detected it right away. Your boss frequently extols your natural abilities when it comes to your line of work. I believe he is correct."

"Thanks, Hadley," I said as he held the door for me.

I stepped outside just as a bolt of lightning flashed through the sky, almost as quickly as Eulalie bolted from the backyard and behind the garage, carrying Hadley's shovel. Though it appeared the shovel hadn't been all she'd borrowed, since she was wearing his rubber boots and a pair of work gloves, too.

I turned to Hadley, and judging from the way he crinkled his eyebrows, I guessed he'd seen her, too.

"Well, it appears one mystery has been solved," he said with a smile. "The whereabouts of my shovel has been uncovered."

I sighed. "If only all our mysteries were so easy to solve . . . I wonder what she was burying now. And for that matter, why is she practically sneaking around our yard?"

"Your guess is likely to be as educated as mine. Though I suspect she may have simply been running to get out of the approaching rain."

Then, as though right on cue, huge raindrops *thunked* onto the back porch, splashing us after they crashed into the flagstone walkway.

"Why don't you stay here where it's dry," Hadley suggested. "I'll go and see if I might assist her."

"Thanks again, Hadley."

I watched for just a moment while he ambled to the garage and through the side door.

Then I went back into the house, ready to return to my room and peruse Freddy's diary. I hoofed it down the hallway, but I stopped when I heard voices in a rather tense conversation. They sounded like they were coming from the vicinity of the kitchen, and while I couldn't quite hear what was being said, I could certainly hear *how* it was being said. First there was Nana's voice, in her usual warm and cordial tone. Then there was Lupé's voice, sounding nervous and apologetic. But the part that struck me as strange was the cold, authoritative voices of a man and a woman that I guessed were coming from the priest and the nun. Again, their demeanor truly sounded off-kilter to me, compared to most people I'd met in such roles.

I couldn't help but wonder—were these people who they said they were? And if not, why on earth would anyone want to pose as a priest and a nun?

I instantly thought back to an older Katie McClue novel, *The Mystery of the Minister's Impostor*, where she had uncovered a band of crooks who had kidnapped a priest just as he was being transferred to a new parish. And since the priest hadn't met his flock yet, no one even realized the man who showed up in a clerical collar was actually a phony. Thankfully, Katie had uncovered the truth, that the fake priest belonged to a gang of crooks who only wanted to obtain the confessions and personal information of the more well-to-do parishioners, in order to blackmail them later for tons of money.

Of course, such a dastardly strategy would never work when it came to Nana or me. Not only did we already have a family minister, but neither one of us had any big secrets to hide.

And now, as I moved closer to the voices, I couldn't help but notice just how tense and uncompromising they sounded. I decided it was time for me to intervene, whether Nana thought she needed it or not.

But then the doorbell rang. So I raced to the front entry and opened the door to find a delivery boy in a damp uniform standing on the portico. He presented me with a dozen red roses, and without waiting for me to sign for them, he ran back to his delivery truck.

I pulled the attached card from its envelope. *Tracy, darling*, it read. *Wishing you a speedy recovery. Hope I'll still see you tonight. Love, Pete.*

For just a minute or two, I paused, and did my best to memorize the beauty and scent of those roses. I closed my eyes and inhaled deeply, because I knew that, one day soon, Pete wouldn't be able to send roses my way. He'd probably be halfway around the world, and the luxury of having flowers delivered would be nothing but a distant memory.

And I was still lost in the perfume of those flowers when the phone rang. Though I knew better than to answer it in a thunderstorm, I decided to risk it. But I was glad I did when I heard Pete's voice on the other end of the line.

He'd barely said hello when I gushed, "Thank you for the lovely roses."

"Beautiful roses for a beautiful girl," he said through the crackling phone line, compliments of the storm. "I thought you might need some cheering up. But you sound like you're feeling much better this morning."

"I am. And you would never believe it, but I'm completely healed."

"Wow, Tracy, that's terrific. I'm so glad to hear it. So I guess that means we're still on for tonight?"

"Absolutely. I'm looking forward to trying out this La-la dancing."

"I'm just looking forward to being with you."

I had to admit, the fella certainly had a way with words.

"Me, too," I told him. "More than you can imagine. I'm also hoping we pick up some clues about Freddy's death."

"That would be swell. Especially since I just got a call from my boss. He and some of the other higher-ups want me to come in this afternoon and have a little chat with them."

"Oh, Pete, I'm so sorry to hear it. But don't go down without a fight. You haven't done anything wrong."

He chuckled. "You and I both know that. Unfortunately, the paper's been doing a pretty good job of convicting me. Now I'll probably have to convince my boss otherwise."

"Keep your chin up."

"I will. And don't forget . . ." he said, clearing his throat. "I still want to have that talk with you."

"I haven't forgotten."

"I'll see you tonight," he murmured, before we said our goodbyes.

And now I had to wonder how I would ever manage to wait until tonight to have this "talk" with Pete and finally find out what he wanted to tell me.

It was going to be a long wait.

In the meantime, I went straight to the kitchen hallway, listening for the tense interaction I'd heard earlier.

To step in if I needed to.

But by now, all was quiet and Nana and the others were long gone. So I headed to my room to delve into Freddy's diary. After shutting the door behind me, I pulled the book from its hiding place and turned to page one. Then it wasn't long before I became completely engrossed and forgot about the world around me.

Because I could hardly believe what I was reading.

CHAPTER 15

Back to the Book and Back to the Museum

Freddy's diary was written in some of the most beautiful script I have ever seen. Each letter and every word were almost works of art in and of themselves. On top of that, I was also astonished by Freddy's command of the English language, though I probably shouldn't have been, considering his apparent love for all things English.

And as I devoured each entry in his diary, I found myself reading faster and faster, absolutely dying to read what he'd written next. Much to my amazement, his diary read more like a best-selling book, and a very scary one at that. As near as I could tell, Freddy had been intent on chronicling the Nazis' rise to ruling Germany, and the horrors he wrote about were only punctuated by the thunder and lightning of the storm outside. Yet while I read from one passage to the next, I had to wonder, what exactly *was* his purpose in recording all that had been going on around him? Had he simply written everything down to read at a later time? Or did he have an audience in mind? Was it possible he planned to use his writings in a book to tell the real story of the Nazis?

Whatever his motives, and whether or not his words had ever been meant for anyone's eyes but his own, he gave a terrifying view of life inside of Germany. It was shocking to read his account of how Hitler and his henchmen had manipulated their way into complete and total power.

One of the first entries read:

Adolph Hitler never should have been in office in the first place. After all, he only received thirty-seven percent of the votes for our presidential election in 1932. Paul von Hindenburg won by a wide margin and got the majority vote. But then Hindenburg made an enormous mistake when he appointed Hitler to be Chancellor in 1933. Of course, Hindenburg only did so to appease Hitler's Brownshirts, who were already acting like thugs and trying to intimidate their way into power. Still, it was a move that proved costly for the German people, because, when the elderly Hindenburg passed away in 1934, Hitler automatically succeeded him. And the minute Hitler was in office, he abolished the role of the president altogether. Then he merged several government offices and gave himself the title of Führer. And from that moment on, the government was run by the National Socialist German Workers' Party—the Nazis.

But it was never the will of the people to have Hitler or the Nazis in power. Hitler knew it and so did all of Germany. Yet Hitler was determined to get all the citizens to go along with his evil plans, either by convincing them through propaganda or coercing them with threats of violence, starvation, or death.

The very thought of it made me gasp. For the life of me, I couldn't imagine being forced to go along with something so evil, at the risk of suffering such horrible consequences.

I shuddered before turning to another entry that read:

Hitler hated the Jews. He had them banned from parks and restaurants and swimming pools. And while he deemed the Jews to be inferior, they were also a convenient target for him. Yes, in order to win the hearts and minds of the German people, Hitler tried to unite us behind the hatred of a common enemy. And since Germany didn't really have any enemies at that time, Hitler created one. Or two, actually. First, he went after the Jews, doing all that he could to convince us that Jewish people were out to destroy Germany and our way of life. Then, Hitler went after the Polish people, claiming they had attacked the Fatherland and were out to get us. But I have it on

*good authority that it was actually the other way around. And since
the Nazis had complete control of the press, they printed Hitler's lies
and not the truth.*

I skipped to a later section in the diary, and was amazed to
read:

> *I find it odd that Hitler has gone to such lengths to
> persecute the church, and has stated that Christianity has
> crippled all that is noble in humanity. He has even done his
> best to remove the Christ child from any celebration of
> Christmas, to the point of rewriting our beloved Christmas
> carols. Yet for one who claims not to believe, he does believe in
> the supernatural power of holy relics, including the* Arma
> Christi, *or the "Weapons of Christ." That's one of the reasons
> why Hitler has been so desperate to get his hands on the famous
> Ghent Altarpiece from the Saint Bavo Cathedral in Belgium.
> He believes there is a coded map contained within the painting,
> a map that leads to the location of the* Arma Christi.
>
> *Of course, when it comes to their quest for supernatural
> power, the Nazis haven't limited themselves to just holy relics,
> and they have a complete fascination with "scientific occultism,"
> including things like witchcraft and glacial cosmogony. Hitler's
> former Deputy Führer, Rudolph Hess, once even had the dream
> of establishing a Central Institute for Occultism. Personally, I
> know very little about such occult subjects, but I do know the
> Nazis will stop at nothing in their quest for supernatural
> power.*
>
> *And that is why the secret Nazi organization, Ahnenerbe,
> has sent archaeologists like me out into the world, to search for
> certain items. Things such as the Ark of the Covenant and the
> Holy Grail, and more of the* Arma Christi. *Probably because
> Hitler believes such objects will help him create an unstoppable
> army. Were it not for that, I wouldn't even be in America,
> while my family is being held captive in Germany to ensure my
> cooperation. And should I defy my orders, and not search for the
> particular object that I was sent out to find, my family will be
> deemed enemies of the Reich and treated as such, even though
> they are not Jewish. Yet my being out of Germany hardly means
> that I am out of harm's way, because the Nazis' tentacles stretch*

*much farther than most are aware. So I go along with a task
that holds nothing but horror for me, since I can't help but
wonder—what will happen to my family once I locate the item
I was sent to find?*

Freddy's words made my heart skip a beat. And it didn't help
when, seconds later, a brilliant bolt of lightning suddenly flashed
through the sky, making me gasp in terror. For a split second, I
forgot where I was and it seemed like Nazi Germany was just outside
my bedroom door, instead of an entire world away.

But I quickly shook off my shock, and I jumped to my feet and
began to pace the floor. While I'd certainly heard plenty about
Hitler, much of what Freddy had written about the fascist dictator
was news to me. And probably news to a lot of people. His diary also
gave a better view of why Freddy was really here. From what I could
tell, he'd been sent to Houston to find some kind of an artifact. And,
according to Freddy's diary, his family was being held hostage until
he found said artifact.

One that the Nazis wanted.

But what?

Could it have been the Greek marble statuette that was stolen
the night of the museum gala? That two-thousand-year-old statue of
a turtledove?

Somehow I found that hard to believe. Sure, the statue was old
and probably worth a lot of money. But from what I knew, it was
hardly on par with something like the Holy Grail or the Ark of the
Covenant. Besides, if that statuette had been so important, I doubt it
would have been on display at the Houston Art Museum, with what
turned out to be inadequate security.

Unless the people at the museum didn't fully understand what
they had.

Though honestly, that seemed highly unlikely to me,
considering the museum probably had their own experts who had
examined each of their artifacts. Even so, was it possible that Freddy
knew something the museum experts didn't?

Which brought up my next question—did anyone else know
why Freddy was really here? Someone like Professor Longfellow? I
guessed that Stanley didn't know, since he'd told me a story of how
Freddy had escaped the Nazis. Probably the very story that Freddy

himself told most people. Yet according to the diary, that must have been nothing but a cover, since Freddy was only in Houston because he'd been forced to come here.

In search of something.

And then I had to wonder—why did the Nazis pick someone as young as Freddy to do the job? Surely they must have had plenty of other archaeologists they could have sent, men who would've participated in Hitler's schemes without coercion.

But I knew the answer to my question the very second it popped into my mind. Freddy was chosen because of his love of all things English, including swing dancing. That meant he could easily fit in over here. He spoke the language as well as anyone, and he knew popular culture like any young adult.

Yet he'd been murdered over here.

Why?

And what about the object he'd been hunting for? Had it been found? Or was it still out there?

Before long, my head started to swim with questions. And I knew the only way to gain any perspective on the situation was to hash it over with my boss. With a lull in the storm, I picked up the phone in my room and dialed Sammy.

"You sound pretty chipper, kid," he said through the line, "for someone who had her mug on the front page of the paper again this morning. How's the burn? You were a little worse for wear when I saw you last night."

"I'm as good as new this morning."

"Glad to hear it. After all that, I figured you'd need some cheering up, so I've got Mildred working her way through that ledger you brought in. I'm hoping she finds a clue or two."

"And I've been working my way through Freddy's diary," I gushed. "You'll never believe what I've learned."

"You've got my ear, kid."

So I told him all that I'd found out so far.

When I was finished, Sammy let out a low whistle. "If the Nazis were forcing Freddy to do their bidding over here, some of Hitler's henchmen must have been keeping an eye on him. Maybe the stolen museum piece was what they were after. And maybe they killed him once he got his hands on it."

"But why would they do that?" I asked.

"To prevent him from spilling the beans to Uncle Sam's agents. Either on purpose or by accident. In case someone figured out his real story and ratted him out."

"Now that he's dead, what do you think will happen to his family?"

"My guess is they're either in a concentration camp or they're dead, kid. Nazis are notorious liars. They've been lying to the world since their very first 'Heil Hitler.' And they were probably lying to Freddy about keeping his family alive. Nazis don't have time to babysit people they plan to kill anyway."

I shuddered. "That's horrible."

"Tell me about it, kid. 'That's horrible' should be the name of their national anthem. But any way you look at it, I think we'd better visit the museum and see what we can learn about that stolen statue. Why don't you head over here to the office and we'll ride over to the museum together."

My pulse picked up. "Won't Ethel have us kicked out?"

Sammy chuckled. "She might. It's a chance we'll have to take. Odds are we won't even run into her."

"Sounds like a plan," I told him, trying to shake the memory of our last "run-in" with the woman.

After Sammy and I said our goodbyes, I hid the diary again and made a beeline for the garage. Thankfully, the storm had moved on by the time I backed the Packard out of its stall and had it motoring toward the corner of Main Street and Texas Avenue.

In fact, I even saw a hint of sunshine when I parked the car at the curb and ran into our building to the elevator. I got off on the top floor, and when I stepped into our office, Mildred Paninsky, our secretary, gave me her usual maternal smile.

I had to admit, I was still getting used to the idea of *even* having a secretary at all. Not that it should have been a problem for me, considering Katie McClue had Rahul running her own office. And while the middle-aged man with an eye patch and several notable scars knew how to take dictation like nobody's business, he'd also taught Katie fifteen different types of self-defense. Including a maneuver that could disable a grown man with a common drinking straw.

Yet the only thing Rahul and Mildred had in common was a fluency in several different languages. That, and they would both guard the sanctity of the office with their dying breath. Him with an iron karate chop and her with a newly acquired Colt revolver.

And even though Mildred was an older, plump woman with curly gray hair, she always dressed in the very latest of styles, and she seemed to enjoy the freedom to wear her high-dollar jewelry. A freedom she didn't have as a Jewish woman living in Germany under the Third Reich.

She immediately got up and came around her desk to greet me, taking one of my hands in both of hers. "Ah, my dear one. My, but what a case you've got going now. To think, someone could accuse that nice boy, Peter, of such a vile act as murder! I'll be pleased to know when you and Samuel have cleared his good name."

"Me, too, Mildred," I said as Sammy strolled in from the back office and nodded to me.

He shrugged into his double-breasted jacket and grabbed his fedora. "You'll never believe what Mildred found in that ledger, kid. Looks like Freddy had tracked a shipment of antiquities that arrived at the art museum back in January of '37."

"1937?" I repeated, dumbfounded.

Mildred nodded. "*Ja,* someone had it marked in the ledger. There was a little circle around it in red ink."

For a few seconds I was too stunned to speak, but I finally managed to say, "Maybe that's why Freddy came to Houston. Could you tell if the missing statue was in that shipment?"

Sammy raised an eyebrow toward Mildred. "It was," he said. "Near as we can make out."

I shook my head slowly. "But judging from what I've read in Freddy's diary, and the kinds of things that Hitler's been looking for, it doesn't quite add up. Why would the Nazis go after something so bland as a marble bird?"

Mildred's face clouded over. "The Nazis are a greedy lot. They want to own anything valuable that they can get their filthy hands on. They stole the possessions and the homes owned by Jewish people. First they declared the Jews to no longer be full citizens. I was there when it happened, and all of a sudden, we Jews were nothing but second-class citizens, without the rights of other people.

And we had to register all our valuables with the government. Then Hitler and his storm troopers simply stole people's valuable possessions, saying they had a right to take them under the law. A law they had just made up."

"I'm so glad you got out of there, Mildred," I said, taking her hand. "Tell me, why didn't more Jewish people leave?"

Mildred sucked in a ragged breath. "It wasn't so easy as people think. Hitler wanted Jewish people to leave, but they weren't allowed to take their money or possessions. So they had to leave with very little to survive on. Because of that, other countries didn't want the Jews, since these penniless Jews would have to live off handouts or government aid. And with the Great Depression, most countries had their hands full trying to take care of their own citizens."

"So the Jewish people had nowhere to go," I murmured.

"That's right, dear one. Though many people didn't leave because they thought things would get better. No one ever dreamed things would become so bad with Hitler." Tears formed in her eyes. "But I digress. I had better not keep you from going to find the clues for your case. Someday you and I can sit and talk, and I'll tell you lots of stories."

"I look forward to that, Mildred." I gave her a quick hug before Sammy and I left the office.

Once we got to the street, I volunteered to drive, since the Packard was already warmed up. We arrived at the museum a few minutes later, and much to my surprise, the place was absolutely jumping. News of the stolen artifact and the so-called "Society Murder" must have been fantastic for publicity.

But Sammy and I carefully avoided the clusters of people as we made a beeline for the first-floor office, the very place where Nana had used the telephone on New Year's Eve to call Pete's dad's attorney.

Sammy motioned to the office door. "Better let me go in first, kid. Keep your head down and stick close to me. Let's hope nobody recognizes you."

"Got it." I tilted my hat a little farther over one eye before grabbing my notepad and pen from my purse. "I'll just pretend I'm your secretary, along for the ride."

"Good plan, kid," Sammy said under his breath as we knocked on the door and entered.

A blond secretary who was sitting behind the front desk squinted at us. "Yes, who's there? It that you, Theodore?" Her nameplate read "Miss Murgatroyd."

"No, ma'am," Sammy said, clearing his throat. "We're here to investigate the burglary a few nights ago."

"Splendid." She stood up and straightened her rumpled dress. "I'm so glad you're here, officer. Though it appears you're not wearing the uniform today. At least, I don't think you're wearing a uniform. I must confess that I can't see you so well, since I broke my glasses this morning and I've been fumbling around all day. In any case, I'm surprised it's taken so long for someone to come over to investigate. The police usually show up right away for any little thing. And I thought the chief would have sent someone before now, considering we've had a serious theft."

"We've been busy," Sammy said quickly, not bothering to mention that we *weren't* the police. "Mind if we borrow a photograph of the statue?"

"Sure, no problem," she said with a smile.

With outstretched arms, she felt her way over to the larger desk in the rear of the office, and then over to a filing cabinet in the back corner. She slid the top drawer open and looked through a file, before pulling out a perfectly focused eight-by-ten glossy photo.

Of a Chinese vase.

"Here you go," she chirped before she presented the picture to us.

"Well, now, ma'am, that's a very lovely photo," Sammy said, turning on the charm. "Almost as lovely as you are. But I'm afraid it's not the picture of the missing statue."

"Oh, I'm so terribly sorry," she gushed. "I wonder where that photo could be."

Sammy put his hand on her shoulder. "Why don't you let me help you out? Since you broke your glasses and all. I gather the picture is in the file cabinet?"

"Uh-huh." The woman nodded and squinted her eyes at the cabinet. "It's in the top drawer. Right near the front. Or maybe it's in the bottom drawer . . ."

"I'm sure I can find it in a jiff," he said in a voice dripping with honey. "In the meantime, would you mind if my secretary here asks you a few questions?"

He raised an eyebrow in my direction, just enough to signal that I was supposed to keep this woman distracted while he had full access to the filing cabinet.

"Oh, not at all," the woman said with an exaggerated nod. "Anything to help with the investigation."

I stood at attention, trying to look official. "What can you tell me about the statue?"

The woman's eyes rolled in the direction of the ceiling and she crinkled her brows, clearly deep in thought. "Well . . . um . . . it was a figure of a turtledove. And it was over two thousand years old."

I scribbled in my notepad. "What was the statue made of?"

"Oh, marble. Beautiful white marble."

"So you've seen it in person? Have you ever held the piece?" I asked, again trying to sound very officious.

She smiled. "Oh, yes. I had that great privilege."

"Was it solid or did it have any hollow spaces?" I glanced toward my boss, who now had an eight-by-ten glossy of the statue in one hand, while he continued to peruse the rest of the files with his other hand.

"Um, no. No hollow places that I could see."

I put my pencil to my chin. "Did it have any symbols or writing on it anywhere? Maybe something in ancient Greek?"

She shook her head. "No. Nothing like that at all."

I returned to jotting down in my notepad. "Did the statue have any kind of special religious significance?" I asked, still wondering why Freddy or the Nazis might have been after it.

If they'd been after it.

She shrugged. "Well, in Greek mythology, turtledoves were considered to be birds of love. But that was about it."

I darted a quick glance at my boss. "How about a curse? Was there any significant legend or curse attached to this statue?" I pressed on, hoping to find some tidbit of information that would help us with our case.

She stared right at me, with confusion etched across her features. "None that I know of. Mostly that statuette was just very pretty. And ancient."

I flipped a page on my notepad. "So can you think of any reason why someone would want to steal it?"

"Lots of people want to own artifacts like that. Because they're so old and extremely rare."

"Very true," I murmured. "And I must commend you, Miss Murgatroyd, for being so helpful. But I have one last question to ask. It's an important question, and it might sound a little odd."

I noticed that Sammy had pulled a file from the drawer. He shoved it under his coat while he dropped a small metallic object into his pocket. Then he picked up the glossy photo of the statuette from where he'd set in on top of the cabinet.

Miss Murgatroyd took a deep breath. "Go ahead and ask your question. I'm more than happy to help."

"Well . . ." I started. "You know there's a war going on and . . ."

"Yes?"

"And we're fighting the Nazis."

She nodded. "Yes . . ."

"Have you ever been contacted by anyone who might be German or a member of the Nazi party? And to your knowledge, is there any reason why Hitler might be interested in the stolen statue?"

To which Miss Murgatroyd responded with a gasp as her eyes went wide. "Why, no! Not at all. I haven't been contacted by any Germans or Nazis. I can't think of a single reason why Hitler would want that statue. Do you really think . . . Are we in danger here?" she asked before she *thunked* her hand to her chest. Then her eyes started to circle and her body began to wobble.

I knew the signs well enough to know what would happen next. So I raced around to catch her, just as she fell into a dead faint. Sammy jumped in to help, too, and we carefully maneuvered Miss Murgatroyd into a chair.

"Here you go," I said softly as I helped her lean forward. "Put your head between your knees and you'll be all right. Try to take some deep breaths."

Funny, but I'd barely spoken the words when I realized I could have taken my own advice. Because my heart started to pound and I suddenly felt a little light-headed myself when I heard a sound that sent chills running up and down my spine.

It was Ethel's voice.

Coming from down the hall.

CHAPTER 16

One Long Line and Two Lousy Intruders

Ethel's voice rang out again from the other end of the hallway, and it sent even more shivers scurrying along my spine. Funny, but since the night she'd accused Pete of murder and Nana of burglary, I hadn't remembered just how screechy her voice really was. Now I realized that it was downright grating.

Amazingly, Ethel didn't have much *official* authority at the museum, except for being a member of the art league, the museum's founding organization. The same organization that Nana belonged to. But Ethel wasn't even the president of the group, and yet she had somehow managed to gain a certain amount of importance and power, most likely by being a bully.

And after our last nightmare encounter with the woman, I didn't much care to tangle with her today. Not on her turf, anyway. And not after we'd just "gathered" evidence in the museum office, so to speak.

That meant Sammy and I had to think on our feet if we wanted to get out of there before she spotted us.

"Quick!" I whispered to my boss. "Give me your coat and hat!"

Without a single question, he grinned and went along with my plan. I donned his trench coat in half a second, before I pulled off my own hat and exchanged it for his. Then I gathered up my hair and stuffed it into his fedora.

I tugged his hat down firmly on my head and leaned into the hallway. "Help! Help! We need a doctor! A lady has fainted."

Which brought Ethel running down the hall like a bowling ball rumbling down a lane. "Where? Where? I am an expert when it comes to first aid. I am superior to many doctors."

"In here!" I yelled from just inside the office.

"Step aside!" Ethel commanded as she came bounding in. She spotted Miss Murgatroyd and ran straight for her, just as Sammy ducked out.

"I'll go call a doctor!" I yelled before I followed my boss into the hallway.

"Young man!" I heard Ethel holler to my back. "The telephone is in this room! You'll need to call from here. And take that hat off! A gentleman never wears a hat inside a building!"

Without responding, I raced down the hallway, right behind Sammy. But I paused long enough to overhear Miss Murgatroyd say, "The police. They were here."

"No, you birdbrain," Ethel chastised her. "The police weren't here. You fainted and you're having some kind of hallucination. It's a wonder you young girls can hold down a job at all."

And that was the last I heard of them as I stepped back onto the first floor of the museum and joined my boss. We quickly exchanged hats and I returned his coat to him. Then I shook out my hair and pinned my own hat low on my head again, while Sammy slipped into his coat, concealing the file he'd taken.

He grinned at me. "I gotta say, kid, you were pretty slick back there. You can bet the fur would've been flying if 'Her Highness' had caught us red-handed."

I shuddered. "I don't even want to think about it."

Sammy chuckled. "You do realize we'll probably have to deal with that dame sooner or later. If we want to solve this case."

I sighed, knowing full well that my boss was right. But in all honesty, I was hoping it would be *later*, rather than *sooner*. So I grabbed the key for the Packard from my purse and held it up. "Ready to get out of here?"

Sammy shook his head. "In a minute, kid. First I've got a key of my own that I'd like to try out."

For a moment or two, I had no idea what he was talking about. And then I remembered the small metal object he'd pocketed while I was quizzing Miss Murgatroyd.

"You found a key in the file cabinet . . . " I said, trying to hide my astonishment.

"Bingo, kid. Right inside a file. And I have a hunch it'll be a perfect fit for the display case that held the statue that's gone AWOL. But I think we oughta check it out for ourselves to make sure. While we're here."

"Sounds like a swell idea to me."

But instead of making a beeline to the cabinet, we took the long way, or the "scenic route," as Sammy said. We glanced at a few other displays as we went, so we didn't draw attention to ourselves, and instead, simply looked like two people who were enjoying the art at the museum.

Once we reached the right cabinet, Sammy glanced from side to side before producing a small brass key from his pocket. Then he slipped the key into the cabinet's built-in lock and turned it. Sure enough, the lock clicked open. Then he twisted the key in the opposite direction and the lock clicked closed.

"Well, that answers that," Sammy murmured.

I could hardly believe it. "Why on earth was that key inside a file? In a filing cabinet?"

"Your guess is as good as mine, kid. But this is one discussion I think we'd better have some place else." He nodded toward the door.

He didn't have to tell me twice. Without another word, I put my head down and strolled straight to the entrance, with Sammy close behind. He held the door for me as we stepped outside.

The cool January air felt refreshing against my face while we walked down the wide stone steps. I couldn't have been more relieved to get out of there. As far as I was concerned, the more distance we put between us and Ethel the better.

"A file seems like an odd place for the museum to keep a key," I said to my boss as I led the way to the Packard. "Seems like they would keep all their keys together. In one place."

"Let's take a look at the rest of that file," Sammy told me as we both climbed into the car. "Maybe it'll give us some answers." He pulled the file from his trench coat and flipped through the contents, passing a few photos to me.

I glanced at them one by one. "They look like random museum photos. Of various art pieces. I don't see a connection to the key."

"That's my take, too, kid. I'm betting someone used that key to unlock the cabinet on New Year's Eve to steal the statue. Then they dropped it into the file."

"Just to get rid of it? In a hurry, maybe?"

Sammy shook his head. "Could be, though it seems pretty strange. If someone used it to take the statue, a betting man would put odds on them keeping the key, too. I gotta wonder why they stashed it in the file."

I inserted my own key in the ignition and turned the engine over. "It doesn't make a lot of sense."

He raised his eyebrows. "Not yet, anyway. Then again, nothing about this case makes much sense at the moment."

I put the Packard in gear, and realized that I hadn't told Sammy about the La-la. So, as my boss would say, I spilled the beans.

He responded with a grin. "Good detective work, kid. But I didn't get a chance to tell you, either—your grandmother told me about this La-la last night. She invited me to be her date. Turns out it was all Eulalie's idea. The Professor got an invitation, too. Looks like we're going to make a party of it, with a swanky dinner first."

"Should we take advantage of this party to question our favorite professor?"

"Great idea, kid, but probably bad timing. After all, we don't want Dr. Longfellow to throw one of his famous fits and ruin our chance of getting to the La-la. No, I think we'd better play this one closer to the vest, and figure out another time to interrogate the Professor."

"Sounds good to me."

We spent the rest of the ride to the office talking about the La-la, and our strategy for the evening. Minutes later, I dropped my boss off in front of our building, and then nosed the Packard back toward River Oaks. I had just reached the edge of Nana's property and was about to pull into the driveway when I noticed a line of people standing to the side.

A huge line of people. One that extended from the back, side door of our house and all the way to the street.

Thankfully, the crowd made room for me so I could pull in. Then I practically walked the Packard to the garage, driving very, very carefully before I eased the car into a stall.

"What in the world . . .?" I murmured to Hadley after I stepped out of the car and turned the keys over to him.

"Precisely my reaction as well," Hadley intoned as he shook his head slowly. "Apparently they've all come to witness the miracle in your grandmother's armoire."

I could hardly believe my ears. "My goodness . . . that news traveled fast! Lupé just spotted that image last night. And all these people are here already?"

"Astonishing, isn't it?" Hadley commented. For once he seemed to be at a loss when it came to reciting one of his favorite, famous quotes.

"I'd say that word pretty much sums things up."

Then much as I tried to remember my manners, I couldn't help but gawk at the line, looking from one end to the other. What a wide variety of people there were! From old to young, and of every shape, size, and color imaginable.

Hadley hung the keys on the rack with the rest. "Maddie and I suggested that your grandmother simply lock the doors and not allow so many unfamiliar visitors inside. But you know your grandmother. From her perspective, if the image in the armoire brings hope and comfort to people in these difficult days of war, then she is happy to allow them in."

"Very generous of her," I murmured. "Unfortunately, it also gives people the chance to help themselves to anything inside our mansion."

"Quite true," Hadley agreed with a sigh. "Though at least she allowed me to put up a makeshift barricade of sorts, to discourage our 'visitors' from going into the rest of the mansion."

Now I had to wonder exactly how much discouragement a makeshift barricade would provide. Especially in light of our most recent break-in.

I'd always heard the expression, "generous to a fault." In Nana's case, I was starting to think the saying was true, especially since I feared her generosity might be putting her in harm's way.

"Maybe I can convince her to close it down for the evening," I suggested to Hadley.

"I think that's an excellent idea, one that would bring me tremendous relief. I shall accompany you."

Minutes later, we entered the very door that so many people had been waiting to go through.

But we'd barely stepped inside when one woman yelled, "Hey! You have to wait your turn, just like everyone else."

"Yeah!" hollered another man. "No cutting in line!"

And that was where *I* drew the line.

"*I* live here," I informed them. "And I am closing down the line for the day. Please leave in an orderly fashion as I will be locking the doors."

My words were greeted with silence. So I went back to the door and held it wide open. Then I repeated the part about the house being closed, so that everyone in the crowd, both inside and out, could hear me.

And that's when someone in the crowd piped up with, "Wait a minute . . . it's her! The dame on the front page of the paper! The one in the museum murder. We'd better do what she says!"

While his alluding to my being a homicidal maniac was certainly annoying, if nothing else, it must have been enough to make people nervous. Very nervous. Because everyone suddenly turned and started meandering down the driveway. And the people inside the house hurried out.

I watched them go, to make sure everyone actually left our property. Most of the people appeared to be decent and upstanding—with a couple of exceptions. A man with a nearly shaved head and a monocle looked back and glared at me a couple of times. The man next to him, who was very tall and thin, appeared to be giving our property the once-over, as Sammy would say.

A couple of suspicious characters if I've ever seen any.

Once everyone had gone, Hadley locked the door behind us. Then together we headed down the hallway, amazed at the mass of flowers, candles, and rosaries placed near our armoire. Suddenly, I wondered if I'd been too harsh in shooing these people away.

But those thoughts quickly changed when I heard voices coming from the other side of what I now realized was Hadley's makeshift barricade.

I let myself through a curtain that was passing for a door, only to find a young blond woman and a man with identical hair on the other side. For a moment or two, I wasn't sure who was more surprised—me or them.

But my surprise quickly turned to anger when I saw through a couple of very poor disguises and recognized the two people standing there.

Polly Jane Montgomery and her cohort, Two-Bit Louie.

Apparently, Polly Jane's motto of "close enough" applied when it came to disguises as well.

I put my hands on my hips. "I'd forget about going any farther into my house, if I was you. Because you're about to be arrested. I'll see to it personally."

Thankfully, Hadley came up behind me. "Did we not have this man arrested last night?"

"Some people never learn," I told him. "This time he's got his partner in crime with him."

Polly Jane gave me a slick smile. "We didn't do anything wrong. We were merely here with the rest of the group and took a wrong turn. We'll be leaving now."

"Oh no you don't! Not until we check every one of your pockets and pat you down thoroughly. *And* take your film," I added.

Hadley pointed to a couple of chairs. "Sit down and do not move."

"You can't force us to stay here," Polly exploded. "This is kidnapping. Entrapment. Extortion."

I fought the urge to roll my eyes. "Nice try, sister. But you'll need to look up those big, fancy terms before you can use them properly. Now hand me your camera."

She complied, but not without practically snarling at me.

Then while I rewound the film in her camera, Hadley called the police. Thankfully, an officer arrived in a matter of minutes, the same one who'd been there the night before.

"This *really* is becoming a habit," he commented.

And he was right. Though it wasn't exactly a fun kind of habit, like shopping at Sakowitz Department Store or eating hot apple pie at lunch. Now I knew I'd have no choice but to talk to Nana about letting so many complete strangers into our house. Maybe I could finally convince her of the danger to us all.

Or maybe not.

Though if nothing else, along with the film from Two-Bit Louie's camera, I also managed to seize a couple of used rolls that he had in his pocket. And I lightened Polly Jane's pockets as well when I confiscated her notebook, where she'd managed to jot down pages and pages of notes. Meaning, she must have been inside our house for quite some time.

"It won't matter," she sneered, while I flipped through her notebook. "Because I have it all committed to memory anyway."

"So . . . did you steal anything from our home?" I asked her. "Like my grandmother's jewelry or perhaps some silverware?"

"The only thing I took was your dignity," she laughed. "Not to mention, your privacy."

"Glad to hear you confess to your crimes," I murmured. "Maybe you'll have time to think about it in a lovely jail cell."

But the police officer was already shaking his head. "I'll see if I can get a trespassing charge to stick, since Louie was arrested here last night. But if they were allowed to walk in with the rest of the crowd, then a breaking-and-entering charge won't hold water," he said as he took them away in handcuffs.

Which I understood to be the officer's way of telling me the pair would likely be out on the street in an hour.

And I could tell from Polly Jane's mocking smile that she probably already knew that.

I sighed to Hadley. "If only I could persuade Nana to take more precautions."

He looked at me with sympathy in his dark eyes. "Our best is all we can do."

"Thanks, Hadley," I said, with a glance at my wristwatch.

The hands on the dial told me it was time for me to get ready for dinner before we all went to the La-la.

I climbed the stairs to the second floor and went straight to my room. Then I dropped the film canisters into the top drawer of my dressing table. Just as I did, I suddenly wondered what images might be on those films. Exactly how far had Polly Jane and Two-Bit Louie gone into our mansion?

Of course, there was only one way to find out. I had to develop those films and see what tales the pictures told me. So I decided to take them with me to the office the next day and use our darkroom to process the films.

In the meantime, I ran to my closet and began to search through my dresses, looking for something that would work for the dance tonight. Though I'd never been to a La-la before, I figured any party dress would work just fine. But I also wanted to wear a dress that would allow me plenty of freedom to move. After all, I was really going out tonight as part of our case, and even though I always loved to go out dancing, something in the back of my mind told me I could be in for a very wild night.

And I might need to be on my toes.

In more ways than one . . .

CHAPTER 17

Dinner and Dancing

Dinner that night turned into a fine affair, considering the table had a few more people around it than it had the night before. Sammy and Nana sat at either end, with Pete and me across from each other. Eulalie was seated next to me, and the Professor sat beside Pete. Having been drilled in table-seating etiquette my entire life, I knew it would have been proper for Eulalie to be seated next to Pete. But my poor fella would have been squirming all night long if he'd been sitting right beside Eulalie.

So I spared him the discomfort by telling Nana ahead of time that we were going to change things up a bit.

And since the night seemed like a celebration of sorts, (which I guess you could say was a little unusual, considering all the turmoil bearing down on us at the moment) Nana had decided to break out two bottles of French wine from her stockpile. Of course, we all knew what that meant, since French wine was a luxury now. So we all sipped and savored it, well aware that we were the lucky ones who had the chance to enjoy this, while men were going off to war and nations were being held hostage by Hitler or Hirohito's war machines.

The Professor took a nice sip from his goblet and then smiled with delight. "Growing good grapes and making fine wine is an art form in and of itself. And the French had certainly perfected that art. Of course, when it comes to the history of French wine making, a turning point was the founding of Marseille—or what was then called Massalia—by the Greeks in the sixth century BC. They, of course, realized that grapevines grew best in the same climate where olive and fig trees thrived. I wonder what will happen to that part of the world now."

"Including all the people and the lovely châteaus," Eulalie murmured.

Sammy raised an eyebrow. "I doubt they'll ever be the same. Not when Hitler's goons don't mind helping themselves to all the art and treasures they can get their filthy paws on."

For a few moments, we all fell silent and stared at our wineglasses. I had no doubt we were all thinking of the French, whose country had been invaded by the Nazis over a year and a half ago. Paris had fallen to the Germans in June of 1940. The horrors that had ensued from that point on were beyond shocking. Or, at least, what stories we'd *heard*, anyway. Since I was certain, for every story that *had* been relayed to the outside world, there were probably plenty of others that *hadn't* been. And after reading sections of Freddy's diary, where he'd chronicled life inside of Germany, I knew the information the general public heard about the Nazis was only the tip of the iceberg.

The thought of it made the little hairs on the back of my neck stand on end.

I took a gulp of my wine, as Nana, always the excellent hostess, reacted to the lull in the conversation. "That's very fascinating," she said to Dr. Longfellow. "Did you study ancient history from that part of the world firsthand?"

He shook his head and smiled. "Alas, no. I learned that tidbit about Marseille from my late student, Freddy. Surprisingly, for his young age, he'd been on many archaeological explorations."

"He must have been a fantastic student," I added, helping Nana to keep the conversation going.

"He truly was," the Professor said sadly. "Some students are naturally born to academic pursuits. Freddy was one of those, a young man who fit the profile of a true genius. Of course, much like many brilliant individuals, Freddy certainly had his eccentricities. He was always running late, as he was too busy reading or writing something to keep track of time. Plus, as far as he was concerned, he had better things to do than bother with organization or any kind of housekeeping. He lived and breathed what might be considered 'organized chaos.'"

This made me smile, having seen Freddy's room firsthand. Though from what I could tell, there was more *chaos* than organization.

The Professor sighed before going on. "Stanley was simply astonished that Freddy's peculiar habits didn't affect his studies."

"How so?" Nana asked.

Dr. Longfellow took another sip of his wine. "The two young men were complete opposites. While Freddy was truly gifted, and things came quite naturally to him, Stanley attained his success purely through hard work. There were several times when Stanley told me he'd stayed up the entire night to study."

Sammy nodded to the Professor. "Sounds like a pretty determined young man."

The Professor shook his head. "They both were. Though Freddy's Achilles' heel actually turned out to be in his head, as he suffered from horrendous migraine headaches. Frequently."

"That's a complete shame," Eulalie added. "Though I must say, it sounds like Freddy lived life to the fullest. A lesson for us all. Especially since, with a war going on, we may not have a tomorrow. These days, it's best not to put things off."

With those words, Pete's eyes met mine. And while the others talked, we merely sat there, staring and communicating, without saying a single word. I knew he longed to pull me into his arms, and I couldn't think of any place I would rather be.

Luckily, I got that chance a few moments later, when Eulalie insisted on giving us lessons in La-la dancing.

"The steps are very similar to modern swing dance," she informed us. "Except you add an extra step to each individual step. Including the rock step."

She demonstrated by taking the Professor into a closed dance position. Pete and I did the same while Sammy took Nana's hand.

Then everyone followed Eulalie's instructions as she continued to teach us the dance. Before long, Pete and I had the basic moves down pretty well.

And I had to say, it was a lot of fun.

Nana and Sammy got the hang of it in a hurry, too. The Professor seemed to be the only one with two left feet, though Eulalie didn't seem to be bothered by this one bit.

As soon as we'd finished practicing, coats and gloves and hats were passed out. Then we all piled into Pete's Caddy for the ride to Frenchtown. The night air was a little chilly and still slightly damp from the thunderstorm in the morning. But thankfully, the clouds had now blown away, so we had a good view of the full moon that was rising over the horizon, this time glowing a brilliant silver.

Under normal circumstances, it would have set the stage for a wonderful night of romance. But in our case, I knew it would likely be a night of mystery instead, since we were heading to this La-la as part of our investigation. Of course, we'd concealed that fact from Eulalie and the Professor, who, judging from their lively conversation in the back seat, were completely oblivious to the real purpose of the evening. Sammy sat next to them, looking out the window, and I could tell from his face that he was keeping his eyes peeled for anything that might seem out of the ordinary.

And, as an Apprentice P.I., I was more or less trying to do the same. After all, it was our belief that Freddy had planned to attend this very dance. But was he merely going to the La-la to dance the night away? Or did he have another reason for wanting to go? We also couldn't rule out the possibility that someone had invited him to come. And if so, was there any special reason why?

So many questions swirled through my mind as I watched Pete expertly drive us along, keeping his eyes glued to the road that was lit by the Caddy's headlamps. His mood all night had been one of constrained emotion, and while he was outwardly polite and cordial to everyone (and certainly romantic to me), I could sense something was churning on the inside. I wondered how things had gone with his bosses. Unfortunately, we hadn't had a moment alone for me to ask.

The trip itself went smoothly enough. We headed east from River Oaks and drove through the city, before turning north and then east, and passing everything our town had to offer along the way. Eulalie gave perfect directions, which led me to believe she'd been there more than once.

We passed a number of cars as we went, mostly heading into town, rather than going out. At long last we drove into the area known as Frenchtown. The houses were deceptively small in front and built in a style known as "shotgun." Meaning, they were long and skinny, with one room behind the next and so on. Clearly the people who lived here took great pride in their neighborhoods, since the houses and porches were beautifully painted with plenty of pretty plants in front. They looked very much like houses I'd seen in New Orleans.

Finally, Eulalie directed us to a parking lot near what appeared to be a gathering hall. Pete parked the car and we all piled out, before we followed Eulalie through the main door and into the hall. Then we waited just inside while Eulalie hailed a woman who appeared to be in charge. A woman who looked like she could have been Eulalie's niece. She had the same black hair and fair complexion. As did many of the people who were out cutting a rug on the dance floor.

I watched the dancers as we waited, and I had to say, they were a joyful bunch, laughing and smiling as they went through lots of different steps. And much like Eulalie had said, the word that best described the music was "infectious." Before I knew it, I found myself bouncing to the beat and swaying from side to side. Pete slid his arm around my waist, and I could tell he was ready to start dancing, too.

It took all the concentration I had to keep my mind on the real reason we were here. But like Sammy had taught me to do, I immediately scanned the room. There were plenty of tables and chairs set close together in the forefront of the room, and a band was set up in the back corner. The area in front of that was designated as the dance floor and was filled with fantastic dancers who were twirling and stepping and spinning.

With so much movement, and with the ladies in a colorful array of party dresses, the effect was mesmerizing. Almost kaleidoscope-like. But once I'd taken it all in, I returned my gaze to Eulalie and kept my eyes on her while she and the other woman had a few minutes of rather exuberant, animated conversation.

Clearly the two were acquainted, if not related.

Finally, Eulalie led the woman back to us. "Please allow me to introduce Miss Felicite Beaumond. She's the organizer of tonight's La-la."

"Goodness gracious," Felicite said with an accent I'd heard many times, whenever we traveled to Louisiana. "So nice to have some visitors tonight."

Nana stepped forward and introduced us one by one. We each shook Felicite's hand before Nana took over again.

"I understand you hold these parties to raise money for your church," she said.

"We do, we do," Felicite answered with a smile. "Would you care to make a small donation?"

"No, I . . ." Nana started to say.

"No matter," Felicite interrupted. "I understand. Times are tough right now. What with the war goin' on. So just come on in and 'laissez les bons temps rouler.' Let the good times roll!"

Nana shook her head and smiled. "I'm afraid you've misunderstood . . . I don't want to make a small donation. I want to make a *large* donation." Then she pulled a folded check from her pocketbook and handed it to Felicite.

Felicite opened the check and her eyes went wide. She gasped and covered her mouth with her hand. "Well . . . I don't know what to say. Is this for real?"

"Real as the rain we had this morning," Nana added.

"Well, thank you, thank you, ma'am," Felicite said with a huge smile. "We need a new roof for our church, and we could use some pavement for the front walkway. So we can certainly put this to good use. May the Good Lord above bless you beyond measure."

Nana smiled and put her hand on my shoulder. "He already has. With this wonderful granddaughter."

"My goodness, Nana," I said with a laugh, all the while wondering why she was being so sentimental. "You're making me blush!"

"It only brings out the roses in your cheeks, darlin'," she told me.

"The girl looks like Betty Grable," Felicite said with a nod toward me, before she pointed to Sammy. "And this fella looks like Humphrey Bogart. I didn't know we were going to get a visit from Hollywood tonight. Now why don't you all come in and we'll get you set up with some punch."

Before we could respond, the band started up with another song. The beat was so beguiling that I couldn't help but take a few dance steps.

Felicite laughed and pointed to my feet. "Except for this one. She needs to La-la."

Seconds later, I found myself out on the dance floor with Pete. And even though the dance moves were still a little unfamiliar, the unusual beat of the music soon made it all feel natural. Before long, Pete and I were moving and twirling along with everyone else.

Step-step, step-step, and a double step into the rock step. While I loved swing dancing, I liked this La-la dancing every bit as much. The French accordion and the washboard and the guitar only added to the rhythm. And kept us moving.

Soon I found myself laughing and smiling, along with the rest of the people out on the dance floor.

When the song was over and the music had stopped, Pete leaned down to my ear. "Let's go outside for a little air, okay?"

So we did. I waved to Sammy and Nana, who were sitting at a table. The Professor was slouched in a chair across from them, looking bored beyond belief and staring into space, while Eulalie was nowhere to be found. I caught Sammy's eye and pointed to the door, and he nodded in return, letting me know he'd gotten the message.

Then I stepped outside with Pete, all the while racking my brain and trying to come up with some dubious reason why Freddy'd had the information about this dance in his pocket. Because, from what I could tell, there really wasn't anything sinister or suspicious going on here. At the moment, my best guess was that Freddy had simply wanted to come to the La-la to dance.

I had to say, *I* was certainly having a swell time, and I figured Freddy would have had fun, too.

I glanced up at Pete as he took my hand, and together we walked a little way, until we spotted a wrought-iron bench that wrapped around an old oak tree. We took a seat and found it was the perfect place to gaze up at the full moon above.

Pete slipped his arm around me and I leaned into him, in what was becoming a very familiar gesture, as though we'd been doing it for a hundred years. He planted a gentle kiss on the top of my head.

"Pete, you never told me what happened with your bosses. What did they say?"

I could feel his heavy sigh as it emanated from deep within his chest. "Well, thankfully they trust me. They have a pretty good idea I'm not a homicidal maniac."

I giggled. "I should think that would be obvious."

"That's more or less what I said. Even so, they want me to keep a low profile for a while. And take some time off. Apparently a couple of people have called in, concerned about working in the same office as me."

"All this from a newspaper story? One with no facts at all?"

"Hard to believe, but it's true. While most of the fellas at work are good guys, there are one or two with a chip on their shoulders. They're not happy that I come from money. They think I should be spending my life sipping mint juleps at the country club, rather than working for a living. So, near as I can tell, they're taking advantage of these lousy newspaper stories."

I wrapped my arm around his waist. "Oh, Pete, I'm so sorry."

He chuckled. "Me, too. But that's not what I wanted to talk to you about. Instead, I want to talk about us. And our future."

Suddenly my heart skipped a beat. "Okay, Pete. I'm all ears."

And then, my heart skipped another beat. Because right at that moment, a movement caught my eye. A young woman raced through the parking lot, dodging between the cars.

A young woman whom I recognized.

"Say, isn't that . . .?" Pete whispered to me.

"Uh-huh," I murmured back, sitting bolt upright. "That's her, all right."

It was the girl who had first danced with Freddy on the night of the museum gala.

CHAPTER 18

A Missing Dance Partner and a Parting Shot

"I've got to catch her," I told Pete as I jumped to my feet. "I need to ask her some questions. And find out her name."

Without waiting for Pete to respond, I raced off after the young woman, the very one who had been Freddy's first dance partner on New Year's Eve. And let me tell you, running across a gravel parking lot in high heels while chasing a lithe girl who must have been half gazelle wasn't exactly easy. I tripped and stumbled the whole way. Even so, I managed to make good time and closed the gap between us.

"Wait! Wait!" I called out to her.

But she ignored my cries and kept on running with the speed of someone who is truly terrified.

"Stop!" I yelled again. "Please, I'd like to talk to you!"

By now we'd moved out of the parking lot and dashed directly into the street. She took a left and ran in front of a row of houses.

But I kept on running, running, running after her. I could hear footsteps behind me, and I glanced over my shoulder to see that Pete had joined in on the chase, and he wasn't far away.

Even so, I didn't slow down. I didn't want to risk losing her. And I was finally getting close to her when she suddenly pitched forward, her arms flailing in the air. She dropped onto the pavement, not moving at all.

"Oh no!" I yelled back to Pete. "She tripped. She's hurt!"

Within seconds, I was on the ground, kneeling beside her. She was trying to roll over, so I helped her onto her back. There were a few scrapes on her face, and her stockings were ruined, but otherwise, she didn't look like she was too badly hurt.

"Lie still," I said gently. "Let's take stock of your injuries."

"You've got to help me!" Her words came out in frantic gasps, and she grabbed my skirt, clutching it as though it were a lifeline at sea.

"Of course I'll help you," I said with my kindest smile. "Now tell me where you're hurt."

"I'm not," she gushed as Pete joined us.

He passed me his folded handkerchief, and I pressed it against a gash on the girl's forehead to stop the bleeding. "You took quite a spill," I soothed. "What had you so scared that you went running off into the night like that?"

"They're trying to kill me!" she insisted.

"Who's trying to kill you?" I murmured softly, wondering if she'd hit her head a lot harder than I thought.

"Them. I think they're Nazis."

A word that had a habit of getting my attention.

I glanced around. "Nazis? What makes you say that?"

"Because I've seen them before," she whimpered.

"Where? At the museum gala? Is that why you tried to hurt the young man you were dancing with that night?"

"What . . . How did you know?" she sort of gasped.

I gave her a small smile. "Someone saw you stab him with the pin from your brooch."

She shook her head as I helped her to a sitting position. "I didn't want to hurt anyone. I only wanted to go to the dance, to get more information. For my group. A group of Catholic Creoles."

"Information about what?"

"Information about who was after *it*."

I crinkled my brow. "I'm afraid you've lost me. What is *it*?"

That's when she responded with pure silence.

Now Pete jumped in. "If you like, I'm sure we could help you back to the dance. Miss . . .?"

"Rosette," she finished. "DeBlanc. Rosette DeBlanc. And no, I can't go back there. It's too dangerous."

"Rosette, I'm an Apprentice P.I.," I told her. "And my partner, a full-fledged P.I., is there at the dance. We can protect you. And if that won't do, we can simply have you wait in our car while we call the police."

She shook her head more vigorously than before. "No, no, no. I can't go back there. Maybe you could help me get out of here and take me some place where I'll be safe."

Pete and I exchanged a knowing look.

"We can do that," I told Rosette.

"I'll go get the car," Pete said. "But first I'll run in to the dance and tell Sammy we're leaving. And let him know I'll come back for the rest of our bunch shortly."

"Sounds good," I told him. "But let's get Rosette out of the street before you go."

Then together we got her up and helped her limp to a nearby front porch, where we carefully set the young woman down on a porch swing. Pete dropped a kiss onto my head before he took off running back to the dance hall.

I took advantage of the time to quiz Rosette further. "I still don't understand why you stabbed Freddy with the pin from your brooch. Did you think he was a Nazi? Or was it because he was dancing so fast?"

She glanced around before answering. "No. It wasn't my idea at all. It was the lady at the art museum. The older lady. The short, gray-haired one. I couldn't afford a ticket, and she said she'd give me one if I did one thing for her."

"Let me guess . . . all you had to do was stick Freddy in the arm, using the pin of your brooch."

Rosette nodded, pressing Pete's hankie to her wound. "That was what she told me to do. She said she wanted me to make a big fuss."

"But things didn't go according to plan."

She shook her head. "Not at all. He was supposed to yell and carry on, so the band would quit playing and there'd be a commotion. People were supposed to jump up and help him. And the security guards were supposed to come in."

I chuckled under my breath. "And you were supposed to pretend it was all an accident."

She nodded, looking more terrified by the second, with her eyes darting from side to side. "Uh-huh."

Now I glanced around myself, since her vigilance was starting to make me nervous, too. "Tell me, Rosette, do you know if there was any poison on that pin? The one you stabbed Freddy with?"

Her eyes went wide. "No, no, nothing like that . . ." But then she gulped. "Well, I don't *think* there was any poison on it. Nobody told me if there was. I just agreed to stick him." Then she let out a little cry. "Do you think I killed him?"

I patted her hand. "We don't know what killed him for sure. Where did you get the pin?"

"That lady . . ." Then, instead of finishing her sentence, she merely gasped.

"The older lady gave it to you? The lady from the museum?"

She bit her lip and nodded.

"You said you just wanted to go to the dance to get information. From anyone in particular?"

She nodded again. "From Frederick. I didn't tell the museum lady that *I* had plans, too. Because after I stuck Frederick with the pin, and after the commotion died down, I was going to get him to leave the hall with me. Then I was supposed to flirt with him. And get him to tell me things."

"But instead, there was no commotion and Freddy went right back to dancing."

A tear slid down her cheek. "I couldn't believe it. He barely even noticed that I'd stuck him. And I'd jabbed him pretty hard. But he only stopped for a few seconds and then he just started dancing so crazy-like. He scared me, and I ran off when the dance was over. Because I thought he was going to hurt me out on the dance floor."

"Was he always like that?"

She wiped at her eyes. "I don't know. I'd never danced with him before."

"How did you know Freddy?"

She took a deep breath. "I didn't. I'd never even met him before. But I knew who he was. He was the archaeologist who came over from Germany. And we were afraid we knew why he was here in Houston."

This confession took me by surprise. "I don't understand. What information were you trying to get from Freddy?"

Her mouth fell wide open and she just stared at me. "Don't you know, Miss Tracy?"

Confusion clouded my brain. Funny, but I hadn't remembered introducing myself.

"Know what?" I asked.

Again, she didn't answer me.

So I tried a different tack. "Earlier you said there were Nazis after you. What makes you think so?"

"Because . . . they want *it*," she whispered.

It was the second time she'd used the word "it."

"What . . .?" I started to ask, when I spotted Pete in the distance, running toward us, with Sammy close behind.

I turned back to Rosette, and the second I did, my eyes barely caught a movement from the tall shrubs on the side of the house. An arm appeared, pointing a long, narrow tube our way. Before I could react, I heard a sudden *whoosh*, followed by a *thwack*, just as Rosette clutched her neck and cringed in pain and terror.

She fell to the porch and I instantly jumped down to her side. My heart skipped a beat when I saw what had caused her to act like that.

A small, feathered dart stuck out from her neck.

I pulled it out just as she gasped for air.

She clutched at my arm, desperate to tell me something.

I leaned down to hear her better.

"The veil, Miss Tracy. Protect the veil," she barely managed to squeak.

And then she was gone.

Pete reached me just as the bright flash of a camera nearly blinded us all.

CHAPTER 19

Another Day, Another Dead Body

"Killer Couple on Crime Spree," announced the headline in the morning's paper. And there, on the front page of the *Houston Star-Journal*, was a picture of Pete and me, kneeling next to Rosette's dead body. But instead of focusing on the sad and untimely death of a young woman, P.J. Montgomery had opted to write her usual hatchet job to sell more papers.

I sighed and shook my head before folding the front page of the paper into itself, wishing I could just make the whole thing go away. But I knew my gesture was useless, and the only way I could put an end to this whole nightmare was to find the person or persons who had killed both Freddy and Rosette.

Yet as I walked toward the kitchen for breakfast (all ready for the day in a smart, forest-green suit) I was beginning to wonder if Sammy and I would ever crack this case. It didn't help that my disposition wasn't exactly upbeat this morning, not after such a long night and a lack of shut-eye. Though, if nothing else, at least Pete and I hadn't been detained at the police department until daylight this time. Despite having to deal with Detective Denton again.

But even after I'd gotten home and crawled under the covers, the Sandman refused to pay me a visit. Not that I should have been surprised. After all, I'd just witnessed the murder of a young woman, and besides that, I couldn't help but wonder if there'd been another dart with my name on it. A dart that might have flown my way had it not been for Pete and Sammy showing up when they did.

Their good timing also made me wonder about the timing of the photographer. After ambushing us and taking what turned out to be the perfect shot of Pete and me, the guy had immediately run off. Of course, I had no doubt about his identity, especially since I saw the outline of a man in a bent fedora moving in the shadows. And, much like my boss would say, I would have bet ten to one that it had been Two-Bit Louie.

Naturally, Sammy did his best to chase after the guy. But the man was practically swallowed up in the darkness, so Sammy returned to where Pete and I were kneeling over Rosette. Then he left to call the police.

That *left* me to check Rosette's body for clues, much like my boss had checked Freddy's dead form at the museum gala. So I took a deep breath, swallowed my fear, and quickly patted her down. But since she was wearing a dress with no pockets, the search proved to be fruitless. The only thing I found was a small gold cross necklace that she'd kept hidden underneath the neckline of her dress.

Shortly after that, Detective Denton was the first on the police force to arrive, and he didn't waste any time pointing one of his stubby fingers at me. "Well, girlie, congratulations. You're racking up quite the body count. Why is it that every time I see you, there's a dead body nearby?"

"Oh, I don't know," I shot back. "Maybe it's because you're a homicide cop?"

His nostrils flared and a vein popped out on his forehead. "Like I told you before, nobody likes a wise guy. Or a wise girl. I oughta run you all downtown and put the lot of you in jail. Then we'll see what kind of a smart mouth you have."

Sammy rolled his eyes. "Put us in jail? On what charge?"

"I'm sure I could think of something," Denton seethed.

Sammy shook his head. "Why don't we worry about the crime scene instead? Let me show you what we know."

Then he proceeded to take Denton through everything step by step, while he pointed out the shrubs where someone had blown the dart gun. The police immediately searched through those shrubs, as well as the side of the house, but didn't find a single clue. Whoever had been hiding there was long gone, and for that matter, had plenty of avenues for escape. Meaning the person who had shot the blow dart could have gone anywhere. Including, doubling back to the dance.

Thankfully though, enough witnesses had seen Rosette take off running right before Pete and I came into the picture. They all claimed she had looked absolutely terrified, but no one knew who or what had scared her so badly. People had also seen her sitting on the porch with me before she'd fallen over dead. Meaning that, for once, no one stood up and falsely accused us of committing a crime.

And, for that matter, at first the police weren't even convinced there was a crime, or that foul play had been involved at all. Not until I pointed out the puncture wound on Rosette's neck and handed them the dart. Judging from what I can only describe as incredulous looks, as near as I could guess, death by poison dart probably wasn't a common occurrence here in Houston.

After that, we'd been free to go. The police had the facts they needed, and none of those facts pointed a finger at us.

Of course, that hadn't prevented Polly Jane from printing yet another false story about Pete and me. Though this time she let the huge photograph do the talking, while the article itself was pretty brief, considering she didn't have someone the likes of Ethel to act as an eyewitness. In fact, from what I could tell, no one who had been there was really interested in talking to the press at all. And the police certainly hadn't given out any information.

Now I had to wonder how Miss P.J. Montgomery's photographer, Two-Bit Louie, had managed to follow us to the La-la in the first place. Obviously he'd been spying on us, since he just *happened* to show up at the right place at the right time. I also had to wonder if he had arrived in time to see the assassin, though somehow I doubted it. If he'd seen the person shooting the dart blowgun, it seemed like that would have been the picture he would have taken. Not ours. And, if he'd witnessed someone kill Rosette, it stood to reason that even a guy as low as Louie would have come forward and told the police what he'd seen.

Yet despite all that, what weighed most on my mind were the last words of a dying woman. For the life of me, I had no idea what she was talking about when she mentioned "the veil."

Was it possible I'd heard her wrong? And what made her think the Nazis were after her? Sure, on another case, we'd had run-ins with the German American Bund members, leftovers from the group of Nazis who'd been active over here. And just because they'd gone underground didn't mean they weren't still in operation.

But if that were the case, why would they be after a young woman from Houston?

I also wondered who had given her the brooch she used to pierce Freddy's arm. Whoever had concocted *that* crazy plan was taking a big risk as to whether it worked or not.

For that matter, it certainly hadn't.

By now this whole case seemed like one big, jumbled-up mess inside my mind. Nothing made any sense, no matter how I put the pieces together.

And unfortunately, none of this helped Pete one bit.

Nana was busy placing cups of coffee around the breakfast table when I walked into the kitchen. But she stopped what she was doing and greeted me with a hug. "What an awful thing this is, darlin'. Why would anyone want to murder a young girl like that? As well as the young man at the first dance? Lately, it seems like every time we go out dancing, someone gets murdered."

I nodded and took a seat. "It's a strange series of events, that's for sure."

Maddie glanced up from dishing out scrambled eggs and bacon onto plates. "I think I should keep the lot of you at home. No more going out."

If only it were that simple.

"Then there was that horrible picture in this morning's paper," Maddie went on. "Goodness, but that reporter has it in for you!"

Without saying a word, Nana merely nodded her agreement. Her eyes met mine, and I could see her gaze was brimming with sympathy and concern.

"She seems determined to make life miserable," I agreed, dropping my chin into my hands.

Nana took the plates to the table, just as Eulalie walked in, carrying Opaline. "There are dark forces at work in the world," Eulalie said, putting Opaline on the floor. "There always have been, throughout the ages."

Nana pulled out a chair for Eulalie before taking her own seat. "That sounds rather ominous. Then again, Hitler and Hirohito are certainly what one might call 'dark forces.'"

Eulalie kept her eyes on me. "Life has always been a battle of good versus evil. We must never let evil win."

"It's a battle, all right," I agreed as I tossed a bite of bacon on the floor for Opaline. "And it sure would be nice to catch a break for once in this fight." My sigh practically filled the kitchen.

"Ah, such a great and mighty sigh . . ." Hadley said as he strolled in. "I heard it from the hallway. If that picture in the paper this morning is any indication, I assume all is not well when it comes to solving your case."

"You can say that again, Hadley. In fact, things are downright awful." Much to my annoyance, I could hear the whine in my own voice. I hated to admit it, but I sounded more like a spoiled brat than a grown woman.

Hadley took a seat and Maddie served him breakfast. "It reminds me of something Vincent van Gogh once said. 'In spite of everything I shall rise again: I will take up my pencil, which I have forsaken in my great discouragement, and I will go on with my drawing.' Now you, my dear young one, must take up your own pencil, as it were. You must go on with your drawing. Figuratively speaking, of course."

For a moment or two, while everyone tucked into their meals, I just stared at my scrambled eggs. I was almost embarrassed when I thought of how childish I'd been acting. Sure, I was only an Apprentice P.I. at this point. But how would I ever get my license and become a successful P.I. if I got discouraged when the going got tough?

Especially since I had more than just myself to think about. After all, if I didn't keep my chin up and do my job, Pete would be the one to suffer. Just like any of my future clients might suffer if I acted like an immature child when I was on the job. I was usually pretty good at looking on the sunny side, and it was high time I stepped back to that side of the street.

I took a big sip of my coffee and smiled at Hadley. "You're right, Hadley. I do need to 'take up my pencil,' so to speak. When it comes to this case, I need to give it my all and solve it."

"That's the spirit," Hadley said with an approving nod.

Then before I could say another word, Lupé slipped into the room. "The father and the sister are here to see you, Mrs. Truworth," she announced, looking directly at Nana. "They would like you to open the doors so the people can come in again. So they can see the vision in the armoire. There is already a line outside."

Nana's gaze flitted to me first and then to Lupé. "I'll go have a chat with them."

"I'll join you," I added.

Eulalie scooted her chair back. "I will as well."

"So shall I," Hadley said before he swiped his napkin across his face.

Nana crinkled her brow. "My goodness. Am I to have chaperones? Apparently no one trusts that *I* can tell the difference between good and evil forces."

I put my hand on Nana's. "We're just concerned, that's all, Nana. You're such a kind and generous person, and we're afraid people will take advantage of you. Especially since there was a gigantic line of total strangers out there yesterday, all just waiting to get into our house."

"They're not waiting to get into our house, darlin'," she said with a gentle smile. "They're waiting to see what they believe is a miracle. And with all the horrors of the war, people need to know that miracles exist right now."

I squeezed her fingers. "I know, Nana. You're right. Most of those people are probably out there for just that reason. But we don't know if they *all* have good intentions. Yesterday, that nasty reporter and her rotten photographer got in and past the makeshift barrier that Hadley had set up. And believe me, the only miracle those two were after was the possibility of catching Pete and me unawares. Just like that photographer did last night. All so Miss P.J. Montgomery can play fast and loose with the truth, when it comes to printing her latest libelous article about us."

Nana frowned. "But do you really think they'll return? After they got caught yesterday?"

"They don't seem to be the type who are easily deterred," Hadley added. "We've had the photographer arrested twice now, and it doesn't seem to stop him. I would suspect he's probably making enough money from his venture that he'd happily invade the sanctity of your home again. Particularly since we confiscated his film yesterday."

Words that reminded me to take those very rolls of film into the office with me today. So I could develop the pictures in our darkroom.

Eulalie poured cream into her coffee. "It wouldn't hurt, Caroline, if we simply asked this priest and nun a few questions. To make sure they are aboveboard, as they say."

Nana let out a little laugh. "All right, all right. I know when I'm licked. Go ahead and ask away. As long as no one is rude about it."

Which was all the permission I needed.

And I decided to start with our new maid. "Lupé, you didn't even tell us how you know this priest. Or the nun."

She looked up at me with wide eyes, and her chin began to tremble. "I know them . . . I know them . . . from the church."

"What church is that?" I asked as gently as I could.

"From downtown. Where I go to the Catholic church," she told us, looking more upset by the second.

"The name, dear," Eulalie added. "What is the name of your church?"

But instead of answering, Lupé merely stood frozen in place, staring at us like she'd seen a ghost.

"The name of the church doesn't matter," the priest proclaimed as he eased into the kitchen, his unblinking eyes on us. "We are all one in the Lord."

"True, but I'm sure the Lord wouldn't mind us taking a few precautions," I said in my most demure, Southern-belle tone. "And as an Apprentice P.I., I've learned to be suspicious of certain situations. Then again, even *you* must realize that anyone could purchase a clerical collar and pretend to be a priest. So, would you mind showing us some identification, please?"

"I'm afraid I left my wallet at home," he said, stone-faced.

"Tracy!" Nana chastised me. "That's no way to speak to a priest."

While *my* words had put the man on the spot, clearly *Nana's* words had provided the precise opening he'd been looking for. And, much as I hated to admit it, I had to hand it to him—he didn't miss a beat when it came to playing on Nana's generosity. Because right at that moment, as though someone had turned on a switch, his features suddenly became etched with outrage.

He puffed out his chest and jutted out his chin. "At the risk of sounding impertinent, would you mind my asking if you always display such hostility toward those of us who have been called to do the Lord's work?"

I gave him my sweetest smile. "No, I don't. I simply want proof that you are who you claim to be."

"That's enough, Tracy!" Nana said in one of the rare times she'd ever raised her voice to me.

She jumped up from the table and stood before the priest. "I'm so terribly sorry, Father. You'll have to excuse my granddaughter. She's had a very long night, and she hasn't had much sleep. She isn't thinking properly."

"Please call me Father Phillip," he said as she led him from the room.

Without a word, Lupé turned and followed them.

Their footsteps echoed from the hallway, and I heard Nana say as they walked away, "If you want the people to see the miracle, then they shall."

Eulalie slipped from her seat and glanced through the doorway. Then she tiptoed into the hallway herself and, as near as I could tell, followed them. Eavesdropping.

Maddie and I just stared at each other while Hadley shook his head.

"I don't believe it," I murmured.

Maddie wiped her brow. "There is something truly odd about that man. I'm not even sure he is a priest a'tall. I don't think a real priest would exploit your grandmother's trusting nature, such as this man seems to do."

Hadley turned to me. "I concur. And while kindness should never be considered a weakness, I fear it may be clouding your grandmother's eyes to the truth."

"Me, too, Hadley. Me, too," I told him. "But if this man isn't a priest, then why is he here? He must have some ulterior motive. And why does he want all these people to come into our house and look at this image in our armoire?"

I had barely asked the question when the answer popped into my mind—if *they* were allowed in, then so was he. As a sort of self-appointed supervisor. Meaning, he could have the freedom to move around our home without anyone suspecting a thing.

I gulped down the last of my coffee. "I'd suggest we all keep the doors to our rooms locked."

"And I'll have the silver and such kept under lock and key," Maddie said with a nod.

I wiped my mouth and got up from my chair. "I need to go to my room for a minute, and then I'll go check on this line of people outside our home."

"As shall I," Hadley said as he scooted back from the table. "In fact, I believe I'll simply sit next to my makeshift barrier, to prevent anyone from entering the remainder of the residence."

"Good idea," I told him. "It would be a big help."

With that, we parted ways and I ran up the stairs to my room. I pinned on a green hat to match my suit and pulled on some matching gloves, before I grabbed the film canisters that I'd confiscated from Two-Bit Louie and Polly Jane. And, just before I walked out, I checked to make sure Freddy's diary was still safe and sound in its hiding place. Satisfied that it was, I left my room and locked my door behind me.

Then I returned to the first floor and headed for the back hallway that led to the now-famous armoire. Hadley had already set up shop as a sentry next to his temporary barrier. We gave each other a salute and a smile as I strolled to the door.

The people who were already inside and standing in line actually did, by all accounts, appear to be there for religious reasons. Some carried flowers or small candles, and some carried rosaries, as they quietly waited in a single-file line for their turn to see the miracle in our armoire.

Once I stepped outside, I saw the nun assisting the priest, as he made the sign of the cross on the foreheads of all who entered. Murmured prayers reached my ears, and for a moment or two, as I scanned the faces, I wondered again if I had been wrong to question Nana's compassion in letting all these people into our home. Maybe seeing this "miracle," such as it was, really would bring hope and faith to those who needed it.

But then I spotted two people about thirty feet from the door. Two people who were doing their level best to blend in with the rest of those waiting in line.

A man with a monocle and a tall, thin man next to him.

The same pair that I'd seen the day before.

Today they both wore fedoras low over their faces and kept their heads down. Trying to hide in plain sight, as Sammy would have said. And if there was one thing I'd learned about people who were trying to hide—they usually *had* something to hide. And because this pair had already caught my eye yesterday, I decided it would be a good idea to ask them a question or two.

Before they set foot inside our home.

So I quickly strolled to the garage, dropped the film canisters into the Packard, and then made a beeline for the two men, taking long strides so I would reach them in a hurry. As I rushed past, I heard gasps and chatter from the crowd.

I was about five feet from the pair when the two looked up, and their eyes met mine. They immediately spun on their heels and shoved the people behind them out of the way, before racing down our driveway.

"Excuse me," I hollered to the men. "Could I please have a word with you?"

But my words only seemed to make them move faster. So I picked up the pace and followed them, now practically trotting in my high-heeled pumps. I could hardly believe it, but it was the second time I'd gone chasing after someone in less than twenty-four hours. I fought the urge to roll my eyes, since I was pretty sure I couldn't run and roll my eyes at the same time.

The men turned into the street and broke into an easy lope. I did my best to keep up, but I quickly realized these two were about to outrun me. That meant I'd never have a chance to question them, or find out who they were and what they were doing at my house.

So I had to do something and do it fast.

Then, in a flash, a trick that Katie McClue had used in one of her later episodes suddenly popped into my mind. In *The Case of the Foreign-Speaking Spectator*, Katie found herself chasing a fleeing witness, one who was about to get away. So she quickly came up with a plan to catch the man off guard and cause him to hesitate. And she did so by simply shouting something to him in another language. Specifically, she yelled, "Je ne comprends pas" or "I don't understand" in French, which she believed to be the man's native language.

And sure enough, just like quick-thinking Katie had planned, the man paused momentarily, giving her time to catch him and quiz him about the case she'd been working on. Of course, during her questioning, he revealed a vital clue that led her to crack the case wide open.

So, as I ran after these two men, I decided to try Katie's trick.

The language I chose? German.

"Guten tag!" I yelled to their fleeing forms.

For a barely perceptible moment, I saw the reaction that told me more than I truly wanted to believe. Both men paused for a split second, as though their natural reaction would have been to respond in kind, purely as a reflex. But they quickly caught themselves, glanced at each other, and took off again.

Then they began to run all out, as though they'd been caught committing a crime. I tried to keep up for a little bit, but I soon realized they were going faster than I could ever hope to run in my high heels.

And while I didn't find out who they were or why they'd come to my house, there was one thing I did know beyond a doubt—they had reacted to my saying "good day" in German.

Not exactly the kind of thing a girl wants to learn when she's already knee deep in a case that makes no sense at all. Especially not after the night I'd had. Yet despite my fatigue and bewilderment, one detail was becoming as clear as day—we were in much more danger than I had imagined. My every instinct practically screamed it.

Because, as near as I could guess, these men were German.

And since they took off running, instead of simply having a nice chat in my driveway, they looked more suspicious than a couple of villains in a *Dick Tracy* comic. Like my boss would have said, I would've bet ten to one those boys were Nazis.

Though what they were doing at my house was beyond me.

Somehow I didn't think they were there to see our armoire.

CHAPTER 20

Miracles and Monocles

A million questions ran through my mind as I walked back to the place where our driveway met the street. By now, the people standing outside our house were all talking in frantic tones. Apparently my having run after two people in line must have given them the impression that I was chasing people away willy-nilly.

Imagine that.

Needless to say, this didn't bode well when it came to the enthusiasm of those waiting to see our "miracle." In fact, an elderly man and woman turned and began to amble down the driveway, before two other women decided to join them. And then a lady and her young daughter left, too.

A part of me wanted to tell them it was perfectly fine for them to stay and see the image in our armoire. But the Apprentice P.I. part of me was now suspicious of everyone. Especially since I wondered if the two men who'd just run off were actually a couple of Nazis.

Last night, before she died, Rosette had insisted some Nazis were after her. Had she been right? And could they have been the same two men who had nearly been on our doorstep this morning?

Nazis on our doorstep. The words played over and over in my mind, like the title of a coming attraction emblazoned across a movie trailer. While it was possible the two men had simply been German, it didn't account for them running off like they did. No, as Sammy had taught me, typically only guilty people ran. People who had done something wrong and were now afraid of getting caught. Of course, it was still possible these two were guilty of something *other* than being members of the Nazi party, but my feminine intuition told me otherwise.

Especially since Sammy and I had come up against Nazi agents before, when we'd had run-ins with the German American Bund. And just because these radicals had been outlawed over here, it certainly didn't curtail their love of their Führer, or their blind obedience to do his bidding. There was plenty of talk that Hitler wanted to conquer America, too, and the Bund boys seemed to believe they were getting in on the ground floor. So if they had visitors from the Fatherland hanging around, it probably only added tinder to their Third Reich fervor.

I shuddered at the thought as I walked up our driveway. I was almost to the door again when something else suddenly struck me—the nun and the priest were missing.

But where had they gone?

I rushed into our mansion, thinking they might have stepped into the hallway and repositioned themselves closer to the armoire, but a quick glance told me otherwise. If nothing else, at least I found Hadley still sitting at his post. While I decided not to tell him about the German men for the moment, I did ask if he'd seen the now absent priest and nun.

He sat up straight and his eyes went wide. "Why, they certainly haven't come through here. Perhaps they've moved around to another entrance?"

"I don't know, Hadley. But I don't like this. Not one bit."

He crinkled his brows. "Nor do I."

I nodded toward the door again. "Well, I know they didn't leave by way of the driveway, so they must still be on our property. I'm going to look for them in the back gardens, and if they're not there, I'll check the garage next."

"That sounds like an excellent plan. Shall I accompany you?"

I shook my head. "Thanks, Hadley, but I think it's best if you stay here. To prevent anyone from going farther into the house."

"Ah, yes, of course. Probably the best line of defense," he responded. "For there is more going on here than meets the eye."

"You can say that again," I said with a sigh.

In fact, as near as I could tell, Hadley's comment could have been the motto for the day.

I bade him goodbye and headed directly to the backyard gardens. I had barely wound around the first path when I saw them—Eulalie, Father Phillip, and Sister Gertrude. And they were all walking my way.

To say I was shocked would be an understatement, since all three were engrossed in what appeared to be an amicable conversation. At least, that's what I thought at first. But when I read between the lines, I picked up on some definite tension coming from the priest and the nun.

Eulalie, on the other hand, was surprisingly high-spirited. "But I simply don't see a problem with creating sculptures of nudes, Father," she chirruped. "After all, God created the human form in His own image, as I understand."

"Well, that He did," the priest said through clenched teeth.

"So why hide it under clothing?" Eulalie went on.

"Perhaps I might tell you about the Garden of Eden, a place that was probably much like this beautiful garden. One where Eve was tempted by a snake and faced a rather difficult dilemma . . ."

And on it went.

In the meantime, I was facing a rather difficult dilemma of my own. The sooner I got to the office, the sooner I could get back to work solving this case. To exonerate Pete. But if I left River Oaks right now, would Nana and our home be safe from ill-intentioned intruders? With her acting as innocent as Snow White, and Hadley only guarding one small section of the mansion, the place was hardly what you could call "secure." Especially now that a couple of Nazis might be running around. Though I doubted the two German men would be back anytime soon, I couldn't say for sure, considering I had no idea why they'd even been here in the first place. Even so, I couldn't help but wonder *who else* might be standing outside waiting to get into our home.

I glanced at my wristwatch, amazed at how quickly the time was ticking by. I knew I needed to go, but I felt like I needed to stay. By now I probably resembled a pushmi-pullyu from a Doctor Dolittle children's book. And much as I'd been nervous about Eulalie coming to stay with us, I realized that, at the moment, she might be my only other ally in keeping the mansion protected.

I waved to get her attention. "Eulalie, would you mind if I had a word with you?"

She smiled at me. "Why, of course not." Her gaze went to the priest and nun who had gone directly to the back door, and her smile suddenly dipped.

I came to stand beside her. "Eulalie, I could really use your help. I need to get to work, but . . ."

She nodded, as though she was reading my mind. "I understand completely. You're concerned about your grandmother and all these strangers coming into her mansion."

I sighed with relief. "Yes. No matter what, I can't seem to make her understand . . ."

"That evil exists in the world? That there are those who would wish to harm others, including her? I suspect you'd like me to help Hadley guard the mansion, in a manner of speaking."

"Yes, please. I would truly appreciate it if you would."

Eulalie put her hand on my back. "You've got a lot on your shoulders these days, dear child."

I stared at my shoes for a moment. "It sure seems like it, sometimes. But others have it so much worse than I do. I mean, think of all the fellas shipping off to fight in this awful war. At least I have a warm bed and food and a nice place to live. And I'm not fighting a war." I looked up to meet her gaze once again.

"Aren't you?" she asked softly.

And all I could do was stare at her, sort of dumbfounded.

After a moment, she broke the silence. "Tell me, young Miss Tracy, do you believe in miracles?"

At first I wondered what had brought on this line of questioning. "Do you mean, things like the image in our armoire?"

Eulalie tilted her head. "Well, I suppose that might be considered a miracle. Plenty of people seem to think it is. But I'm talking about other things. More apparent things. Things like giving sight to a blind man or healing someone who is crippled."

I thought about it for a moment, because, in all honesty, I wasn't sure how to answer her question. Nor did I understand why she'd even brought it up in the first place.

"Well," I sort of murmured in response. "I suppose . . . I guess I do."

"Good," she said with a smile that practically glowed. Then she bowed her head and, without another word, marched off in the direction of the back, side door.

Leaving me standing there alone, stunned.

Even so, with her on our team, so to speak, I felt a little better about leaving Nana and the house. And the longer I dilly-dallied here, the longer it would take me to get Pete out of the horrible jam he was in.

So I went straight to the garage and hopped in the Packard. Then I backed it out very carefully, to avoid hitting anyone in what was left of the line. Once I was safely in the street, I hit the gas and raced out of River Oaks, keeping an eye out for the two German men. All the while, a very big part of me wondered if I should have done more to tail them. Maybe I could have followed them to see if they got in a car, and then taken down their license plate number.

Of course, if I *had* followed them to a vehicle (all alone and probably out of breath from running), I would have been a perfect target for kidnapping. And I could have been tied up and left for dead in a field somewhere.

The very thought of it sent chills racing across my skin.

I was still feeling a little on edge when I walked into the office. My boss, on the other hand, was very energized and animated for someone who'd had as long a night as I'd had. Especially a night with another murder. Mildred also seemed to be full of pep, wearing pearls and an elegant black-and-white suit with matching shoes.

"Glad you made it in, kid," Sammy said as he folded his arms across his chest and leaned against Mildred's desk in the front room. "Because I've got another piece to the puzzle. Hopefully it's one that'll take us down the right road and land us smack dab on our killer's doorstep."

"That *is* good news," I murmured. "Which makes it even harder for me to tell you that I've got news, too . . . since my news is the kind that might put up some roadblocks."

He shook his head. "Don't sweat it, kid. I already saw this morning's paper with your picture on the front page. It was another cheap shot, and a lousy thing for Two-Bit Louie to do. Then again, what can you expect from a louse like him? But once we solve this case, the shoe'll be on the other foot."

"I can hardly wait," I said, trying not to sigh. "But I'm afraid the news I have is something else altogether."

"In that case, don't keep us in suspense," Sammy said. "Tell us your tale first."

And so I did. First I caught him up to speed about the image in the armoire and the long lines to see it, both yesterday and today. Lines that included the two men who had run from me, but responded to my German greeting as I chased them. I also told him my suspicions about the priest and the nun who seemed to be "in charge" of the lines. Then I finished off my story by telling him about catching Polly Jane and Two-Bit Louie inside our house the day before.

"That reporter and her sidekick are like a rash that won't go away," Sammy responded, his dark eyes burning with anger. "But the ones who really get my attention are the two goons you chased off this morning. They sound like Bund boys, all right."

I nodded. "That was my take on it, too. "

Sammy furrowed his brows. "The timing of their visit seems a bit fishy to me. Here we are in the middle of this big, muddled mess of a case and then these guys show up. I'll bet my bottom dollar it's all connected somehow."

"Especially since Rosette claimed the Nazis were after her," I added. "Only minutes before she was murdered."

"Could be the same guys she was talking about," Sammy said, rubbing his chin.

Despite myself, I shivered. "Whoever they were, they were almost inside Nana's mansion. I sure wish I could convince her not to let total strangers into our home."

Sammy chuckled softly. "Good luck with that. I think once Caroline Truworth makes up her mind, it would take a force of nature to change it. But I *would* like to know why your house suddenly seems to be a hotbed of activity. From the break-in to these possible pro-Hitler heavies."

"Nazis are like cockroaches," Mildred added as she very thoughtfully brought me a cup of coffee. "They just keep coming. No matter how you try to get rid of them."

My boss raised his eyebrows. "Wait till they feel the full force of Uncle Sam's army. That'll stop 'em in their tracks."

I thanked Mildred before I took a sip of my coffee. "The priest and the nun seem a little off to me, too. Partly because the nun was wearing bright lipstick."

Mildred's mouth fell open. "That is very odd. I thought such things as makeup were restricted in most orders."

"Did you get the name of this padre?" Sammy asked me.

I frowned. "He claims his name is Father Phillip. And our new housekeeper, Lupé, says she knows him from the Catholic church she attends. Though she was pretty vague about the whole thing, and she would only say that her church was 'downtown.'"

"A likely story," Sammy muttered, before he turned to Mildred. "Be an angel, Mildred, and make some phone calls for us. See if any of our local Catholic churches have ever heard of a Father Phillip."

"I shall do so immediately." She nodded and pulled a phone book from a drawer in her desk.

While she picked up the receiver, I took the film canisters from my pocket and showed them to Sammy.

He grinned and *thunked* his hand to his chest. "Oh, be still, my beating heart. Is that evidence you've brought?"

I shook my head and put the canisters on Mildred's desk. "I'm afraid your guess is as good as mine. They're films I confiscated from Two-Bit Louie, after I caught him and Polly Jane sneaking around our house. And before Hadley and I had them arrested. So I'm not sure what's on these rolls."

"Well, there's only one way to find out," Sammy said, picking up the canisters. "Let's go back to the darkroom and develop these. Maybe we'll get lucky and something will jump out at us."

I followed him into the large back office, where we each had a desk. "But you didn't tell me your good news, about the piece of the puzzle that you found." I left my purse on my desk and unpinned my hat, dropping it onto a peg on the hat rack.

My boss grinned. "I heard back from my buddy who works at a lab."

That made my ears perk up. "Did he find anything?"

"Nope," Sammy said as we walked into the darkroom, which had been converted from a large supply closet. "The guy found nothing suspicious in either the wine glasses or the bottle."

I shut the door after he hit the switch for the red light. "So that means if Freddy was poisoned, it was probably thanks to the pin that Rosette stuck him with."

"Bingo, kid. The pin probably had poison on it, just like the dart that killed the girl. Except she died right away, while Freddy danced like a madman before he hit the floor. My guess is we're dealing with two different poisons."

"But both were poisons on sharp objects," I said as my eyes adjusted to the dim light. "Still, I can't figure out who would want to kill either of them."

"That's where we seem to be coming up short. But there is one thing we do know—it was a short, gray-haired lady who gave Rosette the brooch and told her to create a commotion. So tell me, who is the first person that comes to mind who matches that description?"

"Ethel . . ." I said, seething.

"You got it, kid." Sammy put the film canisters on the counter. "Could be she set up little Rosette to kill Freddy. And then she killed Rosette to keep her from blabbing."

"That would certainly add up," I agreed.

Sammy removed the films from their containers. "And what would you like to bet that Ethel had access to a South American dart blowgun. Along with a nice supply of darts. Probably something the museum had stored in their antiquities section."

I pulled trays from a cupboard. "And since Ethel seems to thinks she owns the place . . ."

"She probably wouldn't mind helping herself." He raised an eyebrow toward the door. "I say it's high time we paid old Ethel a visit. Right after we're done here. Let's find out if she's had a homicidal streak lately."

"Fine by me. Though we'll probably set off a whole bunch of fireworks."

"I've always enjoyed a good show," Sammy chuckled as we went to work on the films.

Soon we had the negatives in the enlarger, and from there, the imprinted photographic papers went into the trays with the developer, fixer, and water bath. Then I hung up all the newly developed black-and-white pictures to dry on the twine that was strung across the length of the room. Almost like hanging clothes on a clothesline. To be honest, I'd learned much of what I knew about developing film from Katie McClue novels. Katie, of course, was an expert at it. For that matter, any P.I. worth her salt knew how to develop her own pictures.

And the minute I saw the pictures we'd just developed, I had to grab the counter in front of me so I wouldn't fall over. Because those photographs showed exactly how far Polly Jane and her pal, Two-Bit Louie, had gone into our house. Much to my amazement, they'd ventured in a lot farther than I'd imagined. While they seemed intent on taking photos of our artwork or anything that probably exuded extravagance, they'd clearly made their way down all the hallways and even up the staircase, to the wall just outside my room.

For all I knew, they might have even gone into my bedroom and searched it. Though I'd probably never know for sure, since they hadn't taken any pictures of my room.

Still, they'd left me with enough evidence to make trespassing charges stick.

And while it was more than a little unsettling to know that Polly and Louie had invaded our home, the final couple of pictures were especially chilling.

Because, these particular pictures showed more than just artwork or the rooms in Nana's mansion. In fact, it appeared that Polly and Louie had knowingly or unknowingly photographed two other people in our house.

Trespassers who had made it all the way to the conservatory in the back.

I grabbed a magnifying glass from the drawer and examined the photographs up close. That's when I saw a couple of familiar faces peeking out from behind the conservatory door. And one of them had a monocle.

It was the two men I'd chased down the street earlier. The men I believed to be Nazis. And they had been right inside our house.

The sight of them made me gasp.

CHAPTER 21

The Plot Thickens . . . and Then Thickens Some More

"That's them!" I practically shouted to my boss as I pointed to the pair in the pictures.

He crinkled his brow. "Who, kid? Who?"

Suddenly words came tumbling out of me at the speed of a runaway train. "The two men who were standing in line at my house! The ones who ran off when I tried to talk to them. The men I believe are Nazis. How on earth did they get into Nana's mansion?"

"Slow down, kid. And think back. When did you first lay eyes on them?" Sammy's own voice was oozing with urgency, something I rarely ever heard from him.

"Well . . ." I began, putting my hand to my chest and trying to calm my breathing. "I saw them outside yesterday, leaving with the rest of the people after we'd shut down the line for the night. Right before we'd caught Polly and Louie inside our house."

Sammy crinkled his brow. "Did you actually see the two men in line? Or did you just see them leaving?"

His question made me pause for a moment, while I tried to recall the scene. "No. I remember seeing them as they were walking away."

Sammy frowned. "They could have been inside the house and gone out another door."

My heart started to pound. "And then they came back again today. But why? Why would Nazis even want to get inside Nana's mansion at all?"

"Your guess is as good as mine, kid. But either way, I don't like it one bit."

"You and me both," I said as we started to clean up the darkroom, leaving the pictures to finish drying.

"I think I'd better have a little heart-to-heart with your grandmother," Sammy murmured. "And try to persuade her to close up shop when it comes to this parade of strangers traipsing through her place. Maybe I need to lay on the charm extra thick."

"Well, if anyone could do it, Sammy, it would be you. I sure hope you have better luck than I've been having. Because, no matter what I say, I can't convince her at all. In fact, she mostly just gets angry with me now whenever I even bring up the subject."

I'd barely spoken the words when it felt like they were practically stabbing me through the heart. Nana and I had always been so close, and I loved her dearly. She had been more of a mother to me than my real mother had ever been. The mere thought of someone trying to harm my beloved grandmother cut me to the core.

And that's when I realized this case had become so much bigger than I had first imagined. Not only was Pete's reputation and future on the line, but now I also needed to protect Nana from "evil forces," as Eulalie would have put it. It was hard to believe, and heartbreaking to say the least, but two of the people I cared about most in this world were in trouble. And maybe even in danger.

I blinked as Sammy turned on the regular light again and we left the darkroom. The frown on his face told me that he was as worried about Nana as I was. Somehow, even knowing that helped a lot.

He caught my eye as he slipped on the jacket of his double-breasted suit and grabbed his fedora. "Don't you fret, kid. We're gonna get them. I won't let anything happen to your grandmother. Or Pete."

And while I knew he was trying to give me a pep talk, I wasn't sure who it was meant for—him or me.

"Thanks, Sammy," I told him as I grabbed my purse and pinned on my hat.

I did my best to put on a smile, too, but I was pretty sure I wasn't succeeding. Some Apprentice P.I. I was turning out to be.

Yet I knew I didn't have the luxury of letting my emotions get the better of me, not when I had people depending on me. So I took a deep breath and pulled together every ounce of courage that I could muster. After all, I needed to be in top form for our visit to Ethel's house.

Then I nodded to my boss and followed him to the outer office.

Mildred stood up from her desk the second she saw us. "You'll never believe it! But I called every Catholic church in the book, and the Episcopal churches, too. And nobody, but nobody, has heard of a Father Phillip. And while there were a few Sister Gertrudes around, not a one of them wore red lipstick."

"Thanks, Mildred," I said with a hug. "That clears up a few things."

Though oddly enough, it didn't. Instead, it simply muddied the waters even more.

At least the cool, fresh air outside brought me a little more vigor as Sammy and I left the building. Minutes later, we were on our way to Ethel's mansion on Montrose Boulevard. I drove the Packard while Sammy kept a hand on his sidearm and an eye out for anyone who might be following us. Now that a couple of Nazis might have entered Nana's mansion, we decided it wouldn't hurt to be a little extra wary.

I had seen Ethel's estate years ago, when Nana had pointed it out to me from the road. So today I immediately recognized the huge building that sported Greek columns and a triangular roofline, which gave the building a Parthenon-like appearance. Her home was in a planned community that had been established before River Oaks, by developer J.W. Link of the Houston Land Corporation. Naturally, Ethel's mansion easily rivaled the one Mr. Link had built for his own family.

We parked in Ethel's circular driveway and marched up the wide steps to the tall double doors in front. Sammy rang the bell and then we waited.

A very proper English butler with perfectly combed white hair answered the door. He scowled and looked down his nose at us through black-framed, round spectacles. Spectacles with lenses that magnified his eyes and made them appear to be about twenty times their actual size.

"We'd like to speak with Mrs. Barton, please," Sammy said, letting his dark eyes bore into the butler's.

And suddenly the butler's wide eyes appeared even wider. For a moment or two, he faltered and seemed to lose all sense of decorum. "*Umb . . . umb . . . umb . . .* I'm so terribly sorry, but if you would please forgive my impertinence . . . but aren't you . . . aren't you . . . him?"

"Yes," Sammy said firmly. "I am. Now, if you would be so kind, my associate and I would like to come in and see Mrs. Barton."

"Yes, yes, of course, sir. I must say, I can't even begin to tell you what an honor it is to meet you in person. While Mrs. Barton certainly entertains her share of celebrities, I never imagined that you might be on our doorstep. I am a great admirer, of course. I've seen every one of your moving pictures. I particularly enjoyed *The Maltese Falcon.*"

"Why, thank you. It's always a pleasure to meet a fan."

Sammy held his hand out to shake and I thought the butler was going to faint. The poor man gasped before he gingerly put his hand in Sammy's, whereby my boss pumped it up and down a few times.

By then the butler was starting to tremble. "Please step inside. I shall deposit you both in the drawing room, where you may wait until Mrs. Barton is available."

"Thank you," Sammy said. "This is the stuff that dreams are made from."

"Made of," I said under my breath, correcting his Bogart quote from *The Maltese Falcon,* as we followed the very giddy butler to the well-decorated drawing room.

Sammy tossed a grin over his shoulder and kept his hat low across his forehead, ignoring the standard gentleman's rule of removing a hat when entering a home.

Ethel's drawing room was located deep inside the mansion, and it was decorated with some of the finest fabrics I have ever seen. And believe me, I was no stranger to elegant fabric, considering the textiles that Nana had chosen for decorating her own mansion. Meaning, I knew quality when I saw it. And Ethel's midnight-blue silk moiré drapes looked positively stunning against a white marble floor with bands of lapis lazuli. The sofas and wing chairs were all upholstered in stunning gold or cream brocades, with many of the threads having a gold metallic look to them.

And though I wasn't sure if Sammy was aware of how beautifully appointed the room was, he gave off the impression that he saw this sort of thing on a daily basis. He strolled in like he owned the place and feigned a bored yawn. Then he flopped into a wing chair near the door, while I slid into another chair that was part of a cluster of four at the far corner. Classical paintings covered every wall, almost making the room into a miniature museum in itself, while a painting of Ethel in her younger years stared down at us from above the white marble fireplace.

The butler pointed to the bar cart in the room. "Shall I pour you both a libation?"

"No thanks," Sammy said. "I don't do my libating until dinnertime. But we'll be quite comfortable here while we wait for Mrs. Barton."

"Very good, sir," the butler said with a trill to his voice. "I shall tell Madame that you are here. She'll be most pleased."

"I wouldn't count on that," Sammy muttered after the butler left and closed the French doors behind him. "In fact, I suspect she'll be downright *displeased*."

I glanced at my boss in amazement. "The butler thinks you're Humphrey Bogart, doesn't he?"

"I'd say so, kid. And as long as everyone keeps telling me that I look like the guy, I might as well take advantage of it every now and then."

I shook my head and laughed. "I only hope you don't start signing autographs as 'Bogey.'"

He grinned. "It got us in the door, didn't it? I'm a little shocked myself that it went so smoothly. I figured we'd have to strong-arm our way in here. But now that we're here, we'd better figure out how we're going to handle this dame. Somehow I don't think she'll be as crazy about us as her butler was."

"Probably not, judging from the way she accused Pete of murder and Nana of burglary. And then practically had Pete and me convicted in the newspaper. No, I think it's safe to say, she won't be crazy about our being here at all."

"So let's come out swinging, kid. Put the woman on the defense. Pull the rug out from under her."

Ethel on the defense? That was something I had to see. Though as we sat there, with the clock ticking away, I was starting to wonder if Ethel would even show at all.

In fact, I was just about to suggest that we call for the butler when the doors suddenly flew open and Ethel framed her body against the doorjamb. She slid one arm up and bent one knee, flamingo-style, in her best Rita Hayworth pose. She was wearing some kind of purple peignoir set with feathers at the cuffs and on the shawl collar. The massive amount of sparkling jewels she wore made her light up like a Christmas tree.

"Humphrey, darling!" she gushed. "I just knew you'd come for me one day! I've dreamed of this moment. Now, take me, darling! Take me into your arms."

With those words, she rushed into the room and slammed the door behind her. She made a beeline for Sammy, with arms outstretched and lips puckered.

Sammy removed his fedora just seconds before she reached his chair. The movement must have been enough to make her open her eyes and look at him.

Really look at him.

That's when she hit the brakes and practically skidded to a stop. "You're not Humphrey Bogart!" she yelled loud enough for the people in the next county to hear. "You're not him at all!"

Sammy put his hand to his chest. "What? People tell me I look just like the man. I hear it once or twice a day. At least." Pretending to be hurt, he turned to me. "You think I look like Bogey, don't you, kid?"

I stood up and gave him my most angelic smile. "Well, of course, Sammy. Everybody does. We hear it all the time."

Ethel's mouth nearly hit the floor when she saw me, and it was clear she hadn't even realized that I was in the room.

Sammy returned his gaze to Ethel. "See? It's true. My associate here wouldn't make something up. Unlike the reporter you've got under your thumb at the *Star-Journal*."

"Out!" Ethel screamed. "Right now! Or I shall call the police!"

"That would be swell, sister," Sammy said. "There's gotta be a phone around here somewhere. If you'd like to call them, that would save me the trouble. After all, we're here to have you arrested for murder."

She slapped a bejeweled hand to her cheek. "Murder? Me? Whatever are you talking about? How dare you!"

Sammy jumped to his feet and took a few steps toward her, until she backed up and dropped into a wing chair. "Oh, save it for the paper, would ya? Your innocent little schoolgirl act doesn't cut it with us. We know you conspired to murder Frederick Hoffmeister. And we know you bumped off Rosette DeBlanc. Or *had* her bumped off. And we even know why. The only thing we don't know is *why* you had Freddy murdered."

"I did no such thing!" Ethel gasped. "Why, I wouldn't hurt a fly."

"No? Probably because you're too busy hurting innocent *people*," Sammy said, not missing a beat. "Don't bother denying it, because we know all about the pin you gave that young girl, Rosette. Let me tell you, sister, she sang like a canary before she died."

Now I moved in closer. "That's right. I heard her myself. Lots of people did. So there are plenty of witnesses."

Sammy raised an eyebrow and glanced around the room. "What do you think, kid? If Ethel hires someone to keep the place up, it should still look pretty good when she gets out of prison."

I shrugged, following Sammy's lead. "Probably. Though her clothes will be out of date by then. And I don't think you can wear evening gowns and jewelry in jail."

Sammy let out an exaggerated sigh. "Not even for New Year's Eve. But with good behavior, Ethel, you might get out in twenty years. What year will that be, kid?"

"It will be 1962," I told him with a smile. "Maybe the war will be over by then."

Ethel clenched her fists and thumped them on the arms of the chair. "You can't do this to me! I want my lawyer!"

"You can see your lawyer if you like," Sammy said, pinning Ethel to her seat with his glare. "Once you're down at the police station, that is. We'll be there, too, of course. Passing along all the evidence we have on you. Cold, hard evidence about a cold-blooded murder."

"I didn't kill anyone!" Ethel yelled again.

This time Sammy yelled back, close to her face. "Sure you did! You just didn't do the actual dirty work. Instead you gave that girl a pin with poison on it and told her to stick Freddy. But murder is murder. Any way you look at it."

"You can't talk to me this way! Don't you know who I am?" Ethel sputtered and leaned forward in her chair. "I don't have to take this."

Sammy laughed. "You'll take it and you'll like it. Now what I want to know is, who did you get to shoot that poison dart blowgun? The one that killed Rosette? I'll bet if we search the museum files we'll find a blowgun listed in the inventory. And I'll bet that blowgun just happens to be missing."

"What are you talking about? I don't know anything about a blowgun!" Ethel's face was becoming almost as purple as her peignoir set.

"A likely story!" Sammy hollered. "Though we don't even need to find the blowgun. We've got enough to lock you away with what Rosette told us. About the pin."

"Tell me, Ethel," I said, jumping right in front of her face. "Where did you get the brooch you gave to Rosette? Was it one of yours?"

By now Ethel's eyes burned with fire. "Oh, you stupid girl! I would expect no less from the granddaughter of Caroline Truworth! Of course I didn't use one of my own brooches. I'd never use something so valuable for such a task as that! I got a cheap one out of the Lost and Found at the . . ."

And then she stopped herself.

Because Ethel Barton knew that we had just caught her.

CHAPTER 22

Fast Cars and Near Misses

Ethel gasped and choked and tried to speak all at once. Then she rolled her eyes and flopped backwards in her wing chair, sputtering a little more as the fight went out of her, like a motorboat running out of gas.

All the while, Sammy and I just stood there, hands on hips, waiting to hear what explanation, if any, she might give us.

"Oh, that stupid, stupid girl," Ethel finally uttered, her nose crinkled in a sneer. "She was only supposed to create a diversion. That was all. And she completely bumbled the whole thing!"

"You bought Rosette's ticket," I prompted, pressing her to continue her confession. "So she'd be there to do your bidding. Where in the world did you get an idea like that?"

She waved her hand before her. "Oh, from that foreign man. The one with the monocle and hair so short it was practically shaved. He bought a ticket for that other girl and paid me a little extra to send it to her."

My mouth fell open. "The other girl . . . Do you mean Dot?"

"Yes, yes," Ethel said, rolling her eyes once more. "That man gave me her address. He wanted it sent anonymously."

I glanced at my boss and caught his eye. At least we had one mystery solved—we finally knew who'd mailed the ticket to Dot. But learning it was the monocle-wearing man only created more questions than it answered.

I scrunched my eyebrows together, doing my best to look fierce as I stared at Ethel. "Do you know why he wanted a ticket sent to Dot?"

"Now how should I know a thing like that?" Ethel smirked.

Sammy folded his arms across his chest and stepped closer to Ethel. "Let's get back to the other girl—Rosette. Seems to me, you figured you could take advantage of a young girl who was short on dough and long on dreams. One who wanted to be at the New Year's Eve gala."

Picking up on Sammy's thread, I added, "And you told her that you would pay for her ticket and she could go to the gala if she did just one little favor for you—she simply had to stick Freddy with the pin on the back of that brooch. But you didn't tell her that you planned to dip that very pin in some poison. It's a wonder you didn't kill Rosette that night, too. She might have stuck herself accidentally. Or maybe that was your plan all along. Maybe you figured you'd tie up any loose ends right then and there."

"Wait a minute!" Ethel hollered. "I did no such thing. And I certainly don't know anything about any poison! I only told that girl, Rosette, to stick him with the pin, a common behavior for girls in *my* day. After all, we used to stick men with our huge hatpins if they got out of line. It usually created a commotion and that's all I wanted to do the night of the gala—create a little uproar. I'd already heard the Professor was coming to the gala with two of his star pupils. And one of them was supposed to be as good a dancer as Fred Astaire himself. In fact, that girl already knew who Freddy was. That's why she wanted the ticket so badly. She knew he was going to be there and she was dying to dance with him. So I figured all eyes would be on them. I knew they'd make such a striking couple. And if she stabbed him with the pin and he bent over in pain . . ."

"Then nobody would notice what you were up to," I said, finishing her sentence.

And for once, Ethel went oddly silent.

Sammy rubbed his chin, watching her like a hawk. "So you didn't want to kill Freddy . . . But you wanted everyone watching Freddy and Rosette upstairs, and then no one would see what you were up to downstairs. And I've got a pretty good idea why. Because you didn't want anyone eyeballing you when you stole that white bird. You must have hid it somewhere in the museum, where you could pick it up later. Then you came upstairs and screamed your head off, giving us some song and dance about the museum being robbed."

Ethel gasped and put her hand to her mouth.

"That's why we found the key to the display cabinet stuck in a file in the office," I jumped in, not missing a beat. "You used the key to open the cabinet and then hid it in a hurry. So anyone who looked for that key in its usual spot would think it had been stolen, too, right after it was used to steal the statuette. Of course, you wanted to keep the key handy for yourself, so you could use it later, when you were ready to put something else in that display case."

"All right, fine!" Ethel shouted, her hands clenched in fists. "But for the record, I didn't actually *steal* that marble statue. I was merely giving it a proper home. It was so pretty, and it belongs in a mansion like mine, where it will be appreciated. Not in a museum where people have no earthly concept of it's value."

Anger rose in my throat. "Yet you falsely accused my grandmother of stealing it. Right after you falsely accused my fella of killing Freddy. To top it off, you even gave false information to that reporter, Polly Jane Montgomery. Do you know how many people you've hurt over this?"

"A mere handful," Ethel huffed with a dismissive wave. "No one important."

I glared at her. "And you have no remorse at all, do you?" I said, fighting with everything I had to keep my ire under wraps.

Ethel snickered. "Well, why should I? I didn't do anything all that terribly wrong."

"Lucky for you, I never hit a lady," Sammy said under his breath. "Though I'm not sure you qualify. So where exactly is this statue now?"

For the second time, Ethel went silent. And that silence told me everything I needed to know, especially when I realized she was having a hard time deciding where to rest her gaze. Meaning, she was doing her very best not to look at anything around us.

But I kept my own eyes trained on her. "It's right in this room, isn't it?"

She swallowed hard, only confirming what I'd already figured out.

Sammy nodded at the phone on a desk near the French doors. "What's it gonna be, Ethel? I'd sure hate to see you get hauled down to the police station in that pretty little purple getup. Might be downright embarrassing if your pals spotted you in the back of a police car. You know, when they drag you down there for questioning. But I'd be willing to go easy on you. If you spill the beans and tell us where the white bird is hidden, then I'll have the police come over *here* to ask you all their questions. So you can change clothes before they take you in. All nice and quiet-like."

"Certainly not!" She jutted out her chin. "I demand that you call my lawyer. I will not go to jail over this."

I put my hands on the arms of her chair and leaned over, until my face was mere inches from hers. "But you would've happily sent Pete to jail and ruined his life forever. I can't even tell you how much I'd like to do the same . . . or worse . . . to you," I said in a voice that was so icy I even scared myself. "Now, I'd suggest you tell us where that statuette is hidden, since my patience has reached its limit . . ."

Apparently, my words and tone did the trick, because Ethel gulped and immediately pointed to a wainscoted wall on the side of the room. "In there. That bottom section of paneling slides back. You'll find a secret compartment."

And without another word, I rushed over to the wall and *thumped* my fist against the paneling, listening for a hollow space. Sure enough, I soon heard a change in the sound coming back to me, in the exact spot that Ethel had indicated. So I quickly slid the section out of the way and laid my eyes upon the ancient Greek statuette that Ethel had stolen from the museum.

"Hello, pretty birdie," I murmured, with a smile inching across my face.

For a moment, I had the strangest sensation that the turtledove before me wanted to "coo" her thanks to me. That beautiful bird had already survived a couple of millennia, and hopefully, once it was back at the museum, it would survive another thousand years or more. And who knew how many lucky patrons would get to view her over the ages?

Behind me, I could hear Sammy on the phone, talking to the police, right before he summoned Ethel's butler and asked him to call her lawyer. Not long after that, thanks to Sammy's request, the police arrived on the scene quietly and without fanfare. Much like Ethel's browbeaten attorney.

Then it seemed like everything went by in a blur. The statue was dusted for prints and photos were taken while Ethel confessed all to the police. Sammy and I made sure of that, much to her annoyance.

Finally, when we were no longer needed, Sammy spoke to the officer in charge. "Mind if Miss Truworth and I take that statue down to the station? That little bird has caused us a whole lotta trouble. We'd personally like to see that it gets to the right place and into the right hands."

The officer nodded to him. "Sure thing, Sammy. These days we could use the help," he added with a groan. Probably because he had his hands full in dealing with Ethel, who now talked nonstop, taking several verbal detours in topics as she kept up her tirade.

All the while, her lawyer sat surprisingly silent. I got the impression he wouldn't mind if she continued her temper tantrum behind bars.

Which would have suited me just fine.

Minutes later, we walked out of Ethel's mansion. Or rather, I should probably say, we were more or less kicked out by her now-indignant butler. Though honestly, I wasn't sure what upset him more—our putting his employer into the hands of local law enforcement, or his learning that Sammy wasn't really Humphrey Bogart.

In any case, if I never saw Ethel's beautifully decorated mansion again, it would not break my heart.

We headed straight for the Packard, where I let Sammy into the passenger side with the turtledove statuette. He covered it as best he could with his handkerchief while I slid in behind the wheel. I put the key in the ignition, pushed in the clutch and brake pedals, and turned the engine over.

"That was quite the performance back there, kid," my boss said with a grin. "You could've given Katharine Hepburn a run for her money."

"Thanks, Sammy. But I have to be honest . . . I had a pretty hard time controlling my temper."

Sammy chuckled. "But you did, kid. You did." He pulled his handkerchief from the top of the statuette and gave it a good, long look. "Ain't exactly the Maltese Falcon, is it?"

I tilted my head back and forth, looking at the dove from different angles. "It's stunning, in a simple, classic sort of way. But it just doesn't seem like something Freddy would be trying to get his hands on for Hitler." I put the car in gear and eased it out of the parking spot and into the flow of traffic.

Sammy shook his head slowly. "You've got that right. It's a pretty bird and probably worth a pretty penny. But other than that, there's really nothing all that special about it."

I paused at a stop sign and waited for a few cars to go by. "And it sure doesn't seem to have any supernatural powers."

"None that we can see, anyway," Sammy said with a chuckle. "But *any way* you look at it, it doesn't look like the kind of thing somebody would kill for. And much as I hate to say it, it takes us right back to the drawing board. We got another piece to the puzzle, but I have a bad feeling we've got two puzzles going at the same time. To top it off, we're still coming up short on the question of, who killed Freddy?"

"And Rosette." I added as I turned onto the main road, which had very little traffic at the moment. "Did you believe Ethel? That she didn't murder either one of them?"

Sammy heaved a great sigh. "I do, kid. I believe the dame. She might be guilty of a lot of things, but near as I can tell, murder isn't one of them."

I felt like sighing myself. "So where do we go from here?"

Sammy covered the marble dove with his handkerchief again. "Let's figure out who else could get their hands on a dart blowgun. My money's on a certain professor of archaeology. Bet he's got some ancient stuff from South America just hanging around his place."

"But why would he kill his prize pupil? The Professor sounded genuinely pleased to have a student who was as smart as Freddy."

"Could be this Longfellow guy found out what Freddy was up to. And maybe the good doctor decided to bump him off, in the interest of national security."

"Which brings us full circle again. We still don't know *exactly* what Freddy was up to. Or *what* he was after. Though Rosette said something about a 'veil.' Or, at least, I thought that's what she said."

Sammy glanced out the rear window. "And again, we're stuck spinning our wheels. Either way, I think we should stick a bee in Longfellow's bonnet and see what shakes loose."

"We'll have a hard time getting the Professor to cooperate with us," I commented as I gave the Packard a little more gas.

We had a straight shot to the police station now, though it was still a few miles away. For the first time in my life, I was suddenly anxious to get there.

"You can say that again, kid. We'll need to come up with a game plan for handling him, just like we did old Ethel back there."

With those words, an idea popped into my mind, like a light bulb over the head of a cartoon character. "I know what we could do! I'll ask Nana to throw a dinner party tomorrow night. I'll invite Pete, of course, and you'll be there as Nana's date. Eulalie will have an open invitation since she's staying with us, and we can invite the Professor to be her date. He's already come over for dinner once, so he won't suspect any ulterior motives on our part. It'll give us a chance to casually quiz him throughout the evening. I know Nana would be more than happy to help out. Especially if we tell her it's for our investigation, *and*, that we need to keep the real reason for the party a secret."

Sammy responded with a huge grin. "Good plan, kid. Your grandmother is a swell gal. Always up for a good escapade."

"She is," I said with a smile, realizing once again just how blessed I was to have her in my life.

Sammy leaned forward and looked out his window, at the Packard's little side mirror that was attached to the spare-tire cover mounted on the fender. "But let's make sure we cover our bases before the party starts. Why don't you run over and have a little chat with Stanley after church tomorrow, since you're pals with him. He might know if the Professor is the proud owner of a dart blowgun. And while you're at it, show him the picture of those two German goons who were inside your grandmother's place. Find out if he ever saw Freddy talking to them."

I pushed in the clutch and shifted to a higher gear. "Sounds like a good idea . . . provided I can get past his landlady. That could be a problem."

"In that case, don't call ahead. Let me go in first and distract the landlady. So you can sneak in."

I smiled. "Are you going to use your Humphrey Bogart impersonation again?"

Sammy returned his gaze to the view outside the rear window. "You got it, kid. I believe Sam Spade said something about not minding a reasonable amount of trouble. Neither do I. And speaking of trouble, looks like we've got some. That black sedan has been tailing us since we left Ethel's."

Chills ran up and down my spine as I glanced in my rearview mirror and spotted the car that Sammy was talking about. It was two car-lengths back, just far enough away for the occupants to remain unrecognizable.

All of a sudden I wished we hadn't volunteered to take that two-thousand-year-old statue to the police station. Especially since we still had a few miles to go.

"Give it a little more gas, kid," Sammy said under his breath, as though the car following could hear us. "Not enough to be obvious. Let's see if this guy sticks with us."

So I did exactly as my boss instructed. And sure enough, the dark car sped up, too. It even had to pass another car in order to keep tailing us.

"We've got a couple of choices here, kid," Sammy murmured. "We could hit the gas and outrun him. Or we could try to lose him on the side streets."

By now my heart had started to pound as I wondered *who* was following us and why. "Let's try outrunning them," I said, fighting to keep my voice steady.

"Good choice, kid."

I was just about to step on the gas when I suddenly spotted an old pea-green car coming up on the sedan. Even from this distance, I could see the green car was full of dents and bumps and rust spots. It picked up speed and passed the sedan in a huge hurry, and before I knew it, it was on our tail.

And I do mean, *right* on our tail. Mere inches from the rear of the Packard.

Not to be outdone by the green car, the dark sedan suddenly hit the gas and came up behind the green jalopy.

"Give it more gas, kid," Sammy told me, just as the sedan sped up and swerved around the green car. He was about to come up on my driver's side when I heard a sound that made the little hairs on the back of my neck stand on end.

It was the *pop, pop, pop* of gunfire.

But who was shooting at whom, I couldn't tell for sure.

"Step on it, kid!" Sammy hollered.

And so I did. I shifted into a higher gear and pushed the gas pedal to the floor. The Packard went racing away. But driving that fast inside the city always made me nervous, especially since there were traffic lights and stop signs I had to deal with.

Not to mention, the possibility of hitting another car.

Such as the blue Buick that was now smack dab in front of me.

Without slowing down, I maneuvered around the driver's side of the Buick and passed him like he was standing still. For the first time in my life, I truly hoped a police officer would show up and arrest me for speeding.

The black sedan and the green car both passed the Buick, too, thankfully without a collision. And so we all raced on. Yet before long, it was obvious the green car didn't have the horsepower to keep up, and it began to fall behind, putting it third in our line of autos speeding toward the police station. Though I had a pretty good idea the two cars following us didn't intend for us to actually *make* it there.

A fact that made my pulse pick up even more.

Especially after my idea was confirmed when the black car managed to slowly creep up on my rear fender. From my side mirror, I could see a man in a black fedora leaning out, and he had an even blacker revolver pointed right at us.

Sammy must have seen it, too. Because he put the statue on the floor and pulled his own gun from its holster. The only problem was, he couldn't get a good shot off from his side of the car. He just didn't have the right angle for it.

"Hit the brakes, kid," he commanded. "And make a sharp right at the next corner."

So I pushed in the clutch pedal with one foot, hit the brake pedal with the other, and downshifted all at the same time. The dark car went flying past, and when the man hanging out the window finally got off a shot, it scuttled across my hood, just missing the metal by inches.

Of course, the green car wasn't ready for my maneuver and it nearly rear-ended me. But it swerved at the last minute and actually hit the tail end of the black car, who'd also found his brake pedal.

That's when I caught a glimpse of a man with a camera in the passenger side of the green jalopy. Two-Bit Louie. As near as I could guess, he'd probably been taking pictures the whole way. Another glance told me the driver of the car was probably none other than P.J. Montgomery herself.

"Okay, here's where you turn right," Sammy shouted. "Turn now, now, now, kid!"

At his command, I cranked the steering wheel as far to the right as I dared take it. I took a quick glance over my left shoulder and saw the black car zooming on down the road, and the man with the gun leaning out and shooting at the green car as it swerved left and right and tried to back off.

Thankfully, I made the turn, kicking up dust and rocks and debris along the way. For a moment, I was pretty sure my two right wheels had gone off the ground, until they landed again and I hit the gas, giving the Packard everything she had.

"We lost 'em, kid!" Sammy cheered. "But not for long. Now to beat them at their own game. Take a right turn up here at the corner."

"But we'll be going away from the police station."

"You got it, kid. They won't expect it. They'll never know where to find us."

"Don't we need to get this statue to the station?"

"Yup, kid. I didn't say we weren't going there. We're just taking the scenic route. Now be a doll and step on it."

Despite myself, I couldn't help but smile. I shifted gears again and gave the Packard some more gas. I took the next corner with just as much speed, but I went wide to give the car a little more stability. Then I sped away in the opposite direction of the police station. By now my heart was racing almost as fast as the Packard's engine.

"I saw who was in the green car," I told Sammy. "It was Polly and Louie."

Sammy let out a low whistle. "Looks like they got themselves in a fine mess. I'll bet dollars to doughnuts our guy with the gun in the other car is a Nazi. Because he looks like one of the goons in those pictures we developed. And I believe I spotted a monocle on the driver."

"So the Nazis are chasing us down?" I asked, unable to keep the astonishment out of my voice. "But why? Do you think they want this statuette?"

Sammy clucked his tongue. "Could be, kid. Your guess is as good as mine. Though for the life of me, I couldn't say why they would want this white bird."

"I sure wish we could find some traffic, so we could blend in somewhere."

"We're outta luck today. But I'm not sure traffic would stop these guys. So take a couple more rights and then go straight to the station."

I slowed down, downshifted, and made a proper right turn this time. "But we'll be on the same road as we were before. The same one where they found us in the first place."

Sammy nodded and kept his eyes glued to the intersection up ahead. "You got it, kid. It's the last place they'll look for us. And besides, if they try to find us, they'll have to backtrack. Meaning they'll be on the opposite side of the street."

I sped up again, heading for the intersection with the very road we'd been traveling on before. "They could turn around and chase us."

"Sure could, kid. But it'll still cost them time. Which *gives* us time. And we don't need much, since the station isn't far. Once we get there we'll be safe. These Third-Reich rats wouldn't dare set foot inside a police station. Not willingly, anyway."

I nodded to my boss and fought to steady my nerves. With my heart in my throat, I stopped at the intersection and glanced both ways, looking for any signs of Polly Jane's green jalopy or the dark sedan that had been chasing us. I was almost giddy when I saw the coast was clear. Or rather, that the road was clear. Then I carefully made a right-hand turn and gave the Packard plenty of gas, until we were speeding toward the police station. All the while, I kept my eyes peeled for an old green car and a dark sedan. We didn't have far to go, but today, it felt like we could have gone to the moon and back in the time it was taking us to get to the station.

Then, we were just a block and a half away from the station when I saw a sight that made my heart skip a beat altogether. Polly Jane's car was on the side of the road, with a nice round bullet hole in the middle of her now-cracked windshield.

And coming right at us from the other direction was the black sedan.

Worst of all, he was driving on our side of the street.

CHAPTER 23

Bootleg Turns and Bad Guys

Even though Polly Jane had become my nemesis, my first instinct was to pull over and see if I could help her. Without thinking, I hit the clutch with my left foot and let up on the gas with my right.

Just as I did, Sammy's voice came through loud and clear. "Don't do it, kid. You'll get us both killed. Get to the police station first. Then we'll send a squad car out to rescue them. If they're not dead already."

The thought of it made me shudder. "All right," I said as I stepped on the gas again and turned my attention back to the black sedan that was still racing right for us. "Any ideas which side of the road I should drive on? So we can avoid a head-on crash?"

"Take it easy, kid, and keep your course steady. He's just trying to scare you and force you to pull over. Let him know you won't flinch."

Which, to be honest, was *exactly* what I wanted to do. In fact, right at that moment, flinching sounded like a *really* good plan to me. And apparently, I wasn't the only one who had that idea. We had finally come up on some traffic, and those cars pulled over the second they saw the black car and my Packard on a collision course.

"Okay, kid," Sammy said. "Time to pull a bootlegger."

"A what?"

"A bootleg turn. Old Prohibition term. It's a turn that bootleggers used when they were trying to outrun G-men. This is gonna go fast, kid, and we'll end up going back the way we came from. Now I need you to follow my directions to the letter. Ready?"

I gulped. "Ready as I'll ever be."

"All right, kid. Shift into second."

So I pushed in the clutch and did as he said.

"Now flick the wheel to the right and then crank it as fast as you can all the way to the left. Then hang on."

With my heart practically pounding out of my chest, I did exactly what Sammy told me to do. That's when everything seemed to happen in slow motion. I held my breath as the Packard went skidding, skidding, skidding around, and the whitewall tires screeched in protest while the world went by in a crazy blur. The car finally ended up on the other side of the road, standing still and facing forward, having made a complete 180-degree turn.

Behind us, the black sedan had hit the brakes, and I guessed the driver was probably a little terrified and unsure of what I had up my sleeve.

Which suited me just fine.

"Now step on it, kid!" Sammy hollered. "Give it some gas and make a sharp left."

And let me tell you, he didn't have to tell me twice. I gave the Packard enough octane to shoot us to the moon. My pulse was pounding like a drum solo in Benny Goodman's "Sing, Sing, Sing," and we were suddenly flying faster than Freddy had been tossing me around the dance floor on New Year's Eve. Polly's car was a blur as we passed it, but at least I noticed it was moving again. That meant they were probably both alive, anyway.

Thankfully, there was no one coming our way when I neared the corner. So I clutched, downshifted, and took a left. Then I shoved my gas pedal to the floorboard and shifted into a higher gear. By now we were going so fast the car would have been airborne if it had had wings.

Beside me, Sammy was cheering me on. "Way to go, kid! That's some pretty fancy footwork! Now let's have a repeat performance when you hang a left up here."

And so I did. But just before I turned, I saw the dark car in my rearview mirror. He'd barely even made the first turn, so by now I had a whole block on him.

Even so, I knew he'd be gaining on us just as soon as he could. I figured we'd be taking another left and then a right, back onto the main road to the station. And my hope was to be out of his sight by the time he came around the next turn, so he wouldn't be sure which way I'd gone.

So I pushed the Packard to the best of its ability. Thankfully, there was no traffic on this block, or at the next intersection. I went through it so quickly I half turned and half skidded around the corner. Before I knew it, I was back to the main road again and ready to make the turn.

And that's when things went haywire.

Because, crossing the street right in front of us was an entire grade-school class, most likely on their way to the police station for a field trip. A crossing guard held up a stop sign in the middle of the crosswalk, letting the students go two by two, from one side of the street to the other. And like so many little children, they were taking their sweet time about it all.

Which gave the dark sedan exactly enough time to catch us. The car came up on our rear bumper just as the last child stepped onto the sidewalk. A very tall, thin man in a dark fedora jumped out of the passenger side of the sedan and made a beeline for us. He reached the back door of the Packard while Sammy reached for his gun, just as the crossing guard lowered her sign and joined the children on the sidewalk. I quickly let out the clutch and gave the car some gas. The Packard's front end lunged past the crosswalk, leaving the thin man in the dust. Then I cranked the wheels to the right, ready to make a sharp turn and head to the police station.

And almost collided with Polly Jane, who had suddenly appeared from out of nowhere and almost t-boned me on my left.

Thankfully, she swerved to avoid a collision and I took the lane just as she pulled ahead of me. Barely a moment later, the sedan was back and on my tail. In front of us, Polly was giving her car everything she could, but her old jalopy just didn't have the power.

So I waited for an oncoming car to pass, and then I gassed the Packard and passed Polly like she was simply out for a Sunday drive. I gunned the engine all the way to the police station, whizzing past the few cars on the road and receiving plenty of loud honks and profanities in response.

I went flying into the police station lot and spun into a parking spot using the same bootleg turn that Sammy had just taught me.

Sammy barely waited for the car to come to a standstill before he jumped out, cradling the statue. "Let's get this bird inside and into the right hands. Before it causes us any more trouble."

I bounded out myself, just in time to see Polly slow down and drive by, with Two-Bit Louie hanging out the window and taking pictures of Sammy and me . . . *with* the stolen statue in hand.

I could already picture the headline in the morning's paper. Sure enough there'd be a fictitious piece on the front page about Pete and me having taken that statue in the first place.

Though I had to say, with as many times as Polly and Louie had been arrested in the last few days, I couldn't believe they'd be so brazen as to drive by a police station while taking pictures.

But some people never learn. And only seconds later, getting arrested again was the least of their worries, when the sound of screeching tires and crunching metal filled the air. The dark sedan had rear-ended Polly's car and sent it straight into a telephone pole. With hardly a dent in its front fender, the black car immediately backed up and raced off down the street.

I signaled to Sammy. "Call for an ambulance! I'm going to check on Polly and Louie!"

"I'm on it, kid!" he said before rushing into the building.

I took off running for Polly's car just as fast as my pumps would allow me to go. I was almost there when Two-Bit Louie stumbled out of the car and limped away, not even bothering to look behind him.

When I reached the green car, I could hear Polly moaning. Her arm was twisted at a grotesque angle, and I knew immediately that it was broken. She also had a cut on her forehead that was sending streams of blood dripping down her face.

It took every ounce of strength I had to yank open the crumpled, driver's side door *and* to put aside my animosity for her. "Hold on, Polly. It's going to be all right. I've got an ambulance coming for you."

"Why?" she asked with a look that was somewhere between a sneer and a cringe. "Why would you bother to help me? I've been nothing but rotten to you."

"That's the kind of person I am," I said gently as I ripped up a blouse she had in the back seat, ignoring the bullet hole in the upholstery.

I fashioned a bandage and wrapped it around her head to stop the bleeding. In the background, I could hear a siren, and I noticed a whole pack of policemen running toward us.

"I'm not a murderer or a criminal or any of the things you've made me out to be in your articles," I said as I tied the bandage. "I'm really a very nice person."

"I know," she replied. "But don't think that will stop me from writing articles about you."

"Lies, you mean?"

"Whatever it takes to sell papers."

"I would expect nothing less," I added as an ambulance pulled up. "Because *that's* the kind of person *you* are. Though with that arm, you won't be doing any typing for a long, long time. Instead, you might spend a little time looking in a mirror, and find out if you like what you see there."

She glared at me before I stepped back and let the medics take over. Sammy soon joined me, and we went back into the police station, so I could wash the blood off my hands. That's when I finally had a chance to *thoroughly* examine the statuette. In fact, Sammy and I both looked it over. From top to bottom and side to side and every way imaginable.

But there were no lightning bolts coming from it, and I certainly didn't feel any sort of holy sensation when I held it. For all intents and purposes, it was nothing but a piece of marble that somebody had beautifully carved into a turtledove a couple thousand years ago.

I shook my head. "I keep wondering if this is what Freddy was searching for. But no matter how I look at it, it just doesn't add up to me."

Sammy raised an eyebrow. "Me, either, kid. I don't see Hitler going to a lot of trouble for a carved rock."

"Is it possible we're missing something? Where this turtledove is concerned?"

"I can't imagine what, kid."

And for that matter, neither could I.

Later, we were both quiet as we drove back to the office, all the while keeping an eye out for the black sedan. Much to my amazement, we didn't see it—or the two German goons who'd been driving it. Now I had to wonder if they were leaving us alone because we'd delivered the statuette into the hands of the authorities. But if that were the case, it meant they really had been after the marble dove. And again, the same question popped into my mind: Why would they have wanted it?

After we got back, we took Mildred out for a late lunch, and over soup and sandwiches, I asked her about something I'd read in Freddy's diary. "Is it true that Hitler not only hates the Jews, but he's worked to convince everyone else to hate them, too?"

Mildred took a bite from her sandwich and nodded vigorously. "Oh, yes, dear one. He hates us Jews with a passion. But not everyone in Germany feels the same way. In fact, until Hitler, the Jewish people lived their lives in Germany like other people did. But when the Nazis appointed Joseph Goebbels as the Minister of Propaganda, he took over the newspapers and magazines. And much of what has been written are lies about the Jewish people. Unfortunately, people who read those newspapers started to believe the lies."

Much like some people believed the lies that Polly Jane had written about Pete and me in her articles.

Sammy shook his head. "You know what they say—you can't believe everything you hear. Or read."

"But people do," I said with a sigh.

Sadness washed over Mildred's face. "And sometimes they will believe the most awful things. There is a newspaper in Germany called *Der Stürmer*, and it's a Nazi propaganda newspaper. Once they even made up an article about Jews kidnapping small children before Passover, saying they needed the blood of Christian children to mix with their matzah."

My mouth fell open wide. "That's horrible."

"Yes, yes, it is," Mildred went on, taking a deep breath. "The Nazis also made a movie where a Jewish man kidnapped and raped a Christian woman. It was just a story, something made up and not real at all. But again, so many people believed it and thought it was the truth. Because of all these things, and so many more just like it, people turned a blind eye to the violence and hatred of the Jews. Even when their Jewish friends and neighbors were taken away or killed."

Sammy raised an eyebrow. "After Hitler got enough people on his side, he treated anyone who didn't go along like they were the enemy. Pure and simple. So you either put up and shut up, or *they* would shut you up."

I hardly knew what to say. It was all so shocking and unbelievable. And yet it was happening. Right here in our modern world.

I was still thinking about it all when we returned to the office and I called Nana, asking if she'd be willing to host a dinner party the next night. Though I didn't give her specifics, I did tell her it was to help with our investigation. Her answer was exactly what I knew it would be. She gave me an excited yes, promising to keep it under her hat, just like I'd asked her to do.

To top it off, she also insisted on inviting Mildred.

Mildred, of course, was delighted, and couldn't stop smiling at the prospect.

Then after I got off the phone, the three of us discussed the best way to approach the Professor at dinner the next night. I left the office armed with a game plan, as well as the photographs that Sammy and I had developed from Polly Jane's camera, the ones of the men I believed to be Nazis. While I planned to show the pictures to Stanley, there were two other people I also wanted to show them to.

And I spotted that pair the minute I pulled into our driveway and put the Packard in the garage. In fact, I made a beeline for them—the priest and the nun—who were standing next to the back, side door, in front of a line folks that stretched clear out to the street.

All waiting to get into our house, supposedly to see the image in the armoire.

I glanced down the long line, to make sure the two Nazis hadn't returned. And though I didn't spot a monocled man standing next to a tall, thin man, my glance was enough to elicit exclamations from others waiting to see the armoire.

"Say, isn't that the girl . . .?" a woman asked.

"The one who committed those murders?" another provided.

"Along with her fella?" a third finished.

And before I knew it, several people turned and practically scurried off our property.

Which was fine by me. At least my notoriety was proving to have some benefit.

"Now look what you've done," Sister Gertrude chastised me as she and the priest stomped over, and met me in the driveway before I could come any closer. "You've scared those poor souls away!"

I stopped and met her glare head on, and my eyes bored into hers. "Speaking of scary, I have some definite concerns about some of the people you've been allowing into my grandmother's home."

She smirked. "Well, I'm afraid you're the only one who has a problem with it. Your grandmother is quite pleased that we're here."

"Probably because you're manipulating a very kind-hearted woman," I shot back. "You certainly don't have her best interests in mind, or you wouldn't be playing fast and loose with her safety and security. Let me warn you, I don't take it lightly when someone does that to my grandmother."

"She's a grown woman who can make her own choices," the priest informed me with a scowl.

"Perhaps I might approach this another way," I said, handing them each one of the photographs I'd brought home. "Have you seen these two characters hanging around? Not only did an unscrupulous reporter and photographer get into our house, but they also caught these two suspicious goons with their camera, probably by accident. Do you recognize these men?"

The looks on their faces told me they did. Because their eyes went wide and they stared at each other, both turning instantly pale.

I could almost feel the anxiety rising from them, like steam from a bathtub. For a moment or two, it seemed like they'd forgotten I was there. They didn't even notice when I retrieved the photographs from their hands.

But before I could get their attention and quiz them further, Nana came strolling from the backyard. "Yoo-hoo, darlin'!" she called and waved to me. "So glad you're finally home. That was such a wonderful idea you had, to host a dinner party tomorrow night. We need to get busy and start planning out the whole soirée."

"Yes, we do, Nana," I said, leaning into the hug she gave me. "Why don't you go inside and I'll join you in a minute. I've got something I need to finish up here first."

Then, as though someone had turned on a switch, Father Phillip suddenly flashed a dazzling smile in Nana's direction. "A dinner party, you say? Why, Sister Gertrude and I would be most delighted to attend! I have a bottle of Chianti that I've been saving for ages. I shall bring it with me tomorrow night."

Nana's eyes registered her surprise for barely a second, yet I knew she was far too polite to correct this so-called priest and tell him he wasn't invited. Instead, she did exactly what I knew she would do—she offered him her most gracious smile.

"How splendid, Father," she cooed. "We will be very pleased to have you both at our table tomorrow night."

I squinted my eyes at the priest. "Not so fast. It's time you finally answered a few questions. You still haven't shown us any identification. My secretary called all the Catholic churches in town today, and no one has heard of a Father Phillip. And for that matter," I said, turning to Sister Gertrude, "I'm curious as to what sect of nuns permits the use of lipstick."

I had barely spoken the words when the priest, the nun, and my grandmother all seemed to suck in air at once. To be honest, I wasn't sure which one of them was more shocked. Though I *was* sure about one thing—any way you looked at it, I wasn't going to fare well in whatever exchange followed. In fact, I guessed I was about to "get it" from all sides. Not that I was too worried about myself, since my biggest concern was for Nana.

Who, by the way, was now livid with a capital *L*. "Tra-cy Tru-worth," she uttered in a harsh stage whisper. "What on earth have you done with your manners?"

Obviously the priest and the nun were none too pleased either, but much to my amazement, the priest managed to counter the animosity in his eyes with an even brighter smile.

"Oh, my heavens!" he exclaimed with a forced laugh. "Of course, none of the local churches would know me. I am merely a visitor and certainly not on the staff of any church here. I've only come to Houston for a brief respite. And I ran into Sister Gertrude, and Lupé, I might add, at a church downtown. Lupé pulled me aside and told me of your miracle here at your home. So we came right over to take charge of the situation, since we knew laypeople wouldn't have the expertise."

"And I don't usually wear lipstick," the nun now gushed. "But I suffer horribly from chapped lips, and since I didn't have any ointment with me, a very kind lady loaned me her lipstick. I didn't realize it was so apparent."

Then before I could respond to them, Nana took me firmly by the arm. "I must apologize for my granddaughter's rude behavior. I'm afraid she's been under a great deal of strain lately. But I assure you, Father Phillip and Sister Gertrude, you are both cordially invited to attend our dinner party tomorrow night."

"Why, thank you, kind lady," the priest said, oozing charm.

And the more charm he oozed, the more the alarm bells went off inside my head.

CHAPTER 24

A Furious Nana and a Nervous Fella

Nana nodded goodbye to the priest and the nun as she took my arm, half pulling and half leading me toward our mansion. Her continued silence let me know that we were about to have words, just as soon as she finished counting to ten. Or, as angry as she was at the moment, for all I knew, she might even count to fifty. Nana didn't have a temper, and she certainly knew how to keep her ire in check. But even so, there was no doubt about it—she was practically boiling over with fury.

And so was I. Not at her, of course, but at these supposed "people of the cloth" who had just played on my grandmother's goodness and pulled the wool over her eyes.

Bringing to mind the whole concept of wolves in sheep's clothing.

Only, the wolves standing in our driveway were dressed in a nun's habit and a clerical collar. And while I had no idea what their real motivation was, I had a pretty good idea it was a whole lot less altruistic than they were letting on. Especially since they had no problem putting my beloved grandmother in harm's way by using the image in our armoire as an excuse to let strangers into our home.

But worst of all, they had driven a wedge between Nana and me, something that hurt me to the core, since we had always been so close. I only wished there were some way I could get Nana to see my point of view and kick this pair out once and for all.

Once we reached the back, side door, I saw that Hadley had been standing there, and I guessed he'd probably witnessed the entire conversation. His eyes met mine and he gave me a grim look while he held the door for us. Then he announced that the "viewing line" for the armoire was officially closed for the day.

The people inside moaned but trudged out quietly. As Nana and I moved along, I glanced back to see the priest and the nun now standing just outside the door. Father Phillip crossed his arms while Sister Gertrude had her hands on her hips. Yet both stood there with angry eyes and mouths stretched into thin, severe lines.

If nothing else, I had a good idea that Hadley would politely but firmly see them off our property for the night.

I turned my eyes forward again and spotted Lupé swishing her feather duster across a hall table—a table that didn't have a speck of dust on it.

She had the same look on her face as the nun and the priest. Clearly she had some kind of connection to them, but what that connection was, I could only guess.

On a whim, I smiled at her as we passed by. "Lupé, tell me again, where did you say you were from?"

She looked so startled I thought she was going to fall over. "Argentina . . ."

South America.

I had the urge to ask her if she'd ever encountered a dart blowgun, but with Nana already upset with me, I thought better of it.

Though I did ask, "Did you meet Father Phillip and Sister Gertrude in Argentina?"

Her eyes went wide, and it seemed the cat had suddenly gotten her tongue.

And speaking of cats, Eulalie's cat, Opaline, joined us after we passed the staircase and finally turned into the hallway that led to the study. In the distance, I could see Eulalie working on one of her life-size sculptures in the conservatory.

Once we got there, Nana shut the door behind us and motioned for me to take a seat on the leather sofa. Opaline jumped up beside me, as though she were there to offer moral support. Then Nana leaned on my father's desk and folded her graceful arms in front of her. By now she had a grip on her anger, and her voice was much more rational.

Funny, but it hadn't been that many days ago when *I* had been the one to pull *her* into my father's study to have a "chat." Now the shoe was on the other foot, so to speak.

"Tracy, darlin', I love you dearly," she began, "but I don't know what to do with you. I raised you to be a kind, generous person. Unspoiled by all this wealth. Yet here you are, being terribly rude to a couple of people who only want to bring hope and happiness to others. I don't understand it. It's not like you."

I sighed. "Nana, there is a lot more going on here than you know about. After all, I told you about the reporters who got in."

"But they haven't been back here, have they?"

"Well, no. But there's more . . . I have reason to believe that two of the men in line today were Nazis. You know the German American Bund was operating openly in our country. Until recently."

"I've heard a little about it. Though I can't imagine why a Nazi would ever want to come to our place. Honestly, there is nothing here that might interest that bunch."

"I'm not so sure, Nana. And I'm also not sure if this priest and nun *are* who they say they are. Frankly, I think they're a couple of impostors. Otherwise, I never would've talked to them like I did."

She shook her head. "Darlin', I think you've just been under way too much strain, what with Pete being accused of murder . . . and our country going to war and your parents both leaving . . . I think you're seeing Nazis and criminals and such where there aren't any. I think you just need a good, long rest."

"Nana, I'm fine. But I *am* really worried about *your* safety."

"Tracy, dear, I'm fine, too. And as long as you live under this roof, I will not have you disrespecting a priest or a nun. Do I make myself clear?"

I sighed again, realizing that it was useless to argue with her any further. "Yes, you do."

"Okay, then. Give me a hug."

So I did. And while I held her slender frame, tears pricked at the corners of my eyes. If only I could make her see what was really going on out there. Or for that matter, in here. Our home.

All of a sudden, I felt an overwhelming urge to protect everyone I loved from the horrors of this modern world. Yet how could I do that, when so much of it was beyond my grasp? Pete was going off to war, and Nana refused to recognize the danger that was on our doorstep. The Nazis had already invaded most of Europe. Were they going to invade my home now, too?

Then again, they'd marched into lots and lots of people's homes, with no respect for the rights of others, and no regard for basic human decency.

Nana and I walked out of my father's study, and we had barely stepped into the hallway when she began to talk about our dinner party the next night. While she saw it as an escapade, or an adventure, of sorts, the whole thing was becoming more troubling to me by the second. And to think, the party hadn't even started yet. Who knew what might happen by the time the hour was upon us? Especially since two of the people who concerned me the most—the priest and the nun—had managed to get themselves invited. But why? I could only guess they weren't interested in the food, and most likely had some other, more sinister intentions, the likes of which I could not decipher just yet.

I instantly remembered one of my favorite Katie McClue novels, *Death of a Dinner Guest*, about a dinner party that had gone terribly awry. As Katie soon discovered, the duck à l'orange had become deadly, after someone slipped some strychnine into the sauce. Katie, of course, had survived the entire ordeal, thanks to her aversion to eating waterfowl, something she had developed after being attacked by a deranged, dive-bombing duck as a child. Funny how a childhood trauma essentially saved her from being the victim of a culinary crime later on. And in the end, she easily cracked the case, mostly through the process of elimination, since the only other survivor of the ordeal also turned out to be the murderer.

The mere thought of Katie's close call made me shiver. Now I only hoped that tomorrow night's gathering wasn't going to be murder.

Or end in one.

I gave Nana one more quick hug before we parted ways in the hallway, with the promise of working out the details of our dinner party later. Then she headed to the kitchen and I followed Opaline, who was walking with her huge feather plume of a tail held high, as she led me to the conservatory to see her mistress. Eulalie was just covering a sculpture with a white sheet when we walked in.

"Mind if I take a peek?" I asked her.

"No, dear child, you shall not see it until tomorrow night. For I plan to do the unveiling right after dinner. When the entire party gathers in here for coffee and dessert."

"You're being very mysterious, Eulalie."

"Life is full of mystery."

"You can say that again," I murmured, shaking my head. "That nun and priest out there are a real mystery to me. I'm not sure whose side they're on."

She gave me a sly smile. "Sometimes it's hard to know the villains from the heroes, and the friends from the foes."

"It certainly is," I agreed with a sigh.

Opaline reached up and stretched against my leg, letting me know that she wanted to be held. I obliged by picking her up and cuddling her in my arms. She, in turn, rewarded me with a purr as loud as a motorboat.

"Have you ever created a sculpture of your cat, Eulalie?" I asked.

"Not as of yet, but I plan to. Next year, for her twenty-third birthday."

I gasped and stared at Opaline. "She's that old? My goodness, I didn't realize cats could live so long. She certainly doesn't look her age."

Eulalie smiled at her feline friend. "She's been such a wonderful companion. I don't know what I would do without her."

"I can see why."

Opaline wriggled in my arms, and I put her down very carefully, now that I realized I was handling such a grande dame.

Eulalie gathered up her art supplies and gave me another smile. "If you'll excuse me, dear child, I need to clean up my things and get dressed for the evening meal."

With that, she went to the washroom and I went up to change for dinner. As I climbed the stairs, I couldn't help but wonder about

Eulalie. Her comment about friends and foes truly hit home. But which one was she? On the one hand, I knew Nana considered Eulalie to be an old friend. On the other hand, there was something odd about Eulalie, something I couldn't quite put my finger on.

In fact, there seemed to be a lot of that going around lately. Especially when it came to solving this case, because, no matter how much I racked my brain, the answer seemed to be just beyond my grasp. And by the time I reached my room, I felt a headache starting to throb along my temples. So I swallowed a couple of aspirin tablets with a glass of water before I changed into my favorite black wool dress, one with reverse pin tucks at the shoulders and waistline, and a gored, flared skirt that gave me a nice hourglass figure.

Then I dialed Pete's number from the phone in my room, to invite him to our dinner party the following night. Naturally, I wanted him to be there, but I also figured it would be good to have reinforcements. People who could help me keep an eye on our so-called "guests" and make sure they weren't up to no good. Even though I already knew Sammy and Hadley would be there and on high alert.

My heart swelled when Pete's voice came through the line. "Hearing from you is certainly the bright spot in my day," he murmured. "I'm hoping you had a better day than I did."

"It was eventful. We caught Ethel with the statuette that was stolen from the museum," I told him, hoping to cheer him up.

He let out a low whistle. "Well, knock me over with a feather. I didn't see that coming. Did she murder Freddy and Rosette, too?"

"That's where we ran into a dead end. Sammy and I don't believe she committed the murders. So now we're following another angle," I explained, before I told him all about the dinner party we had planned. And asked him to join us.

"I wouldn't miss it for the world," he said. "As long as I'm with you, Tracy darling, I don't care what we're doing. Even if you're in the middle of trying to solve a murder mystery."

Words to make a girl go all gooey inside.

"So tell me about your day," I said. "It sounds like it wasn't exactly wonderful. What happened?"

"Oh, you know. The usual." He chuckled, though his laughter rang hollow. "Everywhere I went people recognized me, and they all wanted to know how I could go around murdering innocent people. And why I wasn't in jail."

"That's awful, Pete. And mostly thanks to Polly Jane Montgomery."

"The power of the press. If they print it, plenty of people will believe it."

I sighed. "So true. And from what I've read in Freddy's diary, that's exactly what happened in Germany when the Nazis took over. They used the press to malign the Jews, and make everyone think they were horrible people who deserved to die. Next time we get together, remind me to tell you some of the things I've learned."

"Holy Mackerel! Yes, I'd like to know more about it, especially now that I've been through this firsthand. How does tonight sound? After dinner?" he asked, before hesitating a moment or two. "I'd take you out to an elegant restaurant, but I'm not sure it would be much fun. There's something about having total strangers accuse you of being a homicidal maniac that would probably take the romance right out of an evening."

Despite myself, I smiled. "Yup, that could do it. But I'd rather spend time alone with you anyway. So yes, please come over. I can hardly wait to see you again."

"I'm counting down the minutes."

With that, we signed off.

Yet, as we said our goodbyes, I noticed something different in his voice, a deeper tenderness than I'd ever heard from him before. Though, if I had to be perfectly honest, I wondered if the same sentiment might be apparent in my tone, too.

I dropped the receiver back into the cradle, with my heart already aching to be near him again. The few hours between now and the moment when he would land on my doorstep suddenly felt like the span of a million years.

If I had this much trouble waiting only a few hours to see him, how would I ever survive when he went off to war?

Then from out of the blue, sadness hit me like a gigantic wave, and it almost became overwhelming. I dropped onto my bed, tears rolling down my cheeks. I took several deep breaths and fought to get myself under control. After all, this was a time for bravery, and not a time to fall apart. Sweethearts all over the country were saying their goodbyes as their fellas went off to war. I wasn't the only one in the world who had problems, and I knew I had to be strong, hard as it might be. So I wiped my eyes and did my best to put on a smile. I took a few more deep breaths before I went to my vanity and touched up my makeup. Then I headed downstairs for dinner.

I found Nana and Eulalie in the dining room, engaged in a lively conversation as they planned the menu and décor for the following night. I joined them at the table and did my best to add my two cents, especially since I'd been the one to ask Nana to host the dinner party in the first place. And she had been so gracious to agree.

Needless to say, it made me happy to pay her back, in a sense, by breaking the good news to her about Ethel being arrested for stealing the statuette from the museum.

Her eyes went wide and she let out an excited squeal. "That's splendid, darlin'! You're a natural born detective. You've got a lot of your grandfather in you. He was a Pinkerton detective once," she said, turning to Eulalie.

Eulalie tilted her head and barely raised her brows. Her mild response surprised me.

I took a sip of my sweet tea. "But Sammy and I still have to figure out who murdered Freddy and Rosette."

"It's just a matter of time, darlin'," Nana replied with a sparkle in her eyes.

I only hoped she was right.

After dinner, and with all the plans in place for the party, I excused myself from the table. Then I strolled to the back, side hallway, to grab a coat from the armoire before Pete showed up.

The very armoire that people had been lining up to see.

I pulled a wool jacket out and shut the door, and I couldn't help but notice how vivid the image in the burl wood seemed to me tonight. Funny, but since the night when Lupé had spotted it, this was the first time I'd really stopped and taken a good look at the image.

Alone. Face to face.

That's when it hit me—could this be the item that Freddy was after? Somehow, it didn't seem very likely. After all, the armoire had been in our family for years. It hadn't come from a church and it wasn't a famous artifact. And honestly, it wasn't even old enough to be considered an antique, let alone an antiquity.

No, it was nothing more than a lovely piece of furniture with a very well-defined image on the door.

And a rather brilliant, lifelike image at that.

"We could sure use your help right now," I sort of murmured to the face whose eyes met mine with great kindness. "I don't mean to complain when I know you've got more important things on your plate. Things like Hitler and Hirohito and all the horrible stuff they've been doing to people. But if you've got a spare moment or two, my boss and I could really use your help solving this mystery . . . Because Pete Stalwart is a really good man, and I don't want to see him accused of murder. And well, we seem to be finding an awful lot of dead ends in trying to figure this all out. So, if you could give me a sign and let me know if I'm on the right track, I sure would appreciate it . . ."

"That would be swell," I heard a male voice say.

And for a few seconds, I thought the image in the armoire had answered me back. Though to be honest, I wasn't sure if God would talk in modern slang and use words like "swell." He seemed more like a "thee" and a "thou" and a "shalt" kind of guy.

But then I realized that God wasn't the guy talking to me. Instead, I turned to see my own fella standing in the hallway. I hadn't even heard the doorbell ring.

"Pete . . ." I said just under my breath. "When did you get here? And how long have you been standing there?"

"Long enough to think that was a pretty nice prayer."

"I hope you know I don't always talk to our furniture."

He smiled as he came closer. "Oh, I've seen a few pieces around here that are definitely worth talking to."

His words made me laugh.

He reached me and took me into a warm embrace. "Is there some place where we can sit and talk?"

"How about the parlor? I'll have Maddie bring in some sweet tea."

Minutes later, there we were, cuddled up on one of the sofas with the lights down low as we watched the glowing embers of the fire in the fireplace.

Being next to Pete felt like the most natural and magical thing in the world to me. And the happiness that enveloped me soon made me forget all the cares that had been weighing so heavily on my mind.

Pete, on the other hand, seemed surprisingly nervous tonight. His hands were sweating and shaking, and I wondered if he might be more upset than I realized, after so many random strangers had approached him throughout the day, and accused him of being a murderer.

He touched my hair and then pulled back and stared into my eyes. "Tracy, there's something I've been wanting to talk to you about."

"I'm all yours."

"That's a good start," he said with a chuckle. "Because, like I started to say the other night, I know we haven't been going out for a long, long time. But, well . . . these are different times. And with this war going on, none of us knows who will be coming home and who won't. Plenty of guys have already been killed, and they'll never have a chance to finish out their lives and do the things that most guys would get to do."

And that's when the truth about this war really and truly hit home for me, and I realized the courage it would take for him to go off and fight, and for me to stay back and keep the home fires burning, as they say. Then there would be the heartbreak of the two of us being apart, maybe for months and maybe for years. And maybe forever, if he didn't make it back.

All of a sudden, I felt like I couldn't breathe.

Pete paused and took a big gulp of his tea. "And . . . well . . . sometimes a fella doesn't need a lot of dating and going to dances and all that before he knows when something is right, and when someone is the right one for him . . ."

At that very moment, I had a pretty good idea what Pete was driving at, and what he was trying to tell me.

My heart skipped a beat as I waited for him to say the words he'd come here to say.

And he probably would have said those very words.

Had it not been for someone screaming bloody murder.

CHAPTER 25

Swing Heil and Sammy's Subterfuge

Without thinking, Pete and I were on our feet and running into the hallway. There we found Nana, her skin tones terrifyingly pale, as she sat bent over on the bottom step of the staircase. Just then, she seemed so tiny and helpless, like I'd never seen her before.

Maddie stood nearby while Eulalie held Nana's wrist, checking her pulse. And judging from the tears that streamed down Maddie's face, and the way she had a hand pressed to her heaving bosom, I guessed Maddie must have been the one who had screamed.

"Nana!" I reached her side and slipped down beside her on the stairs. "Are you all right? What happened?"

"No need to fuss," she said weakly. "I'm fine. I just got a little dizzy, that's all. Right after dinner. I need to go to my room and lie down, if you would help me, please."

"She fainted," Maddie said through sobs. "I saw her. She fainted dead away!"

"I'll help her upstairs, if you'll call the doctor," I told Maddie. "Nana, can you stand?"

"I'll do one better," Pete said. "Let me carry you upstairs, Mrs. Truworth."

This brought a smile to Nana's face. "Normally I would refuse, young man. I haven't had a man carry me up to my bedroom since my wedding night. Okay, well . . . maybe a time or two after that. Or three, possibly."

All the while, Eulalie ogled Pete in a way that was almost embarrassing. Thankfully, he had his back to her, so he had no idea that she was staring at him—even when he lifted Nana in his arms and carried her up the stairs, as though she were light as a feather.

I followed them up the stairs while Maddie rushed off to telephone the doctor. Once we reached Nana's room, Pete laid her gently on the maroon satin bedspread of her four-poster bed. I grabbed the blanket folded at the foot of the bed and covered her up.

"My, my," she teased. "If I had known I would get this much attention from everyone, I would have fainted long ago."

I sat on the bed beside her. "Nana, what's wrong? When did you start feeling ill?"

She shook her head. "It was the strangest thing. It just came over me right after dinner. Before that, I felt fine. Fantastic, even."

Maddie knocked on the door and stepped inside. "The doctor will be right over. He's on his way now."

Thankfully, Dr. Watkins lived just a few doors down.

"Oh, goodness," Nana groaned. "I surely hope I haven't interrupted his dinner."

"If so, we'll feed him," Maddie said. "Don't you worry about a thing, Mrs. Truworth."

Nana laughed. "I must be dying if you're going to start calling me Mrs. Truworth now. It's always been Caroline to you, Maddie. And yes, please offer Dr. Watkins a beverage and something to eat."

"Most certainly," Maddie told her, fighting back tears. "We'll take care of him right after he takes care of you."

And minutes later, Dr. Watkins—a rounded, middle-aged man—arrived with his well-worn doctor's bag. Pete, ever the gentleman, stepped out of the room while the doctor gave Nana a thorough examination.

"I'm fine," Nana insisted, again and again.

Until she threw up.

And that was enough to send everyone into a flurry of activity. Lupé appeared from out nowhere to clean up the mess while the doctor filled a rather large hypodermic needle and gave Nana a shot. Eulalie arrived to supervise, though her efforts were hardly necessary, since everyone was already fussing over Nana like she was Princess Elizabeth of England. Opaline even jumped up on Nana's bed and sat protectively on the end, swishing her tail.

Finally, Dr. Watkins pronounced that Nana simply had a stomach bug, most likely caused by something she ate. He then pulled me into the hallway and gave me strict orders to check on her throughout the night. Of course, I promised I would, before I walked the doctor down the stairs and directed him to the kitchen, where Maddie had gone to prepare a snack for him.

After that, I went in search of Pete, and found him sitting and waiting patiently in the foyer.

"How is she?" he asked, getting to his feet.

"The doctor thinks she'll be fine, but he wants me to keep an eye on her. So I'm going to stay with Nana in her room tonight. Though it scares me so much to see her like this . . . I doubt I'll get much sleep."

"Probably not," Pete agreed as he slipped his arms around me and planted a kiss on my forehead. "I should probably vamoose, so you can get back to your Florence Nightingale duties."

"I suppose so," I said, wishing we could return to that intimate moment in the parlor.

But I knew that moment had passed. For now, anyway. So instead, I walked him to the door where we enjoyed a long, lingering kiss.

"See you tomorrow night," he whispered, when we finally stepped apart.

"It's a date."

Though I truly wondered if we'd still be having our dinner party, with Nana feeling under the weather.

I held the door for Pete and watched him walk out into the darkness. He blew me a kiss goodbye when he reached the end of the driveway, and then he turned and disappeared down the street. All the while, I couldn't shake the feeling that someone was out there, hidden from view, spying on us. I even shuddered as I closed the door, right before I ran upstairs and changed into my pajamas.

Then I grabbed Freddy's diary from its hiding place and headed back to Nana's room.

"Won't this be fun, darlin'?" she cooed with a feeble smile when I walked in. "It'll be just like our very own slumber party."

"It'll be swell, Nana."

Seconds later, she closed her eyes and fell fast asleep. Which was probably the best medicine of all for her.

I pulled the covers up around her shoulders and turned off her nightstand lamp. Then I climbed into the other side of the bed, turned on my reading lamp, and began to peruse more of Freddy's diary.

One entry read:

The Nazis hated us, the Swing Youth, with a passion. We were defiant of the Nazis, the opposite of the Hitler Youth, with their short hair and uniforms, and their blind devotion to Hitler, a demagogue. We wore our hair longer, and we dressed differently from everyone else. We lived for swing music and dancing, and instead of devoting our time to rallies and being on the lookout for people to turn in to the Gestapo, we went out dancing every night, and we welcomed Jews and half-Jews into our group. Instead of saying "Sieg Heil!" we said "Swing Heil!" which infuriated the Nazis even more. Plus we spoke English more than we spoke German, since we loved English and American music.

Then hundreds of us were arrested and everything changed. Our freedom was gone. And while I watched many of my friends, the leaders of our group, being taken away to concentration camps, where I knew they'd be beaten and tortured and starved, I was singled out for a special purpose. The Nazis, of course, knew who my father was, and they knew what my studies had been. And with my command of the English language, they knew I'd be perfect for their plan. I could be placed in America as a graduate student of archaeology and no one would be the wiser. I could say I had escaped from Germany, and the Americans, with their good hearts, would believe me and take me in. Of course, I didn't wish to cooperate with the Nazis, but what choice did I have? And when I arrived here, I knew I was being watched from the shadows, and a bad report back to Germany would mean the death of my family.

I put the book down for a moment, tears forming at the corners of my eyes. The idea of being arrested simply because a person went out swing dancing or listened to swing music shocked me to the core.

If Pete and I had lived in Germany, we would have been arrested long ago.

I set the book on my nightstand, turned off the lamp, and tried to go to sleep. But I hardly slept a wink. Mostly because I couldn't stop worrying about Nana. And I couldn't stop missing Pete. And I couldn't quit thinking about what Freddy had gone through. Sadly, I also had a pretty good idea what had become of his friends and family. The thought of it nearly made me sick to my stomach.

When I finally did fall asleep, Nazi soldiers marched through my nightmares, and swastikas loomed large. By the time the morning sun peeked through the curtains, my headache had returned with a vengeance. In fact, my headache could have been featured in full-length horror movie of its own, since it had practically become a living, breathing creature in and of itself.

Nana, on the other hand, jumped out of bed with the vim and vigor of a woman half her age. Amazingly, there was little or no sign that she'd even been sick the night before.

"You look terrible, darlin'," she clucked softly when she saw me. "Why don't we put you back to bed with some aspirin? I think we'll skip church this morning."

I moaned. "Aspirin sounds good. And I do think I'll stay in bed for a while. But I'm supposed to meet Sammy after lunch today. It's important that I make it."

Nana looked at me like I had probably looked at her the night before—with concern etched across her features. Funny, but it had been less than twelve hours since *I'd* been the nurse and *she'd* been the patient, so to speak. Now our roles were completely reversed.

She brought me some aspirin and a glass of water. "Take three," she said softly. "It's a better way to treat a bad headache."

I managed to nod before I swallowed the tablets and the entire glass of water.

And that was the last I could remember. I was barely aware of her pulling the covers up over me, and then I was off to dreamland for hours. I felt better when I woke up, and after I got some tea, toast, and broth inside of me.

But my headache was threatening again by the time I donned my favorite navy suit and matching hat. I'd been told the skirt made my gams look great, but today I couldn't have cared less whether the seams in my stockings were straight or how good my legs looked. Instead, I just tried to focus on driving the Packard and being on time to meet Sammy. Though if nothing else, at least Nana had agreed to keep the house closed from strangers coming in to see our armoire today.

Naturally, that didn't mean it wouldn't be up for discussion later.

And "later" was exactly when I intended to deal with it as I gave the Packard some gas and drove out of River Oaks. By the time I parked the car at the curb behind Sammy's sedan, about a block away from Stanley's boardinghouse, my headache was pounding in time to the Glenn Miller song on the radio.

Sammy got out of his car and raised an eyebrow when he saw me. "You don't look so hot, kid."

I slid out of the Packard and took a deep breath. "So I've been told. And as near as I can tell, it seems to be going around. Nana was violently ill last night, and now here I am. With a horrible headache."

"Hmmm . . . That does sound a little fishy. Let's get this wrapped up and over with so you can get back home. Think you'll still be up for our little dinner party tonight?"

The thought of food made me feel as sick as Nana had been the night before.

"Sure, I'm up for it," I lied.

Given the way my boss rolled his eyes, I guessed my fib must have been pretty feeble.

"Uh-huh . . ." he murmured. "Don't sweat it, kid. I can pull off an inconspicuous interview of our professor pal if you can't make it."

"Not on your life. I wouldn't miss it for the world," I said with about as much conviction as I could muster. "Besides, you probably haven't heard the latest. The nun and the priest are coming, too."

Now Sammy raised both eyebrows. "You don't say. So what's the scoop?"

"They very skillfully managed to get themselves invited," I told him as we walked toward the boardinghouse.

Sammy shook his head. "Why doesn't that surprise me? Let me guess, they played up to your grandmother's goodness. They must have something up their sleeves, if they went to so much work to wrangle an invitation."

We paused and partially hid behind a huge oak tree. "My thoughts exactly."

"Well, let's hope that sore head of yours gets better. Because it sounds like we're gonna need you tonight, kid."

Didn't I know it. If only I'd thought to bring some aspirin with me, because I was due for another dose. Especially since my headache was getting worse by the second.

Sammy peered around the tree. "I've already given the joint the once-over, kid. I'll go chat up the landlady while you wait at the front door. I'll pretend I'm looking for a place to stay, and when she takes me off to see a room, you make your move. Got it?"

"Got it."

With that, Sammy jumped out from behind the tree and strolled up the walk. He paused for barely a moment at the front door, standing as tall as he could while he pulled his fedora down over his forehead. Then he entered the house, without removing his hat, as was customary for a man upon entering a building. Of course, I knew this was only because he wanted to pull off his Bogart impersonation.

I scooted closer to the framed-glass front door to catch Sammy's act. I knew I was taking a risk that Mrs. Chapman might spot me, but I couldn't resist seeing my boss in action.

Though this time it didn't take much action on his part, since Mrs. Chapman started to gush the second he walked in. "Oh my, oh my. You're . . . you're . . ."

". . . in town for a short time and looking for a room to rent," Sammy said with a grin as he finished her sentence for her, though probably not in the way she'd intended. "But it's a secret. You can keep a secret, right, dollface?"

To which Mrs. Chapman gasped, and then stammered and stuttered to the point where she could no longer connect syllables to form actual words.

"I'd like something on the ground floor, if you've got it," Sammy went on.

Mrs. Chapman blushed to her roots and flashed him a radiant smile. "Right this way. I've got something perfect at the end of the hall. Right next to my room."

As they left, I caught the tail end of the conversation, when Sammy said, "Next door to your room, you say? Well, that's just an added bonus."

Once they were out of sight, I wasted no time before running inside and up the stairs. I knocked on Stanley's door and prayed he would be home. After all, when it came to getting the information we needed to question Professor Longfellow tonight, Stanley was our best hope.

CHAPTER 26

Headaches and Freemasons

My heart was pounding along with my head as I stood before Stanley's door, hoping and praying he was home. Thankfully, I didn't have to wait long. He answered mere seconds after I'd knocked. Today he was dressed in nice slacks and what appeared to be a new sweater.

"Tracy!" he said with a wide smile. "What are you doing here? And how on earth did you get past old Lady Chapman?"

"Guess I was just lucky," I told him. "Would you mind if I came in and asked you a few questions?"

"Umm, well . . . okay," he hemmed and hawed before he opened the door and let me in. "I was just about to go out." And then he blushed, making me think he might be on his way out to visit a girl.

"Going anywhere special?" I asked with a smile. "Or should I say, seeing anyone special?"

"Well . . . yes. I think you've met her. Dot?"

I stepped inside the apartment and shut the door behind me. "The girl who was dancing with Freddy on New Year's Eve?"

"Uh-huh. That's her. I was studying at the library the other day when she came up to me. We started chatting and I walked her out, since I didn't want us to get kicked out of the library for being too loud. So we went to the drugstore and had an ice-cream soda."

I fought the urge to give him a hug. "That's swell, Stanley! I hope the two of you get along fantastically."

"I hope so, too."

"Then I promise I won't take up too much of your time. So you can be on your way."

"It's okay. I've got a few minutes. But say, you look a little under the weather. Are you feeling all right?"

I shook my head. "No, I'm not. I've got a horrendous headache."

His mouth dropped wide open. "Freddy had a headache the night he died. A bad one."

"You wouldn't happen to have some aspirin, would you?"

Stanley stepped over to a small desk and pulled the top center drawer open. He reached for something, but then he stopped and his face fell.

He slammed the drawer shut and turned back to me. "Freddy took some aspirin that night, too. I told him to take three of them."

"My grandmother told me the same thing. To take three. It's the best way to treat a headache."

Stanley shook his head. "I'm not giving you any aspirin. Not after, well . . ." He bit his lip.

"Stanley, I'm not going to die, though it sure feels like it at the moment."

"I'm sorry, but the answer is still no."

"Okay, then." I sighed, trying to get my eyes to focus as I pulled the photo of the man with the monocle and his tall, thin partner from my purse. "Maybe you could tell me if you recognize these men."

Shock registered in his eyes when I passed him the picture, letting me know that he *had* seen the pair before. Even so, he completely clammed up, as Sammy would say.

"Did you ever see Freddy with these two?" I asked gently.

He frowned but stayed silent.

"It's okay, Stanley. Freddy is gone."

"I'd never rat out a friend."

"You're not, Stanley. In fact, if you help us find Freddy's killer, you're actually *helping* your friend, by bringing his murderer to justice. Now, if you would, please tell me—did you ever see Freddy with these two men?"

This time he nodded his head.

"Were they speaking German?"

He nodded again.

"Did the men see Freddy on a regular basis?"

Once more he nodded in silence. I could tell by the way he fidgeted with his hands that I was making him more uncomfortable by the second. Not only did I hate putting him through this, but I also feared he might ask me to leave if I kept on pressing him.

So I switched subjects. "Stanley, have you ever seen a South American blowgun in any of Dr. Longfellow's things?"

"Now you want me to talk about Dr. Longfellow? Why, he's one of the best professors around. I'm lucky to have him as my faculty adviser. And he's a brilliant teacher. I would never say anything bad about him."

"Even if he killed Freddy?"

Sparks flared in Stanley's eyes. "Professor Longfellow did not kill Freddy."

"So he doesn't own a dart blowgun, then?"

Stanley went silent once more.

If only I could have said the same about my headache. By now it was pounding so loud that I could barely hear Stanley speak. When he did speak, that was.

"Tracy . . . You really don't look so good," he said, with his voice sounding like it was coming from somewhere far, far away.

Stars danced before my eyes, and I was pretty sure I was wobbling just a little bit.

Stanley took my arm. "Maybe you should sit down."

I waved him off. "No thanks. I'd rather stand. But judging from your reaction, I gather Dr. Longfellow does own a blowgun."

He sighed and threw his hands up. "Of course he does! Lots of archaeology professors own them. If they've ever spent any time out in the field, and most of them have, they've gotten artifacts from South America. It's not uncommon. That still doesn't mean he murdered Freddy."

"I know. And I'm sorry to upset you by insinuating anything against your mentor. I have just one more question and then I'll get out of your hair."

"Another question?" he moaned. "All right. Fine."

"Someone mentioned something to me about a veil, that it might be something Freddy was searching for. Do you know anything about a veil? From an archaeologist's perspective?"

Stanley crinkled his nose. "Well, do you mean v-e-i-l or v-a-l-e? V-a-l-e can be a valley. Or vale is Latin for 'farewell.' Vale is also a type of language. And, Vale could be short for Valentina, a common Italian name for a girl. But personally, if I were to guess, and if I were looking for artifacts or anything hidden, I would think about the Galveston Valley of the Scottish Rite."

"The Galveston Valley of the what?"

Stanley smiled. "Of the Scottish Rite. They're Freemasons."

"Freemasons . . . ?"

And that was when the room began to spin. Just when I thought things couldn't get any more complicated, we now had the Freemasons joining the party. And by party, I meant this case that Sammy and I were working on. One that was making me so sick I wondered if I'd be throwing up soon, just like Nana had been the night before.

I put one hand over my mouth and ran to grab Stanley's trash can from beside his desk.

His eyes immediately went wide. "I've got something about the Galveston Valley of the Scottish Rite in a book in my bedroom. Let me run and get it for you."

As he did, I reached for the trash can. And then, out of sheer desperation, I did something else. Something I wasn't proud of. Instead of grabbing the can, I pulled the center drawer of his desk open, the very one that Stanley had opened when he'd almost gotten me some aspirin. In a flash, I snatched a little aspirin tin from the drawer, dropped it in my pocket, and slid the drawer shut again.

I could hardly believe my headache had driven me to petty theft, but there I was, committing a crime. Minor though it may be. And I immediately had the guilt to go with it. Though I did fully intend to return the tin to Stanley later on, filled with replacement aspirin tablets, I thought of a way I could repay him even sooner. Because, if there was one thing a strapped-for-cash graduate student would appreciate, it was a hot meal. And a fancy, full-course dinner would probably be a dream come true.

"My grandmother is hosting a little dinner party tonight," I said as he walked back in, carrying a book. "Would you care to join us? The Professor will be there. And you could invite Dot, if you like."

A huge smile crossed his face and his eyes went wide. "Are you serious? That would be terrific! I'm sure Dot would love to come. It'll almost be like a dinner date. She's mentioned you a few times, and I bet she would love to see you."

I leaned over his trash can again, trying to breathe through the nausea from the headache. "Wonderful!" I said as I gave him our address.

He repeated it once, which apparently was all it took for him to commit it to memory.

Then he opened the book he'd brought in and held it up for me to see. "Here, this is what I was talking about. Here's the Scottish Rite Cathedral, built in 1929."

The picture before me was of a stunning, art-deco type building in Galveston. In fact, I was pretty sure I'd even seen it once or twice before, when I'd been on the island not far from Houston.

"They have a huge library and an Egyptian room," he said, his eyes dancing with excitement. "If someone told me about some 'vale,' or 'valley' around here, this would be the first place I'd look. And now that I think about it, I'm pretty sure Freddy mentioned something about wanting to go down there."

"He did?"

"Uh-huh. It's all coming back to me. He mentioned something about a rumor that an ancient Egyptian artifact was buried under the cornerstone. One that was supposed to have supernatural powers. You can borrow this book if you like. Just bring it back when you're finished with it."

"Thanks," I said, taking the book from him. "Now I'd better run. We'll see you tonight."

"I can hardly wait to tell Dot," he gushed.

Then he walked me down the stairs, making sure the coast was clear so I didn't run into Mrs. Chapman. He stuck with me until we'd left the building, and then he headed in the direction of Dot's boardinghouse while I went the other way, to the Packard.

When I got to the car, I leaned against the door, waiting for my boss to break away from Mrs. Chapman's attentions. And while I knew I was supposed to be thinking about our case, the only thing on my mind at the moment was the aspirin I had stolen. I pulled the tin from my pocket, all ready to take some tablets so I could get some relief, until I realized I was missing one key ingredient—a glass of water. And as desperate as I was to quiet my headache, I simply couldn't swallow aspirin without something to drink.

That's when it dawned on me—Freddy probably had the same problem. The night he had died, he probably needed some water to take the aspirin he had downed.

Aspirins and water. Aspirins and water. Freddy must have gotten some water from somewhere on the night of his death.

I glanced down at the aspirin tin and noticed the label was written in German. This container must have been Freddy's, one he'd brought over from Germany with him. Or maybe he'd gotten it from those two German goons, the men I believed were keeping track of him.

Which led me to wonder about those two men. If they were supposed to be watching Freddy and making sure he did his job, then why on earth had they come to Nana's house after Freddy had been killed?

I shook my head. If there was one common denominator in this whole case, it was that none of the pieces of the puzzle fit together. No matter how I arranged them and rearranged them. And my head was pounding much too hard for me to make sense of anything.

At long last, Sammy showed up. Apparently Mrs. Chapman had kicked him out when she finally realized he wasn't Humphrey Bogart.

"Happens every time, kid," he said with a chuckle. "One minute they love me, and the next minute they want me outta there. Women can be so fickle."

I laughed, before I quickly relayed all that I'd learned from talking to Stanley. Then I showed him the aspirin tin and opened it. Thankfully, there were three aspirins inside, identical to the pills my grandmother had given me this morning.

"Any ideas where I might get a glass of water?" I moaned. "So I can take these? Somehow I don't think Mrs. Chapman would be happy to help me out if I went back to the boardinghouse."

"You're in luck, kid. I've got a flask of water in my car, and you're welcome to it."

Needless to say, I took him up on his offer right away. Seconds later, I had those aspirin down. Now I wondered how much time would pass before I felt better.

"This theory about the Freemasons has got me curious," Sammy said. "The Gestapo put a halt to the Freemasons in Germany. They confiscated their libraries and stole anything valuable."

"So maybe they're after Masonic treasure over here, too?"

Sammy shook his head. "And maybe the Masons killed Freddy. And Rosette. Could be, kid. But it just doesn't have the right ring to it."

"I know what you mean."

"Let's put the screws to Dr. Longfellow tonight and see what happens. If that doesn't pan out, we'll take a look at the Freemasons tomorrow."

"Sounds like a plan to me."

"Now, go home and get some rest," he commanded. "So you'll be in tip-top shape for tonight."

Which was exactly what I intended to do.

Right after I made a little detour.

Because there was something Freddy had written in his diary that was nagging at my aching brain. While Stanley seemed to think Freddy was after an Egyptian artifact, Freddy's diary had referred to *Christian* artifacts. More specifically, the *Arma Christi*. The Weapons of Christ. And sure, Stanley was much more educated in the field of archaeology than I would ever be, and his theory about the Freemasons and an ancient Egyptian item buried under a cornerstone could certainly hold water. But my feminine intuition was trying to tell me something, and it was speaking to me even louder than the headache still pounding inside my skull.

I instantly thought of one of my favorite Katie McClue novels, *The Case of the Clearly Confusing, Clever Clues*. It was probably Katie's most difficult case, where she was hot on the trail of a medieval emerald ring. Throughout the book, she'd managed to uncover a whole slew of clues that clearly pointed her in one direction. To top it off, everyone around her agreed it was the way she should go, and while a lesser detective might have listened to that logic, Katie's famous feminine intuition told her to think again. And because she listened to her feminine intuition, she reinterpreted the clues and found a different route. One that led her straight to the ancient artifact.

So, on my way home, I decided to take a different route, too. And I popped into one of the oldest churches in town, an Episcopal Church, Christ Church Cathedral.

I headed straight for the Very Reverend's office, only to have his secretary tell me he was out for the moment and would return shortly. So I decided to wait in the nave, where I genuflected and slid into a pew. Then I closed my eyes and tried to relax my headache away. All the while, I said a prayer for Nana and Pete, and all the men going off to fight in this horrible war. And I prayed for the people who were under the rule of the Axis powers. I also asked for help in finding the answers to this case.

Apparently I'd been talking out loud, for someone behind me suddenly cleared his throat. That's when I realized I wasn't alone. I turned and saw an elderly gentleman, a bald man with a rather pronounced hump. A priest. Sitting a couple of rows back.

He leaned forward in his pew and offered me a kindly smile. "You sound rather troubled, my child."

I returned his smile. "I didn't see you sitting there."

"I like to sit here in the afternoons after the morning church services. It's quiet and peaceful, and I can be alone with my thoughts. I'm retired, you understand. And the church has been rather kind in providing me food and lodging."

"That's very nice."

"It is. Now tell me, what is it you're searching for, my child?"

Funny, but I wished I could have posed that very question to Freddy. If only I knew *what* he'd been searching for, then it would have made this case a whole lot less complicated. Now, oddly enough, it seemed I had stepped into Freddy's shoes and *I* was the one doing the searching. And my search hadn't exactly been successful, considering I'd been going in circles, because, unlike Freddy, I couldn't even name the item I was after.

Now I wondered if the priest behind me might just be able to give me some clues, given his age.

Still, I wasn't quite sure how to broach the subject. "I have an odd question," I told him.

He chuckled. "My child, I am a very old man. In my time, I think I've heard almost every question imaginable. I'm sure I shall hardly find yours to be all that odd. So please, ask away."

"Well . . . I was wondering if you might know about objects of religious significance. Things like the Ark of the Covenant, or the Holy Grail."

"I'm quite familiar with the Ark of the Covenant, but I'm afraid the Holy Grail is an Arthurian legend, and probably more myth than reality."

"Do you know anything about a veil, by chance? Something that is believed to have some kind of supernatural power?"

He tilted his head. "Well, I do know of one veil that might fit your description."

I felt my eyes go wide. "You do?"

"Why, yes, my child. Veronica's Veil."

"I'm afraid I've never heard of it."

He smiled again. "Many people haven't. And, like the Holy Grail, the veil is probably more myth than reality. But plenty of people do believe in its existence. Last I knew, the veil was thought to be in Europe somewhere, most likely locked away in a Vatican vault. Though again, that is certainly questionable."

"What is the veil?"

"When Christ was forced to carry his cross to Calvary Hill, where he was crucified, it is said that a woman named Veronica was terribly distraught when she saw his suffering. And when he fell, she offered her veil so he could wipe the sweat and blood from his face. He gave it back to her, and later, when she examined it, she saw the perfect image of Christ in the cloth."

"Ooooh . . ." was all I could say.

"And according to legend, much like the Holy Grail, the veil is believed to have great healing powers. And it is said that anyone who touches the veil will be healed from any illness or injury."

"Sounds like a great thing to keep in your first aid kit."

He nodded with a smile. "Which is why the veil, if it is real, has always been a highly coveted item."

"I could see that. But if the veil exists, wouldn't a hospital own it? A place that could use it to make people well?"

He shook his head. "These situations are never so simple as they sound. Of course, there are those who think such items should be available to heal the masses. But if it were, that would most certainly make the veil vulnerable to theft by those who would want to own it for their own selfish purposes."

I crinkled my eyebrows. "So is there any reason the military might want it?"

He rubbed his chin. "Well . . . I suppose so. If the veil were real and it did have healing powers, it could be used to heal wounded soldiers."

"And they could keep on fighting," I sort of muttered.

"Perhaps. But by the same token, if it were to fall into the wrong hands, it could be devastating."

I looked straight into his rheumy eyes. "What do you think about this veil, Father? If it is real, do you think it could have healing powers?"

To which the priest nodded toward the altar. Remember the woman in the Bible who touched the robe of Jesus so she would be healed? I believe you'll find the answer to your question in the words of Luke 8:48 of the King James Bible. 'And he said unto her, Daughter, be of good comfort: thy faith hath made thee whole; go in peace.'"

By the time I left the church, my headache was gone. Dark clouds formed on the horizon as I drove back to River Oaks, though I hardly noticed, considering my mind had been doing a mental jigsaw puzzle the entire way home. I only had one major question left unanswered, and I knew exactly who could answer that question for me—Mildred.

So I called her the minute I got upstairs to my bedroom. She happily provided me with the information that I needed as she told me about life in Germany before she had escaped.

I thanked her before we said our goodbyes and signed off. And as I dropped the receiver into its cradle, I couldn't decide whether to be happy or terrified. Because I had a pretty good idea who had killed Freddy and Rosette.

And why.

CHAPTER 27

Dinner and Deception

A thunderstorm was in full swing by the time I finished getting ready for the dinner party, having donned a long black dinner dress trimmed with a row of gold sequins down the neckline. It was one of my favorite dresses, but tonight I chose to wear it mostly because it had side pockets. They weren't quite large enough for me to carry a gun, but they were big enough for me to hold a few items that I was going to need later in the evening.

I had just started to apply my red lipstick when a huge bolt of lightning flashed and sizzled outside my window, followed by an explosion of thunder, making it sound like we were in the middle of a war zone. Yet oddly enough, from what I'd learned in the last week, the idea that we here on the homefront were also in a war zone didn't seem all that far-fetched.

It was hard to believe it had been less than a week since Pete and I had gone dancing at the museum gala. Yet with all that we'd been through, it felt more like a month had passed. And now I hoped and prayed that, after tonight, we could put all the drama and danger behind us.

Provided, of course, that everything went according to my very loosely organized plan—a thought that made my stomach turn somersaults, since, in my experience, things rarely went according to plan.

I only wished I could have told Sammy what I'd cooked up. After all, I was still just an Apprentice P.I., and my boss was the one with years and years of experience. But since tonight's storm was so much more severe than most, I didn't dare risk using the telephone. Meaning, I didn't want to end up *being* cooked. Electrocution by phone was rare enough, but Ben Franklin and his kite-flying experiments had more than proven it was possible. Lightning was just as happy to travel down a telephone wire and into a home as it was to travel down a kite string and into a jar.

And the storm outside was doing its level best to come into our home tonight. I was halfway down our staircase when the loudest thunder I'd ever heard in my life suddenly rocked our mansion. It nearly sent me tumbling down the rest of the stairs, but thankfully I was able to grab on to the staircase railing and hold on for dear life.

That's when I realized just how rattled I really was. Not only was the storm putting me on edge, but the plans I had for later in the evening—after everyone had gathered in the conservatory for coffee and dessert—were making me extra jittery.

Of course, our guests would only be told that we were gathering there for the purpose of unveiling Eulalie's newest work of art.

But that wasn't the only thing that would be unveiled.

No, much like Katie McClue had once gathered her entire cast of suspects in the drawing room to reveal the identity of the murderer in *The Old-Fashioned Drawing Room Mystery*, I planned to unveil the murderer in this very convoluted case.

Now I only wished I had Katie's years of experience when it came to dealing with such situations.

Especially when the simple act of descending the stairs seemed to be a challenge tonight. I kept a tight hold of the stair railing all the way down, while the thunder outside kept up a constant racket. Once I made it to the marble tiles of the main floor, I headed straight for the dining room, where I found Nana putting the final touches to the table. For a moment or two, as I glanced around, I stood frozen in place, almost overwhelmed by the dazzling décor. I had to say, Nana had turned the room into a magical place. Bouquets of red roses and evergreen sprigs caught my eye from the center of the table and on stands in the corners, while the gold-rimmed white bone china and Fostoria crystal glasses gleamed with elegance. I also noticed two candelabras had been placed on either end of the table. Though the crystal chandelier gave off plenty of light, with a thunderstorm of this magnitude, we had to be prepared in case the lights went out.

Nana rushed over to give me a hug. "I'm so happy to see that you're feeling better, darlin'."

"Thanks, Nana. I love what you've done with the place. And I'm so relieved that you're feeling better, too. You really had me worried last night. I'm not sure what made us so sick, but one thing I do know—I'd be absolutely lost if anything ever happened to you."

She chuckled. "I feel the same way, too, darlin'. It scared me to death to see you as white as a sheet, and in such pain. I know you've had a lot on your shoulders these days, and while I don't completely understand why you've been so worried about all those people coming in to see our armoire, it's enough for me to know that it *does* worry you. So I've decided to put a halt to all that."

I gave her my brightest smile. "I can't even begin to tell you how happy I am to hear that."

She smiled back. "So no more worrying, right?"

That's when I gulped. "I umm . . . I sure hope not . . ." I sort of stammered. After all, I was about to reveal a murderer tonight, in our very own conservatory. And from my experience, murderers didn't exactly like it when you pointed out to the world that they'd committed a horrible crime and were about to go to jail.

But that was a detail I didn't want to reveal to my grandmother at the moment.

Thankfully, I was saved by the bell—the doorbell, that is. My boss was the first to arrive, and I quickly pulled him aside to give him the scoop and tell him how I'd managed to make the pieces of the puzzle fit. Then I gave him the specifics about my plan for the evening.

He grinned from ear to ear. "I knew you had it in you, kid. You're a natural at this. Once we get to the entertainment portion of the evening, I'll let you take the reins and I'll wait for your signal. I've got my piece, just in case." He patted his pocket.

"Good," I said with a nod. "Hadley said he'd be happy to pitch in, too, if we need him. He'll be helping Lupé serve in the conservatory. And he'll keep it all under his hat."

Sammy glanced from side to side, as though someone might be watching us. "Good plan. No need to scare your grandmother."

With those words, he headed for the parlor.

Just in time for me to answer the doorbell. I opened it to find a handsome face smiling down into mine.

It was Pete.

I went warm all over.

"Hello, beautiful," he murmured before planting a kiss firmly on my lips. "Fancy meeting you in a swell joint like this."

I laughed and let him in. "Pete, I need to talk to you for a minute before everyone gets here."

"I need to talk to you, too. But I'll probably have to wait until everyone *has gone.*"

"I'll be looking forward to it," I said as I took his hand and led him to my father's study.

Then I took one of my father's handguns from the locked cabinet and passed it to him. "Pete, I can't tell you exactly what's going on tonight, but it has to do with this case and . . ."

Before I could finish, he raised his eyebrows and nodded. "No need to say more. I'm happy to lend a hand if you and Sammy need me." He checked to see that the gun was loaded. "But I have this funny feeling you're about to unmask the person who killed Freddy and Rosette. And we might be holding that person until the police arrive."

"Yup. That's about the size of it."

"And you don't have room for a gun in that stunning dress," he said with a smile.

I shook my head. "Nope. I'm afraid not."

"I'll be ready when you need me. Are you nervous?"

"A little," I lied, as thunder boomed outside and the lights flickered. "Okay, *a lot.*"

"You'll be wonderful, Tracy. And after this, we won't have a murder accusation hanging over us. I never thought I'd have a girl who is a detective. I'll be bragging about you to all the other fellas in my unit. When I enlist."

Tears suddenly pricked at my eyes. "I'll be bragging about you, too, Pete."

He folded me into his arms. "I love you, Tracy," he murmured into my hair.

"I love you back," I whispered into his ear.

Only seconds before the doorbell rang. Again and again and again. Everyone arrived amidst lightning flashes and booming thunder that constantly interrupted the flow of the conversation. After cocktails and hors d'oeuvres in the parlor, the entire group moved to the dining room, where we were seated at our huge table. Eulalie, the Professor, Pete, Nana, Dot, Stanley, Father Phillip, Sister Gertrude, Mildred, Sammy, and me. All dressed in our evening finery. Sammy sported his white dinner jacket with the shawl collar, and Dr. Longfellow and Pete were both decked out in their tuxes. Nana and Dot had chosen lace dresses for the evening, while Eulalie had donned an apple-green satin gown. Mildred wore an elegant garnet-colored dinner dress, along with her best ruby jewelry. Only the priest and the nun were the exception, and they sat stiffly in the same outfits they'd worn the day before.

At my request, and since Violet had the night off, Maddie had asked Lupé to serve. And apparently Lupé was taking her job quite seriously, considering she rarely left the room at all. Though of course, any absence on her part would have made it tough for her to keep track of the conversation, and judging from her facial expressions, she wasn't even trying to conceal her attempts at eavesdropping.

Though to be honest, it wasn't a good night for eavesdropping, considering she served the soup course with plenty of thunder booming in the background. Yet despite the storm, everyone quickly settled into the conversation, with the Professor taking the lead.

"Ah, yes, I remember my first expedition to Egypt," he said with stars in his eyes. "Oh, the joy of crawling through tombs and finding one's first burial chamber. There's nothing quite so exhilarating. I certainly do enjoy a good pyramid. I went from pyramids in Egypt to pyramids in Peru. Oh, how I miss those days of great exploration."

I offered him my brightest smile. "Professor, did you perhaps come across any ancient dart blowguns? And any poisonous frogs?"

He laughed and waved his hands. "Well, most certainly! I brought back an ancient blowgun and a set of darts from the Amazon. And I have observed many a frog. You can find them in Central and South America, and they really are most colorful."

From across the table, Stanley shot me an angry look.

But I persisted anyway. "Did Freddy ever go with you on any of those adventures?"

The Professor sighed. "Alas, no, he did not. Most of his archaeological field work was in Europe."

"That would make sense, considering the kid was born and raised in Germany," Sammy interjected so casually he might have been talking about the weather. "I understand he escaped Hitler's clutches and showed up on our shores."

The Professor stared into his wine glass. "That was how I understood it as well. At first."

"Poor Freddy," Dot added. "No wonder he always looked so sad."

"Anyone would be sad, if they were still under the thumb of the Nazis," Sammy commented.

"Understandably so," the Professor intoned. "And I do not believe that Frederick had ever truly escaped their grasp."

Nana put a hand to her chest and Dot gasped. The priest and the nun shared a knowing look, while Eulalie had a slight smile on her face.

Stanley's eyes met his mentor's. "You knew?"

Agitation rose in the Professor's voice. "Well, I suspected as much, of course. Most recently, anyway. How could I not? It's very rare for someone to escape Germany and have the kind of funds that Freddy had, with plenty to pay for his schooling and his work. Naturally I began to question his story and wondered if the Nazis might have sent him here for some reason. But I certainly did not have any proof. If I had, I would have had no choice but to contact the authorities."

Sammy took a sip of his wine. "Gotta be pretty tough to rat out your prize pupil."

Stanley continued to stare at the Professor, as though he were actually seeing him for the first time. "You mean, you wouldn't have tried to help Freddy? You would have just turned him in? How could you, when you were a father figure to him?"

Instead of answering, the Professor turned to my boss and, if looks could kill, Sammy would have been a goner. "You seem to know an awful lot about the situation," the Professor seethed.

Sammy shrugged. "You learn things when you investigate a homicide."

Then before anyone could say another word, a gigantic boom of thunder echoed all around us, causing the entire mansion to rattle. Seconds later, the lights flickered and went out. In response, all the women in the room, including me, let out a little cry. All except for Lupé, who suddenly seemed to be absent. Thankfully, the candelabras had been lit, and while they did their job in providing some light, it wasn't the same as the bright glow of the chandelier.

Much to my amazement, I could feel my heart thumping. From across the table, Pete looked into my eyes. And as near as I could tell, he was trying to make sure that I was all right. Funny, but I hadn't even had time to process the fact that he'd told me he loved me.

And that I'd said it back.

A moment later, Lupé reappeared, carrying a platter with beef Wellingtons and a serving dish with potatoes au gratin.

Despite the undercurrents of unease in the room, Nana got to her feet, ever the perfect Southern hostess. "I hope everyone enjoys this exquisite Texas tenderloin. I fear it may not be available to us much longer. With this war going on, we'll likely see rationing of certain foods. Especially beef. As I'm sure we'll want to keep our fighting men well fed."

Pete grinned. "Well, I guess there've gotta be a few perks about joining the armed forces. I may be sleeping in a tent, but at least I'll be eating a nice, thick steak."

His words brought laughter and broke the tension in the room. With the exception of Stanley, who sat sullenly glaring at the Professor.

"I'm afraid you may be too low on the totem pole to get steak, son," Sammy said with a grin, shaking his head. "You might need to make general first."

"Then I'll aim high," Pete put in.

We all had another laugh, but after that, the conversation became stilted. In fact, Nana, Sammy, Mildred, Pete, and I did most of the talking. The rest of the bunch became completely guarded, only giving a bare minimum of responses while we all ate the delicious food.

When we had finished and Lupé had cleared the plates, I stood and addressed the group. "We'll be having dessert and coffee in the conservatory, so please follow me."

"Why are we going in there?" Sister Gertrude finally spoke up.

"So Eulalie can show us her latest work of art," Nana explained.

Then the whole group trudged out, as though on a death march, rather than as part of a dinner party. I tossed a knowing glance to Sammy and Pete, and both gave me a barely perceptible nod. Just enough to let me know they were with me. I also caught Hadley's eye once we entered the conservatory, and at the same time, I noticed Lupé was watching me like a hawk. She immediately jumped in and helped Hadley serve, taking plates with slices of white layer cake to the priest and the nun first.

Thankfully, Hadley had candles lit in the room already, so we weren't completely in the dark. But since several of the walls were made entirely of windows with a wrought-iron framework, we had an up-close view of the lightning and raindrops. And I had to say, the storm outside was putting on a spectacular show.

I only hoped things didn't become as stormy on the inside as they were on the outside.

Once everyone was seated, Hadley helped Eulalie roll the platform with her sheet-covered sculpture forward, until it was front and center.

"I'm so excited," Nana gushed. "I've never had a work of art unveiled in my own home before."

Dot took a dainty bite of her cake. "I've never even seen anything *unveiled* at all. This is a whole new experience for me."

She smiled at her date, whose eyes were dark with anger and whose frown was almost frightening. Then again, the priest and the nun had the same look to them. And Lupé's hands were noticeably trembling as she delivered more plates of cake and cups of coffee.

Eulalie, on the other hand, appeared to be oblivious to it all. Instead, she smiled as she addressed the group. "In art, as in life, one finds inspiration everywhere one looks. But occasionally, a subject crosses one's path and lights the way to more beauty than one could have ever imagined. So now, without further ado, I give you my newest work, entitled, 'A Pirate for the Ages.'"

With that, she pulled away the cloth covering her clay sculpture. And there, before us, stood a life-size statue of Pete, wearing nothing but a pair of very torn and barely there breeches.

I gasped, and Pete's mouth fell open wide, horror filling his eyes. Even from where I stood, I could feel him blushing to his roots. Sammy choked on his coffee while the priest dropped his plate. The Professor looked like he was going to explode.

Nana, still in the role of the consummate hostess, plastered a smile on her face. "It's lovely, Eulalie. Clearly you've put a lot of work into this, and you certainly are talented."

Sammy coughed and then cleared his throat. "Well, we're off to a good start here this evening. And now, boys and girls, please gather round for the second part of tonight's entertainment, when my associate, Miss Truworth, tells us all a tale of intrigue. I think you'll find her story has you on the edge of your seat."

"What kind of a story?" the nun asked with great irritation in her voice.

"She's about to tell us who murdered Frederick Hoffmeister and Rosette DeBlanc," Sammy said with a grin.

Gasps rose from the group as my boss turned to me. "You're up, kid."

Yet as I stood there, still in shock over the nearly naked Pete statue that Eulalie had created, suddenly, for the life of me, I couldn't remember a single thing I was going to say.

CHAPTER 28

Revealed and Concealed

Let me tell you, if I had thought I was unnerved before, it was nothing compared to how I felt now. I more or less dragged my feet as I moved to the center of the room, battling the bewilderment that fogged my brain. All the while, I tried to divert my eyes from the almost bare Pete statue standing there. I was all in favor of art, and I was hardly what you might call a prude. Not to mention, I had certainly seen my fair share of nude sculptures, including Michelangelo's statue of David in Italy.

But this had crossed a line. Pete hadn't posed for this piece, and he certainly hadn't given his consent. And for that matter, *I* hadn't even seen Pete with his *shirt* off, let alone in ripped breeches. And while I was well aware that Eulalie had been ogling my fella, it truly bothered me that she had pictured him wearing next to nothing.

Much like it clearly bothered Pete, too.

And now here I was, supposed to be doing my job as an Apprentice P.I., with all eyes upon me. Or maybe all eyes were on the mostly naked Pete statue. I couldn't tell for sure.

"Well . . ." I sort of stammered. "Let's start with the night of the museum gala, when Freddy was killed. That night, everyone noticed

Freddy on the dance floor. I think we can all agree, he was a regular Fred Astaire out there. And he danced with Dot first."

Dot put her plate down on a side table and shifted in her seat.

I kept my eyes on her as I spoke. "Dot had a crush on Freddy, and for some time, she had been wishing he would ask her out. She thought her dream had come true when someone sent her a ticket for the gala, because deep down in her heart, she thought Freddy was the one who had sent it. Especially when, much to her delight, she found herself dancing with him that night. Only, dancing with Freddy in real life wasn't anything like she'd imagined. Because Freddy wasn't a considerate dance partner that night. In fact, he hurt her while they were swing dancing and . . ."

Before I could say another word, Stanley jumped to his feet. "I can save you a whole lot of trouble, Tracy. Because I know who killed Freddy, and it wasn't Dot. Dot wouldn't harm a fly."

I smiled at Stanley. "I'm sure she wouldn't."

His eyes met mine. "Do you remember when you came to my apartment and asked me about a dart blowgun? And whether or not Professor Longfellow owned one? Well, I'm here to tell you that he does own one. I've seen it myself and I will be happy to testify to that in court."

Sammy raised his eyebrows. "Keep your shirt on, young fella," he said. Then he immediately started to choke, no doubt regretting his choice of words, given the half-naked Pete statue in the center of the room.

In the meantime, poor Pete rolled his eyes and looked at the ceiling.

Once he'd recovered, Sammy continued with, "Dr. Longfellow admitted as much at dinner. We've got plenty of witnesses."

But Stanley wasn't about to be appeased. "That may be, but I know *why* Professor Longfellow killed Freddy."

The professor slammed his coffee cup into its saucer. "That is absurd! You are spreading fallacies, young man! I shall have you dropped from the archaeology program!"

"Let him talk," Sammy said, as he got to his feet in one smooth motion.

And that was all the encouragement that Stanley needed. "Professor Longfellow killed Freddy because he was after the Veil of

Veronica. His search was supposed to be a secret. But Dr. Longfellow found out, and he didn't want Freddy to find the veil."

"The Veil of Veronica?" Dr. Longfellow scoffed. "Have you gone completely and utterly mad? The veil is nothing but a myth. Sure, Freddy may have asked me about it from time to time, but I steered him away from such nonsense."

"So you knew about the veil, and that Freddy was searching for it?" I interjected.

"Well . . . yes." The Professor laughed with condescension.

Stanley pointed a finger at him. "You know and I know the veil is no myth. Lots of people have been looking for it. And you killed Freddy because you knew he was getting close to it."

The Professor snorted. "That's absurd. Why would it matter to me?"

"Think about it," Stanley went on, with all eyes upon him. "The veil is said to have great healing powers. An army with the veil would be unstoppable. Injured soldiers could be healed and back in action immediately. You didn't want the Germans to get their hands on it."

Now I jumped back into the fray. "But there were others who were after the veil. Right, Father Phillip and Sister Gertrude?"

Without speaking, the two of them glanced at each other.

"And you were in on it, too, weren't you, Lupé?" I said to her, just as she was about to duck out.

She turned and stared at me with tears in her eyes while Stanley returned to his seat.

I took a step toward Lupé. "You were supposed to come into our home and get a job as a maid, weren't you? After all, my grandmother is known for her generosity. And you were sent to take advantage of that, since it was a pretty good guess that she would hire you. Whether we needed a maid or not."

Without speaking, Lupé nodded.

"You were the front person," I went on, "and it was your job to find a reason for these two to be allowed into our home without question. I think you originally planned for them to come in as boarders or refugees or something. It must have been a real stroke of luck for you when you spotted that image in our armoire. Then your cohorts here could enter as a priest and a nun, since the costumes would be easy to find, and because who, in their right mind, would argue with . . . a priest and a nun?"

"Sí, sí," Lupé whispered.

"I'm afraid that's where you're somewhat mistaken," Father Phillip piped up. "I am a real priest, but not associated with any local churches. Though the rest of your information is accurate."

I looked directly at the so-called nun. "But you're not a nun, are you?"

She removed the headpiece of her habit and shook out her dark hair. "No, I'm not. My name is Francesca, and the three of us belong to an . . . um . . ."

"Organization," Father Phillip finished for her.

"What organization?" I asked. "Surely not the Freemasons."

"Hardly," Father Phillip scoffed. "Though ours *is* a secret society, of sorts. The Holy Order of the Divine Protectors. Lupé came to us from a branch in Argentina, where they'd been keeping an eye on Nazi activity down there."

"The Holy Order of the Divine Protectors," Mildred repeated under her breath, as though she'd heard of them before.

Father Phillip kept his gaze on me, unblinking. "We've been hunting down the lost Catholic treasures, the *Arma Christi*."

"The Weapons of Christ," I said.

Father Phillip gave me a slight smile. "That is correct. And the Veil of Veronica just happens to be one of those lost treasures."

Francesca nodded, just as a bolt of lightning lit up the sky. "And like all the *Arma Christi*, the veil needs to be protected and hidden away, so it can never fall into the wrong hands. If the Nazis were to get hold of it, the world might be controlled by evil."

Thunder rattled the windows before Father Phillip added, "And though the veil has been lost for a long, long time, we believe we have located it. Right here, in this house."

"You see," Francesca went on, "Freddy wasn't the only one who was close to finding it. We have been on the trail for quite some time, too. The quest for the veil is a race against the dark forces in the world."

Dot and Mildred sat spellbound, while Nana clutched her hand to her chest.

Despite myself, I shuddered before I soldiered on. "But there was another group trying to make sure the veil didn't fall into the wrong hands. Isn't that right, Eulalie? Do you have a name for your organization, too?"

She offered me a demure smile. "I'm afraid our association is much more loosely organized. We're simply a group of Catholics, mostly Creoles, who moved here from Louisiana, and all with a strong connection to France itself. And you, Tracy, could have joined us. Your heart is certainly true enough, and we couldn't think of a better person than a detective, such as yourself, to ensure the veil would always be safe. We planned to recruit you the night Rosette was murdered."

"Because she was one of your group," I went on.

Eulalie suddenly became interested in her nails. "Yes, she was."

"And your group knew that Freddy was after the veil," I went on, realizing my voice had now taken on the tone of a narrator in a radio-mystery show. "That's why Rosette was willing to go along with Ethel's ridiculous plan. Not only did she get a free ticket to the museum gala—an event she'd heard Freddy would be attending—but she also agreed to stick Freddy in the arm with the pin of a brooch. Then she planned to pull him aside afterward so she could find out exactly what he knew."

Eulalie lowered her lashes. "And we could find out precisely how close he was to finding the veil. Unfortunately, Rosette wasn't able to get any information from Freddy that night, since he barely even noticed she'd stuck him, and Freddy went on dancing like a madman. We probably learned more when I read his diary."

I folded my arms across my chest. "So you're the one who took the diary from my car and later returned it to my room."

"Yes, that is correct. It was such an interesting work, almost like a book rather than a diary. The young man was such an eloquent writer," Eulalie said, as though she were enjoying herself.

Stanley started to choke. "Freddy had a diary? Where did you get it?"

I turned to face him. "It was hidden under a floorboard beneath his bed."

"I can't believe I didn't know . . ." Stanley muttered.

But I wasn't finished with Eulalie, and my gaze met hers. "You were the one who arranged to have the veil transported over to this country in the first place. In a shipment of artifacts that came over in 1937 to the Museum of Fine Arts. But the veil wasn't an official part of that shipment. No, instead it had very cleverly been hidden inside, as nothing more than packing material."

"Which I easily pocketed minutes after it was tossed aside," Eulalie announced with a flick of her fingers. "Nobody was the wiser. And you could hardly blame my group for getting the veil out of Europe after our French counterparts located it. Especially when we, like so many others, saw this war on the horizon."

"Freddy must've caught the scent of the veil in Europe," Sammy interjected. "Since he was being forced to find it for Hitler."

"And Freddy tracked it to Houston," I murmured as I stepped toward Eulalie. "That's how he ended up in Houston, and you found out that he was hot on the trail of the veil. Which is why you took advantage of my grandmother's generosity. You knew that a mere mention of needing a place to work on your art would prompt her to extend an invitation to stay here. In her mansion. With so many places to hide something like an ancient veil, no one would ever find it. Not in a million years."

Now Eulalie glared at me. "Tracy, you are dealing with forces far greater than any of us. There is much more at stake here than you can imagine, and I would advise you to tread lightly."

"Where is the veil now?" Dot finally asked.

I glanced around the room, at all the faces before me. "I believe the veil is nearby."

The Professor threw up his hands. "Oh, all these fairy tales!"

Stanley leaned forward and pointed at Dr. Longfellow. "Could we please just get this over with? Have that man arrested for murder! Now!"

And that's when I turned to Stanley. "Why would we do that, Stanley?"

Stanley's eyes were wild. "Because he murdered Freddy, of course!"

"Did he?" I asked, just as a flash of lightning punctuated my words. "I think you know better, Stanley."

Stanley crinkled his eyebrows. "What are you talking about?"

I tilted my head. "No one knew Freddy better than you did, Stanley. You first met him in Germany, where you actually admired the Nazis and their way of life. So much so that you couldn't understand why Freddy didn't appreciate all that he had. Things *you* didn't have."

"That's nonsense," he said, his words barely audible above the thunder that rattled the glass panes of the walls.

I shook my head. "Not really. Because Freddy's school and his expeditions were all paid for by the Nazis. Since they were after certain archaeological artifacts, they were footing the bill. You envied your friend for that."

I started to pace the floor. "You even met the two German men, underground members of the German American Bund, Nazis, who were keeping an eye on Freddy for their German counterparts. And you had the idea that, with Freddy gone, you could simply step into his shoes. Only, where Freddy was being *forced* to do the work, you would have done so willingly."

Stanley leaned back in his seat. "The Germans aren't all bad. They're actually quite efficient, when you think about it."

Shock registered through the room like the next wave of thunder that jangled the windowed walls.

Dot turned to him. "Stanley, how can you say that? Don't you know how evil the Nazis are?"

Stanley laughed. "Oh, that's only what people want you to believe. I've seen the other side of them."

I took a deep breath and persisted. "I have to say, you really played your role well, Stanley, and you had everyone fooled. You even did a great job trying to mislead me and send me off the trail this afternoon, when you brought up your theory about the Freemasons."

He gave me a condescending smile. "You're going to regret this, Tracy. Because one day the Nazis will rule the world. You're just too dumb to know it. That, and you haven't got an ounce of proof against me."

"Oh, but I do have proof," I went on, as I pulled two little pill tins from my pocket. "On the night that Freddy died, he had a horrible headache. And you said you gave him three aspirin tablets. Here is the aspirin tin you gave him that night. We found it in his pocket, and the writing on it is in English." I held it up for everyone to see.

"And here is the tin that I took from your desk drawer in your apartment today," I went on.

Stanley scooted forward to the edge of his seat. "You took something from my apartment?"

"Oh, yes," I said, speaking above the rain that now pelted the ceiling of the conservatory. "And you almost had me fooled, Stanley, with your little routine about not wanting to give me any aspirin, because it reminded you of how Freddy had died. That memory was supposedly painful for you. But the real reason you didn't want to give me any aspirin was because you didn't want me to see this tin." I held up the little pill tin with the German writing, just in time for another bolt of lightning to illuminate it.

Stanley snickered. "That's ridiculous."

I shook my head. "No, it's not. Because this second tin says 'Pervitin.' And when I asked Mildred, a woman who had escaped from Germany, she explained to me what Pervitin is. It's a drug called methyl-amphetamine. Hitler has been giving it to his soldiers, because it gives one man the energy and stamina of four men. It also makes them impervious to fear and pain. And you probably got this tin from the Nazis who were keeping track of Freddy over here. I'm guessing you took a pill once in a while, whenever you had to stay up all night to study. Freddy, on the other hand, didn't need to stay up all night to study, and he never would have taken this drug."

"So?"

"You knew Freddy suffered from frequent migraine headaches, and the odds were good that he'd have a headache the night of the gala, too. So you switched out the aspirins in the other tin and put in three Pervitin tablets instead. Then you gave the aspirin tin with the Pervitins to Freddy, and that's what he unknowingly took the night of the gala. It made him move with the speed of Superman, and it made him oblivious to the suffering he was inflicting upon any of his dance partners."

Stanley shrugged. "So maybe I got confused and did it by accident. What's the big deal?"

I stared directly into his cold eyes. "You know full well what the big deal is. Pervitan is a very strong drug. The dosage on the tin says to take one pill and one pill only, and only from time to time. Any more than that could be dangerous. But you told Freddy to take three at once. And so he did, thinking he was merely taking aspirin. But three Pervitan tablets were enough to give him a heart attack, and that's exactly how he died."

Stanley chuckled. "This is quite a work of fiction you're telling everyone, Tracy."

Slow, rolling thunder rumbled through the dark clouds above us

I shook my head. "I'm afraid not. Especially when you went a step further. You wanted to *make sure* that Freddy danced himself to death that night. So you somehow convinced your new Nazi pals— the ones who were supposed to be keeping an eye on Freddy—to send Dot a ticket to the dance. My guess is you probably gave them some song and dance about this being necessary in the hunt for the veil. And since Dot had a crush on Freddy, and Freddy loved to dance, you knew he'd be dancing till he dropped. Everyone would simply think he had died of natural causes. And once you had Freddy out of the way, you planned to take his place, going after artifacts for Hitler and the Nazis while they paid for it all."

Stanley snickered. "Freddy had no idea how lucky he was. He was such a prodigy and everything came so easily to him. So, of course the Nazis wanted him. But instead of appreciating it, he fought them every step of the way. He was a spoiled pain in the rump."

His words shocked me. "Yet you pretended to be his friend."

Stanley laughed. "Freddy, who was supposed to be such a genius, had no idea what I was up to! I completely outsmarted him. And I outsmarted you, too, Tracy. You didn't suspect a thing. You, the great detective!"

"Which is why you killed Rosette, isn't Stanley? Because you didn't want her to talk to me," I said, chomping on my words as I fought to keep my anger under control. "Since much like Eulalie's group had learned about Freddy, *he'd* also caught wind of their group. And he planned to go to the La-la in hopes of finding out more about them. That was his next step in his search for the veil."

"Well, aren't you smart, Tracy?" Stanley snorted. "Yes, when we learned you were headed for that silly dance yourself, we guessed you'd probably run into Rosette. Of course, we knew you'd recognize her from the museum gala. Then you'd start in on your endless, annoying questions."

"And you were afraid she'd tell me everything she knew," I added. "About Freddy and the veil."

Stanley shrugged. "Let's face it, I couldn't let her blab. Or else you would have put the pieces together. So Rosette had to be silenced. But no big deal. After all, there are casualties in every war."

"But I *did* put the pieces together, Stanley. And I not only figured out that you're a murderer, but you're also a traitor to your country. You thought you had a bright future, but I'm afraid it's not looking too wonderful at the moment."

Stanley laughed again, loudly, as though he found my deductions to be amusing. "Oh, but you are so shortsighted, Tracy. When the Nazis take over America—and they will—you will be very, very sorry. You will not be treated kindly."

Now, all eyes were on Stanley, and it suddenly occurred to me that he was a little too smug for a man who was about to be arrested. Plus, he was admitting to much more than most cornered suspects ever would.

Seconds later, I figured out why, when the sky above us went dark and another bolt of lightning flashed, nearly blinding us all. By the time our eyes had adjusted to the dim light again, there were two men standing in the room, holding revolvers. One with a monocle, and the other very tall and thin.

The Nazis whom I had chased down the street.

Mildred and Dot screamed.

"You are too clever for your own good, Fräulein," the man with the monocle said to me, though he pointed his gun at Pete.

Everyone gasped in terror, including me, as we all feared this man would shoot my fella on the spot. That was, until Nana let out a little scream and grabbed her neck.

And I suddenly noticed that Stanley was holding a narrow wooden tube, one decorated with painted symbols. A dart blowgun. He must have had it concealed in his pocket the entire evening. And I would have bet it belonged to Dr. Longfellow.

Nana slumped over in her chair, and I spotted a little dart on the side of her neck.

"Nana!" I screamed and rushed over to her.

Sammy was right behind me.

I carefully removed the dart and felt her neck for a pulse. She was still alive.

Stanley stood up. "She will die slowly. I used a different poison this time. Which means you have maybe ten to fifteen minutes to save her."

"Save her?" I cried.

"Yes," Stanley said with a laugh. "You're a detective. You know how to save your grandmother. Of course, you'll need to find the veil to do that. So I would suggest you get to work, before it's too late."

My heart started to pound about a million miles an hour. How would I ever find the veil in time to save Nana? Provided the veil would even save her life at all?

CHAPTER 29

Lousy Night and a Leap of Faith

Though I didn't think it was possible, the thunderstorm became even more ferocious and louder than before. Lightning bolts blazed across the sky as rain pelted the conservatory in angry torrents. Yet despite the deluge outside, we had a storm of our own raging right there inside the conservatory.

Especially after Hadley hollered, "Someone broke in to this room days ago, and they must have been looking for that veil! It has got to be in here! Start searching!"

I glared at the monocle-wearing man while I held Nana's hand. "And I'll bet we have you and your tall pal to thank for that break-in."

"Naturally, Fräulein," he said, sounding proud of himself.

Then while he and the other Nazi stood guard, everyone else—with the exception of Eulalie, Pete, and Stanley—broke into a full-blown frenzy, as they frantically moved furniture and plants and more, all in search of the veil.

And that's when I looked up at the one person who could help me. The person I knew had been harboring the veil the whole time.

Eulalie.

"Please," I begged her. "Please save my grandmother. I know you can. Because you know where the veil is."

She glanced away. "I'm afraid I haven't a clue where that veil is now, dear child. I may have retrieved it after it was shipped here, but I certainly didn't keep it. I passed it on to someone else who could protect it."

I stood up and moved directly in front of her. "You're lying, Eulalie. You know exactly where the veil is. You used it to heal my burns the night I spilled the hot chocolate. And it's the reason Opaline has lived to such an old age for a cat. It's also the reason you've got the health and stamina of a woman half your age."

"But if I turn it over, they will steal it," she said calmly. "And if one person dies to prevent the veil from getting into the hands of the Nazis, I think your grandmother would say it was well worth it." She gave me a radiant smile, one that seemed so out of place, given the life-and-death drama going on around us. "After all, I am ready to die to protect it. All is right with my soul."

"Well, it's not worth it to me!" I cried. "You've been using my grandmother and putting her in danger from the moment you moved in here. Now it's time for you to pay her back by saving her life!"

Before she could say another word, the priest raised his hand and hollered, "The sculpture! She probably hid it in the sculpture!"

Then all at once, people started to pummel the semi-naked Pete statue and break it apart just as quickly as they could. Yet Pete himself was forced to sit still, since the man with the monocle kept his gun pointed right at my guy. I could feel the tension in the room building, almost like some invisible hand had turned an invisible dial, especially once the sculpture was destroyed and the veil was nowhere to be found. Clearly Eulalie hadn't hidden it in her latest work.

With obvious annoyance, Stanley got to his feet and started to pace the room, keeping an eye on his pocket watch.

I turned back to Eulalie. "Please, Eulalie. Please help us."

But Eulalie just gave me a sly smile.

And I was about to beg her again, but as I stood, studying her features, the light finally dawned. "Actually, Eulalie, I don't even need you to tell us where you hid the veil. Because I already know." I glanced outside to the garden.

A jagged bolt of lightning ripped across the sky, illuminating her face just long enough to show me that she had now turned pale. "You wouldn't . . ." she uttered in disbelief.

"Hadley, I'll need a shovel," I countered, as my words were drowned out by another explosion of thunder.

But apparently Hadley only heard part of what I'd said, because the next thing I knew, he pulled a shovel from behind a potted palm and wacked the tall, thin man on the head with a loud *thunk*! The sound was enough to cause the monocled man to turn his head, giving Pete the perfect opportunity to sideswipe the man's leg while also grabbing his gun hand. And his gun. At the same time, Sammy tackled Stanley, shoving the blowgun out of the way.

Hadley pointed at the unconscious man lying on the floor. "Much like Mark Twain once remarked, 'When everyone is looking for gold, it's a good time to be in the pick and shovel business.' I had a hunch I might need a weapon tonight, and this seemed like an excellent choice."

"Good work, Hadley," Sammy said. "Maybe you and Pete can help me cart these characters out so Eulalie can show Tracy where the veil is. Longfellow, you go and help them. Mildred, I want you to stay with Caroline." He glanced at Nana with grave concern in his eyes.

Then as Pete, Hadley, and Sammy took the two Nazis and Stanley from the room, the Professor stood up and brushed some cake crumbs from his suit. "I shall be leaving now, since I have endured more than enough for one evening. I shall take my ancient blowgun and go home."

I gasped. "But my grandmother will die if we don't find that veil."

"I've got bad news for you," he scoffed. "That veil won't save her. It is nothing but a myth. Your grandmother is as good as dead."

His words were like knives stabbing at my heart. Still, I knew I couldn't believe what he'd said. I couldn't give up hope in trying to save her.

The Professor strode out of the room while the priest stepped over to me. "There is still hope, child, but only if you have faith. For your faith shall make her well. Now take a leap of faith and go find that veil."

To be honest, in that horrible moment when I knew Nana was so close to death, faith was all I had left to cling to. And if this veil, the one that was supposed to have touched the face of Jesus, could heal people, I had to have faith that God would use it to save her, too.

But first I had to find it.

I snapped my fingers. "Eulalie, move it! Now! Right now! If you've got any decency in you at all, you'll save your friend. The Nazis are gone and they can't take the veil from you anymore."

With those words, she finally got up. Then I grabbed Hadley's shovel and a flashlight before she and I dashed out the door and into the storm. Cold rain pelted us, making me shiver and soaking me to the skin. I knew we were taking an awful risk, running out into a lightning storm like that, but what other choice did I have? I couldn't let Nana die.

Eulalie held the flashlight before us, but with the huge droplets blowing sideways, and right into our faces, we had almost no visibility at all. Even so, we managed to slip and slide over the flagstone path, around the bend and all the way out to the back garden.

That's when Eulalie pointed to a flat rock in the garden. "There!" she yelled above the roar of the wind. "It's under there."

I didn't waste a second before I started to dig. The soil was wet and heavy, and came up in big globs of mud. I knew my shoes were ruined after just a couple of shovelfuls. But I didn't care. I could always get a new pair of shoes. Replacing my grandmother was a different matter.

I had just dug in for the third shovelful when the flashlight went out. Eulalie smacked it a few times, but it was no use. So I merely started to dig on instinct, getting a glimpse of the garden every now and then when more lightning momentarily lit up the sky. The soil seemed to be getting heavier, and water quickly filled the hole.

By now my hair was plastered to my head and rain ran down my face, making it even harder to see.

"Are you sure this is where you buried it?" I yelled to Eulalie over the deluge.

When she didn't respond, I looked behind me and saw that she was gone. So I just kept on digging, desperately. Right at that moment, I couldn't remember ever feeling so alone.

Especially with the idea of never seeing Nana alive again. To think, I'd been so worried about her safety, ever since the night of the gala, and now here she was, mere moments from death. The idea of losing her cut me to the core. My grandmother had been my rock when I was raised by a society woman who became abusive when she drank. And my grandmother had been there for me when I endured my first failed engagement. In fact, Nana had always been there for me.

And now I needed to be there for her.

So I did the only thing that I could do—I prayed and kept on digging. I just had to save her. I couldn't lose her now. Not like this.

Before long, my arms felt leaden, and it seemed like every shovelful of mud weighed more than the last. At the rate I was going, I wasn't sure how much longer I could keep digging. My muscles ached to stop, as the rain pelted my whole body, making me shiver. I cried out with one last prayer, asking for the strength to carry on.

And mere seconds later, big, strong hands encircled mine, taking the muddy shovel from me. I looked up to see Pete, and I couldn't remember ever being so happy to see him before in my life. Tears rolled down my cheeks, hot in comparison to the cold, drenching rain.

Thankfully, Pete didn't waste a moment before he began to dig with the speed of Superman. The next thing I knew, I heard a *clunk* as the shovel hit metal. I got down on my hands and knees, and dug around the edges. At long last, we pulled a little metal chest from the muck.

Which wasn't easy, considering the chest must have weighed at least a ton. Apparently Eulalie really *had* buried her gold in there, too.

Pete picked up the box and together we raced through the rain and the lightning, until we got back into the conservatory. We were both dripping water and mud as we practically slid over to where Nana was slumped in her chair. Much to my amazement, Father Phillip and Francesca sat stoically observing it all, as though they were merely watching a movie on the silver screen. Eulalie, on the other hand, was nowhere to be seen.

Pete pulled the lid off the box, and there, tucked away on the side, was what looked like a very old piece of linen. I pulled it out and gasped when I saw the rust-brown image on the cloth. It was of a face that I recognized. By now, Nana's breathing was shallow, and her skin was very pale as Mildred and Dot kneeled on the floor next to her, with tears rolling down their cheeks.

I placed the cloth on top of Nana. "Let's pray this works."

Father Phillip came to stand next to me. "It will work, all right. Your faith will make her well," he repeated.

And sure enough, Nana blinked a couple of times and coughed once or twice, before she stretched and came to life.

She saw Pete and me and laughed. "My goodness, what have you two kids been up to?"

I hugged her like I'd never hugged her before, while salty tears flowed freely down my face. "Oh, Nana, I'm so happy to see you again!"

"That's good to hear, darlin', but you're dripping water all over me," she said with another laugh.

Mildred plumped up some pillows behind Nana. "I think we'd better keep her dry," she said softly.

So I let Pete pull me up, whereby I promptly collapsed into his arms.

Then I heard Father Phillip's voice coming from behind us. "As touching as this is, I'm afraid I must interrupt. I'll be taking that veil, if you please."

"What . . . .?" Pete started to ask.

We both turned to see that Father Phillip now held a gun, and he had it pointed right at us. Francesca quickly snatched up the veil, folded it, and shoved it into her nun's robe. "We must make sure this never, ever falls into the hands of the Nazis. Rest assured, we will hide it where no one will find it."

Then without saying a word, Lupé opened the very door that Pete and I had just come through. A huge gust of wind blew rain and leaves into the conservatory, and for the first time, I noticed Lupé was holding a small revolver herself.

"You can't just take that away, not when there is so much good that could come from it," I pleaded. "What about using it for people who need to be healed? It could even help our own soldiers."

Father Phillip shook his head as Francesca stepped outside. "They're all lovely ideas, but I'm sorry, we simply can't take that chance. If it's placed where the public has access to it, without a doubt, the Nazis will get to it. And we can't take that risk."

"But it's not up to you to decide," Pete said with great firmness. "After all, Tracy and I dug up the veil. And Eulalie had possession of it. You have no right to take it from us."

"Again, son, I'm sorry," the priest said with one foot out the door. "But the veil must be protected at all costs. Like the lady said earlier, we are dealing with forces much greater than any of us. And we must think of the greater good."

Still keeping the gun trained on us, he fully exited the room. And with another flash of lightning, all three disappeared into the night.

CHAPTER 30

Goodbyes and Swell Times

After Lupé, Father Phillip, and Francesca had more or less vanished, I knew I didn't have the strength to go after them. And to be honest, I wasn't convinced they wouldn't shoot us. Exhausted, I fell back into Pete's arms.

Later, I barely remembered Nana being helped upstairs by Maddie, who'd been surprised when Sammy, Pete, and Hadley had marched Stanley and the two Nazis into her kitchen for safekeeping. My boss and Hadley held them there until the police arrived.

As usual, Detective Denton led the charge.

He jabbed one of his stubby fingers in my direction. "Are you still playing at being a detective, girlie?" he asked with a sneer.

Sammy took a step toward him. "That would be Miss Truworth to you, fella. And she's turning into a first-rate detective. She solved this double homicide when you boys didn't even get your feet wet."

Which in this case, may have been more literal than what my boss had probably intended. Even so, it was enough to stop Denton from harassing me further. Who knew? Maybe Detective Denton and I would learn to play nice someday.

After he and Sammy had gone, I gave Pete a goodnight kiss and a very soggy hug, with the promise of talking the next day. Then I went upstairs, got out of my damp and muddied dress, and slipped into a nice, hot bath.

Yet before I went to bed, I had one more task to complete. So I sat down at my father's Royal DeLuxe portable and typed up the whole sordid story, from start to finish.

I woke up the next morning with a song in my heart, the sun shining through my window, and a written account of the crime in my hand. Well, at least the parts of the crime that I could write about, anyway. I didn't actually mention the veil, for fear everyone and *their* grandmother would be looking high and low for it. Instead, I only referred to it as an ancient, religious artifact, which was plenty of information for the sake of the story. Of course, I was careful to leave out anything that might jeopardize the case when it came to prosecuting Stanley for the murder of Freddy and Rosette. As for the man with the monocle and his tall, thin cohort, last I'd heard, they were headed for FBI custody. I wasn't sure, but I figured Stanley might end up there, too.

Either way, I was happy to leave it all to the G-men—including Freddy's diary, which I asked Sammy to pass along in hopes they might gain some knowledge that would help Uncle Sam win the war. Somehow, I had a hunch that J. Edgar Hoover's boys would find it interesting reading.

That left me with one last thing to get off my hands. Literally as well as figuratively. And with the morning sun bouncing off the hood of the Packard, I donned my sunglasses and drove to the other paper in town, the *Houston Register-Tribune*. I strolled in and placed my typewritten account into the hands of a very happy City Desk reporter. Then she, Ruby Goodwin, a young woman with red hair and even redder lipstick, promised to print it, along with pictures of Pete and me. Soon all of Houston would know the entire story of how we'd been falsely accused of crimes we didn't commit.

Not only did Ruby and I hit it off (and make plans for a lunch date later in the week), but I also believed she'd hold true to her promise.

In other words, Pete and I were about to be exonerated, once and for all. That meant Pete wouldn't have to worry about getting fired from his job. And he would also be free to enlist in the service, whenever he decided to go. Just the thought of it tugged at my heartstrings, especially when I realized how soon his departure might be. But any way you looked at it, it was better than being tried and convicted in the court of public opinion. Besides, if we didn't all make sacrifices and fight the evil trying to swallow up our world, who else would?

I gave Pete the good news shortly after I got back home, when I walked in just in time to pick up the ringing phone. And that's when he asked me out for dinner and swing dancing at the swankiest nightclub in town. Naturally, I said yes. For the first time in days, I felt like whistling, especially when I went to the back hallway and realized something was missing—namely, the long line to view our armoire.

Hadley explained the situation to me. "I proposed a solution to your grandmother, one that I believe will make all parties happy," he said with a smile. "Thus she has agreed to loan the armoire to Christ Church, where it will be displayed behind a velvet rope at a safe distance, to prevent any possible damage to the piece. So all who wish to see it may do so."

"Oh, Hadley, that's brilliant!"

I had to admit, it really was the best of both worlds. We wouldn't have a constant stream of strangers coming into the mansion, and yet people who wanted to see the image could do so. And if that image gave people a sense of hope, well, I was all for it.

I gave the image in the armoire one last look, and I smiled before offering up a silent prayer of "Thank you." Then I headed to the staircase, and along the way, I found Eulalie packing up and moving out. To be honest, I had a hard time even speaking to her after the way she'd almost let Nana die the night before. Especially when she'd knowingly put Nana in danger in the first place, since she was well aware that evil people were after the veil and that the rest of us might get caught in the crosshairs.

Though I guess when it came right down to it, I knew I'd have to find it in my heart to forgive her. Misguided as I believed her motives might have been, I figured we were all on the same side.

I gave her the most cordial smile I could muster. "What about your art exhibit?"

In return, she gave me one of her usual sly smiles. "I'll be able to use my old space now."

And I let it go at that, before I said goodbye to her and Opaline. To be honest, I was truly going to miss my new feline friend.

That night, I donned a midnight-blue satin evening gown and matching gloves. Pete arrived at my door right on time, looking more handsome in his tux than I could ever remember. He took my hands in his, and I gazed up into his eyes, realizing how very much I loved him. And how lucky I was to have a fella like him.

At the nightclub, Pete had reserved a table for two on the balcony overlooking the dance floor. We dined on ribeyes and creamed spinach and baked potatoes. Then we hit the dance floor as soon as we'd finished our delicious dinner. The big band music was fantastic, with lots of brass and plenty of octane. Pete led me into a rock step right away, and soon I was spinning and twirling while we had the time of our lives. It seemed like Pete and I had reached a point with our dancing where we really moved together, working as a team. And I relished every single second of it.

It was a swell time to go swing dancing.

Near the end of the night, he took me outside for a moonlit stroll in a nearby park. We stopped at a little bench where we sat and stared at the brilliant stars in the sky.

"Tracy," he murmured, "I was hoping we could finish having our talk."

"I'd like that," I said just above a whisper.

But then he jumped to his feet and glanced around. He looked left and then right, and finally made a complete turn, his stance like an athlete about to take off running, while his eyes were wide and alert.

"Oh no! Now what's going on?" Anxiety rose in my chest, especially after the week we'd just had.

"Nothing . . . yet. But I'm just looking around to make sure no one is about to scream bloody murder, or that some suspect isn't about to go running by. Because every time I try to talk to you about this, we get interrupted. And these aren't any old run-of-the-mill interruptions, either. They involve everything from the sudden appearance of religious images to people trying to commit murder with poison darts. Not the typical things that most fellas run into when they're trying to have a serious discussion with their girl."

He leaned over and winked at me.

Which sent me into gales of laughter. I grabbed his hand and pulled him back down next to me.

He leaned into me. "Though to be honest, I wouldn't have it any other way. Life with you, Tracy Truworth, will never be boring."

"I sure hope not," I told him. "But whatever you're trying to say, maybe you'd better spit it out quick, just in case . . ."

He laughed. "Okay, here goes. Let's start with this . . ." And without another word, he planted his lips firmly onto mine and kissed me.

And took my breath away.

Then he pulled back slightly. "You know I love you," he murmured. "And there's no doubt in my mind that you're the girl for me. The only girl. And if we lived in a world without war, I'd say we should date for a year. Or two. And then make a commitment."

"Uh-huh." My heart started to pound like the pistons in the Packard.

"But . . ." He paused and took a deep breath. "These aren't normal times. I'm going to be enlisting soon and going off to war. Who knows how long I might be gone? And who knows if . . .?" He let the words drop.

Yet we both knew how that sentence might end. Because there would likely be many, many soldiers who would never come back from the war. In fact, there were already men who had been killed, leaving their sweethearts behind to grieve.

"Anyway," he went on, "what I'm trying to say is, we don't know if we'll even have a tomorrow."

"I know, Pete." Tears welled up in my eyes, and I fought with everything I had to stop them from spilling over and onto my cheeks.

Funny how a girl could go from laughing to crying in a matter of seconds. But this awful war had us all on such a roller coaster ride of emotions.

Pete took my hand. "I don't want to leave town without knowing that we'll be together for as long as we can. Whether it's for one year or forty, I just want to make our relationship more . . ." He paused again, as though searching for the right word.

"Devoted?" I supplied.

"Yes, that works. But how do you feel, Tracy? Do you feel the same way I do?"

I nodded and wiped away a tear. "I do, Pete. I really do. I love you, too. And I'd like to know where we stand . . ."

He nodded. "So do I. I want to know where we stand, too. But for this next part, I'm afraid I'm going to have to kneel."

And the next thing I knew, he was down on one knee. "Tracy, would you do me the honor of being my wife? Will you marry me?"

I gasped. "Oh . . . Pete . . ."

"Before you give me your answer, let me assure you, I don't want to run off and get married at the Justice of the Peace in the morning. Like so many couples do these days." He paused for a moment and took a deep breath. "Instead, Tracy, I want a proper wedding. I thought we might get engaged now, and then later, months from now, if I can get some time on leave and come home, then we could have a real wedding. In a church. So what do you say?"

"It sounds wonderful, Pete. Just wonderful. And the answer is yes, I will marry you."

I had barely taken a breath when his lips were on mine and he pulled me close to him. And I kissed him as my "fiancé" for the very first time. Right there under the stars.

"Oh, wait, I almost forgot," he said with a laugh. "I've got something for you. Hope you like it."

Then he pulled out a little red-velvet box with the most beautiful emerald-cut diamond ring I had ever seen. He placed it on my finger and we kissed again, never wanting to let go.

Later, when we returned to Nana's mansion, I invited him in for a nightcap. Because I wasn't quite ready to let him go for the night. In fact, I wasn't sure if I'd ever be ready to let him go.

We walked into the house to find a little celebration was going on in the parlor. Nana was the first person I spotted when we entered, and I couldn't get over the way she was smiling and laughing, and showing no signs at all of her near-death experience. In fact, if I didn't know better, it looked to me like she had the energy of a woman half her age.

And I, for one, couldn't have been more relieved. Not to mention, overjoyed that she was still with us.

I saw Sammy, Maddie, and Hadley next, and then finally, the reason for the festivities.

My father was home from Washington.

I cheered and was about to run over and hug him when Nana yelled, "Stop right there, darlin'! Wait just a minute . . ." She glanced from me to Pete and then back again. "Something's different about you two . . ."

Pete and I gazed into each other's eyes and smiled, without saying a word.

That's when Nana let out a little squeal. "Oh my goodness! You kids got engaged, didn't you?"

I barely got in half a nod before it was hugs and kisses and congratulations all around.

"I couldn't ask for a better son-in-law," my father said, beaming.

"Welcome to the family," Nana gushed, kissing Pete's cheek.

After that, champagne was passed around and it turned into an even bigger celebration. A moment of happiness after so much turmoil for so many days.

Later, Sammy pulled me aside. "Why don't you take tomorrow off and spend the day with Pete. After that, I'm going to need you in the office. I've been hearing some rumblings, and it looks like we've got a new case about to land in our laps, kid. This one could be a real doozie."

Right away I thought of Katie McClue and one of her most recent episodes. She had been at a party, commemorating the two thousandth criminal she'd put away, when suddenly the case of a lifetime came crashing in. Literally. When a dead body smashed through the skylight above and fell at her feet.

I grinned and gave my boss a little salute. "Sounds swell. I'll be there."

"Good deal, kid," he said before we both rejoined the party.

Then as I looked around at my family and friends, and my boss and my new fiancé, and as I thought about the case that Sammy and I had just solved, all of a sudden, I couldn't help but think—maybe 1942 was getting off to a roaring good start, after all.

THE END

Author's Note

This book is a work of fiction, and created for entertainment. While it is not intended to be a history book, there are many historical facts incorporated into this work.

Including . . .

Thanks to a wonderful and hardworking group of visionaries, known as the Houston Art League, the first section of the Museum of Fine Arts was opened in Houston in 1924. Even so, I'm sure they never had members the likes of Ethel Barton or Eulalie Laffite, who are characters created purely by my imagination. The original section of the art museum building still stands, and it is a work of art within itself.

Annette Finnigan was a real and true Houston heroine, and her contributions to the newly built art museum were legendary. Not to mention, incredibly generous. She did take several trips abroad, in search of treasure to bring home to the museum. Without her, the museum might not have become the fantastic institution it is today.

The area once known as Frenchtown in northeast Houston is considered the home of Zydeco. While most of the original buildings are gone, a plaque honoring that important time in history remains.

Packards were some of the coolest cars ever built. They were the cars of the movie stars back in the day, and you can still see these fine automobiles at vintage car shows. Thank you to all those wonderful people who restore them back to their original glory.

And despite the years that have passed, swing dancing is alive and well today. If you're in need of a pick-me-up, I highly recommend it. Because it's always a swell time to go swing dancing.

About the Author

Cindy Vincent was born in Calgary, Alberta, Canada, and has lived all around the US and Canada. She is the creator of the Mysteries by Vincent murder mystery party games and the Daisy Diamond Detective series games for girls. She is also the award-winning author of the Buckley and Bogey Cat Detective Caper books, and the Daisy Diamond Detective book series. Though she lives in Houston with her husband and an assortment of fantastic felines, people often tell her she acts like she's from another era, and that she *really* belongs back in the 1940s . . .

CPSIA information can be obtained
at www.ICGtesting.com
Printed in the USA
LVHW04s0920050618
579639LV00001B/1/P